THE KING'S MAN

THE
KING'S MAN

(The Zero Enigma, Book VII)

CHRISTOPHER G. NUTTALL

The characters and events portrayed in this book are fictitious. Any similarity to real persons, living or dead, is coincidental and not intended by the author.

Text copyright © 2020 Christopher G. Nuttall

All rights reserved.

Printed in the United States of America.

No part of this book may be reproduced, or stored in a retrieval system, or transmitted in any form or by any means, electronic, mechanical, photocopying, recording, or other-wise, without express written permission of the publisher.

ISBN: 9798614637521

Book One: The Zero Blessing
Book Two: The Zero Curse
Book Three: The Zero Equation
Book Four: The Family Shame
Book Five: The Alchemist's Apprentice
Book Six: The Family Pride
www.chrishanger.net
chrishanger.wordpress.com
www.facebook.com/ChristopherGNuttall
https://mewe.com/page/5cd32005dc9f631c9973f058

Cover by Brad Fraunfelter
www.BFillustration.com

All Comments Welcome!

AUTHOR'S NOTE

I've done my best, as always, to make this story as stand-alone as possible. However, a number of characters made their debut appearances in earlier books. Adam, Saline and Louise first appeared in *The Family Pride*, while Rebecca and Jill starred in *The Alchemist's Apprentice*.

CGN

HISTORIAN'S
NOTE

The Thousand-Year Empire dominated the twin continents of Maxima and Minima through two advantages, an unmatched command of magic and the development of Objects of Power, magical weapons and tools that made them seemingly invincible. But the Empire fell and the secret of making Objects of Power was lost.

Hundreds of years later, a young girl—Caitlyn Aguirre—was born to a powerful magical family. Caitlyn—Cat—should have been powerful herself, like her two sisters, but she seemed to have no spark of magic at all. She lacked even a sense for magic. In desperation, her parents sent her to Jude's Academy for the Magically Gifted in the hopes that exposure to magical training would bring forth the magic they were *sure* lay buried within her. There, she met Isabella and Akin Rubén, children of her family's greatest enemy. Isabella became her rival, while she formed a tentative friendship with Akin.

Cat developed no magic, but she discovered something else. Uniquely, as far as anyone could tell, she had no magic at all. She eventually discovered that a complete lack of magic was necessary for forging Objects of Power. Far from being useless, her talent made her extremely valuable and utterly irreplaceable. As far as anyone could tell, Cat was the only true 'Zero' known to exist. This led to her—and her friends, Akin and Rose—being kidnapped, then targeted by Crown Prince Henry and Stregheria Aguirre, Cat's Great

Aunt, when they launched a coup against the Great Houses and the King himself. Their subversions—which turned Isabella against her family—nearly led to complete disaster...and perhaps would have done just that, if Cat and Akin hadn't become friends.

In the aftermath, Cat proposed that she and Akin should be betrothed, creating a marriage bond between their families and making it impossible, at least for the next few years, for the two houses to come to blows. This was—reluctantly—accepted, with the proviso that either Cat or Akin could reject the agreement if they wished, when they came of age. Cat left Jude's to found her own school, where other Zeros—when they were found—would be taught.

Meanwhile, the Great Houses had to deal with the repercussions of the attempted coup and the sudden shift in the balance of power. Isabella Rubén, condemned as a traitor, was exiled to Kirkhaven Hall, where she discovered a secret her family had sought to bury...and a new secret, one of her own. Others took advantage of the chaos to stake a claim to power themselves, plots that were only foiled through sheer luck and outside intervention. The city remained unstable...

Six years passed, slowly. Akin Rubén went back to school for his final year, to discover—thanks to his father—that he had to compete in the Challenge, a contest to find the 'Wizard Regnant.' Reluctantly, Akin complied, forming a team consisting of his cousin Francis and a handful of misfits, including merchant's daughter Louise Herdsman and Saline Califon, a distant relative who was under a spell cast by her wicked uncle. Despite Francis's betrayal—the result of a shadowy figure from the family's past—Akin managed to realise the true nature of the Challenge and forge a last-minute alliance with Alana Aguirre, Cat's sister, that allowed them to share the victory.

This did not please everyone, most notably common-born student Adam Mortimer.

That was five short months ago. Now, Adam is on the verge of finishing his education...

PROLOGUE

If there was one lesson my father—and my experience at Jude's—had hammered into me, time and time again, it was this.

Never, *never*, trust an aristo.

It wasn't that all aristos were bad. I'd met some who were good, who were decent and kind and generous...as long as it didn't impinge upon their interests in any substantial way. And I'd met some who seemed to take delight in looking down on the commoners and making us beg, for everything from food and funding—and patronage—to simple survival. They'd been taught to put their interests of their class ahead of everything else, even simple human decency. They were just too different. They could never be trusted.

Father had sworn he would never call upon an aristocrat and he'd kept his oath. He'd worked his way up from the docks through sheer talent and a gritty willingness to do whatever it took to build up a merchant trader business by himself. He could have had everything on a platter, if he'd become an aristo's client. They would have given him everything he could handle, at the cost of losing his independence. Once they had him in their clutches, they would never have let him go. The price was too high. And Father had proved it could be done without them. He'd made me swear the same oath when I went to Jude's.

I'd kept it, as best as I could. It came with a price. I could be friendly to anyone and everyone, but I could never truly be *one* of them. I wasn't an aristo, of course, and I was unwilling to submit to them. They knew I wasn't useless, but they also knew I would never be their client. I studied as hard as I could, determined to make a name for myself that relied on no one else. I was going to be the greatest sorcerer in the world. It was why I'd entered the Challenge.

And then, everything changed.

I'd chosen not to form a team. There just weren't many students, like myself, who didn't have ties to the aristos. Even *trying* to put together a group would have exposed me to humiliation. I was good too, good enough to think I could do it on my own. I thought, as I heard the rumours echoing through the school, that I'd have some advantages if I was alone. I wouldn't have to fear my allies putting a knife—hopefully just metaphorically—in my back. One never knew with aristos.

The Challenge itself seemed absurdly simple. Capture the Flag, writ large. I suppose that should have tipped me off. Nothing is ever quite as simple as it seems. I woke up in the middle of a forest, miles from anywhere. No worries. I was good at being sneaky. I'd spent my nights at school sneaking around, stealing food from the kitchens or feuding with other students. I stayed low, keeping my head down as I inched through the forest towards the castle. I didn't want to encounter the other teams, not when I couldn't afford to take a single hit. If I was frozen, stunned, or trapped in a useless form…I would lose. No one was going to liberate me before time ran out. It would just make life harder for themselves.

I watched and waited as two other teams reached the castle, only to start snapping spells at each other instead of splitting up or trying to collaborate. They took each other out, more or less. There were only a couple of students left free by the time I spelled them both and walked into the castle. The wards felt stronger than I'd expected, strong enough to confuse my senses. The building's interior kept shifting. I was impressed, as well as worried. I knew it would be very easy to get turned around and pointed in the wrong direction. I was sneaking down the corridor when I saw someone moving ahead of me. I hexed him...

...And promptly got hexed in the back.

My body froze, my muscles locking stiff. I wanted to shout, to roar in fury, but it was too late. I'd been tricked and...I'd lost. Francis Rubén walked past me, sniggering like a depraved loon. He'd been separated from his team, but...it had worked out for him. He'd taken me out of the game. He dropped his trousers and mooned me, then walked on into the shadows. I stood there, helplessly. There was nothing I could do but wait for the game to end.

I'd been beaten before. It happened, no matter how hard I tried. There's always someone better or luckier or...simply in a position to take advantage of my mistakes. I didn't take losing personally. If I was beaten according to the rules, I didn't mind. It happened. But Francis...I felt tricked, belittled, and humiliated by how he'd rubbed my nose in it. And it didn't help that others snickered at me too as they passed. I was frozen, but I could *hear* them. They pointed and laughed, the commoner who'd tried to do the Challenge alone. Alana was particularly cruel. She'd never liked me, ever since I'd asked her to walk out with me. She didn't pay attention to anyone unless he—or she—could trace their bloodline all the way back to the Thousand Year Empire.

It felt like hours before I was freed. The Challenge was over. Akin Rubén—one of the few decent aristos—had won. Alana had come second, sort of. Francis was dead. I never heard the full details, which led me to suspect he'd done something embarrassing. I would have liked to think that he'd hexed someone else in the back, but I doubted it. Aristos didn't get thrown out for cheating commoners. That was how most of their ancestors had risen to power in the first place.

But the whole affair left me unsure of what to do with my life. I was a good magician—I knew that—but what would I do after I graduated? What *could* I do? There were few careers open to me that didn't involve asking for patronage, pledging myself to an aristo and following my patron's orders slavishly. The system had little room for the truly independent. Father had worked hard, but he'd run up hard against the limits. He couldn't grow his business any further without their help and it was the one thing he refused to do.

The weeks and months that followed were frustrating, to say the least. *Everyone* knew I'd been humiliated. They learnt not to snigger so loudly after I claimed Scholar's Rights and hexed two particularly annoying students until their own mothers couldn't have recognised them, but I knew they were still laughing. Of course they were! I was a safe target. They wouldn't get embroiled in a family feud by laughing at me. Whatever I did to them, it wouldn't last. I forced myself to work hard, putting my all into the exams. And then…

I waited, bored. I had to do something to liven things up.

Ironically, my decision to commit a string of pranks was what opened the door to a whole new world…

CHAPTER ONE

It was going to be the greatest prank ever.

I smiled as I carefully picked my way into the Charms classroom. Jude's had a tradition of pranksters, students who pushed the limits as far as they would go without crossing the line into bullying. I'd gleefully embraced the tradition over the last few months, devising newer and better spells to make everyone—even the victim—laugh. But I hadn't come up with anything *new*. My pranks were little more than modified or improved versions of older pranks. They'd be saying I was a copycat. And that was intolerable.

This time, I told myself, it would be different. I was *really* going to do something new. I was going to upset the aristos, shock them…my smile grew wider as I slipped into the empty classroom and made my way to the storeroom beyond. I'd borrow a handful of supplies, use them in the prank and—afterwards—take whatever punishment came my way. Magister Hugh Von Rupert wouldn't be too annoyed, I thought. The old geezer barely knew what year it was, let alone the names and faces of his students. He had a first-class mind for magic—I'll give him that much—but little else. I honestly didn't understand why students like Caitlyn Aguirre had paid so much attention to him.

The wards on the storeroom parted after a few moments of careful effort. I nodded to myself as I gingerly opened the door—I wouldn't put it past the charms tutors to rig a surprise on the far side for any thieving students—and peered inside. The small collection of tools, supplies and textbooks seemed to shimmer in welcome. I stayed where I was, casting a handful of detection spells. Getting caught after the fact was one thing, but getting caught in the act would make me a laughingstock. Being laughed at was worse than detention, or writing lines, or volunteering at the local soup kitchen. If there were any more charms inside the compartment, I might be in some trouble.

But there were none.

I frowned, torn between the urge to get on with it and the sense I should back away now. The storeroom wouldn't have been left *completely* undefended. I could hardly be the *first* student who'd thought of raiding the charms classroom for supplies. The potions cabinets were heavily defended—most students tried to raid *them*—but really…the storeroom should have been warded better than this.

Yet…there was nothing.

I narrowed my eyes, then inched inside. I'd come too far to back out now. I'd know, even if no one else did. I would know I'd been a coward, rather than taking what I wanted and withdrawing before lunch was over and the tutors had returned. I reached for the nearest box of tools…

…And sensed, more than heard, someone behind me.

I tensed, bracing myself as I turned slowly. If Magister Von Rupert had caught me…I might be able to talk my way out of *serious*—and humiliating—trouble. Boys will be boys and all that guff. My heart sank as I saw Magister Grayson, hands crossed over his chest and a grim expression on his face. Magister Von Rupert was easy-going, but his partner was vindictive, vicious, vile and a number of other things that also started with V. No one ragged on Magister Von Rupert—much—for fear of Magister Grayson. I was doomed, unless…I groaned. Tradition decreed that any student who managed to get past the tutors and escape was allowed to go free, but I knew I wasn't going to get past *him*. Magister Grayson was the toughest tutor in school. A student who tried to give him the traditional black eye would be lucky if he *only* spent the next few weeks in the hospital wing.

"Adam Mortimer," Magister Grayson said. I tried to look for a hint of mercy in his dark eyes, for an awareness that we were nearing graduation, but saw none. "What do you think you're doing?"

A hundred answers ran through my mind, all discarded before they were fully formed. I couldn't lie, not to him. I couldn't escape either. There was nothing for it, but to take my punishment like a man. I wondered, as I forced myself to relax, what it would be. Tutors weren't allowed to hit or hex students, unless the students hit or hexed them first, but they had wide latitude for punishment. I was an upperclassman. Maybe he'd humiliate me by assigning me lines, as if I were a lowly lowerclassman. Or maybe he'd tell me to spend the next few days helping the kitchen staff.

"I was borrowing supplies for a prank, sir," I said. I didn't bother to pretend I was sorry, not about anything other than getting caught. He wouldn't believe me if I'd tried. "I...how did you know I was here?"

"That's none of your business." Magister Grayson glowered at me. I wondered, suddenly, if he'd swapped shifts with his partner. I'd thought Von Rupert was on duty today. I would never have dared raid the storeroom if I'd known it was Magister Grayson. "You're meant to be graduating, are you not?"

"Yes, sir." I felt a flicker of fear. Could Magister Grayson tamper with my exam results? I didn't think so—the exams were administered by independent proctors, sworn to neutrality—but it was impossible to be *sure*. Magister Grayson was *good*. "I'm due to leave for good in two weeks."

"How lucky for us," Magister Grayson said, his voice dripping with sarcasm. "I suppose giving you a year's detention is a *bit* out of the question."

"Yes, sir." I tried not to smirk. Whatever punishment he gave me, it wouldn't linger past graduation day. "I'll be gone soon."

"Quite." Magister Grayson smiled, coldly. I felt another *frisson* of fear. "Go to the detention hall. Supervise the detentions until dinnertime. And if I catch you in here again, you'll regret it."

I tried not to wince. Supervising detentions was *boring*. An hour supervising the detention hall was almost as bad as having detention itself. Worse, perhaps, because the supervisor had to keep an eye on the detainees. He wasn't allowed to read or do his own work or do *anything*. I'd done a few shifts, an hour at a time, and I'd hated it. I had never been *quite* sure who was *actually* being punished. The lowerclassmen in detention, or the poor upperclassman who was meant to be watching them.

"Yes, sir," I managed. There were worse punishments, weren't there? "Thank you, sir."

Magister Grayson pointed at the door. "Go."

I walked past him, gritting my teeth as I strolled into the corridor. There was no point in *not* doing as I was told. Magister Grayson would report the punishment to higher authority and if I didn't attend the classroom...I snorted, rudely. *That* would get me in *real* trouble. It might not affect my exam results, but it would *certainly* affect whatever reference Jude's gave me after I graduated. Getting caught trying to break into the storeroom was one thing; disobeying orders and welshing out of punishment was quite another.

And Father would not be pleased, I reminded myself. I didn't *want* to work for my father, after I graduated, but I might not have a choice. And... my actions would reflect badly on *him. Everyone would be saying he raised a coward who couldn't look himself in the eye.*

I dawdled as much as I could as I walked through empty corridors and into the detention hall, trying to convince myself the hall would be empty. The exams were almost all over, save for a handful of exams intended for specific career paths. I hadn't taken any of them, if only because I wasn't sure what my career path *was*. Everything I wanted to do would have required pledging myself to *someone*...I put the thought aside as I peered into the hall and winced. The Head Girl—Alana Aguirre—sat at the head desk, bored. A handful of younger students sat at other desks, doing their work. They looked too scared to talk out of turn. I didn't blame them. I'd been like them too.

"Adam?" Alana glanced up at me. "*You* have detention?"

I tried not to stare. Alana was *beautiful*, with dark skin, darker eyes and hair so perfect I *knew* she used magic to keep it in line. I'd found her attractive from the moment I'd started noticing girls as more than oddly-shaped boys. She looked as though she wouldn't harm a fly. But I knew she not only *could* harm a fly, she was perfectly capable of turning someone *into* a fly too. Rumour had it she'd been *really* terrible to her sister, the Zero. I believed it. I'd asked her out once, and she'd laughed in my face.

And it doesn't help that people keep asking if we're related. I resisted the urge to roll my eyes at the thought. *They really can't believe my talent came from the commoner ranks.*

"Yeah." I had the satisfaction of seeing her eyes widen before I explained. "I've been ordered to take over from you. Lucky you."

Alana smiled. It lit up her face. "What did you do? Throw a tomato at the Castellan?"

"Something like that," I said, vaguely. I wasn't going to admit what I'd actually been caught doing. Magister Grayson might not be very specific when he reported me to higher authority. Alana had access to the punishment books. If I was lucky, they wouldn't tell her very much. "The Magister was not best pleased."

"Hah." Alana stood, brushing down her skirt. I tried not to stare at her shirt as she donned her uniform jacket. "Akin's due to take over in an hour or so. Should I tell him not to bother?"

"I'm here until dinnertime," I told her. The more I thought about it, the more annoyed I grew. "Tell him to do whatever he wants."

Alana nodded stiffly, then turned and headed to the door. I resisted the urge to watch her as I took the seat and checked the detention roster, casting my eyes over the list of names. I knew some of them from tutoring, but—as an upperclassman—I was obliged to pretend I didn't. It was lucky my sister wasn't in the crowd. I'd have had to be extra hard on her, just to make it clear I wasn't favouring her. I settled back into my seat, raising my eyes to study the detainees. They made a show of not looking back at me, save one. Penny Rubén.

I held her eyes until she looked down, her cheeks burning with humiliation. Penny was a fifth-year student who'd been caught bullying—openly bullying—one of her first-year charges. *Akin*, her cousin, had caught her. He'd surprised and outraged many of his peers by ensuring Penny had the book thrown at her, rather than dealing with it himself or burying the truth to protect the family name. I wasn't sure *quite* what had happened—and not all of the rumours reflected well on Akin—but he'd certainly ensured the problem could not be quietly forgotten. Penny might spend two more years at school, yet...she'd always be treated as a lowerclassman. One of her former peers had probably given her lines. She couldn't have been more humiliated if she'd been forced to clean cauldrons like a skivvy.

Serves you right, I thought. Upperclassmen were not supposed to pick on lowerclassmen, certainly not first-years who were meant to be under their supervision. But Penny was an aristo. Her father, who'd left his family under mysterious circumstances, had probably raised her to suck up to her superiors while sneering at everyone below her. *It isn't as if your punishment will follow you when you graduate.*

I scowled. I'd been assured that wasn't true. Penny's reputation would follow her, wherever she went. But it wasn't a *formal* punishment. She'd probably find a way to parlay her birth into an advantageous match, or convince her family to give her lots of money in exchange for taking herself out of Shallot. Her family wouldn't punish her unless she *really* stepped over the line. Akin's sister had been sent into exile for high treason. Anything less would probably be quietly ignored.

Someone coughed. I glared at him, then turned my attention back to the list. A boy who'd been disobedient in Defensive Magic. I was surprised he'd been sent to the hall instead of being put to work by the tutors. A pair of girls who'd been given detention for talking too loudly in the library. Personally, I thought they weren't being punished enough. I'd always hated chattering brats when I'd been trying to study. And seven others, girls and boys, who'd been ordered to write some variant of *'I will do as my tutors tell me without talking back.'* I had to smile at one of the notes—a first-year boy who'd charmed a piece of chalk to write lines on the blackboard for him—and made a mental note to suggest to my sister that she kept an eye on him. Someone with that sort of talent might be worth watching.

He's probably got a patron already, I thought, sourly. Aristo students were expected to start recruiting clients *young*. It just wasn't fair. I could have had anything I wanted, as long as I pledged myself to someone barely older. If they couldn't give it to me themselves, their parents certainly could. *And even if he doesn't, that will change before too long.*

I leaned back in my chair, wishing for something—anything—to happen. The rules were clear. I wasn't allowed to read, I wasn't allowed to write…I wasn't even allowed to engage my charges in conversation, unless one of them did something I could object to. I waited, half-praying for Penny to step out of line so I could stomp on her, but she did nothing. I guessed she knew just how bad things would be for her, over the next two years. She deserved no less. It wasn't justice—personally, I would have expelled her—but it would have to do.

The door opened. I glanced up, just in time to see a brown-haired firstie girl inching into the room. She looked ashamed, as if she was already regretting whatever she'd done. It was probably her first detention. I concealed my amusement as she sneaked forward, as if she could avoid being noticed as long as she stayed quiet. She was already too late to escape notice. Hell, she was ensuring she *was* noticed by trying *not* to be noticed. I wondered, idly, how long it would take her to learn that there was nothing more conspicuous than someone trying to hide.

Probably a commoner, I decided, as she stopped in front of the desk. She looked so tense that I was tempted to shout *BOO. An aristo would be a little more confident even if she was walking to her doom.*

I dismissed the temptation—I wasn't *Penny*, damn it—and took the slip she offered me. It was clear and concise. The poor girl—her name was Gayle—had been given lines for a poorly-written essay. I guessed she'd been having problems with her handwriting, rather than whatever she'd actually written. I'd had problems too, when I'd been a lowerclassman. Father had made sure I knew how to read and write, but I'd never been a particularly good writer. My tutors had made hundreds of sarcastic remarks as I'd struggled to learn the ropes.

"Take a seat," I ordered, as I passed her a pencil and paper. "Write your lines, then you can go."

It wasn't the nicest thing I'd ever done, but the last thing she *needed*—when she had six more years of schooling to get through—was me going easy on her. The other students might be pretending to ignore us, but I knew they were listening. They'd talk if I went easy on her, if they thought I let her off...her classmates would hear, eventually, and take it out on her. It wouldn't be her fault. It wouldn't be as through she'd begged me to let her go or something along those lines. But they'd take it out on her anyway. There was nothing I could do about it.

I watched her sit down, then forced myself to think of something—anything—else. I had only two weeks before I needed to start job-hunting in earnest. I knew my father. He'd put me to work in the shop, or kick me out if I refused. And the longer I took to get a proper job, the harder it would be. I glowered at my hands, magic prickling just under my skin. It just wasn't fair.

Life isn't fair, I reminded myself. *All you can do is play the cards you're dealt and hope for the best.*

The door opened, again.

I blinked in surprise as *Akin* stepped in. Alana should have told him he wasn't needed...right? I didn't *think* she'd take the risk of letting the Head Boy embarrass himself, not when their families were in alliance. Her parents would be *furious* if she caused a rift between the two families. And her sister Cat, perhaps the most important aristo amongst her generation, would be angry too. She and Akin were betrothed. They seemed to get on better than most betrothed couples.

"Akin," I said. "I'm stuck here until..."

Akin cut me off. "The Castellan sent me to take your place," he said. "You've been summoned to his office."

I blinked. "Why...?"

"I have no idea." Akin smiled, humourlessly. "But you'd better get there quickly."

"Will do." I stood, wondering if I should be relieved or worried. "Have fun."

CHAPTER TWO

I tried to look confident, as I strode through the corridors and up the stairs, despite the fear gnawing my soul. It was uncommon for students, even upperclassmen, to be summoned to the Castellan's office unless they were in *real* trouble. I couldn't think of anything I'd done, or anything I might reasonably be suspected of doing, that might have earned me a summons from the school's master, but…I couldn't think of any *other* reason why I might be summoned either. Even Akin and Alana weren't important enough to be offered a *social* invite. Caitlyn Aguirre was perhaps the only student of my generation to merit one and *she'd* left Jude's five years ago, after the House War.

Maybe he just wants to yell at me for breaking into the storeroom, I thought, although that didn't seem likely. Tradition insisted that a person could only be punished *once*, no matter what he'd done. Magister Grayson had foreclosed *that* possibility when he'd sent me to supervise detention. *Or maybe something else has happened.*

Ice gripped my heart as I knocked on the half-open door and stepped into the antechamber. The Castellan's secretary, a woman with an glower that could curdle milk, scowled at me, then pointed to the inner door. I set my face in a carefully-neutral expression, then walked into the Castellan's chamber. He sat behind his desk, glaring at a sheet of official-looking paperwork. Another man sat in a chair front of the desk, turning to look at me. I tensed, despite myself. My instincts recognised a threat when they saw one. He had the air of a man who knew himself so well there was no room for doubt or scruple. His face was handsome, but oddly bland. It was the kind of face that looked as if it would go unnoticed in a crowd.

I met the Castellan's eyes. "You called me, sir?"

"Yes." The Castellan sounded irked. "Sir Gareth?"

I blinked as the stranger stood. He was taller than I'd thought, wearing a dark suit that marked him as a king's messenger. I hesitated, suddenly unsure of the proper protocol. Was I meant to bow or go to one knee…? The thought burned. I hated bending the knee to *anyone*. Magic seemed to grow stronger as Sir Gareth studied me. He was a powerful magician. His spells seemed to be spreading out, touching the entire office.

"We'll have the room now," he said. His voice was aristocratic, but oddly accented. I had the feeling he was from the capital, rather than Shallot or one of the border cities. I'd never been outside my hometown. "I'll speak to you later."

The Castellan nodded and stood. I stared in disbelief, unable to wrap my head around someone ordering the Castellan out of his own office. The Castellan might not be the supreme ruler of the school—that was the three lords above him—but he ran the building. It was hard to believe that someone—anyone—would show him so much disrespect. Sir Gareth had to be *very* important. And if he was a king's messenger…

My thoughts ran in circles. Did Sir Gareth work for the *king*? Or was he representing another aristocrat? Or…what did he want with me? Was I in trouble? Or…I couldn't think of any explanation that made *sense*. I wasn't Caitlyn Aguirre, or someone else with a unique talent, someone who might have drawn the attention of the king himself. I was just another common-born magician, with neither money nor connections. There was no reason anyone should be interested in *me*.

"Take a seat." Sir Gareth lowered his voice as he indicated a chair. "We have a lot to cover."

I sat, trying hard to focus. What was going on? Sir Gareth snapped his fingers, summoning two decanters and a jug of water from the sideboard. I watched, numbly, as invisible forces manipulated the three items, filling the decanters with water and returning the jug to the side. I took the glass I was offered and eyed it, unsure if I dared to sip. It was both an impressive display of power and a warning. Sir Gareth was clearly someone to take seriously.

Sir Gareth sat back. "Why did you take the Challenge alone?"

I felt my cheeks heat. "I thought it would give me a chance to make a name for myself," I said, truthfully. "If I won, if I became Wizard Regnant, I thought I could get an apprenticeship without any pesky strings attached."

"Indeed?" Sir Gareth didn't smile. "And that was what you wanted?"

"In part." I didn't want to tell him the rest, but I had the feeling I should. "I wanted—I needed—to make a name for myself. I didn't—I don't—want to be just another client."

"I've reviewed your grades," Sir Gareth said. "And your exam results. You'd hardly be just another *client*."

"I would be." I eyed him, sourly, as a thought stuck me. "Are you *encouraging* me to talk?"

"Yes." Sir Gareth didn't sound remotely sorry. "I wanted truthful answers."

I glared. "You didn't trust me?"

"In this line of work, most people will bend over backwards to tell me what they think I want to hear," Sir Gareth said, unemotionally. "The truth is often far more important."

"I won't lie to you," I snapped. It crossed my mind that I shouldn't be talking to him like that, but I was too angry to care. "What do you *want* with me?"

"I've reviewed your grades," Sir Gareth repeated. "You have top marks in everything practical, from Advanced Charms to Forging. Your marks in more abstract studies are poorer—clearly, you don't take *that* much interest in history or current affairs. And a couple of your sports masters have remarked that you're not a team player. What would you say to that?"

I bet Francis wrote one of those assessments, I thought, nastily. Francis had never liked me. I'd been a good enough player to stay on the field, but not good enough to write my own ticket. *And what he meant was that I didn't spend enough time kissing his unmentionables.*

"I argued that positions within a team should be allocated by skill, not family connections," I said, coldly. Francis hadn't liked *that* argument. The little bastard had genuinely believed he'd won his post though skill, rather than the family name. He'd been good, but not *that* good. "And my arguments didn't please the aristos."

"I'd wager not," Sir Gareth agreed. I thought I saw a flicker of amusement cross his face. "You have *excellent* marks as a duellist. Why didn't you join the league?"

"I couldn't afford the dues," I said, reluctantly. "It was impossible on my allowance."

"An unfortunate problem," Sir Gareth said. "But not an insurmountable one. You could look for a sponsor."

"Which would mean giving up my independence," I pointed out. "Whoever sponsored me would certainly want *something* in return."

"Quite." Sir Gareth nodded, curtly. "And where do you see yourself in five years?"

I frowned. The sudden shift in subject seemed designed to confuse me. "I don't know," I admitted. "It isn't as if I have many prospects."

"Really?" Sir Gareth lifted his eyebrows. "Is that true?"

"Yes," I said. "The only *real* prospect is going to work for my dad."

I stared at my hands, unwilling to admit how little I wanted that. Father wasn't a *bad* person—perish the thought—but I wanted to be more than just a merchant tradesman and shopkeeper in Water Shallot. And yet, where could I go? What sort of job could I do without surrendering to the aristos and becoming just another client? I couldn't imagine *anything*, save perhaps signing on to a clipper ship and sailing to distant Hangchow. But even the clipper ships belonged to the Great Houses. I wouldn't have a hope of commanding my own ship, unless I sold myself to the aristos.

Sir Gareth leaned forward. I had the sense the *real* discussion was about to begin. "Every year, my office looks for students such as yourself. Skilled magicians, with brains and power...and independence. People who know Shallot, or the other cities, without being part of the local power structure. I dare say that's true of you?"

"I dare say," I echoed. "Father has a tiny power base, too small to matter."

"Quite," Sir Gareth said. "I have a job offer for you. The training is hard; some would say brutal. You might wash out within the first few weeks or die, if things go wrong. The pay is good, but don't count on having much time to spend it. You'll have respect, and support, as long as you uphold the law. And you'll be *challenged* every day until you retire."

I cocked my head. "What sort of job is it?"

"A King's Man," Sir Gareth said. "We're always looking for new recruits. And we think you have the right stuff."

I forced myself to say nothing. My thoughts were a churning mess. I'd heard all sorts of stories about the King's Men, from damsels in distress being rescued to angry dragons being slain before they could lay waste to entire towns and cities. The King's Men had done *everything*, if the stories were to be believed. They'd stopped invasions, put down rebellions, protected commoners, defeated crime lords and aristocrats and generally upheld the law. The stories made them sound like supermen. And they wanted me? I was tempted. By the Ancients, I was tempted.

And yet, the king was just another aristocrat. Wasn't he? I didn't want to pledge myself to *any* aristocrat. But...I stared down at my hands, unsure of myself. I wanted the chance to take on a newer and better challenge, whatever the price. What choice did I have? I *really* didn't want to spend the rest of my life as a glorified shopboy. Father might not even leave the shop to *me*. My older sister was first in line and *she* was determined to turn our small business into a massive enterprise. I had the feeling I'd be spending the rest of my life serving her, when Father finally joined his ancestors.

I swallowed, hard. "What...what's it like?"

Sir Gareth smiled. "Like I said, the training is hard. And it never stops, even when you graduate. You'll spend the rest of your life on the cutting edge of magical and military research, learning spells and techniques you will hopefully never have to use. Your word will be enough to save or damn the accused, to settle disputes and comfort the afflicted. One day, you may find yourself brokering a truce and ending a House War; another, you may find yourself tracking down a murderer or chasing a fugitive across the border. Or you might lead troops into battle, holding the line for reinforcements to arrive. Or...you might be on the far side of the border, doing whatever you can to slow an enemy army. The only thing you can be sure of, young man, is that each month will be different."

"And you want me to pledge myself to the king," I said. It was hard to keep the bitterness out of my voice. "I don't want to surrender everything..."

"You don't have to," Sir Gareth said. "The king understands the importance of *listening* to his advisors. And his loyal servants."

I frowned. "I don't know," I said. It was almost—if not quite—a lie. "What...I...someone came to you, didn't they, and made the same offer. What do you wish *you'd* known before you started?"

Sir Gareth nodded. I had the feeling he was pleased. "It can be a lonely life," he admitted, slowly. "You're obliged to cut all formal ties of obligation. You can stay in touch with your family—many of us do—but you can't use your position to help them. Should you get married, your wife will have the same issue. She will not be allowed to manipulate you or your position for any reason whatsoever. And...you may find yourself spending months, if not years, away from her.

"And you'll make enemies. There are hundreds of lords and ladies, with power both magical and mundane, who hate us. A couple of us have met with suspicious accidents during the course of an investigation. We never managed to prove who killed them, or even if their deaths weren't accidents, but...we know. You might wind up dead, your ashes scattered in a graveyard no one outside the order knows exists.

"And...there will be times when there will be no satisfactory end to an investigation. You'll find the suspect has enough power and influence to escape judgement. Or that the entire issue is hushed up, with agreements made for compensation behind the scenes. Or...that you'll be ordered to do something off the record, to ensure there is punishment even if it is never formally acknowledged. If you're wedded to a happy ending, all the time, you may find this job a little frustrating."

I let out a breath. "And warlocks?"

"Yes." Sir Gareth nodded, curtly. "You'll certainly encounter warlocks."

He smiled, thinly. "I understand you don't like the aristocracy, young man. I don't blame you. Consider this your chance to keep an eye on it. Who knows? Maybe you'll find a way to teach them a lesson."

I frowned. "How many people did you talk to before you spoke to me?"

"Enough." Sir Gareth shrugged. "We do a background check before revealing our hand. It saves time. If a candidate is deemed unsuitable... well, they never know they had our attention in the first place."

"I see," I said. "What did they say about me?"

"I can't answer that question," Sir Gareth said. "Suffice it to say they said nothing to make us rethink our interest."

He smiled, rather humourlessly. "Are you interested? Or should I give up?"

"I'm interested," I said. Father might not be pleased...I told myself I'd have to discuss it with him. Technically, I was old enough to make such decisions for myself, but I didn't want to blindside the old man. I certainly didn't want to be disowned. "When do I need to give you a definite answer?"

Sir Gareth smiled. "Intake Day is one week from today," he said, as he dug into his briefcase and removed a large envelope. The runes sketched on the parchment promised an unpleasant surprise for anyone who tried to open the missive without permission. "You'll find all the details here. If you're interested, after you read the papers and consult with your family and friends, just turn up for training as ordered. If you change your mind...

don't bother. We'll log you as another reject and proceed to the next set of candidates."

"I understand," I said.

"Tell the school you're moving out early," Sir Gareth added. "Don't count on coming back within the next couple of months, unless you wash out. If that happens,"—he shrugged—"you might as well try to apply yourself elsewhere."

"Yes, sir," I said, reluctantly. "I'll be there."

"Consult with your family first," Sir Gareth urged. "You're doing *far* more than just getting a job. It's a *calling*. And things will never be the same again."

"I see, I think," I said.

"I'd be surprised if you did," Sir Gareth said, coolly. He placed the envelope on the Castellan's desk. "It took me *years* to truly understand what I'd joined, and how it would consume my life."

I stared at him. "Is it worth it?"

"I've saved lives. And cities." Sir Gareth sounded pensive, his eyes looking into a past only he could see. "So yes, it's worth it. But it does come with a price."

"I understand," I said.

"Hah." Sir Gareth smiled, rather coldly. "If you can tell me that again, a year from now, I'll buy you a drink."

I kept my thoughts to myself. I knew I'd have to talk it over with Father, but...I already knew I was going to be reporting for training on Intake Day. My fingers itched to reach for the envelope, open it and read the papers, to plan my journey to...to wherever I would be trained. I felt torn between my hatred of surrendering even *some* of my independence and hope—new hope—of doing *something* about the aristos. Catching some of them with egg on their face would make everything worthwhile.

Sir Gareth stood. "I have a final test for you," he said. "A warning, as well as a test. Are you interested?"

I blinked. "I don't..."

He jabbed a finger at me. I sensed the surge of magic, a second too late. I'd had defences in place, but they melted like snow in the face of the sun. My body warped and twisted—I felt a surge of pain, the unmistakable sense of being transfigured—my eyesight twisting and bending as the world grew larger. The magic boiled around me. I tried to cast a counterspell, but it refused to work. I looked down at myself and gulped. I'd been turned into a frog! I'd been turned into a frog, as easily as a firstie who knew no magic before he came to school. And all my defences had proven worthless.

That's what he's trying to teach me, I thought, numbly. I hadn't been so easily defeated since I'd been a little boy, playing in the gutter with the other snipes. *There are magics beyond the fields I know.*

"Free yourself, before the Castellan reclaims his office," Sir Gareth ordered, coolly. "And if you're still interested, report to the hall on Intake Day."

He turned and strode out of the room, leaving me behind.

CHAPTER THREE

I forced myself to calm down and *focus*, even though panic yammered at the back of my mind. I was not a little kid, unused to magic. I'd been transfigured hundreds of times over the past decade. I shouldn't be panicking, not when I was in a form that could move and wave its hands to cast the counterspell. I'd plenty of experience of breaking spells from the inside, freeing myself and going on to strike back at my tormentor. I shouldn't have any trouble breaking free this time.

But *this* spell was different. It roared around me in a manner I'd never sensed. The sheer power was terrifying, as if it was forcing me into another shape through naked *will* alone. I tried to focus, to pick out the spellform and dismantle it from the inside, but it refused to hold still long enough to let me analyze it. I'd seen all kinds of spells designed to make life difficult for anyone who wanted to take them apart, yet…this was different. It shifted so often that I found it hard to believe it had *just* turned me into a frog. It could have done something else…

I held still, a giant weight pressing me down. My back felt uncomfortable, as if I'd been forced to the floor in a wrestling match. I knew from bitter experience that if I felt *that* bad, if someone had me trapped so completely, I'd lost. I'd have no choice but to tap out in surrender. And yet, there was no one to surrender *to*. I inched forward, feeling the pressure move with me. The spell wasn't going to let me go *that* easily.

The spell can't be unbreakable, I told myself. I looked around, trying to spot anything that might help. The Castellan might have a spellbreaker in his office. If he did, I couldn't see it—or anything else. *There has to be a way out.*

I gritted my teeth, trying to push the spell away. It was a raging torrent of energy, pushing me down...it barely budged, even when I threw everything I had into the effort. I couldn't even begin to untangle it. And yet...a thought stuck me and I forced myself into new effort. I pushed the spellflow back as hard as I could, while inching forward until I fell off the edge of the chair. My concentration snapped the moment I hit the floor, but it didn't matter. I was outside the spell's influence. My body returned to normal seconds later. I stumbled to my feet, sweat trickling down my back. That had been too close. The Castellan would certainly have told Sir Gareth if I'd failed.

The envelope called to me. I picked it up, stuck it under my arm and headed for the door. The secretary nodded coldly as I wobbled out of the office, feeling like someone had cast an instability jinx. I hadn't felt so bad since I'd gone out to a party, drank a *lot* more than I should and wound up nursing a hangover through my first classes of the day. I shuddered as I made my way through the empty corridors. No one had said anything about going back to the Detention Hall. I was sure that meant Akin was going to handle the duty until the bell rang for dinner.

I put the thought aside as I reached the upperclassman dorms and unpicked the hex on the lock. The sixth years had been trying to sneak into *our* section of the dorms now that their exams were over, picking out the rooms *they* wanted when the next term rolled around. I'd heard that some of them were competing to become Head Boy and Girl, although I had a feeling they were wasting their time. The decision wouldn't be made at Jude's. Akin was a decent person, for an aristo, but neither he nor Alana had *really* deserved the honour. There were others—better students, kinder students—who should have been offered the job.

I heard footsteps behind me and blinked as Louise Herdsman hurried up to the dorms. We should have been friends—we came from similar backgrounds, with similar stories—but we'd never really gotten along. Louise had spent her first few years at Jude's acting like a know-it-all who didn't, trying to boss everyone around when she wasn't questioning why things weren't organised to suit her. I understood her frustration, but ... she could be very wearying at times. Her blonde hair hung down to her shoulders, a reminder that she was now a legal adult. She was pretty, yet...there was something cold and hard about her. I tried to ignore the part of me that suggested I should ask her out.

"Adam," Louise said. "I heard you were in trouble."

"Foul lies," I said, wondering what she'd heard. Alana had probably told everyone I'd been given detention. "I am never in trouble."

Louise gave me a look that suggested I was something particularly unpleasant she'd scraped off her shoe. Given that she was about as aristocratic as myself, it *was* very impressive. I would have been cowed if I hadn't known her as a little girl.

"What are you doing this evening?" Louise sounded indifferent. I had the feeling it was an act. "Are you going to be free?"

"I don't know," I admitted. "I have to go back home."

"Ah." Louise backed off. "I'll see you later."

I watched her go, trying not to let my gaze linger on her behind. Louise... she hadn't been trying to ask me out, had she? I didn't think so. She'd never shown any interest in *anyone*, as far as I knew. I frowned, then opened my door and stepped into my bedroom. I'd never *minded* the dorms, where there had been little privacy, but I had to admit the private bedrooms were *much* better. It was just a shame that I'd be going back to the family home—and a complete lack of privacy—if becoming a King's Man didn't work out. I was too old to share a room with my sisters or father, wasn't I?

If we had room to spread out, we would, I thought, as I poured myself a mug of juice and sat on the bed. There was barely enough room to swing a cat, but the chamber was still better than anything I'd had as a youngster. *Back home, there's no way we can make the chambers bigger without magic or money we don't have.*

I sipped my drink as I opened the envelope and read through the set of leaflets. They weren't as informative as I'd hoped, although they did manage to answer a couple of questions I hadn't thought to ask. The Intake Day was going to be held at Haddon Hall, an estate thirty miles north of Shallot. I picked up a map and studied it, trying to understand how I was meant to get there. There was a stagecoach passing through Haddon itself, but the estate was a mile or two south of the town. I might have to get off at the town and walk to the estate. Or go to Haddon the day before and rent a room for the night. It wasn't as if it would be hard.

Just expensive, I mused, tartly. *They could have offered to pay my travel expenses.*

I frowned as I worked my way through the rest of the papers, then stood and started to pack up. I didn't have much, thankfully, but I couldn't afford to leave anything behind. I had to report for training in a week and…I didn't want to lose anything. I glanced back at the list of items I was supposed to bring and frowned. A handful of clothes and nothing else. No spellcasters, no spellbreakers, no toys and games…not even any books! I wondered, sourly, if we were going to be kept so busy there would be no time for fun. Probably. I didn't know much about the King's Men, beyond the fact they'd tried and failed to stop the House War, but I had the feeling we were going to be worked hard. Very hard.

The room looked oddly bare when I'd finished. I stood, feeling a twinge of disquiet. I'd lived in the room for nine months and…I hadn't really made any impression at all. The walls were as barren as they'd been when I moved in. I sighed, remembering how the aristos had decorated *their* rooms. Even *Akin* had hung a huge painting of himself and Caitlyn in pride of place. I wondered, as I headed for the door, what Alana made of it. As a reminder her sister was marrying before her, it could hardly be bettered.

I heard the dinner bell ring as I made my way up to the library, ignoring the handful of lowerclassmen running to the dining hall as if the food was going to run out. They probably expected to be tossed out, a few short seconds after they entered. Upperclassmen lorded it over lowerclassmen. It was the way of things and, now that the exams were over, the upperclassmen were free to be jerks. If they wanted to be. I'd never felt the urge, myself.

Probably because I spent too much time fetching and carrying when I was a lowerclassman myself, I thought coldly. The librarian was shutting his office, but he had no qualms about leaving an upperclassman in the library. *I don't want to be a jerk too.*

I smiled, then turned my attention to the careers section. There was no shortage of information on apprenticeships, from potions and alchemy to healing and financial wizardry, but almost nothing on the Kingsmen. I read through what little there was, frowning in dismay. The Kingsmen were definitely more than *just* a career, but there were almost no specifics. There were certainly no testimonials from people who'd joined, served their time and retired. I put the papers aside with a sigh. It was clear I wasn't going to find anything here, not when I wasn't sure what I was looking *for*.

The door opened behind me. I glanced back, just in case. I'd learnt, back in first year, to be wary of anyone behind me. Saline Califon entered the library, shot me a bright smile and headed down the stacks towards the section on law. I smiled again, then returned my attention to the files. Saline was an odd duck and no mistake. She'd started well, with an academic career everyone envied, then gone sharply downhill. And yet...she'd started doing better—much better—after the Challenge. I didn't understand it. She was an aristocrat, with all the power and connections she could possibly want. Why would she slack off in the middle of her schooling? I supposed I might have cared more about it if she'd been common-born. I'd tutored younger kids. I could have tutored her too.

I put my thought aside as I found the archived newspapers and started to work my way through them. There were hundreds of stories about the Kingsmen, but it was impossible to sort fact from fiction. The Kingsmen were wondrous supermen, who could go anywhere and do anything; the Kingsmen were buffoons, useless fools who couldn't even find a trio of missing children. They could do anything, but did nothing; they threw their weight around, but it was all for a good cause. My head throbbed by the time

I finished reading the stories from the last couple of years. There seemed to be nothing *solid* in the papers, nothing more than rumours and innuendo. The Kingsmen themselves didn't give interviews.

Which probably isn't a bad thing, I thought, as I returned the stacks to the shelves. *The media would probably tinker with whatever they said to make it more newsworthy.*

I snorted at the thought, then stood and looked around the library. Saline had her head in a book, her pretty face frowning. She looked up and met my eyes, challengingly. I looked back, silently kicking myself for getting into a pointless contest. I didn't want to back down, but I didn't want to make *her* back down either. The second dinner bell rang, making me jump. I looked away, smiling as I headed back down the stairs. I'd been saved by the bell.

And now I have to go see Father, I thought, as I returned to my room and picked up my bag and the envelope. *And see what he has to say.*

I hurried down the stairs and strode out of the main doors, heading to the gates that led to the city. It wasn't uncommon for older students to leave the grounds for a few hours, now that the exams were over, but I still felt oddly exposed as I passed through the gates. Something had been lost when I'd become an upperclassman. The challenge of scrambling over the back wall, with the prospect of being caught and marched to the office by the groundskeeper, was gone. Skullion had given me a black—well, blacker—eye once. I didn't mind. I should probably have given up instead of trying to fight, but I'd never been the sort of person to simply give up.

A figure hurried away from me, heading for the bridges that led to Water Shallot. I blinked in surprise as I recognised Louise. Where was *she* going? Her family had a shop on the far side of the river, but…she was heading for the wrong bridge. I opened my mouth to hail her, then told myself—firmly—that it was none of my business. Louise was a qualified sorceress in all but name. She could take care of herself. Any footpad or predator who tried to grab hold of her would find himself sitting on a lily pad, snapping at flies. And yet…it was odd for a young woman of her age to head to Water Shallot alone. Didn't she *care* about her reputation?

People will talk, I thought, as I crossed the road to head to a different bridge. I didn't want her to think I was following her. *And her parents will be furious.*

I felt a twinge of sympathy for Louise, mingled with a grim awareness that it could be a great deal worse. People *would* talk. It was all they ever did. And she would find herself painted as everything from a scarlet woman to an outright whore. She wouldn't have to do the crime to serve the time. It would suddenly be very hard for her to get married, if she *wanted* to get married. Or if anyone wanted to marry her. She *did* have a very disagreeable personality.

And she'd probably say the same about me, I told myself. *And people have been saying that about my father and sisters too.*

I put the thought aside as I walked along the riverside, staring down into the murky waters. A pair of barges were navigating through Shallot, carrying valuable goods from the docks to the warehouses on the far side of the city. The goods would be on their way to the capital—or somewhere else further up the river—before too long. I'd had a summer job working on the barges, for a couple of years. It had been fun, but I wouldn't have wanted to make a career out of it. The dockworkers guild was harsh to anyone who refused to bend the knee. I smiled as I turned onto the bridge and crossed into Water Shallot. The city didn't look any different, not here. The aristos didn't know what they were talking about.

Idiots, I thought. *They talk about slumming, and yet they never see the real slums.*

It would have been funny, if it hadn't been so tragic. I'd heard dozens of aristo brats drop hints of roguish dealings in Water Shallot, just to impress girls. They made it sound as if they were travelling to the Desolation, or the jungles of Minima. And they never went to the deep dark places, particularly after nightfall. There were limits to their bravery. I wish I could say I'd been surprised.

Water Shallot wasn't *that* different to the lower-class regions of South Shallot. The riverside streets were being gentrified, forcing out everyone who couldn't afford to live there any longer. I wondered where the former residents had gone, now that the newcomers had taken their homes and shops. A handful of guardsmen were on patrol, eyes nervously swinging from side to side as they made their way down the street. I was sure they'd run when trouble *really* broke out. The City Guard was kept deliberately weak by Magus Court. The Great Houses didn't want to create a rival, or a check on their power. Father and I knew, at base, that the only people who'd defend our home and business were ourselves. We couldn't rely on the City Guard.

The streets grew a little more decayed as I walked east, passing through growing crowds of fishermen and dockyard workers who'd finished for the night and now intended to drink themselves into a stupor. I shuddered, knowing how easy it would have been for Father to fall into the same trap. Some of my friends, back when I'd been a child, hadn't been so lucky. Their fathers, treated badly at work, had taken it out on their wives and families when they'd gotten home. I'd seen the bruises.

It could have been worse, I told myself. *I could have joined them too.*

CHAPTER
FOUR

My father's shop—and warehouse, as he put it—started life as a fairly small corner shop, one of a dozen under a giant tenement block. He bought it, then took a loan and purchased the two shops next to it and converted them into a single, much larger, shop. His empire had kept expanding until he'd laid claim to most of the block, with an option to buy what little he didn't already hold. I had the feeling he'd never gain *complete* control of the block, but it didn't matter. He held enough territory to veto anything he didn't like.

I stopped in front of the window, inspecting the display of goods intended to entice customers. Father sold *everything*, from clothes made by part-time seamstresses to meat and fish from the local farms and fishmongers. He'd told me, once, that he intended to make it easy for everyone to shop, for them to come to a single place to do it. I hadn't been convinced—his neighbours would have pushed back hard if they'd thought he was underselling them with the intention of driving them out—but it seemed to be working. The old man always had a lot of satisfied customers. Who knew? Maybe, by the time he died, he'd have taken his empire right to the limits.

Father doesn't believe in limits, I reminded myself, as I pushed open the door. A handful of anti-theft spells buzzed around me, then faded into the background. *And neither do I.*

"Adam!" I glanced up and smiled as I saw my sister, sitting behind the counter. "Welcome home!"

"Toni!" I grinned at her as she motioned me to the backroom door. "It's good to be back."

I felt my smile grow wider as Toni directed the shopgirl to take the counter and led me into the backroom so she could put the kettle on. My older sister looked *strikingly* like Alana Aguirre, although there was a faint scar on her face that Alana would have had removed the moment the raw magic faded. I'd watched hundreds of boys pay court to her, only to be thwarted by her demeanour and father's tongue-in-cheek demands for massive dowries. Alana could hardly have done it better. I grinned, then sat on the overstuffed armchair. It might have passed through a dozen hands before it came to our shop, but it was more comfortable than the fancy armchairs I'd seen at Jude's.

"You'd better have done well on your exams," Toni said, as she poured hot water into the teapot. "Father will be cross if you don't have good marks."

"I have it on good authority that I've done very well," I said. "How is the shop?"

"Good enough." Toni passed me a mug of tea, keeping one for herself. "The new assistant is shaping up well, certainly better than the *last* one. Poor girl was trying to steal food to feed her family. Dad was a boozer and mother…" she shrugged. "I had to let her go. We just couldn't afford the losses."

My eyes narrowed. "Are we making a profit?"

Toni frowned. "Barely. Father keeps finding new things to sell, which is great when they actually *sell*."

"I know." I sipped my tea thoughtfully. There was nothing we could do for the former shopgirl. "Some things simply don't take off."

"And others do," a new voice said. "Welcome home, Adam."

I put the mug aside and stood to receive a hug from my father. He was shorter than me, with dark chocolate skin and curly black hair he'd never bothered to straighten. I wouldn't have either, if it hadn't been the fashion. Alana and her sisters—and my younger sister—had it worse. Their hair was meant to be long and straight, not short and curly. I had the feeling they spent hours each day just smoothing it down.

"Father," I said, stiffly. "It's good to see you again."

My father nodded. "What? No tea for me?"

"You weren't around," Toni said. "There's tea in the teapot, if you like."

"No wonder no one's prepared to pay a massive dowry for you," Father grumbled. His smile took the sting out of his words. "Let me know when you want me to reduce it."

I looked from one to the other, realising—for the first time—that Father had set the dowry so high to make it easy for Toni to say no. It would be easy for her to blame the failure of any courtship on her father, who held the purse strings and had veto rights as long as she worked for him. She couldn't be blamed if her father refused to let her go, could she? I wondered, grimly, if anyone *would* come along she'd actually want. Water Shallot wasn't a good place to meet men. Or women, for that matter. I could easily see her deciding she'd prefer to stay single.

Mother died in childbirth, I recalled. *And she was one of the lucky ones.*

Father poured himself a mug of tea and sat down. "It's great to see you again, Adam," he said. "But why *did* you come home so soon?"

"Did you get kicked out?" Toni smirked. "Or were you simply bored of loitering around the school?"

"Neither." I resisted the urge to make sarcastic remarks as I opened my bag and removed the envelope. "I got a job offer."

I felt my heart start to pound as I passed the demagicked envelope to my father. If he said no...I could take off on my own, and perhaps I would, but I could hardly come back after a very public break. I wasn't sure *what* I'd do, if he said no. I didn't want to give up the chance to do something *great*, but...I knew he wouldn't be keen on me doing *anything* for the king. The king wasn't a normal aristo...

"I see." My father's voice betrayed nothing of his feelings. "Do you want to do this?"

"Yes, father." It was hard to speak definitely, but I had no choice. "It might give me a chance to make a difference."

"Might," Father repeated. He passed the papers to Toni. "Knocking down a building would *also* make a difference, but not a particularly good one."

I scowled. Father was fond of dropping little sayings like that into the mix whenever we argued. It was never easy to tell what he meant—what he *actually* meant, as opposed to what he *said*. I'd never known anyone so good at giving mixed messages. Even *girls* weren't so good at confusing me. I had the feeling he wasn't inclined to support me, but…how could I be sure?

"I might catch someone with their hand in the till or their pants around their ankles," I said, pushing as hard as I could. "And that person might be very important indeed."

"Which would put you in danger," Father pointed out, coldly. "You don't *need* to be a Kingsman to catch someone with their pants down."

"Of course not," Toni agreed. "You can just go to the brothel."

Father gave her a sharp look. Properly brought up young women weren't supposed to know the brothels existed, although pretty much all of them *did*. I'd heard plenty of chatter about that too, in both Jude's and Water Shallot. Any young woman born and bred in the poorest part of the city had to know the brothels were an option, if she had to put food on the table or if there were debts she couldn't repay. I swallowed, hard. The thought of Toni or Nora ending up in one of them was sickening.

"Father," I said. "What *else* am I going to do with my life?"

Father waved a hand at the wall. "You could work here. For me. For *us*."

I shook my head. "I don't want to be a shopboy," I said. "And it would be a waste of my education."

"You could go into tutoring," Toni pointed out. "If you're as good as you say…"

"I'd never get a magic licence," I said. There were some loopholes in the system, mainly covering parents teaching their children, but not ones I could exploit. "The Great Houses have the system all sewn up."

I met her eyes. "And besides, can you imagine me trying to teach a little brat? I'd go mad within the week."

Toni smirked. "A little brat like you, you mean?"

"Yeah." I conceded the point without rancour. Tutoring lowerclassmen was easy. Tutoring children promised to be hours of pure hell. "I don't understand how Father refrained from brutally strangling me."

"You got too big, too fast," Father said. He sipped his tea. "There are other options."

"Not many." I met his eyes, evenly. "I don't want to be a shopboy. I'm not going to inherit the business, even if I wanted it. Toni will do that..."

"Thanks a bunch," Toni muttered.

"...And Nora and I will have to find something else to do with our time," I continued. "I have the grades to seek an apprenticeship, but that would mean pledging myself to an older sorcerer and his family. There aren't many other options for me, are there? The careers I might want, the careers that might allow me to build a life for myself, come with strings attached."

"Strings that will be used to hang you, if you refuse to toe the line," Father said, evenly. "You'll be so tied up you won't be able to move."

"Yes. I *know*." I shook my head. "At least *this* way, I might have a chance to accomplish something for myself."

"Not for yourself," Father said. "For the king."

He scowled. "And the king was pretty useless during the House War, wasn't he?"

I shrugged. I'd never heard a clear explanation of just *what* had happened during the House War, even though I'd fought beside the others to retake and defend the school. Stregheria Aguirre had been plotting a coup, some said; Crown Prince Henry had been her dupe, her pawn. Or, perhaps, her *partner*. It seemed unlikely—the Crown Prince would inherit everything when his father died—but I'd heard stranger stories. I didn't really care. It was more important to look to the future.

Father let out a long breath. "That said, the Kingsmen have done some good. It was one of them who took Biddy Murphy away from her wretched husband. Saved her life."

I nodded. I should have remembered that.

"And you're sure of this," Father said. He took back the papers and thumbed through them. "You've made up your mind."

"Yes, Father." I breathed a sigh of relief. "I do intend to try."

"Best you can do," Father grunted. "You'll be taking yourself out of the line of inheritance"—he held up a sheet of paper—"but you didn't stand to inherit much anyway. I think I can still leave you my trousers, if nothing else. The girls aren't going to want them."

Toni rolled her eyes at me. I snorted. Young ladies weren't supposed to wear *trousers*. Maybe that would change, one day, but I doubted it. Toni wasn't going to be blazing a trail. It would have to be someone with real clout, someone like Alana...I snorted, again. No one was going to see *her* in trousers anytime soon.

"And perhaps a little money," Father added. "And guest-right."

"I don't want anything," I said, carefully. "Father..."

"That's what I said, when I was your age," Father said. "And do you know how close I came to utter disaster before you two and your sister were born?"

"No," I said.

"Yes," Toni said. "You've told me often enough."

I blinked. "You never told me."

"No." Father shook his head. "There were things I didn't want to discuss, not until you were an adult. Call me a coward if you like."

"I wouldn't dare," I said, truthfully. Calling someone a coward, in Water Shallot, was a guaranteed fight. Father had a mean right hook and years of experience at fighting dirty. I'd once seen him pick up a would-be mugger and throw him into a brick wall with tremendous force. "But shouldn't we be discussing them now?"

"This evening, if you stay." Father took one last look at the documents, then passed them back to me. "I don't think you should be doing this, Adam, but you're enough like *me*—when I was your age—that I know you won't listen if I forbid it. So go and be careful, and make sure you get everything in writing."

"And write to us," Toni said. "I'll be sure to write to you."

"And send you pointed little reminders if you fail to write back," Father said. "She picked up that habit from your grandma."

I nodded, remembering how my paternal grandmother had used to write sarcastic notes when we didn't answer her letters quickly enough. The old lady had had quite a sharp turn of tongue. I hadn't met anyone quite so sarcastic until I'd gone to school, where I'd discovered that making mistakes could draw an equally sharp comment—and detention—from my tutors. And, somehow, my grandmother had been far more fearsome.

"Thank you, Father," I said. "I just couldn't spend the rest of my life here."

"You don't know how lucky you are," Father said, curtly. "Do you?"

"I do," I said. "But..."

"Hah." Father shrugged. "What else do you have to tell me?"

"Nothing much," I said. "What about yourself?"

"There's lots of chatter about Prince Jacob of North Cairnbulg coming to town," Toni said. "Miss Higgins was insisting the prince is going to visit Water Shallot."

"I doubt it," I said. I'd heard rumours about Prince Jacob, but nothing felt really solid. It was very easy to get nasty rumours in Polite Society. For one thing, Polite Society wasn't really *polite*. "Unless they *want* to get him killed."

"You never know," Father said. "There's also stories about a challenge to the merchant guild's representative on Magus Court. Someone else might be putting their hat in the ring."

I frowned. "You, Father?"

"I don't have the backing," Father said. "It could be just a pointless challenge, something designed to get concessions from the guild rather than deliberately trying to unseat their representative, but it's hard to be sure. The guild normally has things sewn up well before voting rolls around. Everyone knows which way to cast their votes and all's well on the night.

But this time, there are odd rumblings from the working men's clubs. They might have a new leader."

"They might?" I shook my head. "I thought they were impossible to lead."

"So did I." Father looked down at his dark hands. "The working men's clubs have numbers, but they've never been a coherent political force. They've had too many problems remaining stable for *that*. If that's changed, they could swing the voting balance through weight of numbers alone."

"Which would be hard luck for the merchant's guild," I mused. "They can't beat up dissenters if the weight of the working men is on the other side."

"It might be hard luck for us too," Father said. "If they start demanding higher wages, we might be in some trouble. We don't hire many people ourselves, but our suppliers certainly *do*. If they have to raise wages, they'll have to raise their prices too. And we'll have to pass it on to our customers."

"Who are already unhappy at rising costs," Toni commented. "If we were the only ones raising charges, Father, we'd lose all our customers. Believe me, it would be pretty bad."

"I don't doubt it," Father said. He scowled. "Perhaps it's for the best, Adam. You'll be away from the city by the time something blows."

"If it does," Toni said. She smiled. "I'll be sorry not to have you working for free, but…"

"Go boil your head," I said, with more maturity than I thought the jibe deserved. "I'd be plotting to remove you within the week."

"You would, too," Toni said. She snorted as she stood. "Do you want something to eat, before you go back to school?"

My stomach rumbled. "If you don't mind," I said. I hadn't told them I was coming. I could hardly expect them to be ready for me, not with a three-course meal. I didn't want them to think they *had* to provide. "But don't worry about it. I have food waiting for me at school."

"I should hope so, given the fees," Father grumbled. "You make me proud, alright?"

"Yes, Father." I stood and shook his hand. "Thank you. For everything."

"My son joining the king," Father said. "Alack the day!"

Toni put a frying pan on the fire, produced a packet of bacon and eggs and started to cook with practiced ease. "You'd better drop in and see Nora before you take off," she said, as the bacon started to sizzle. "She'll miss you when she gets home for summer."

"I'll have to keep it on the down low," I said. I took the bread and started to slice and butter it. "She won't thank me for visiting her in public. Upperclassmen are supposed to ignore lowerclassmen."

"Really." Toni shot me a sharp look as she started to fry the eggs. "I guess that explains a lot about your school, doesn't it?"

"I suppose," I agreed. "I'll find a way to approach her without being noticed. It won't be easy, but I can do it."

"You should just ignore tradition," Toni said. "What would you do if she was in trouble? Or if there was an urgent message from home?"

"That would be different," I said. Toni hadn't gone to Jude's. She didn't know the rules. "But if I speak to her without a good reason, I'll just make life harder for her."

"Bah," Toni said. She ladled bacon and eggs onto a plate, then thrust it at me. The smell was heavenly. "Eat up. Then you can go."

I nodded. I knew she was upset. And there was nothing I could do to make her feel better.

CHAPTER FIVE

I wasn't sure what I'd expected, the day I took the stagecoach to Haddon and walked my way down to Haddon Hall, but what I saw was nothing like it. The estate was further from the town than I'd realised, surrounded by a high brick wall that was topped with spikes and nasty-looking curses to deter intruders. I kept walking, clutching the paperwork in my hand until I came across a solid-looking pair of wrought-iron gates. The guard greeted me, inspected the paperwork and then pointed me up the driveway to the mansion itself. It looked as if someone had been trying to make an elegant-looking fortress and dismally failed.

Magic crackled all around as I walked up the steps and into the entrance hall, unable to escape the feeling I was strikingly out of place. I was sure they knew I was coming—the wards wouldn't have let me enter if I wasn't invited—but there was no one inside the hall. The walls were lined with statues and portraits, including a large painting of the king and his grandson. There was no sign of the king's son, not after his role in the attempted coup. I wondered, morbidly, what that meant for the poor *grandson*. Was he still in line to inherit the throne?

A tall man stepped out of the shadows. "Adam Mortimer?"

"Yes, sir," I said. I was fairly confident he already knew. "I'm sorry I'm late…"

"You're not *too* late," the man grunted. He opened a door that hadn't been there a moment ago. "Step right in, pour yourself a glass, take a seat and wait."

I nodded and stepped through the door into what looked like a comfortable sitting room. A large drinks trolley dominated the rear wall, crammed with bottles labelled with everything from dockside rotgut to the finest wine. I reached for a bottle, then hesitated. It might be a test. I poured myself a glass of water instead and sat down, grateful I'd thought of it before swilling wine like water. Getting drunk on the first day would be embarrassing, even if it didn't get me kicked out.

The armchair was surprisingly comfortable. I nearly drifted off as I waited. A handful of others—five in all—joined me over the next few hours, all clearly as nervous as myself. They had a lean and hungry look—I guessed I must have it, too—that spoke of a desire for new challenges. Magic flickered as they took drinks and sat down. We didn't speak. We were too nervous to say anything.

I studied them, carefully. There was a tall girl with light chocolate skin and long brown-black hair that fell to her hips. She was striking, holding herself in a manner that suggested utter self-confidence. There were two pale-faced boys, both as muscular as myself. Another girl, with a sour expression that suggested she thought we were all below her. And an odd-looking boy who might have been foreign. I wasn't sure. Shallot had inhabitants from all over the known world, including half-caste children descended from Hangchowese sailors, but I'd never seen anyone like *him*. I wondered, suddenly, where the other five came from. I'd never seen *any* of them. They couldn't have come out of Jude's, or I would have known them.

Particularly the girl, I thought. *I couldn't have missed her.*

We straightened up as a tall man wearing a long black robe stepped into the room. "Stand up," he ordered with authority. We were on our feet before we knew it. "Let me have a look at you."

He studied me for a long moment, his eyes seeming to gaze into my soul before he turned his attention to the others. I tried to stare back at him, but it was hard. I'd never met anyone quite so sure of himself, even among the aristos. There was no doubt in his eyes that we'd do whatever he told us, whatever it was. I felt a sudden desire to prove myself to him, as if the newcomer's approval meant more—all of a sudden—than anyone else's. I wanted him to be proud of me. And yet, I knew it wouldn't be easy. This was a man who'd been there and done that, and come home to tell the tale.

"I am Sir Muldoon," the man informed us. "For your information, *princelings*, I am your training supervisor. My job is to get you ready to serve, first as a squire and then as a Kingsman. You'll find me a harsh master"—he grinned, challengingly—"but if any of you want to leave, just say so. There's no shame in admitting you can't handle it."

Except the shame of knowing we quit, I thought. I would sooner die than quit. *I don't want to go home a failure.*

"This estate serves as our first training centre," Sir Muldoon continued. "You'll spend the next three months, give or take a few days, learning how to handle yourselves in all kinds of situations, from basic brawling to high society dinners. If you complete your exams, you'll be handled over to a qualified Kingsman and serve as his assistants until he believes you're ready to be raised to Kingsman status yourselves. If that happens, we'll welcome you into the brotherhood and—from that moment on—you will be one of us till you die. If you fail, on the other hand, you will be returned home. There are no second chances."

I swallowed, hard.

"If you want to leave, say so," Sir Muldoon repeated. "If you want to stay, you have to work for it."

He gave us all a sardonic smile. "There are rules to living and training here. If I—or one of the others—gives you an order, we expect you to obey. Immediately. If you disobey the order, you'd better have a damn good reason. If you fail to convince us that you had a good reason, you're out. If you put someone else in danger, without good reason, you're out. I'm going to be drilling these rules into your head time and time again over the next week, just so you know what *not* to do. After that...if you break the rules, you're out."

I tried to keep my face under tight control. It wasn't easy. Jude's had never been so blunt, never warned me so sharply that I could lose everything in a moment. I'd never even been *threatened* with expulsion, even after pulling a whole string of pranks. But here...I tried not to show my dismay. The slightest mistake could get me kicked out on my ass. I wondered if I'd have the nerve to go home and show my face after I failed so badly. Father wouldn't be impressed. My sisters would laugh. I promised myself, silently, that I wouldn't fail.

Sir Muldoon waved at the chairs. "You can sit down now," he added. "We'll work on proper respect later."

I hesitated, then sat. My fingers itched to take the glass of water, but I didn't dare. It would just have drawn Sir Muldoon's attention. He was studying us, thoughtfully. I was sure he was trying to determine which of us was going to fail first. I hoped he wasn't thinking about me. I really *didn't* want to fail.

"The Kingsmen are the eyes, ears and hands of His Majesty," Sir Muldoon said, when we were all seated. "In the Crown Lands, our authority is absolute. We answer only to the king himself. Outside the Crown Lands, in semi-independent cities like Shallot, our authority is bounded by treaties that were signed hundreds of years ago. We still have authority, but it's limited. Bear that in mind at all times. There's a great deal of flexibility built into the treaties, but also some pretty hard limits. The Great Houses see us as a check on their power, and they don't like it."

Of course not, I thought, sourly.

Sir Muldoon gave us a sardonic smile. "You'll learn more about our history and traditions over the next few weeks," he informed us. "All you need to know, right now, is that you are *princelings*. Recruits, in other words. Whatever you accomplished back home, you are—right now—at the very bottom of the ladder. Should you climb up a step or two, you will become squires and find yourself apprenticed to a master. And then you will become a Kingsman or find yourself shuffled sideways, into the auxiliaries. Don't take that too badly, if it happens. The auxiliaries do a lot of useful work."

His smile tightened. "And don't look down on them either," he added. "Like I said, they do a lot of useful work."

"But they're not Kingsmen," someone muttered.

Sir Muldoon looked at him, coldly. "No, they're not," he agreed. "But without them, we couldn't do our jobs. So...be polite."

He smiled. "Now, in a few minutes, I'm going to show you to the barracks. You're going to be living there, until you either become squires or get kicked out. I'll give you an hour to get settled in before we start training in earnest and"—his smile grew colder—"don't expect me to be so generous next time. You'll learn to dress within five minutes, when the bell rings, or you'll be doing your training in the nude. You won't enjoy that."

Of course not, I thought.

"Talk amongst yourselves, if you wish," Sir Muldoon concluded, sternly. "But don't pry too much. Wherever you came from, whatever you were back home, you're all princelings now."

He stood. "Follow me."

The six of us followed him down a long corridor, past a dozen doors that were firmly locked and warded closed, and into the barracks. I'd thought my first-year dorm was bad, but this...there were twelve bunks, each one barely large enough for a child. Six of them had been made, with mattresses and thin sheets to cover us at night; the remaining six were nothing more than frameworks, as if they were intended to serve as a climbing frame. It struck me, a moment too late, that all *six* of us—boys as well as girls—were going to be sharing the same room. I blushed, furiously. I was glad, very glad, it didn't show on my face.

"There are showers in the next room," Sir Muldoon said, as he opened a door. "When the morning bell rings, go straight down the corridor and into the dining hall. Do *not* open any of the locked doors. That's more than you can handle, at this stage. Don't worry. They'll be unlocked soon enough."

I felt a shiver as Sir Muldoon went on and on, detailing rules I could barely remember. I'd always had a good memory, but this…? I didn't know how to cope. I felt intimidated as hell, and it was only the first day! I picked one of the bunks, dropped my knapsack on the mattress and opened it up, feeling hopelessly out of place. How was anyone meant to cope? I'd thought my days of sharing bedrooms were over. Clearly, I'd been wrong.

Sir Muldoon gave us a final set of instructions, then withdrew. I watched him go, then turned my attention to my knapsack. It felt as if I hadn't brought anything like enough, even though I'd gathered everything on the list. The Kingsmen had promised to provide everything else I needed. I let out a breath, feeling overwhelmed as I sat on the bunk. How was I meant to cope? All of a sudden, quitting didn't seem such a bad idea after all.

"Hey." I looked up. One of the boys was waving at me. "I'm Chance. Who are you?"

"Adam," I said. I frowned. "Did your parents *really* call you *Chance*?"

"That's a matter of opinion," Chance informed me. "I say they did. They say they didn't. And now I'm eighteen, what I say goes."

One of the girls leaned forward. "And they just let you put *Chance* on the application form?"

"Let's just say they didn't mind, as long as I lived up to my promise," Chance said. "Who're you?"

"Jean," the girl said. "Who else do we have?"

"Archie," one of the other boys said. "And the strong silent dude beside me is Hector."

"He talks enough for both of us," Hector said.

"And I'm Caroline," the pretty girl said. Her accent reminded me of Shallot, although I still didn't recognise her. She didn't *look* that much older than me. She couldn't have been in the year above me without me knowing. Maybe she simply hadn't been to Jude's. There *were* other schools, even though Jude's liked to pretend they didn't exist. "I guess we're all overachievers."

"Pretty much," Archie said. "I nearly overachieved my way to getting expelled."

I blinked. "What did you do?"

"I proved my teachers wrong," Archie said. "It wasn't a harmless little prank like murder, I'll have you know. They wanted to expel me for it."

"Sounds about right," I said. Teachers didn't *like* being upstaged by students, particularly when their students made them look like idiots. "Are we all in this together?"

"Maybe we're competing," Chance said. "How many slots *are* there for squires?"

"Probably more than they have recruits...*princelings*." Caroline smiled at our questioning looks. "Think about it. Wouldn't they recruit more than six candidates if they could? This room alone is designed to take *twelve* people. There might be others too. But they only have six princelings in our class."

"As far as we know," Archie pointed out. "We might still be in competition."

"But we don't know we are," I disagreed. If it was anything like the Challenge, the rules might not be what we thought. "And even if we are, how do we win? Or lose?"

"Good point," Caroline agreed. "We'll have to ask."

Chance blinked. "Ask?"

"They didn't tell us we couldn't ask questions," Caroline reminded him. "And I think we should know if we're actually supposed to wage war on each other, instead of just trying to pass our exams."

I sighed, then shook my head and stepped into the bathroom. There was no privacy, not even basic concealment wards. I wondered if we were meant to sort out bathroom rotas for ourselves, then decided it probably didn't matter. The odds were good we were going to be too busy—and too tired—to notice that we were sharing facilities with the opposite sex. I splashed water on my face, then headed back out. The bell rang a second later. We exchanged glances, then hurried to the dining hall. The chamber was immense, but there was only one table. I wondered, morbidly, where Sir Muldoon and the other instructors ate.

"Take all you can, but eat all you take," Sir Muldoon said. I jumped. I hadn't seen him standing by the door. "And then we'll be burning it off in a forced march around the lake."

"Yes, sir," I managed.

Sir Muldoon nodded as we took plates and sat down. "Do you have any questions?"

"Yes, sir," Jean said. "Are we really meant to share the barracks with the boys?"

"Yes." Sir Muldoon didn't smile. "And you know what? You're going to be working too hard to care."

I thought as much, I reminded myself, as I crammed scrambled eggs and bacon into my stomach. The food tasted slightly odd, as if it had been spiked with *something*. I knew there were potions for building muscle mass and endurance, but I'd always been discouraged from using them. They tended to be dangerous, if misused. I trusted Sir Muldoon and the Kingsmen knew what they were doing. *They probably want to get us ready as quickly as possible.*

Sir Muldoon jumped to his feet as soon as we were finished. "Put the plates in the racks, then follow me," he said. "We're going on a forced march."

"Sounds like fun," Archie said.

"You'll see," Sir Muldoon said. I didn't like the look of his smile. "You'll see."

I shared a worried glance with Caroline as we jogged out of the hall and onto the estate. It was bigger than I'd realised, bigger than anything I'd seen in the city. Shallot was a big city, but even the richest aristo couldn't afford a giant estate in the centre of town. Here...land was relatively cheap. An aristo—or the king—could purchase hundreds of square miles for the cost of a small estate back home.

And probably purchase the people who live on it too, I thought, sourly. The estate appeared to be empty, but I wasn't so sure. *The aristos can purchase people like cattle.*

"Pick up the pace," Sir Muldoon shouted. He was old enough to be my father, but he seemed to be having no trouble leading the pack. "Don't slip too far behind!"

I gritted my teeth as my muscles started to ache. I'd played football and dodgeball back home, but they didn't seem to have given me anything like enough endurance. I saw sweat on Caroline's back as she ran past, shirt clinging to her skin. I was too tired to care as I forced myself on, wondering how an old man could stay ahead of us. Sir Muldoon was laughing. I didn't understand. He seemed to be having the time of his life, urging us to run faster even as we stumbled over rocky outgrowths and patches of turf that threatened to send us sprawling to the ground. No matter how fast I ran, it wasn't fast enough to suit him..

I'd thought I'd known pain before. I was wrong.

CHAPTER
SIX

I won't bore you with too many details of my training. The days simply blurred together as we were pushed to the limit—and beyond. Every day, we spent the mornings exercising—we ran, we fought, we played games that helped to develop our muscles and magic—and the afternoon learning more about the law, the cutting edge of magical development and everything else our instructors thought we needed before sending us out for yet more exercise. I couldn't tell you what we did on any specific day. Our bodies ached as we sweated the weaknesses away, while our heads pounded as we stuffed them full of facts which we then had to use to solve puzzles. We were too tired to notice, every day, that we were sharing a barracks with two pretty girls…and, I assume, the girls felt the same way too. We bonded over shared adversity as our instructors upped the pace. There was no time for anything else. I barely even had a moment to scratch out a note for my family.

There was some competition, although less than I'd expected. Sir Muldoon gave a handful of tiny rewards for those of us who completed our tests first, none of which would have meant anything if we hadn't been pushed right to the limit. He paired us up, searching for partnerships that could solve mysteries or survive brief but savage attacks from the shadows. I found myself working with Caroline, learning to rely on her even as she learnt to rely on me. It wasn't easy—I'd always preferred to work alone—but there was no choice. A number of the puzzles they gave us couldn't be solved without teamwork.

"There's a dead body in this room," Sir Muldoon said, one afternoon. "I want you to figure out how he was killed."

I shivered as he opened the door. I'd seen enough tableaus by now to find them chilling, even if they were *just* very realistic fakes. The next one might *not* be fake, I'd been warned. They were all based on real cases...I wished, as my eyes swept the room, that I'd spent more time studying true crime stories. The newspapers had made them all sensational as hell, with more action and adventure and drama than Sir Muldoon seemed to think existed in real life, but it might have given me a hint. But there was nothing. A single body sat in a chair, slumped over. A smashed glass of blood-red wine lay on the floor. I glanced at Caroline as the door closed behind us. Sir Muldoon wouldn't open it again until we solved the problem.

"You know, this could be anyone," Caroline said. "Right?"

I nodded, studying the body without touching it. The murder victim—it *was* terrifyingly realistic—wore a simple black suit, suggesting he was upper middle class. His hair was black shading to grey, cut short enough to suggest he wasn't particularly vain. He probably wasn't an aristo or someone with dreams of reaching such heights, not when he wasn't aping their style. A lone Device of Power hung around his neck, scattering my spells. I examined it carefully, trying to determine what it did. It seemed to be designed to cancel smaller spells, making it impossible to hex or jinx the wearer as long as it stayed in contact with his skin.

"Interesting," Caroline said. "I imagine he was wearing it for protection."

"Probably," I agreed. I slipped my gloves on and carefully removed the Device of Power. It was neatly designed, very professional. I didn't know anyone who could do a better job. "It didn't work though, did it?"

"No." Caroline cast a pair of detection spells. "It looks as if he was poisoned."

"If he was paranoid enough to wear this"—I put the Device of Power on the table—"surely he would have thought to check anything he drank for poison?"

"Maybe he made a mistake," Caroline said. She tested the spilled wine. "The wine seems perfectly fine."

"Yeah." I could imagine some of the sots from Water Shallot licking the liquid from the floor. The thought made my stomach churn. "Maybe he just drank too much and his heart gave out."

Caroline shot me an odd look. "You don't like drinking?"

"I've seen too many people drink themselves to death," I told her. I'd joined in a few drinking contests at school, but Father would have killed me if I'd made a habit of it. "They end up in the gutter, begging for coin to buy a cheap bottle of rotgut."

I scowled as I paced the room, looking for clues. It was barren, save for the table, the chair and the dead body. I wondered if *that* was a clue. A drunkard would sell everything he had, just to get another bottle to make the pain go away for a while. But...the victim didn't *look* like a drunkard. He looked successful, within his sphere. I studied the body thoughtfully, trying to determine how it had been done. The Device of Power wouldn't have been cheap. A man so paranoid would hardly have failed to check for poison. And that meant the murderer managed to sneak something through his defences.

Think like a murderer, I told myself. *How would you do it?*

I tossed a handful of possible scenarios around as I studied the body. It didn't look to have been *that* strong, but magic made physical strength meaningless. The man could have been held down and forced to drink poison, yet there were no signs of a struggle. It looked as if he'd drunk the wine quite willingly. A spell, designed to mimic the effects of poison? I couldn't see how the murderer had gotten it past the Device of Power. They would have had to remove it, which would have led to a fight...

It hit me in a moment of insight. "I think I know what happened," I said, as I picked up the Device of Power and placed it next to the spilled wine. The liquid shimmered, ominously. I sensed magic fading back into the ether. "Someone cast a spell on the wine."

Caroline frowned. "What sort of spell?"

"It wasn't wine." I cast a spell of my own, just to check. "It was poison, but someone transfigured it into wine. When it came within the Device's field, it snapped back to poison and killed the victim."

"And then snapped back to wine, when it fell out of the field," Caroline finished. "Brilliant, Adam."

I smiled at her. "Brilliant—and deadly."

The door opened. "Well done," Sir Muldoon said, as he stepped into the room. "You solved the case."

Caroline straightened. "How much of this is real?"

"It's based on a real case, like I told you," Sir Muldoon said, patiently. "It took us longer to figure out how it had been done, the first time. You cracked it faster than the original team."

I allowed myself a moment of pleasure. "Thank you, sir."

Sir Muldoon nodded. "You can get back to the others now," he said. "And *don't* talk about your mystery with them. They'll have their own shot at the locked room murder before too long."

"Yes, sir," I said.

The days went on and on. I found myself growing stronger and sharper than ever before, my brain honed with puzzle after puzzle that—I was told—had real-life applications. The teams were broken up, reformed and then broken up again, ensuring we all had a chance at taking the lead before we headed towards our exams. I discovered that I was better at taking orders from people I respected, something I hadn't realised at Jude's. But then, I'd never respected any of the sports masters at Jude's. Francis had been a prat even before he fell off a tower and hit the ground.

"Someone in this village is a spy," Sir Muldoon informed us, one afternoon. He'd shoved hundreds of briefing notes at us over lunch. "Who is it? And why?"

I felt my head start to hurt. There was so much data in the briefing notes that I was suffering from information overload. The village—a border town that kept changing hands so often the inhabitants probably paid taxes to both sides—was extensively detailed, from the headsman who was afraid of the sky falling on his head to an elderly gentleman who had a beautiful wife a scant couple of years older than myself. I guessed he was very wealthy as well as very old. Every last inhabitant was detailed, so completely that I couldn't bear to look at the files. Who was out of place? They *all* looked to be precisely where they belonged.

"There's a bard who can't sing," Archie commented. "Maybe he's the spy."

Jean snorted. "Just because he can't sing?"

"Yeah." Archie laughed. "They kept making fun of his singing, so he got sour and started to spy on the villages for money. Or kicks. Or…"

I stroked my chin. I wasn't so sure. People went sour easily—I'd seen it happen—but villagers, at least, didn't turn to betrayal so quickly. They were part of a bigger community. I scanned the files, looking for the ones who stood out. Someone who felt excluded completely might turn into a spy, but…there was no one. No girl who'd been isolated for daring to get pregnant out of wedlock, no boy who'd been badly injured and was nothing more than a burden…nothing, as far as I could tell. And yet, Sir Muldoon was convinced there *was* a spy. I scowled. Of *course* there was a spy. I knew there was a spy. They'd put it in the training material.

"It's the teacher," Caroline said. "This…woman with the unpronounceable name."

Sir Muldoon lifted his eyebrows. "And your proof?"

"No proof, not yet." Caroline smiled. "You didn't write *spy* into her dossier. But she's an outsider. She might have entered the village ten years ago, but she's still an outsider. She has no family connections to the villagers and no real hope of getting them. She's the only person, as far as I can tell, who has no obligation to protect the villagers."

"I always knew teachers were traitors," Archie muttered.

"Really?" Sir Muldoon gave him a reproving look. "And what do you think we're doing here?"

"Training, sir," Archie said. He gave a shit-eating grin. "Trainers are not *teachers*."

I rolled my eyes at Caroline as Sir Muldoon gave Archie push-ups. Lots of push-ups. I had a feeling he'd be making up new numbers soon. We'd all done so many, over the past few weeks, that we'd developed muscles on our muscles. Archie didn't seem to mind. He was used to his smart mouth getting him in trouble.

"Good thinking," Sir Muldoon informed the rest of us. "The teacher is indeed the spy, planted there to keep an eye on the villagers."

"It seems a little pointless, sir," Hector said. "Why would anyone *bother*?"

"The village sits in the middle of the border," Sir Muldoon reminded him. "An incident there could lead to outright war. We have to tread lightly."

"So does the other side, I assume," Caroline put in.

"Yes," Sir Muldoon said. "But we have to assume they'll push things as far as they'll go."

He ordered us to put the paperwork away, then join him for another run around the hall. I was almost relieved. The puzzles were fun, but I always had the feeling I was on the verge of failing. I couldn't understand how some people could be so bitter and twisted that they devised impossible plots, just to get their hands on their inheritance or take their revenge or… something. It made me glad I wasn't in line to inherit much of anything. If I'd wanted what little my family had, I'd have needed to murder my sister as well as my father…

I shuddered. There were people who'd done exactly that—and worse, far worse. I couldn't wrap my head around some of the truly *ghastly* crimes. Perhaps that was why they'd gone unchallenged for so long. No one could force themselves to believe they'd actually taken place. Feeding someone love potion…or compulsion potion…or slamming a slave collar on their necks without permission…it was sickening. And some people had done even worse. I felt sick just thinking about it. I'd thought I was wise to the way of the world, but there had been limits to my imagination. And things I didn't want to imagine.

Two days later, we were invited into a previously-locked room and told to peer through a sheet of one-way glass.

"The hell?" Caroline sounded shocked. "What is *she* doing here?"

Archie nudged her. "You *know* her?"

"No!" Caroline elbowed him. "But she's clearly not in her right mind."

I peered through the glass. A young woman—a year or two older than me, I guessed—was sitting on a chair, her eyes curiously blurred. She was wearing a tight white dress that left nothing to the imagination, her dark hair falling in ringlets around a strikingly pale face. And...she was smiling sloppily, as if she was deeply—madly—in love. I felt my stomach churn. The feelings weren't real. They couldn't be.

"Watch," Sir Muldoon ordered, curtly.

The girl looked up as another woman entered the room, wearing a healer's gown. She didn't look interested, merely...I wasn't sure how she looked. Her face was so slack that it was hard to tell what she was thinking or feeling...if she *was* thinking or feeling. The healer sat down next to her and touched her hand lightly. The girl snatched her hand away, as if the healer's touch had burned her. I thought it seemed a bit of an extreme reaction.

"Tell me about Cooper," the healer said.

The girl smiled in a manner I would have found arousing if it hadn't been so disturbing. "Cooper is the most wonderful boy," she said. Her dreamy tone chilled me to the bone. "He's the sexiest, the loveliest, the cutest, the dreamiest, the handsomest, the most charming..."

Archie snickered. "Did she swallow a dictionary at some point?"

"I can't wait to give myself to him," the girl continued. "I will be his and he will be mine and I will do anything for him and he will do anything for me and..."

Sir Muldoon tapped the glass. It went black.

"Do *any* of you," he asked, "think her condition is natural?"

"No, sir," I said. No one disagreed.

"No," Sir Muldoon agreed. "Cooper—who is currently serving his time on Skullbreaker Island—fed her an advanced love potion. It has bonded with her, creating a permanent effect that we have not—so far—been able to remove or refocus on something a little less harmful. If Cooper called for her, she'd go."

"She sounds stupid," Archie commented.

"She isn't." Sir Muldoon nodded at the dark glass. "She's actually quite intelligent, as long as Cooper isn't mentioned. Bring him into the picture and she becomes…well, what you see. A love-sick girl who will do anything, no matter how degrading, for her lover."

Jean made a retching noise. "Why can't you *tell* her that her feelings aren't real?"

"We've tried, obviously." Sir Muldoon shook his head. "She doesn't believe it. The feelings appear to be completely natural, from the inside. She thinks we're lying to her. And no matter what the healers do, they can't burn the potion out of her. The obsession is so all-consuming that we've been unable to even get her fixated on something harmless."

"Shit." Caroline sounded stunned. "Can she live a normal life?"

"Not really." Sir Muldoon looked from face to face. "This is why we're necessary. This is why we exist. There will always be people who will use magic—dark magic—to get what they want. Our job is to stop them. When the next Cooper comes along, you're going to be ready."

I stuck up my hand. "How do you tell the difference between someone under a love potion and someone who's just madly in love?"

"There are signs," Sir Muldoon said. "The majority of love spells have an unpleasant effect on the victim's ability to *think*. They'll start having problems adding two plus two without getting five. Most people know to watch for friends and family members becoming grinning idiots. Love *potions* can be far more insidious. There are tests you can perform—which we will teach you how to perform—to check if someone is under the influence. If they are, you hold them and wait for the potion to wear off. If not, you have to let them go. There's no law against making a fool of yourself in public."

"And if it won't wear off?" Caroline waved a hand at the glass. "What do we do with cases like her?"

"Like I said, the vast majority of such victims can be refocused on something else, something harmless," Sir Muldoon said, patiently. "There are brute-force ways to reprogram the potion. You'll cover those later on, although you'll hopefully never have to actually do it. For those who can't... there are asylums. They're well-treated, if their family has the cash, but they can never be let free. They cannot live a normal life."

He scowled. "That's why we're necessary," he said, again. He tapped the glass, lightening it. The poor girl was telling the healer, in great detail, about what a wonderful person Cooper was and how he was waiting for her. It made me sick. "Do you understand, now?"

I nodded. "Yes, sir."

CHAPTER SEVEN

"We're moving onto more important matters now," Sir Muldoon said, after breakfast. "I trust you're ready to try something new?"

I nodded, blearily, as we lined up in front of him. I'd lost track of time over the past few weeks. I honestly wasn't sure how long it had *been* since I'd entered Haddon Hall and started my training. My life before the Kingsmen was starting to seem like a dream. Did I have a father? Sisters? I was no longer prepared to swear to anything. My world seemed to have shrunk to the four corners of the estate. I wasn't even sure there was anything beyond the brick walls.

"This is something new," Sir Muldoon said. He held up a strange device. "What do you think it is?"

I frowned. The device was nothing more than a strip of silver metal. It didn't look anything like as exciting as the spellcasters we'd learnt to use, or the wardcrackers, or the skeleton keys or even the protected armour that was supposed to ward off anything that might threaten us with death. The Kingsmen had all the best toys. And yet, the device didn't seem important. I couldn't understand what I saw.

"Let me have a volunteer," Sir Muldoon said. "Who wants to give it a try?"

We glanced at each other, silently coming to the conclusion that it was *my* turn to volunteer. It probably was. Sir Muldoon made sure we *all* got a chance to volunteer, even if we didn't *want* to. I didn't mind it that much, not really. It was always interesting, although it was almost always hair-raising as well. I supposed being on the streets would be even more hair-raising. Sir Muldoon had regaled us with countless tales of Kingsmen who'd died in the line of duty.

"I will, sir," I said.

"Very good," Sir Muldoon said, as I stepped forward. "Hold out your hand."

I did as I was told and watched, alarmed, as he folded the metal strip around my wrist. The moment it snapped closed, I felt oddly heavy. My magic crumbled into nothingness, as if it no longer existed. The world felt dull and old and…I stumbled back in shock, my free hand scrabbling at the strip. It refused to come free. I was deaf and blind and…and on the verge of panic. I bit my lip, hard. My thoughts steadied, but the magic refused to come. I wondered, numbly, if this was what Caitlyn Aguirre felt like *all* the time.

"The cuff is designed to make it impossible to use magic, as long as it's wrapped around your wrist," Sir Muldoon said, calmly. "The unlocking spell is actually quite easy to cast, but—as long as you have the cuff on—quite beyond you. There are more complicated designs that are harder to remove, magic or no magic, but we won't be looking at those now."

He took a step back. "Once you put the cuffs on someone, you are placing them under arrest," he continued. "They have the same rights as every other prisoner. They are in your custody until you turn them over to the City Guard or let them go. You are, amongst other things, required to defend them against attack. They won't be defending themselves without magic."

I looked down at the metal strip. "Can you take it off?"

"Of course." Sir Muldoon removed the strip and passed it to me. "You'll be wearing them again, later. There are sections of the exams where magic is forbidden."

I swallowed, hard. I'd had magic all my life. I'd never tried to live without it. I only knew one person who didn't have magic at all. And…I stared at the cuff, feeling an odd frisson of fear. The cuff wasn't as dangerous as the spellcasters, or so easy to misuse as the wardcrackers, but it could cripple me. I felt as if I was holding a poisonous spider. I wanted to toss it away, or slice it up for potion ingredients, or do something—anything—other than holding it in my hand.

"Today, we will be running a set of different exercises," Sir Muldoon informed us. He passed out five more cuffs, ensuring we each had one. "One at a time, this time. Adam? Do you want to go first?"

No, I thought.

I didn't bother to say it out loud. Sir Muldoon had already made up his mind. I was going to go first and that was that. It probably wasn't going to be bad, merely...*a learning experience*. Sir Muldoon passed me a spellcaster, which I checked automatically. He'd handed out push-ups like candy every time we failed to check the spellcaster to see what it was designed to do. This one was designed to kill.

"Your mission is simple," Sir Muldoon said, once he'd dispatched the others to the backroom. "The wards have detected someone sneaking into the estate. Your job is to catch them, put the cuffs on them and get them back up here for interrogation. Do you understand me?"

"Yes, sir." I knew what was happening. Someone—one of the Kingsmen or their auxiliaries—would be sneaking across the wall, trying to get to the hall before I caught him. I'd be in real trouble if they made it to the hall. Or if they saw something sensitive and got out before it was too late. "I won't let you down."

"Use the compass to track them down," Sir Muldoon told me. He clapped my shoulder. "Good luck, Adam."

I felt my heart start to pound as I picked up a ward-attuned compass and headed outside. The compass needle swung around, seemingly at random, before finally coming to a halt pointing west. I scowled. The western side of the estate was crammed with ancient trees, each one providing more than enough cover for someone to sneak up to the hall. The intruder could get pretty close before they had to come into the open. I started to walk down the path, keeping the spellcaster raised. I'd have to be careful not to accidentally use the weapon on the intruder. Sir Muldoon would be furious if I killed one of his comrades.

The compass kept twitching as I made my way through the abandoned hamlet—it had been enclosed generations ago, as far as we'd been able to tell—and down towards the trees. It crossed my mind that the intruder might be waiting for me, ready to attack the moment I came into view...I stayed low, wishing I could get a sense of just how far away the intruder actually *was*. They had to be on the near side of the wall, but...the forest was big enough to hide a small army of intruders. I stared into the gloom, wondering if I dared go into the shadows. Whatever advantages I'd have would fade once I was within the gloom.

Something moved by the edge of the forest. I dropped down, staring as a figure emerged from the shadows. A young girl, no older than myself. She glanced from side to side, but didn't seem to see me. I stared, unable to believe my eyes. She didn't *look* like a Kingsman. Caroline and Jean were both far more muscular than the intruder. I was sure a graduated Kingsman would be even tougher. Sir Muldoon was tough enough to kick me around the training field with one hand trapped behind his back. He'd done it too. For a moment, I was sure there'd been a mistake. The girl couldn't be dangerous...

She could have powerful magic, I reminded myself, sharply. Alana hadn't looked that tough, but she could turn me into a frog with a snap of her fingers. Or worse. *She might have enough magic to stop me in my tracks.*

I crawled forward as the intruder started to sneak away from the forest, heading up towards the hall. She *had* to be my target, unless we had a *real* intruder. I braced myself, clutching the spellcaster in one hand, then stood and fired a single spell. She jumped as a fireball rocketed over her head and slammed into a tree. The trunk exploded, sending the remnants of the tree crashing to the ground.

"HANDS UP!" I shouted as loud as I could. "TURN AROUND! KEEP YOUR HANDS IN THE AIR!"

The girl looked terrified as she spun around, dropping something on the ground as she put her hands in the air. I felt a pang of guilt, which I ruthlessly suppressed as I ran forward, cuff in hand. She yelped as I grabbed her arm and wrapped the cuff around her wrist. She was helpless now. Without her magic, she was helpless. I started to search her...

...And she swung around and punched me in the chest. Hard.

I doubled over, coughing and retching. Sir Muldoon had taught me how to take a punch, but the girl had caught me completely by surprise. She didn't give me any time to recover, either. She brought her foot up, kneeing me in the nose. I felt bones break as I stumbled and hit the ground, in too much pain to put up a fight. She grabbed my hands, yanked them behind my back and wrapped a cuff around them. My magic faded, again. I struggled, but the cuff was unbreakable. I couldn't get free.

"Well," a very familiar voice said. Sir Muldoon was standing right behind me. "Did you learn anything useful from this experience?"

I coughed, trying to roll over so I could see him. Had he followed me, cloaked behind an illusion spell? Or had he worn one of the invisibility cloaks he'd taught us how to use? Or...I felt a wave of shame as the girl helped me to my feet. I'd made a complete and total fool of myself. The girl had kicked my ass as effortlessly as...as Sir Muldoon himself. Whoever she was, she was clearly someone to take seriously.

"Yes, sir," I managed. It hurt when I tried to breath. "Don't assume she's helpless because she doesn't have magic."

"A useful lesson, to be sure." Sir Muldoon smiled. "What did you do wrong?"

"I should have stunned her, rather than relying on the spellcaster to intimidate her," I said. I knew plenty of spells that could have stunned her, if only for a few seconds. She was no common-born student, unable to counter a spell most aristos learnt from their parents. It would still have kept her out of it long enough to keep her from battering me into submission. "And I shouldn't have gotten so close to her. I just thought..."

"That an absence of magic renders someone powerless," Sir Muldoon finished. He cast a stasis spell on my nose, then patted my shoulder. "I trust we've cured you of that little mistake?"

"Yes, sir," I said. "What now?"

"You go back to the hall." Sir Muldoon removed the cuff and passed it back to the girl. "Go straight to the Blue Room and work on the exercise there. Do *not* speak to any of your comrades. Let them have their chance to make the same mistake."

Or see how many of them realise the danger and take more care, I thought. My cheeks burned with humiliation. I'd been bested before, but this was terrible. In a sense, I'd bested myself. *Caroline will spot it, won't she?*

I put the thought aside as I turned and forced myself to walk back to the hall. My chest hurt, despite the effort. I had a feeling I was going to be covered in bruises by the time I got a shower. It was all I could do to get into the hall, find the stairs and stumble my way up to the Blue Room. Someone had already laid out an exercise and a small bottle of potion. I was in so much pain that I had to force myself to check it was safe to drink before I took a swig. Sir Muldoon had told us that people had tried to poison Kingsmen in the past, even though it was an automatic life sentence. They'd been too desperate to care.

The exercise itself looked simple, but—the more I worked through it—the more I realised it was nothing of the sort. I had to get a body of troops from Point One to Point Two within a short space of time, without losing any along the way. I rubbed my eyes as I contemplated the map. The shortest route was actually the most treacherous, the most likely to cause an entire string of delays. They'd have to take the longest route if they wanted to reach their destination in any kind of fighting order. I felt a flicker of pity for the soldiers, mingled with gratitude Sir Muldoon had forced us to study the land by marching us over it. I wouldn't make *that* mistake in a hurry. Better to take the longer route and arrive without any trouble.

Caroline joined me an hour or so later, looking faintly put out. "That guy zapped me," she said, as if she was personally offended. "I had him and he *zapped* me."

"I got beaten halfway to death," I said. The pain had faded to a dull ache, but it hadn't vanished. "At least you didn't get clobbered."

"I got cuffed with my own cuff," Caroline said. "I still don't understand how he zapped me. I got the cuff on him."

"He probably had a spellcaster concealed up his sleeve," I guessed. Did a cuff block a spellcaster from being triggered? I didn't know. I could think of a couple of ways around it, if so. It would be relatively simple to build one that didn't need magic to trigger the spell. "It could have been worse."

"I wound up looking a bloody fool," Caroline insisted. Her gaze sharpened. "I should have seen that coming."

"So should I." I snorted. My sister was certainly strong enough to break my nose. I knew better than to think girls were weak and harmless. "I guess we're both fools."

Archie staggered into the room, gasping. "Drink, drink."

"Three fools," Caroline said, as she picked up a glass of water and waved it under his nose. "I guess it'll be six fools, soon enough."

"Well," Sir Muldoon said, an hour later. "I guess Jean was the *only* one of you who thought to be careful."

Jean looked smug. I didn't really blame her. The rest of us had been battered or enchanted into submission. We'd all thought we'd had the edge. Jean had been the only one practical enough to stun *her* intruder and *keep* stunning him until she'd slapped the cuff on his wrist and dragged him back to the hall. The rest of us...I shook my head. My nose was starting to hurt again.

"Five fools," Caroline muttered. "I guess we all could have done better."

"You can spend the next hour practicing your healing spells," Sir Muldoon said, coolly. "Caroline, why don't you fix Adam's nose?"

"He looks so much better with a battered nose," Archie put in. "Doesn't he?"

"I must say the black eye really suits you," I told him. "Do you want a matching pair?"

I leaned back as Caroline carefully pressed her fingertips against my nose and cast a healing spell. My bones seemed to scrape against each other, sending shivers down my spine, before finally returning to normal.

I felt a surge of magic running through me, a flash of attraction I knew I must ignore as our magics blurred together. Caroline licked her lips, then removed her hand and stepped back. I did my best to dismiss her. There was no point in getting into trouble.

"Thanks," I said.

"Good work," Sir Muldoon said. "Jean, why don't you fix Archie's eye?"

I stood shakily and brushed myself down. "I...how many people know how to fight without magic?"

"You might be surprised." Sir Muldoon watched Jean, never taking his eyes off her as she cast the spell. "The average longshoreman is far more likely to settle things with his fists than his spells. The Great Houses are the only ones that discourage physical violence, and that's only because they think that gives them the edge."

"It does," Caroline said. "Doesn't it?"

"Matter of opinion," Sir Muldoon said. "And don't forget the Zero. *She* has no magic. But that didn't stop her escaping an inescapable prison and finding her way back to Shallot. By the time we found her and her friends, they were already well on their way home."

"So I heard," I muttered. I'd heard the stories. I just wasn't sure how many of them I believed. "She's supposed to be tough."

"She is," Sir Muldoon confirmed. "And she forges some really nice toys for us. If you behave, I'll even let you play with them."

He smirked, rather coldly. "You get a nice relaxing evening tonight," he said. "Isn't that nice of me?"

We shared worried glances. We didn't *get* nice relaxing evenings, not here. We worked until late at night, then stumbled into bed only to be woken—seconds later—by cockcrow. If we were being allowed to relax... whatever was coming tomorrow morning had to be *really* awful. I gritted my teeth, reminding myself just how much I'd survived in the last few months. I could do it. Whatever it was, I could do it.

Archie took the silent cue to speak. "Are you planning to hang us tomorrow morning?"

"Of course not," Sir Muldoon said. "You're going on survivalist training. All you have to do is get from Point A to Point B without being caught."

"We're dead," Hector said. "I'd sooner be hung."

I scowled. It was hard to escape the feeling he was right.

CHAPTER
EIGHT

Cold air wafted across me, blowing raindrops into my face.

I stirred, certain that *something* was wrong even though I wasn't sure *what*. I was cold and uncomfortable and…it dawned on me, blearily, that I was no longer in my bunk. I wasn't even in the hall! My eyes snapped open, staring up into a gloomy overcast sky. It looked as if it was about to rain. I sat up, looking around in horror. I was in the middle of a clearing, as naked as the day I was born. It felt like I'd been thrown back into the Challenge.

"Ancients," a voice breathed. "What *hit* me?"

I turned before I could stop myself. Caroline sat there, bare breasts bobbling. She had no baby fat left after weeks of intensive training, nothing but solid muscle and flesh. I stared, then forced myself to look away. She had looked back at me, her eyes wide and staring. I cringed, cursing the instructors under my breath. It was bad enough getting naked in the barracks, where we were normally too tired to notice … or care. Here…

A cold gust of damp air blew against me. I reached for my magic to cast a warming spell and cursed, again, as the magic flickered out. Someone had wrapped a cuff around my wrist, taking my magic. I didn't have to look at Caroline to know she'd been cuffed too. Our hands were free, but we had no magic. I glanced around, remembering our orders. We had to get somewhere, didn't we? A compass lay on the ground, positioned neatly on top of a nasty-looking knife—it looked more like a small sword—and a single flask of liquid. I picked it up and checked the contents. Water.

"Water," I told her. "We live in luxury."

"No belts, no scabbards, no nothing." Caroline picked up the knife and held it with practiced ease. "I guess someone forgot the rule about running with swords."

"Looks that way," I agreed. I slowly turned, scanning the desolate landscape. Where were we? I was having flashbacks to the Challenge. "You think they've taken us off the estate?"

"Looks that way," Caroline echoed. She picked up the compass and pointed north. "Shall we go?"

"I guess." I wanted to take the lead, if only to keep my eyes off her. She was very distracting. I also knew she'd kill me if she caught me staring at her. Literally. "I'll go first. You keep the knife at the ready."

I shivered as we walked, doing my best to ignore my nakedness. Where *were* we? If we'd been asleep, we could be anywhere. We could be on the other side of the country. I looked at the distant hills, as barren as an aristo's heart, and groaned. We could be hundreds of miles from the hall. I wondered if there were any civilians, if they were watching from a distance. It was hard to believe someone could eke out a life for themselves in these surroundings, but humans were endlessly adaptable. I saw a white spot moving on one of the hills and frowned, before realising it was a sheep. Perhaps we weren't *that* far from civilisation.

My bare feet ached while we walked. Water droplets soaked my hair and skin. Cold water slid down my back, splashing to the muddy ground. The cuff seemed to grow heavier as we moved, taunting me. The compass vibrated in my hand as we slipped down a rocky gorge, the barren interior suggesting the entire region would flood when the rain finally came in earnest. I glanced back at Caroline and saw she looked as bedraggled, too. We certainly didn't look like Kingsmen!

"They said it was a survivalist test," Caroline said. "But how are we meant to survive here?"

I scowled. It was quite possible to live off the land on the estate, but here? I wasn't sure the gorse was edible. The water trickling down the streams might be poisonous. There were spells to check if something was safe to eat or drink, but—without magic—there was no way we could use them. I glanced up at the darkening sky. Perhaps we should walk with our mouths open. It might be the only way to be *sure* the water was safe.

"I guess we keep our eyes open for food," I said. The sheep were a long way away, but…we could catch a lamb and turn it into food. Couldn't we? Or would that be cheating? Or…were we allowed to ask a civilian for help? Sir Muldoon hadn't set the rules very clearly. "Do you think we're allowed to seek help?"

"I don't know." Caroline snorted, behind me. "We might not have a choice."

Thunder crackled, high overhead. I jumped, reaching for a spellcaster I wasn't carrying as the skies opened. It felt as if someone high overhead had tipped a bathtub over us. I cursed and started to scramble for higher ground as the trickle of water became a flood, washing down the gully and threatening to take us down with it. Caroline followed, cursing too as we reached the top of the gully and looked around. Rain washed us clean. We huddled together, too cold and miserable to care that we were naked. The rain seemed never-ending.

"We've probably failed," Caroline predicted. "You think they'll rescue us or just leave us to die here?"

"I think they'll come for us," I said. We hadn't lost yet. We certainly hadn't been *told* we'd lost. "I…"

The rain stopped. I brushed water off my arm as I let go of her and stumbled to my feet. We stood on a hill, staring into a gloomy fog. Visibility was so poor that I was tempted to suggest we stay where we were, at least until it got better. But I knew we couldn't wait. Sir Muldoon hadn't mentioned a time limit, but I was damn sure there *was* one. And besides, we didn't have anything to eat. We might starve to death before we were rescued if we stayed still.

They're probably watching us and laughing, I thought, as we started to make our way down the trail. *And telling themselves we'll never make it to the far side.*

The compass vibrated again, drawing us on. I kept walking, despite a growing tiredness that threatened to bring me down. I hadn't eaten anything. My stomach growled ominously, warning me that I needed to find something to eat before I collapsed. We'd been told we could go several days without eating, if necessary, but I found it hard to believe we could go without eating while hiking our way across rough country. I started keeping my eyes open for sheep or something—anything—we could eat. I wasn't proud. I'd eat a rat or two if the only other option was starvation.

"Let me take the lead," Caroline said, stiffly. "It's my turn."

I tried to think of a good argument against it, but came up with nothing that wouldn't annoy her. Instead, I shrugged and traded the knife for the compass. Caroline grinned challengingly, then struck out at terrifying speed. I forced myself to keep up, knowing she was making a point. Neither of the girls were inclined to let the boys baby them. Caroline was tougher than many people I'd met. I tried to keep my eyes fixed on the back of her head as she moved, heading down a rough path. She didn't seem inclined to slow...

The ground gave way under her. I jumped as she fell into a pit. I heard a crash, followed by a grunt of pain. A trap? Or...or what? I inched forward, ready to hop back if the ground threatened to collapse under my feet too. My head felt thick, thick and dull. The cuff had worn me down. I pulled at it with my free hand as I reached the hole and peered down. Caroline had collapsed at the bottom, staring up at me. I didn't need to be a trained healer to know her leg was broken. It simply *couldn't* bend in that direction *without* being broken. And she was bleeding.

"Keep back." Caroline sounded as if she was in dreadful pain. Blood spilled from her chest. "Adam, keep back."

"I'm not leaving you there," I said. I tried to find a way down. The pit was cunning, clearly designed to keep someone—or something—trapped until the hunter could return to see what he'd caught. Thankfully, he hadn't lined it with spikes. "I'm not leaving you there."

I forced myself to think. If I had a rope...I had no rope, nor did I have a place to put it. I could get down, easily enough, but how could I get *up* again? It didn't matter, I told myself as I swung my legs over the side and started to lower myself into the pit. Caroline might bleed to death before help arrived, if we were being watched. I shuddered. If we *weren't* being watched...

I lost my grip halfway down the wall and fell the rest of the way, hitting the stony ground hard enough to hurt. The impact jarred me, sending pains up and down my legs. Blood ran down my legs as I forced myself to stagger over to Caroline. Her leg was definitely broken. And her chest wound was far worse than I'd feared. I pressed my hands against her bare skin, trying to staunch the bleeding. It didn't work.

"They have to be watching us." Caroline sounded dazed, as if she was drifting away. I wanted to slap her, in hopes of keeping her focused, but I didn't dare. A single spell would have been more than enough to save her life. I tore at the cuff, but it refused to budge. "They'll come for us, won't they?"

I swallowed, hard. I hadn't seen anyone before lowering myself into the pit. It would take time—perhaps too *much* time—for help to arrive, even if it was dispatched the moment Caroline got hurt. I knew a dozen spells that would save her life, that would get us both out of the pit effortlessly, but I couldn't use them. The cuff was too tight to remove. Caroline was dying, and there was nothing I could do about it.

"Caught you staring," Caroline managed. Her breath came in fits and starts. "Just you wait."

"Caught you staring too," I tossed back. There had to be something I could do, but what? "You plot your revenge. You'll live long enough to punch me in the balls."

Caroline laughed. The sound became a choking cough. Blood splattered around her mouth. I put more pressure on the wound, but it seemed useless. She was bleeding out in front of me and I could do nothing. I looked up, hoping to see the instructors peering down at me. But there was no sign of them. A thought struck me and I reached for the knife, trying to act before I could think better of it. This was going to hurt...

"What?" Caroline coughed again, spitting up more blood. "Adam..."

I took the knife in the cuffless hand and sliced down, cutting off my other hand. The cuff fell to the ground. Blood spilled everywhere. I felt the magic return, followed by a wave of pain and ghostly sensations that suggested my body hadn't quite realised I'd lost a hand. I cast a painkilling spell I'd been warned never to use unless the situation was desperate, followed by a spell to cauterise the wound and keep me from bleeding to death. Caroline let out a sound, something between a giggle and a cry of pain, as I bent over her, casting an entire string of healing spells. If this was cheating, I'd make the most of it. I sealed up the wound, fixed her broken bone and replenished her blood. By the time I was finished, I was so weak and drained that it was all I could do to remove *her* cuff. I should have thought to do that *first*.

"You saved my life," Caroline said. I almost laughed at her astonished tone. "Adam, you saved my life."

"I guess that means you can't punch me in the balls, then," I said, as she helped me to stand. Blood—hers and mine—trickled down our bodies and pooled on the stony ground. "I saved your life."

"Oh, I don't know about that," Caroline said. I was suddenly very aware of her breasts pressing against my arm. "You *were* staring."

I leaned against her as she cast a levitation spell, lifting us both out of the pit and landing us neatly on solid ground. I lay there for a long moment, staring up at the dark sky. Had we failed? We hadn't been told we could remove the cuffs. I looked at my stump and shuddered. A hand could be reattached, or regrown, if someone was willing to pay. I didn't know if the instructors would agree. Technically, I'd probably broken the rules. But if I hadn't, Caroline would have died.

Caroline swore. I glanced at her. "What?"

"The fucking compass is broken," she said. "We don't know where to go!"

"It doesn't matter," a new voice said. I looked up to see Sir Muldoon. I didn't know how he'd managed to get so close without us spotting him. "You've both passed."

I stared at him in shock. "That was a *test*?"

"Of course." Sir Muldoon looked back at me, evenly. "What did you *think* it was?"

"You...you arranged for her to get injured as a *test*?" I glared at him, balling my fist. I hadn't been so angry since Francis had hexed me in the back. "She could have died!"

"But she didn't, thanks to you," Sir Muldoon told us. "And between you, you escaped a trap."

"You..." I threw the punch without thinking. "You..."

Sir Muldoon sidestepped the blow. "You have been told, time and time again, that you will be tested," he said, sternly. He didn't seem worried that I'd taken a swing at him. I suppose it would have been a different story if I'd actually *hit* him. "This was just another test."

He turned. "Come with me," he said. "We'll get back to the hall, then assess your conduct during the test."

"I'm not sorry," I said. "I *needed* to remove the cuff."

"We know." Sir Muldoon glanced back at me. "There wasn't any other way to save yourselves."

I glared at his back as we resumed walking down the trail. The entire area seemed to be glowing with magic, now the cuff was gone. I wondered, sourly, if we'd been walking in circles the entire time. There was enough magic in the air to make sure of it, particularly as we hadn't been able to sense it when we awoke. The compass could have been programmed to lead us over the pit, just to ensure that one or both of us was injured. I clenched my fist, struggling against the urge to throw another punch. The bastard could have killed us! I wasn't sure he would have bothered to rescue us if we'd been permanently trapped.

Caroline touched my hand, lightly. I scowled at her, unsure how she could take it so calmly. She'd nearly died. She would have bled to death—or worse—if I hadn't cut off my own hand. My thoughts ran in circles. The others might be facing their own challenges—or worse. Who knew what *they'd* be facing?

"Next time, it might be you who gets injured," Caroline predicted. "Or one of the others."

"We'll see." Sir Muldoon didn't look back as the hall came into view, but I could hear the irritation in his voice. "There's a certain element of chance in the exercises."

"You're a bastard," I said, crossly.

"That's *you're a bastard, sir*," Sir Muldoon corrected. "And these tests are designed to make sure you can handle yourself under pressure. Which you did."

"Hah." I wanted to clutch Caroline's hand as the excitement steadily drained away. It was suddenly very easy to envisage all the hundreds of ways everything could have gone wrong. "I nearly panicked."

Sir Muldoon stopped and turned to face me. "You want to know something important?"

He went on before I could say a word. "There aren't many men without fear. Those who claim to be fearless have often simply never run into anything to fear. When they do, they tend to come apart at the seams. They don't learn how to handle fear until it's too late. For us? The key is not being unafraid. The key is learning how to work *through* it, to keep your fear from rendering you helpless and alone. Today, you took an important step towards mastering your fear."

"And learning how to mutilate myself," I muttered.

"Get up to the healer's chamber and have her check you out—both of you," Sir Muldoon ordered. "She can grow you a new hand. You can report to the dining hall afterwards and get some food. Tomorrow is another day."

"Is that your way of saying there's going to be another test?" Caroline asked. "A nastier one?"

"How many times do I have to tell you, princelings?" Sir Muldoon sounded amused, rather than angry. "The only easy day was yesterday."

CHAPTER NINE

I'd thought Sir Muldoon was joking. He wasn't.

The next two weeks—or what I thought were the next two weeks, as it was hard to tell—grew harder and harder. Sir Muldoon and the other instructors pushed us as much as possible, forcing us to develop our skills or risk being left behind...or worse. I sweated though combat training—with and without magic—and relaxed by studying social etiquette and how to handle myself in High Society. Caroline seemed to find it easy, but the rest of us struggled. We honestly didn't know how to wear a proper suit or tie our ties. I almost felt sorry for Akin and Alana as we worked our way through wine lists, learning how to bluff our way through social encounters I would have considered unthinkable. If they'd spent their childhoods memorising millions of useless facts, I could almost see why they acted as if they had a giant stick wedged up their behinds.

"You have to be comfortable everywhere," Sir Muldoon pointed out, when I protested. "We need you to be a social chameleon, as comfortable at a wealthy man's table as you are in a dockside pub."

I shuddered. I'd never *been* in a dockside pub. Father had threatened to thrash me to within an inch of my life if I so much as *looked* at a dockside pub. I'd heard enough horror stories to understand the old man had a point. They were crammed with hard-living men, drinking and whoring to forget the horrors of their lives. I knew I could have been one of them, if things had been different. It didn't mean I had to feel sorry for them.

"You'll be visiting all sorts of places," Sir Muldoon said, dryly. "Believe me, you're going to be fitting into all of them."

"I still don't understand why I have to wear a suit," I protested. "It's obvious I haven't worn one in...like, *ever*."

"You'll get used to it," Sir Muldoon assured me. "Now, in what order do you use the cutlery?"

I groaned. "From the outside in, at a formal dinner," I said. "There should be a set for each course. Asking for replacements is a sign of lousy upbringing."

"Quite," Sir Muldoon agreed.

I did my best to pay attention as he launched into a long lecture covering the symbolism of using the right cutlery for the right occasion. It made no sense. Father was relatively wealthy, for someone born and bred in Water Shallot, and *he* couldn't afford hundreds of sets of cutlery. He'd have had a heart attack if I or my sisters suggested it. I tried to imagine how much it would cost to buy so much just for my small family, and scowled. It would cost more than we'd make in a decade.

"It makes no sense," I complained to Caroline. "The aristos are *mad*."

"If you belong, you know the rules," Caroline pointed out. "It's astonishing how much you can get away with if you don't *look* out of place."

I nodded, sourly. We'd studied the case notes. Some of the greatest con artists in history had pretended to be aristocrats, without making even a single slip until they'd completed their plans and slipped back into the shadows. High Society didn't seem to *like* talking about how it had been fooled, even though it had happened dozens of times. I found it rather amusing. Alana might talk about how blood tells, but...blood didn't seem to be any more talkative than water. And if an aristo couldn't tell the difference between another aristo and a commoner aping his betters, was there any difference at all?

The thought made me smile as we were ordered upstairs into one of the training rooms that had been—until now—firmly locked. I looked around with interest as Caroline and I stepped through the door, spotting a heavy wooden desk and a young woman sitting behind it. She looked harmless, although I knew—by now—that was meaningless. The Kingsmen had taught me that some very dangerous people looked utterly harmless, until the time came to lower the boom. She looked bland, wearing an outfit that made her look more like a secretary than a secret agent. I reached out with my magic and sensed nothing. She was masking very well.

"Greetings," the woman said. The door banged closed behind us. "Look at this…"

She moved her hand in a complicated gesture. Green light flashed. I felt my will drain away. I could hear her speaking, but the words seemed muffled. I knew, at some level, that something was dreadfully wrong, yet…I couldn't force myself to care. It felt like a dream, or a nightmare. I'd heard stories of people who were hag-ridden in the depth of the night and were never the same afterwards. But…I just couldn't force myself to care.

The trance snapped. I started, feeling my senses reel. Beside me, Caroline swayed. She would have hit the ground if I hadn't put a hand on her shoulder. What had she *done* to us? I glared at her, sitting behind her desk. My head was starting to pound, but…it felt like a ghostly headache. It felt as if it wasn't really there.

I found my voice. "What did you do to us?"

"This." The woman's voice was very cold. "Chicken."

I felt my entire body jerk, then start to hop around like a chicken. Horror flowed through me as I clucked and squawked helplessly, flapping my hands as if they were wings. Caroline did the same, eyes wide as her body betrayed her. I'd faced compulsion spells before, but this…I struggled, desperately, to stop my treacherous body, but nothing worked. Whatever she'd done to us, it made the little spells I'd learnt as a student seem weak and ineffectual. *They* could be brushed off by someone with a very strong will.

"Stop," the woman said. I sagged in relief as I felt the compulsion vanish. "I trust you learnt an interesting lesson?"

"Who are you?" Caroline demanded. She sounded badly shaken. "And what gives you the right to…?"

"To answer your first question, I am Lady Grey," the woman said. "And to answer the second, it's part of your training."

She motioned to a pair of chairs, pressed against the far wall. "Take a seat," she said. "We're going to be quite busy here."

I gritted my teeth as I chose a chair and sat down. "Why did you…?"

"So you would take this seriously," Lady Grey said, without giving me a chance to finish the question. "Many people choose to overlook the more subtle compulsion and dominance spells, even though they're incredibly dangerous. They don't realise how easy it can be for someone to worm their way into their mind—or how easily their perceptions can be warped, once there's a hole in their defences. Making you two act like chickens is harmless, compared to some of the other tricks people can play. It isn't impossible for someone to find their mind so full of holes that they have almost no free will of their own."

"Shit," I said.

"Quite." Lady Grey eyed me severely. "You will be authorised to use such spells yourself, if you feel it necessary. Should you use the spells without good cause, you risk spending the rest of your life in exile—or worse. The mere *existence* of such spells is not common knowledge. You will have to weigh the risk of using them against the dangers of *not* using them. And the risk of being thrown to the wolves by your superiors in order to prevent a greater disaster."

"Like General Dyer," Caroline said.

I scowled. General Dyer had opened fire on rioting crowds, ten years ago. He'd claimed, at the time, that he'd restored order. But he'd killed upwards of ninety people and the public had demanded his head. I wasn't sure how I felt about it. Dyer had been a shithead, but it had been clear—when I'd studied the records—that he'd been denied the right to a fair trial in the haste to disavow him. The wrong thing for the right reasons? Or the right thing for the wrong reasons? I honestly wasn't sure.

"Correct," Lady Grey said. "There *are* strict rules for using such spells. If you break them, you will be in some trouble even if you are found to be completely justified. Do you understand me?"

"A little too well," I muttered.

"Good." Lady Grey smiled and raised her hand. "Let's try that again, shall we?"

I hastily gathered my mental defences as she cast the spell. My shields shivered, then shattered under her pounding. I felt her mind press into mine, reading my thoughts and scanning my memories. A surge of shame shot through me as I forced her back out, cursing her as savagely as I knew how. She didn't seem displeased as she nodded to me, then turned her attention to Caroline. I watched, terrified, as Caroline's defences weakened and broke in front of Lady Grey. She could have done a lot worse to us than make us cluck like chickens.

"This is how you cast the spell," Lady Grey said, an hour later. "Do *not* practice without both prior permission *and* supervision."

I studied the spellform, feeling sick as I realised just how simple it truly was. The compulsion spells I'd seen at school were a *lot* more complicated. It made me wonder if they'd been kept *deliberately* complicated, just to make it harder for students to master. But this spell...I cast it on Caroline, time and time again, before she cast it on me. It grew easier to resist, as we practiced. And yet...

"We'll continue this tomorrow," Lady Grey said. "Sir Muldoon will be lecturing you over dinner."

I rubbed my forehead. "Can I draw a headache potion?"

"If you need one," Lady Grey said. "It's never a good idea to leave a headache unattended."

Caroline caught her eye as she dismissed us. "How many people know these spells exist?"

"Too many," Lady Grey said. "Us, the Great Houses…they keep being reinvented, even when we try to keep them out of the textbooks. And you'll be learning how to watch for people who've been influenced by magic over the next few days too."

I collected a headache potion from the healer, then made my way down to the dining hall. The food seemed to have gotten better over the last week, although we were kept so busy it was hard to be sure. It was certainly hard to eat while listening to the evening lecture, covering a wide range of subjects from healing magic to history and current affairs. I wasn't sure how many of the subjects were actually important, but I didn't dare ignore them. We had to be getting close to our exams.

Caroline had the same thought. "How long have we been here?"

I shrugged. "Years?"

"I think it's been around two months," Caroline said. She smiled at my questing look. "I've…bled twice, as far as I can tell."

I nodded, stiffly. I knew the facts of life. I'd grown up with two sisters. I just didn't want to think about them.

"Today, we will be considering the intricacies of truth spells," Sir Muldoon informed us. I filled my plate with food, then sat down as the instructor continued to talk. We knew from experience that he wouldn't repeat himself. "There are two different classes of truth spells, one that merely makes it impossible to speak a lie and one that actually *compels* the victim to speak. The latter category is actually forbidden without a court order, although someone can volunteer to waive their rights and have the spell cast on them to prove their innocence."

He paused. "Why would the former category be less effective?"

Caroline stuck up a hand. "Because the victim can choose his words to give a truthful, but misleading impression."

"Correct, in part," Sir Muldoon agreed. "It's also worth noting that the victim may genuinely *believe* he's telling the truth, even though he's clearly *not*. It isn't uncommon for one person, in a dispute over sexual consent, to believe he *had* consent while his partner—equally truthfully—believes that consent was withdrawn. They would both pass the truth spell test, even though they would both believe the other was either mistaken or lying."

He paused. "You have to be careful, even when the truth spell is firmly in place, to watch what you ask. Experienced interrogators tend to triangulate around the subject, asking the same question in several different ways to limit the risk of being misled. A couple of murderers nearly escaped justice because we thought we were looking for a single murderer, not two murderers with two separate victims. We asked each of them if they killed both victims and—of course—they answered no. Perfectly truthfully, yet totally misleading."

I rubbed my forehead as the lecture went on and on. It was growing harder to think these days, as if I was reaching my limits. I couldn't face the thought of stuffing more facts and figures into my brain, of trying to pull all the spells into a coherent whole...I tried to think of a way to get my hands on some memory-enhancement potion, but nothing came to mind. Sir Muldoon had warned us that such tricks wouldn't just be useless, they'd be actively harmful. I believed him. He'd shown us enough ways to tell if someone was under the influence that I *knew* there was no hope of getting anything past him.

Caroline is doing well, I thought, as I surveyed the room. She was, too. I had the feeling she had reserves of bloody-mindedness and gritty determination the rest of us lacked. *But the rest of us...*

My headache grew worse, despite the potion. Hector and Archie looked grim, as if they were nursing headaches too. Jean's face was blank. Chance looked ready to jump out the window, something they'd actually taught us to do safely. I wondered what Sir Muldoon would do if we went to him in a body and told him we needed a break, then sighed as I realised he'd consider us quitters. I felt my muscles starting to hurt too, a grim reminder that I'd lost the last bout in the training circle. Archie had struck me a mighty blow and nearly caved in my ribs.

"The only easy day was yesterday," Sir Muldoon said. I felt a flash of naked hatred. Ancients! I was getting sick of hearing that...that saying. "Tomorrow is another day."

He cleared his throat. "Next week, you'll hit the qualifying exams. Should you pass, you'll be raised to squires. Should you fail"—he gave us a completely sweet, completely fake, smile—"try not to fail. Please."

Caroline caught my arm. "This is it!"

I felt a flush of excitement, mingled with fear. We'd been pressed so hard, over the past few weeks, that I couldn't imagine anything worse. And yet, I knew it *could* be worse. I was sure of it. Sir Muldoon's horror stories had grown even more gruesome. We'd probably have to fight a dragon stark naked or pretend to be an invited guest at the aristo ball. I'd sooner have faced the dragon. At least it would probably have killed me quickly.

"You'll make it," Caroline said, reassuringly. She grinned at me. "We'll all make it."

"Yeah." I tried to sound confident, though I was nothing of the sort. It had taken me longer than it should have to realise that the tests had been steadily growing harder. I'd felt as if I was making no progress at all. "And then the *real* pain begins."

"Not really." Sir Muldoon had overheard me. "If you pass the exams, we'll know we can rely on you. We won't press you *that* hard."

"We'll be pressing ourselves, sir," Caroline guessed. "Right?"

"Yes." Sir Muldoon smiled. "If you're not self-motivated by now, you won't be self-motivated at all."

I mulled it over as we were dismissed. Sir Muldoon no longer escorted us back to the barracks, now that we were experienced enough to understand that we needed as much sleep as possible, but we headed back to the bunks anyway. Was I motivated? It was growing harder and harder to remember my life before Haddon Hall. Did I really have a father and two sisters? Or was my family the one surrounding me now? I glanced at Caroline. She glanced back. She seemed as tired as I felt.

"Do you think they'll give us some leave, afterwards?" I met her eyes. It was surprisingly easy to ask her out, unlike the girls I'd known back home. "We could go home and see our families. Or visit somewhere new."

"I have no idea," Caroline said. She shot me a wistful look. "My family probably doesn't want to see me again. But it would be nice to go somewhere new."

I blinked. "They don't?"

"Yeah." Caroline didn't seem inclined to talk about it. "We can go see your family, if you like."

"Just get through the exams first," Hector advised. He nodded to Archie, who winked. "They'll probably make you take them again if you fail. Or retake the entire course from the start."

"Or boot you out completely," Jean said. She stripped and clambered into her bunk. "What will they do with us if we fail?"

I shrugged. "We'd better not fail," I said. "It might be the end."

CHAPTER
TEN

I lay on the wooden floor, feeling terrible.

The last week—the exams—were a blurred nightmare. I felt as if I'd drunk myself senseless, then walked into a dockside pub and issued an open challenge to a fight. My body felt as if I'd been beaten black and blue, with no patch of skin left untouched by my invisible opponents. I wanted to move, to get off the floor, but I couldn't muster the energy. It no longer mattered if I passed the exams or not. I just wanted to lie still and die.

"Drink this," a quiet voice said. I recoiled as I felt a gourd pressed against my lips. "Please."

I forced myself to drink. The potion tasted awful, as always, but it was soothing. I breathed a prayer of thanks as it banished the pain and calmed my thoughts. I rolled over and sat up, looking around as Lady Grey fed the potion to the other recruits. Caroline lay next to me, looking as bad as I felt. Her hair was strewn around, as if she no longer had the energy to cast a grooming charm; her tunic was tattered and torn, as if she'd come off the worst in a dispute with a lion. I imagined she no longer cared about her appearance. I was pretty sure I was no longer at my best either.

Lady Grey helped me to my feet, then gave me another drink. "When you're ready, you and Caroline have an appointment through there," she said, indicating a door. It glowed ominously. "Good luck."

I stared blearily after her as she gave Caroline a drink. Had we passed? Or failed? I couldn't swear to anything, not any longer. Hector and Archie snored loudly, unable to stay awake. I wondered if they'd failed too. There would be a certain kind of freedom in *knowing* one had lost, I supposed. They could go home or shuffle sideways, if they wished. I wondered, suddenly, what had happened to Jean and Chance. They hadn't made it back.

Caroline stumbled to her feet. "I suppose we'd better get it over with," she said, coughing loudly. I coughed too, feeling like a fifty-cigar-a-day man. "Coming?"

"Yeah." I took a long breath, trying to ignore my aching lungs. Father had never let me smoke. Now, I understood why. "Let's go hear the bad news."

The door opened into a whole new room. Sir Muldoon stood beside a desk, with another man standing beside him. He was taller than Sir Muldoon, wearing silver armour studded with carved runes and crests I didn't recognise. His beard was strikingly red. He looked at me for a long moment, then turned his gaze to Caroline. We managed to look back, somehow. His gaze was warm, but very sharp.

"Congratulations," Sir Muldoon said. "You passed."

I blinked. "We passed?"

"Yes." Sir Muldoon seemed oddly amused at our astonishment. "You passed. Congratulations. Again."

Caroline laughed. "I told you we'd make it."

"I never doubted it for a moment," I lied.

Sir Muldoon nodded, no longer amused. "You two are both squires now," he said. He took a small pouch from his belt and opened it to reveal a pair of silver rings. "Take these rings and put them on, gingerly. Once they bond with you, they won't work for anyone else."

I reached for the nearest ring and picked it up. It tingled against my bare skin. I turned it over and over, spotting the king's crest worked into a set of runic diagrams I could barely follow. The ring grew warm, just for a second, as I pulled it onto my finger, tightening until it was almost impossible to remove. It felt like part of me. My eyes slipped over it, as if it wasn't there at all. The charms woven into the metal would make it difficult to see unless one already knew it was there.

"Neat," Caroline commented.

"We try." Sir Muldoon smiled, coldly. "From this moment forth, we expect you to uphold the honour of the Kingsmen. You will be *trusted*. I strongly advise you not to let us down."

"We won't, sir," Caroline said.

Sir Muldoon indicated the stranger. "This is Sir Griffons," he said. "You two will be apprenticed to him until you become Kingsmen in your own right."

Sir Griffons? I had an odd memory of hearing something about Sir Griffons. *Where have I heard your name before?*

Sir Griffons leaned forward. "Welcome," he said, stiffly. He had a gruff voice that spoke of a man who had no need to prove himself. "Tomorrow morning, the three of us will be heading to Shallot. We'll be based there over the summer, unless there is an urgent need for us elsewhere. I'll expect you to handle yourselves well, remembering—at all times—that you represent His Majesty the King. Should you embarrass me, or him, you'll regret it."

I swallowed. "Yes, sir."

"Very good," Sir Griffons said. He produced a sheaf of papers from his pocket and held them out to us. "You have authority to speak for me, within limits, and to serve as an officer of the law. Don't abuse it. The last thing we need is a dispute with the City Guard and the Great Houses over who *really* writes the rules."

"Yes, sir," Caroline said.

I leaned forward. "What happens if there's a disagreement?"

"Then the diplomats earn their pay," Sir Griffons informed me, stiffly. "There are precedents that can go one way or the other, whenever there's a disagreement. And they won't matter in the slightest, if people want to put them aside and press a different case. Understand?"

"Yes, sir," I said. I'd studied how Shallot related to the rest of the kingdom. The city was practically a law unto itself. "I understand."

"Good." Sir Griffons turned to Sir Muldoon. "I'll collect them tomorrow morning. Give them the rest of their briefing notes, then feast them well tonight. They've earned it."

I watched him stalk out the room, then looked at Sir Muldoon. "Why Shallot?"

"You want to be somewhere else?" Sir Muldoon cocked an eyebrow. "You already know the city. You and Caroline make a good team. Sir Griffons is a pretty good trainer, with a track record of raising a dozen men to knighthood. And...for political reasons, there are limits to how many fully-qualified Kingsmen we can send into the city. Sending *you* in gives us a chance to take advantage of a loophole."

"Ouch," I said. I thought I saw the logic. "Do the Great Houses know?"

"Of course they do," Sir Muldoon said. He led us towards another door. "They just can't rewrite the treaties. Not now."

I glanced at Caroline as we found ourselves in the dining hall. The rest of the recruits—squires now, I supposed—were taking their seats, surrounded by the instructors. I smiled as I hurried forward to shake hands with the others, who all seemed to have passed. I wondered, vaguely, where they were going, now they were squires. They couldn't all be going to Shallot.

"We're off to Caithness," Archie proclaimed. "It's going to be fun!"

"As long as you remember to do your work too," Sir Muldoon said, indulgently. "You have to qualify as a knight before too long."

Jean looked up. "What happens if we don't qualify?"

"You'll probably be moved sideways, to the auxiliaries," Sir Muldoon said. He motioned for Caroline and I to sit down. "Or advised to transfer somewhere else."

I nodded. King Rufus wanted as many Kingsmen as possible, according to the briefing notes, but Parliament had demanded a hard limit on numbers. Technically, squires weren't knights and weren't countered as full-fledged Kingsmen; practically, reading between the lines, I had the feeling Parliament wasn't impressed with the loophole. A skilled squire might be *almost* as good as a knight, without the rank that would put a target on his back. I told myself, firmly, that I wasn't *that* good, not yet. I had a long way to go before I won my spurs.

Caroline sat next to me as the instructors served the food. My mouth watered as I saw the giant roast turkey, surrounded by all the trimmings. I'd never eaten so well at home. I was suddenly ravenous. I tucked in, eating as much as I could while the instructors told us stories of life on the front lines. Some of them were hard to follow—Lady Grey's story of a murder mystery where everyone claimed to be guilty was confusing—but I thought I understood. They were welcoming us to the brotherhood. We might be inexperienced—Sir Muldoon had made it clear that training could only go so far—but we'd taken one hell of a step along the road to knighthood.

I found myself grinning at Caroline as the instructors brought out the pudding. "What are we going to do now?"

Caroline gave me a smile that was full of promise. "We'll see."

"I won't keep you much longer," Sir Muldoon said, once we'd finished the pudding and refreshed our glasses. I was pleasantly tipsy. "But there are some matters we need to cover."

He paused, dramatically. "For the past three months, you have been worked hard. We feared some of you would quit, would drop out and leave, but none of you did. You suffered—you grumbled and complained like soldiers always do—yet you kept going, even when the pressure became unbearable. We are proud of you, all of you. And we hope that you complete your path to knighthood before too long.

"We exist to serve the kingdom. We exist to uphold the rule of law, to fight for justice and honour and—above all—the ancient rights and freedoms of our land. Our order existed well before the current dynasty came to power. We have survived by serving the land as a whole, not individual monarchs or great noblemen. Many of us have died in service. Others have retired and stepped out of public life.

"You will find it a heavy responsibility. Duty is often a burden. There will be times when you will find it easier to step back, to put your duty down and walk away. And you will think—then—that you can get away with it.

And it is then, when the chips are down and everything rests on you, that you will discover what you really are. Will you uphold the honour of our order? Or will you bow to temptation and walk away?"

I shivered. I didn't think I'd walk away. But I knew how easily someone could be pressed into doing the wrong thing.

"You won't understand me, not really." Sir Muldoon smiled. "You won't understand until you face the question yourselves. And then you will know if you're truly worthy to wear our rings.

"I'm going to end this speech with a joke. It's a funny joke..."

"Uh-oh," Archie muttered, a little too loud.

"...But it has a serious point," Sir Muldoon said, shooting Archie a look that should—by rights—have blasted him into dust and ash. "Once upon a time, there was a really chaste girl. She promised everyone that she would remain chaste until she married. And then...along came a rich man, who offered her a million crowns if she would sleep with him."

"Anyone rich enough to have a million crowns isn't going to have any trouble finding someone to share his bed," Caroline muttered. "He'll be beating them off with sticks."

I couldn't disagree. The aristos I'd met hadn't been *that* handsome, but they'd never been short of female company. The only one I knew who *hadn't* been surrounded by eager young girls had been Akin, and *he'd* been betrothed. Francis had had so many girlfriends that I didn't know how he'd managed to pass his exams. Perhaps he'd bribed the examiners. He'd certainly been rich enough to do it.

Sir Muldoon scowled. "She thought about it. A million crowns is a hell of a lot of money. She didn't want to sleep with him, to surrender her virginity, but...she wanted the money. So she said yes.

"And the rich man, instead of pulling out his wallet, asked her if she'd sleep with him for a single crown?"

He laughed, humourlessly. "And she objected, strongly. Certainly not! What sort of woman did he think she was? And so on and so on. And he took the wind out of her sails with a simple sarcastic—and completely truthful—remark. They'd already established what sort of woman she was. They were just haggling over the price."

His eyes swept the table, lingering on each of us. "Once you give up your integrity, you will never get it back," he said. "Remember that. You'll just be selling out for the best you can get."

I looked at Caroline. She looked thoughtful. I wondered what was going through her head as the instructors dismissed us, with a final reminder to be ready to depart tomorrow. Archie and Hector returned to the food, somehow finding room for more. Jean and Chance seemed inclined to stay too, drinking wine as the fire burned down. I caught Caroline's hand and tugged her towards the door. She followed me, a faint smile crossing her face as we headed towards the barracks. My heart was beating so loudly I was surprised the others couldn't hear it.

"I..." I found myself suddenly unsure of what to say as I stopped just outside the barracks. "I..."

Caroline leaned forward and kissed me. I wrapped my arms around her, feeling the pulsing muscles in her arms as our kisses grew more passionate. I could feel her breasts pushing against my chest, her hands slipping down my back and into my trousers. She let out a long breath as my hands roamed too and...

"And what," a cold voice said, "do you two think you are doing?"

I jumped, nearly banging my head into the wall as we disentangled. I hadn't been so embarrassed since I'd been caught with Nancy Parkinson, two years ago. We'd been given detention for a month. She'd never looked at me again, unsurprisingly. Caroline, on the other hand...

"We were making out, sir," Caroline managed. She sounded badly shaken. "I..."

Sir Griffons cocked his head. "Are you aware, perchance, that relationships between squires are strictly forbidden? You are not allowed to develop *any* sort of romantic relationship with another squire. Or did they somehow manage to skip that part of the briefing when they told you about becoming a squire?"

I felt my face heat. "Sorry, sir," I said. "It was my fault."

"No, it was mine too," Caroline said. "Sir, it was me."

"It was both of us," I said, shortly. I wasn't going to let her take the blame. Girls always had it worse, if someone got the impression they were loose women. "Sir..."

"I'm glad to hear you're prepared to admit your fault," Sir Griffons said, nastily. "And I'll overlook it, *this* time. If I catch you making love again, before you rise to knighthood, you'll regret it. We're not allowed emotional entanglements before we're ready to handle them."

"Yes, sir," Caroline said.

Akin's going to be getting married at the end of the summer, I thought. It wasn't fair. I wanted a partner I could love and respect too. It wasn't as if my prospects had been good, even before I'd travelled to Haddon Hall. *And if he doesn't get married, two houses will probably go straight back to war.*

Sir Griffons eyed me, sharply. "Do you understand, Adam?"

"Yes, sir," I said. "Sorry, sir."

"Hah." Sir Griffons didn't sound as though he believed me. "If you want to get your rocks off, go to the brothels. Or find someone who is discreet. Or take matters in hand yourself."

I flushed. Thankfully, my skin hid it.

"I understand the urge," Sir Griffons added. My flush grew worse. Father had explained the facts of life to me when I'd turned twelve and that had been bad, but this was ghastly. "But don't indulge it with your comrades. It never works out well."

"No, sir," Caroline said.

"Good," Sir Griffons said. He looked from me to Caroline and back again. "I'll see you both tomorrow morning."

He turned and marched down the corridor. I watched him go, feeling my cheeks flush with shame and guilt. Sir Muldoon hadn't banned relationships amongst recruits, but he hadn't needed to bother. We'd been worked so hard that none of us had been in any state to so much as think about it. I supposed it was a minor miracle. Normally, it was hard not to think about sex.

"That could have been worse," Caroline said, as we stepped into the barracks. Her lips were slightly puffy. "If we'd…"

She trailed off. I understood. If we'd gone much further, Sir Griffons wouldn't have been able to let it pass. And then…I didn't know what would have happened then. We might have been kicked out, or separated, or…or something. I didn't want to think about it. My hands itched, remembering the feel of her in my arms. It was hard, so hard, to let it go. I liked her, more than I cared to admit.

"Friends," Caroline said, firmly. "All right?"

"Friends," I agreed, sombrely. I undressed quickly and climbed into my bunk, careful not to look at her. "I'm sorry."

"Yeah." Caroline's voice was muffled as she undressed. I heard her clambering into her bunk, muttering a word to dim the lanterns. "I'm sorry too."

CHAPTER
ELEVEN

Sir Griffons said nothing else to us about our would-be indiscretion, the following morning, as we carried our bags into the courtyard. Three horses waited for us, their beady eyes glowering as we dumped the contents of our bags into the huge saddlebags before scrambling up into the saddles. The horse shifted, trying to test me. I pushed down, making it clear to the beast that I knew what I was doing. I'd never liked horses, but I knew how to ride. I'd just never imagined I'd be using the skill after I left school.

"Say goodbye," Sir Griffons said. He waved a hand at the hall, then pushed his horse forward. "We'll be back home within a few hours."

I groaned as the horse started to trot forward, following the other two. Caroline seemed to be having no trouble with *her* horse. We cantered through the gate, magic flickering as we said goodbye, and headed down the road to Haddon. I'd expected to travel around the town, but Sir Griffons led us right into the settlement. I stared with interest, noting the handful of shops, the single small schoolhouse and the market. My sisters would have liked it. Haddon was far smaller than Shallot, but...it had a sense of community the bigger city lacked. I shivered, unsure if that was a good thing. Mother had come from a similar town. My aunties had had all sorts of horror stories about growing up in a place where everyone knew their names. No wonder they'd gotten away as soon as they could.

The horse picked up speed as we raced out of town and down the road towards Shallot. It had been a slow trip, when I'd taken the stagecoach to Haddon, but now…the beast ate up the distance as if it were nothing. We cantered past dozens of coaches and wagons, from aristos heading to their summer estates to farmers transporting goods and supplies to the city itself. A line of wild pigs was being marched down the road, grunting unhappily as they neared their doom. I'd seen them sold in the marketplace. The housewives could make a single pig last for weeks, once they killed the brutes and chopped them up. I'd helped my father and sisters slaughter them, too. It had never been pleasant, but there'd been no alternative. We couldn't afford a full-time cook.

I saw Caroline's hair blowing in the wind as we crested the hill and headed towards Shallot. It wasn't fair. I wanted her—and I knew she wanted me—but Sir Griffons had blocked us as effectively as a father with a spell-caster in one hand and a sharp blade in the other. I was tempted to suggest we find a room, once we were in the city, but I knew Sir Griffons would notice. The Kingsmen were *sharp*. They'd taught me how to study my surroundings and deduce what was *actually* going on. I wasn't sure what Sir Griffons would do, if he caught us in bed together, but I didn't want to find out the hard way. I sighed, inwardly. It didn't help that Caroline had barely spoken a word since we'd clambered out of our bunks for the final time.

She's probably embarrassed, I thought. Girls tended to take the brunt of it, when they were caught making out. *Her parents will not be pleased.*

I put the thought aside as I stared at the city. Shallot was huge. I'd known it, but I hadn't really *grasped* the sheer size of the city until I'd seen it from the outside. The Shallot River ran down to the city, splitting into three as it lanced through the waterways and canals before finally flowing into the sea. I could see giant ships making their way up the river to the capital or heading out to sea, travelling to distant places like North Cairnbulg or far Hangchow. I felt a flicker of envy, mingled with a droll awareness that I should be happy to be where I was. How many young men in the city before me wanted to become a Kingsman?

The wind shifted. I took a breath, tasting the faint but unmistakable stench of the city on my tongue. It had always been part of my life, but I'd never really been aware of it until I'd travelled away from Shallot. I swallowed hard, wondering—suddenly—just how many people *liked* travelling to the city. Did the aristos stink of fish when they headed north to the capital? The thought made me smile, as we cantered down the road to the city gates, even though it wasn't *that* funny. Maybe the *real* reason the city had so much independence was that no one wanted our leading men and women at court.

Sir Griffons slowed his horse as we trotted up to the gates. A team of City Guardsmen were at work, checking papers as farmers and merchants moved in and out of the city. Their leader glanced at Sir Griffons, then waved him through without bothering to search us. I frowned, wondering what Sir Muldoon would have said if *we'd* let us through the gates without checking our papers. He wouldn't be pleased. And yet...I cast my eye over the line of farm wagons waiting to be checked. There simply wasn't *time* to check them all for contraband. As long as the smugglers were careful, they could slip anything they wanted past the Guardsmen without being noticed.

Caroline caught my eye as we followed Sir Griffons into the city. "Welcome home, Adam," she said. "Has it changed?"

I frowned. The city didn't *look* to have changed—much—but...I felt different. I studied the crowd, my eyes noting a handful of half-naked youngsters who were almost certainly pickpockets. They'd take their pickings back to their master, if they didn't get caught. If they did...I felt sick, remembering my father's lectures. There was never any shortage of poor kids willing to steal for a living. Their masters wouldn't care if a handful were caught. I spotted a young boy—no, a young girl; her hair cut short in a distinctly masculine manner. It was safer to pretend to be a young boy on the streets. I wondered, sourly, what she'd do when puberty finally hit.

I looked away, feeling a pang of guilt as I turned my attention to the wealthier strollers. A trio of young women, hunting for wedding gowns. I couldn't tell which of them was getting married—perhaps they were *all* getting married. A pair of young men eying them with predatory interest, perhaps hoping to get lucky before the girls married. Older men, strolling around as if they didn't have a care in the world; an older woman, clearly trying to provide *some* semblance of chaperonage. And a pair of kids—they couldn't be more than twelve—from the Great Houses, wearing their family colours as they moved from stall to stall. The pickpockets gave them a wide berth. I didn't blame them. The Great Houses would tear the entire city apart to find someone who stole from their kids.

My horse neighed as we moved onwards, cantering over the bridge into North Shallot. I looked around, noting how the houses and mansions steadily grew older and more expensive...if they were up for sale at all. Most of the mansions would be entailed, if I recalled correctly. They couldn't be sold, as long as a single family member remained alive. I wondered, as we cantered past a low wall bristling with deadly charms, where Akin or Alana lived. I'd never bothered to look it up. They'd certainly never invited me to their mansions. Why would they? It wasn't as if I had anything to offer.

I do now, I thought. *But I still don't want to offer myself to them.*

The thought calmed me as we cantered past Magus Court itself. The building shimmered with magic. It looked as if magic was the only thing holding it together. The structure was elegant, I supposed, but it should have collapsed long ago. Sir Griffons tossed a salute towards a statue of the king, then led us onwards until we reached a mid-sized building a few short metres from Magus Court. I winced as we cantered into the courtyard, powerful spells crackling around us. Sir Griffons chuckled, humourlessly, and pulled his horse to a stop. My horse stopped so sharply that I nearly went flying over its head. I had to grab the reins tightly to save myself.

"Welcome," Sir Griffons said, gravely. "This will be your home for the next few months."

I clambered off the horse, aches and pains in muscles I hadn't known I had. I was dirty and sweaty and probably stank of horse. Caroline seemed utterly unaffected, somehow. I didn't understand it. Sir Griffons glanced at us both, then waved a hand at the building. It felt empty, even as the wards withdrew to allow us entry. I had the feeling we were completely alone.

"There are stables 'round the back," Sir Griffons informed us, as he led his horse around the building. It looked more like an inn than a secret service base. "You'll be responsible for taking care of the horses until they're needed elsewhere."

I groaned, inwardly. I'd never liked mucking out the school's barn. I supposed I was one of the lucky ones. Alana and Francis had had their own horses at school and they'd had to do all the mucking out themselves. I'd never heard them complain. Having a horse of their own made up for one hell of a lot. Besides, the horses were only supposed to bond with their riders. My horse shifted behind me, as if it was considering the virtue of kicking me in the back. I had a feeling it certainly wasn't going to bond with me.

Sir Griffons showed us where to find the tools, then watched as we stabled the three horses and left them to eat their food. My stomach was rumbling angrily, reminding me that I hadn't eaten for…hours? I wasn't sure. I'd been good at keeping track of time, before I'd started intensive training. Now…how long had it been since breakfast? Sir Griffons nodded to us, then led the way into the building itself. The wards buzzed around us, before parting at his touch. Someone had gone to a lot of trouble to make sure the building was secure. I didn't recognise half the protective wards woven into the wood. They seemed designed to keep everyone out.

"There are offices and a pair of prison cells on the ground floor," Sir Griffons informed us, as we moved through the building. "You'll each have an office—or a prison cell, if you misbehave." He chuckled, as if he'd cracked a joke. "The first floor has a kitchen, a pantry, a training circle and a lounge; the second floor has bedrooms, a large bathroom and a handful of other things we'll discuss later. The two of you will be sharing a bedroom. I trust you won't do anything stupid before you attain your knighthoods."

I scowled. "Yes, sir."

Sir Griffons shot me a warning look, then led us up the stairs. "I suggest you both get a bath and change into your tunics," he said. "I'll prepare something for us to eat."

"Yes, sir," Caroline said. She sounded astonished. "You don't want us to make the food?"

"There are no staffers here," Sir Griffons said. "We'll take turns to make the food."

And you probably want us washed and dried before we stink the place up, I guessed. I wasn't fool enough to say *that* out loud. *You probably stink too.*

Caroline led the way upstairs. I followed, noting that there was plenty of room for the three of us. The bathroom was huge, large enough to pass for a public bathhouse. We could have shared the tub, if it hadn't been a terrible idea. I waved for her to go first, then dumped my saddlebags in the bedroom and searched through them for a change of clothes. I didn't have much. Sir Griffons had promised we'd be able to get more in Shallot.

I wandered over to the window and peered over the city. My family wasn't *that* far away. I could walk to Water Shallot in less than an hour, if I pushed it. I felt an odd sense of wistfulness, combined with the grim awareness that Sir Griffons wouldn't be pleased if I left without telling him. I promised myself I'd ask permission to go before too long. I hadn't had time to write a single letter, not over the past few months. My father had to be wondering if I'd dropped off the face of the world.

He knew I wouldn't be able to write much, I thought, as I heard the sound of splashing behind me. *But I did manage to write at least once.*

I put the thought aside as I stripped down, then waited for Caroline to emerge from the bathroom. I didn't blame her for taking so long, even though I wanted a bath myself. It had been so long since I'd visited the public bathhouses, let alone had a proper shower at school. I'd been spoilt at Jude's. Father hadn't been able to afford anything more than a very basic shower.

"The water's lovely," Caroline said, as she emerged with a towel wrapped around her. "But my entire body was covered in layer upon layer of dirt."

"I didn't want to know that," I said. I hurried into the bathroom, then stuck my head through the door and grinned at her. "What do you think we're going to be doing?"

"Eating something." Caroline's stomach growled. "I'm hungry."

I laughed, closed the door and scrambled into the bath. The hot water felt fantastic, even though I could *feel* dirt drift off my body. I scrubbed myself, muttering a pair of spells to cleanse the water, then leaned back and allowed the warmth to soak into my muscles. I could have closed my eyes and drifted off to sleep. Only the grim awareness that Sir Griffons would have been annoyed kept me awake.

Caroline banged the door. "Food's ready!"

I muttered a curse as I pulled myself out of the tub, dried myself with a spell and stumbled back into the bedroom. Caroline was already heading downstairs. I pulled on my tunic and followed, despite the aches and pains pervading my body. I *really* didn't like horses, but…I had the feeling I'd be doing a lot more riding in the future. The Kingsmen were expected to get from place to place as quickly as possible. I didn't think we'd be reopening the teleport gates any time soon.

Sir Griffons looked up as I entered the kitchen. "Take a plate," he said, as he ladled out scrambled eggs and sausages. "Eat as much as you can."

"Thank you, sir," I managed. It felt odd to have a full-fledged knight cooking my lunch, but neither Caroline nor myself were in any shape to do it. "What are we doing this afternoon?"

"Training exercises," Sir Griffons said. He smiled at our downcast expressions. "And then the City Guard will be taking you out on patrol."

I blinked. *That* didn't sound very exciting. "Just that?"

Sir Griffons shrugged. "Something will happen," he said. "It always does."

He pointed a finger at me. "And when it does, young man, you'll regret complaining about patrolling with the Guard."

"Yes, sir," I said. "I just…I want to do something."

"You will." Sir Griffons shrugged, again. "Believe me, something will happen. And then we'll be investigating…a murder, a theft, an elaborate con designed to steal money from a fool with more gold than sense. It could be anything."

"It sounds like fun," Caroline said. She chewed her food slowly. "Do we have time to explore the city?"

"You might have time to go out tonight," Sir Griffons said. He finished his plate and put it in the sink. "But right now, you need to work out those muscle kinks and practice your skills now you know you're not going to wash out. There are levels you have to master before you attain your knighthoods."

If we ever do, I thought, morbidly.

"We have to work fast," Sir Griffons said. He poured himself a mug of water and took a long swig. "*Something* will happen."

Caroline cocked her eyebrow. "How do you know?"

"I told you," Sir Griffons said. He met her eyes, evenly. "Something *always* happens."

I nodded. Shallot wasn't the safest place in the world, particularly if you weren't an aristo with magic to burn. I'd heard there were ten murders every day in Water Shallot, if not more; I'd been told the genteel politeness of High Society was a cover for malicious manoeuvring that left countless daggers planted in victim's backs. And...I recalled the pick-pocketing kids and shuddered, helplessly. Sir Griffons was right. *Something* was going to happen. It was just a matter of time.

And I'm completely out of touch, I thought. I had the impression Sir Griffons hadn't been in Shallot for a few years, if not longer. I wasn't sure about Caroline. *I suppose that's why we're going to be working with the Guard. We have to get a feel for the city before the shit hits the fan.*

Sir Griffons stood. "You two can do the washing up," he said, brushing down his tunic. "I'll be in the training circle. When you're done, come find me."

I shared a glance with Caroline. "Yes, sir."

CHAPTER TWELVE

The training circle was oddly disappointing, compared to the circle we'd used back at Haddon Hall. It was a large room, one wall covered with training blades and devices I didn't recognise; a handful of protective runes had been drawn on the wooden floor, hopefully ensuring the combatants took their lumps without being seriously injured. I felt my heart start to race as I followed Caroline into the room, spotting Sir Griffons on the far side of the chamber. He was holding a pair of training blades in his hands. I could sense the magic around them from a distance.

"The two of you have worked closely together, over the past three months," Sir Griffons said, without looking around. "You've saved each other's lives time and time again. Are you ready to move to the next stage?"

I exchanged puzzled looks with Caroline. "Yes, sir."

"Good." Sir Griffons turned, balancing the blades in both hands. "Take your blades from the wall and stand ready."

"Yes, sir," I said, carefully. "Why…?"

"Do as you're told," Sir Griffons said. His voice was very flat. "All will be revealed."

I frowned as I tested a handful of blades before choosing the one that felt right in my hand. The training blades were heavily charmed. They weighed the same as *real* blades, from what I'd been told, but they wouldn't do more than give someone a nasty bruise. The blades simulated injury rather than inflicting it. I wasn't sure what would happen if someone struck me in the neck. Would I collapse until the training bout was over? Or would I be able to keep fighting even though I was technically dead?

Caroline hefted her blade. "Is there any prospect of us getting *proper* blades?"

"Bonded swords? Objects of Power?" Sir Griffons shrugged, his eyes moving from me to her and back again. "You never know. And even if you have to settle for a Device of Power, they're far from useless."

He stood, raising his blades. "Stand on guard," he ordered. "I'm coming."

Sir Griffons lunged forward, lashing out with his blades. I barely had a moment to get my blade up to block. Sparks flashed as the two blades collided, the force of the impact driving me back. Sir Griffons kept moving, putting himself between us. I couldn't believe he could fend us both off, but he did. He struck my blade again, then darted forward and slapped his blade against my side before turning to do the same to Caroline. The charmed blade sent me to the floor, grunting in agony. Caroline dropped her blade and reached for her magic, too late. Sir Griffons smacked her on the head, sending her to the floor too.

"So," Sir Griffons said. "Learn anything useful from the bout?"

I staggered to my feet. "I thought we weren't supposed to wield two blades."

"It's astonishing what you can do, if you try." Sir Griffons shrugged. "What did you learn from the bout?"

"That we should have been working together," Caroline offered. "You caught us by surprise and we had no time to work together."

"True enough," Sir Griffons said. "The two of you are going to learn to work together without speaking. I want you focused on each other as we go through the dance again. You have to be *aware* of each other..."

I picked up my training blade and nodded to Caroline, reaching out with my magic to touch her. It felt as though I was overshadowing her. She pushed back a moment later, as if she didn't like my touch. I didn't like hers either. She was trying to control me...no, we were trying to find balance.

It wasn't easy. I honestly wasn't sure where I was or where *she* was. It made my head hurt...

"Go," Sir Griffons said, quietly.

He lunged forward again, blades raised. I tried to move to meet him, but my head was spinning so badly I nearly fell over without his help. Magic boiled around us, confusing us to the point we practically defeated ourselves. Sir Griffons had no trouble at all knocking our blades to the ground. This time, he didn't bother to hit us. He didn't have to.

"I wasn't expecting you to get it on the first try," he said. He didn't sound unhappy, but I had the feeling he was disappointed. "You'll be trying it again and again until you get it right."

Caroline snorted. "Should we be holding hands?"

"It won't work unless you learn to combine your magics," Sir Griffons said. "You need to be *very* intimate."

I frowned. How intimate? I wasn't sure I wanted to know. A partnership, rather than a romantic relationship? Or...I wondered, suddenly, how many knights were sleeping together. It wasn't as if there were many outsiders who'd understand the life of a knight. But it would have to wait. We'd been told we couldn't sleep together until we were knighted.

"You can keep working at it for the rest of the day," Sir Griffons said. He sat, motioning for us to sit too. "For the moment"—he held up his ring—"what do you think this can do?"

I looked down at the ring on my finger. It was easy to forget it existed. I wasn't sure what to make of *that*. The charms woven into the metal seemed to be affecting me too. Somehow, I didn't think that was a good sign.

"The rings are part of a communications network," Sir Griffons informed us. "You can use them to talk at a distance."

Caroline blinked. "But they're so small!"

"We still don't know how the Thousand Year Empire did it," Sir Griffons said. "They used Objects of Power, of course. We had to come up with Devices of Power that could do the same."

He tapped his ring. "Adam."

I felt my ring grow warm. "Sir?"

"If you can talk, just press your finger against the ring," Sir Griffons said. The warmth faded away. "It's charmed to make it difficult for anyone to hear what the caller is saying, but anyone in the area *will* be able to hear what *you're* saying. They might or they might not find it interesting, depending on where you are. A number of criminals have come to realise that the charms exist, despite our precautions. They may take drastic steps if they think you're in touch with higher authority."

I swallowed. "Yes, sir."

"You simply speak the name of the person you want to call," Sir Griffons said. "You'll have a chance to practice later. Right now, you two can only call each other—and me. You'll be permitted access to the rest of the network when you're knighted."

Caroline cocked her head. "What if we need to contact someone else?"

"Then you're in some trouble," Sir Griffons said. He stood. "I need to talk to the Guard Commander. You two can continue practicing your magic. I'll see you in a couple of hours."

He turned and walked out. I watched him go, feeling confused. It had been a long day, and it wasn't over yet. The clock swore it was only three o'clock in the afternoon, but I didn't believe it. It felt like midnight. Caroline laughed—I wasn't sure what the joke was—and rested her hand on my shoulder. I wanted to relax, but I didn't dare. I was fairly sure we weren't unobserved. The training circle was crawling with monitoring spells.

"I could have used this when I was a little girl," Caroline said, looking down at the ring. "My parents would have loved to be able to call me home."

"It sounds like a nightmare," I said, remembering days I'd come home late and sworn blind I'd lost track of time. "You'd have no deniability at all."

"Hah." Caroline shrugged, then leaned forward. "What did you spend your childhood doing?"

"Working in the shop, when I wasn't at school," I said. I couldn't bear the thought of going back to working in the shop again, particularly as I wouldn't inherit anything. And besides, I'd probably drive customers away. Toni could have the shop, and welcome. "What about yourself?"

Caroline looked lost, just for a second. "Studying," she said, finally. "And trying to be what my parents wanted."

I felt a wave of sympathy. I wasn't sure what my father had wanted either. I had no doubt the old man had wanted three business-savvy children, who'd grow the business and marry well until they—and the family—were completely unchallengeable. Toni was good—I gave her that much—but Nora and I were less interested in standing behind the counter and trying to sell overpriced crap to people. Father's dream seemed as unattainable as ever. I put the thought aside and smiled, grateful I'd found a new life. Father would be happier with one less mouth to feed, now that I'd left school.

"I don't think we need to worry about making our parents proud," I said, as I sat back on my haunches. "We just have to attain our knighthoods."

"And make Sir Griffons proud," Caroline said. She reached out and held my hands. "I think I have an idea."

I shivered as she pushed magic through her skin, into mine. It felt like an intimate touch, but…one I didn't want, one that creeped me out as it grew stronger. I flinched, pushing back. I sensed a wave of revulsion from her as my magic brushed against her. She didn't like the touch any more than I did. I was suddenly very aware of her beating heart, of every fibre of her body. I forced myself to pull back as she gasped and let go. We were no longer touching, but I could still *feel* her. It was hard, so hard, to put the sensation into words.

"Close your eyes," Caroline ordered. "And reach for me."

I nodded and obeyed. My eyes were firmly closed and yet…I could see her. Sense her. The magic was calmer now that we were growing used to the sensation. It felt almost as if we were one person. Caroline lifted a hand and threw a punch. I blocked it with almost casual ease, as if I'd had all the warning in the universe, then threw a punch back at her. She deflected it, giggling. I felt her amusement brushing against my magic. I couldn't help being amused too. Perhaps, just perhaps, we were on the right track.

My eyes snapped open. The connection broke. I reeled, feeling almost as if I was drunk. The floor seemed to move...I had to take a deep breath and focus before I could convince myself that the floor *wasn't* on the verge of collapse. I could still feel her, but...the connection was gone. It was all I could do not to reach for her again. Her dark eyes met mine. I could tell she felt the same way too.

Caroline let out a long breath. "This is dangerous."

"Yeah." I stood, pacing the room. "And yet he wants us to do it?"

"I guess they wanted us to be partners." Caroline picked up her training blade and stood. "Stand on your guard."

I grabbed my blade, an instant before she swept forward. I *knew* she was coming. I wasn't sure how or why, but I knew it. I blocked her, parrying the blow, then lashed at her. She didn't try to block me. She just jumped back, carrying herself out of range. I came forward, slashing at her blade time and time again. She blocked me effortlessly, as if she knew what I'd do before I did it. I grunted as she thrust back at me, trying to block her. She seemed more capable of hiding her intentions than myself. I wasn't sure how she did it.

The strange feeling grew stronger as we cut and thrust at each other. I tried to ignore the intimacy, even as I depended on it. I wanted her. I needed her. And yet...we'd been given strict orders not to get *too* intimate. I pressed forward, finding it harder and harder to remember why I should listen to Sir Griffons. Caroline smiled widely, sweat dripping down her face. She'd never looked more beautiful. I wanted her, yet I couldn't have her.

I sensed something shift, an instant before Sir Griffons thrust himself into our dance. I jumped back, stunned. Where had *he* come from? It felt as if we'd been duelling for hours. Sir Griffons laughed and raised his blades, lashing out at both of us. This time, I wasn't surprised. Caroline and I moved as one, raining blows on him from both sides. We thrust our blades at him, parrying his counterblows as we struggled to bring him down. He had the edge, in strength and skill, but we were one. I threw myself forward, forcing him to concentrate on me. His sword struck me in the chest—I grunted in pain, stumbling to my knees—as Caroline stabbed him in the back. Sir Griffons laughed as he joined me on the floor. I swallowed, hard. The fencing master at Jude's would have called *that* a dirty trick. He'd have given us both detention for years. But here...

"Very good," Sir Griffons said. He pulled himself to his feet, grinning down at us. "You could have pressed your advantage a little more, both of you, but you did well."

"Thanks." It felt almost like a dream. My memories were hopelessly scrambled. "Does *everyone* manage to make it work?"

"Not everyone." Sir Griffons met my eyes evenly. "Some people are better at it than others. We try hard to spot people with the power to make it work, but...we're not always successful."

"Great." Caroline watched as I stumbled to my feet. "What's the point of it?"

"Being able to fight as one comes in very handy, if you're badly outnumbered," Sir Griffons said. "Didn't they make you study the Defence of Duffer's Drift during training?"

I nodded. I wasn't sure I believed the story. The defenders had been outnumbered a hundred to one. Odds like that didn't care how good you are. But they'd woven a complex network of wards and traps to force the enemy to come to them a few at a time, ensuring that they could be picked off one by one. The story had impressed me, when I'd heard it, even though two-thirds of the defenders had been dead by the time the relief force arrived. They'd stood their ground, despite being massively outnumbered. They'd probably saved the entire kingdom from defeat.

"They all fought as one," Caroline said. "But will we need it here?"

"You might." Sir Griffons gave her a warning look. "The City Guardsmen will be taking you on patrol tomorrow. They don't like us, unless they want us to solve a mystery for them. Expect to be tested."

"Yes, sir." I sighed. It was an article of faith in Water Shallot that only thugs, bully-boys and incompetents joined the City Guard. The *honest* guardsmen were the ones who stayed bought after collecting their bribes.

I wondered—sourly—if any of them would recognise me. Father was one of the merchants who paid through the nose for extra protection. "Are we allowed to hit them?"

"Only if they hit you first," Sir Griffons said. "We *really* don't want an incident, if it can be avoided. Our superiors will not be pleased."

Caroline leaned forward. "Sir…how many Kingsmen *are* there in the city?"

"As far as I know, just me." Sir Griffons smiled, humourlessly. "You two don't count. Not yet. And there's a strict cap on the number of Kingsmen who can enter the city at any time."

"So we were told," I said. "It just doesn't make sense."

"There are agreements. Treaties." Sir Griffons met my eyes. "And those treaties have been in force long enough to make them extremely difficult to evade. What few loopholes there are have been exploited so heavily that *everyone* knows they exist."

"Ouch," I said. I rubbed my aching sides. Sir Griffons had hit me hard enough to hurt, despite the charms. I wanted a hot bath and a painkilling potion. I had the feeling I wasn't going to get either. "What now?"

"You two can have the afternoon to yourselves," Sir Griffons said. "I suggest"—I knew it was an order—"you spend it familiarising yourselves with this building, before you go out to get the lie of the land. Or the *lie* of the land."

"Yes, sir," I said, resisting the urge to groan at the terrible pun. We'd been taught we needed to know what was normal in the city, before things became *abnormal*. "Can I go home?"

"I'd advise against it," Sir Griffons said. "Get yourself used to being here first, before you tell your family you're back in town."

"Yes, sir," I said, reluctantly.

"You can show me around instead," Caroline said. She shot me a smile. I had the feeling she wanted to get out of the building for a while. "And then we should probably go to bed early."

"Quite," Sir Griffons said. "You're expected to be ready to depart at seven in the morning."

"So we'll be leaving at nine," I guessed. The City Guard wasn't known for being punctual. "Or maybe even *ten*."

"Be ready for seven," Sir Griffons said. His voice was very firm. "I won't have you two showing me up in front of the City Guard."

"Yes, sir," I said. There was no point in arguing. "We won't let you down."

CHAPTER THIRTEEN

"That's the City Guard?"

"Probably," I said. Caroline was peering out the window as I tightened my tunic and checked my spellcasters. "It's only eight o'clock. They're being remarkably efficient."

I stepped up next to her and looked down. Five tough-looking men stood just outside the wards, wearing rusty armour that looked as if it would shatter under a single spell. The armbands they wore were the only things that marked them as guardsmen. Otherwise...I thought I might have mistaken them for mercenaries or hired thugs. I scowled as I glanced at their weapons—their swords looked as rusty as their armour—and then led the way down the stairs. There weren't many people in Shallot who respected the City Guard. They were widely seen as nothing more than deeply corrupt bully boys.

Sir Griffons opened the door as we reached the ground floor. "Captain Dale," he said, indicating a man who looked like a half-shaved gorilla. "Allow me to introduce my new squires, Adam and Caroline."

Dale looked at me—his eyes managing to give the impression that he'd seen more impressive people in the bars, drunk out of their minds—then at Caroline. I saw a hint of a leer cross his face before he thought better of it. I gritted my teeth as he held out a hand for me to shake, then bowed to Caroline. This wasn't going to be fun. Dale nodded politely to Sir Griffons and then led us out of the building. The remainder of the guardsmen eyed us with a mixture of indifference, fear and amusement. I tried to ignore the way they looked at Caroline.

"Stay close to us," Dale ordered, as the patrol started to move. "Don't draw your weapons without my command."

I glanced at Caroline as we fell into step. The guardsman didn't so much march as *amble* down the street. Despite Dale's command, they kept their hands close to their weapons. I had the feeling they expected trouble, even though the streets weren't that busy. But then, we *were* in North Shallot. Things would be busier—and more exciting—in Water Shallot. Dale kept up a steady line of chatter as we took the long way around, staying well clear of the mansions. The aristos didn't want the guardsmen lingering around. I didn't blame them. I had no doubt the guardsmen would drink the wine, leer at the staff and do as little as possible if they were called. Besides, the aristos had armsmen of their own. They were hired to do the dirty work and keep their mouths shut afterwards.

The streets grew busier as we crossed the bridge into South Shallot. Children were heading to school, looking about as enthusiastic as convicted criminals heading to the gallows. Their parents were walking beside them, glancing nervously at the guardsmen as they ambled up the road. The shops were already open, shopkeepers waving to potential customers and shaking their fists at independent stallkeepers and hucksters running up and down the street trying to make sales before the locals drove them away. The guardsmen ignored the growing tension as they turned up the next road, walking past a potions' store I recalled visiting—once or twice—when I'd been in school. Caroline touched my hand lightly, indicating a pair of young men on the corner. They looked ready to commit some kind of mischief.

"They're back," Dale said, stiffly. "Look."

I followed his pointing finger. Someone had stuck a poster to the wall, inviting all and sundry to the local Working Men's club for…for what? The bottom half of the poster was already torn, obscuring the message. The guardsmen didn't look impressed. I heard them muttering about socialists and garbagemen as they tore the remnants of the poster from the wall, crumpled it up and dumped it in the gutter. I exchanged glances with Caroline as the guardsmen resumed their march, heading further up the street. There were four more posters waiting for us. They were rapidly torn down and destroyed.

"What's going on?" I wasn't sure I could trust whatever Dale said, but there was no one else to ask. "Who are they?"

"We have orders to shut down all socialistic chatter," Dale snarled. "The bosses told us to make sure the posters are destroyed before..."

His voice trailed off as he spotted another poster. I watched him tear it down, muttering a spell to burn the paper to ash. I didn't understand. The Working Men's clubs were hardly a problem. They kept men off the streets, men who might be eating the sawdust in dockyard pubs or picking fights with the City Guard. I'd been in a couple of them, when I'd been a child. They'd been far safer than the average pub. The customers had been surprisingly friendly.

"Why are they putting up posters?" Caroline leaned forward. "And why do you have orders to tear them down?"

"I don't ask questions," Dale growled. The look he gave her was far from friendly. "I just carry out my orders."

I shrugged as we resumed our march. We weren't going to get any good answers from Dale. I guessed he didn't have the seniority to understand the rationale behind his orders. I made a mental note to follow it up with Sir Griffons later, then put the thought aside as we marched across another bridge and into Water Shallot. I felt a twinge of shame at marching next to the guardsmen. The locals eyed us warily, their eyes burning with hatred. I knew they thought we were the enemy. We were right *next* to the enemy.

The sense of unfriendly eyes following our every movement grew stronger as we marched through the gentrified side of the island. I saw tough-looking men watching us, shadowing us; their heads popping in and out of alleyways as if they were plotting to lure us into a trap. A handful of women—prostitutes—turned their heads away, refusing to make eye contact. I didn't blame them. The guardsmen would demand freebies, in exchange for not harassing the streetwalkers. And then they'd probably arrest the poor girls anyway. The hell of it was that a night in the cells would probably be better than another night on the streets.

One of the guardsmen muttered something unpleasant as we turned and headed back to the bridge. I ignored him as best as I could. We weren't going *really* deep into Water Shallot, then. I wasn't surprised. There were places towards the docks where no one would willingly go, not without a small army at his back. The City Guard knew better than to trespass in gangland territory. The smugglers would hand them their heads if they so much as *peeked* into the docks. Even the Great Families trod lightly there. The guardsmen might go in, but they wouldn't come out again.

We'd be better off going alone, if we had to go, I thought. A gust of warm air struck me as we marched back into South Shallot. The streets were even busier, somehow. *The guardsmen would just draw attention like moths to flame.*

"Interesting," Caroline said, as she pointed to another poster. "What's that?"

Dale sounded annoyed, although not with her. "Prince Jacob of North Cairnbulg is campaigning for support," he said. "He wants Shallot and the Great Houses to fund his bid for power in North Cairnbulg. Or something like that. He's currently trying to drum up support in Magus Court."

I blinked. That was a more useful answer than I'd expected from Dale. "Why did he come here?"

"He thinks the Great Houses will support him." Dale spat, rudely. "He's sitting on his ass, eating and drinking at taxpayer's expense, while we have to protect him against his enemies because we can't let him die here or we'll look like bloody fools. Or worse."

"He's actually here?" I remembered hearing about Prince Jacob, but I hadn't thought he'd moved to Shallot. "Why?"

"Like I said, he thinks we'll help him." Dale gave me a look that suggested he thought I was stupid. "And you know what, there's a whole bunch of aristos who think helping him is a *really* great idea."

Caroline nudged me. "Wouldn't that be a treaty violation?"

"Probably," I agreed. I had the feeling it wasn't our problem. "We should probably ask Sir Griffons and…"

"Move," Dale snapped. "Run!"

The entire patrol started to run, chasing a young boy who clutched a handbag in one hand. I realised, as I picked up speed, that he'd stolen it from an elderly woman. I heard her screaming curses and spitting magic in all directions as we ran past her, chasing the boy. He was fast, but not fast enough. I hit him with a tangle spell, sending him crashing to the ground. The guardsmen jumped him before he could recover. I stared in horror as they punched him again and again.

"Stop," I snapped. "You got him!"

"Teach the little bastard a lesson," Dale snarled, as he hauled the thief to his feet. Blood was streaming from a cracked jaw. "He won't be stealing again…"

"No," I agreed. I stepped past him and inspected the damage. It looked worse than it was, but it was still pretty bad. I muttered a couple of healing spells, ignoring Dale's swearing. The boy stared at me, eyes wide. "I think you gave him enough of a beating for that."

"We have to take him to the cells," Dale said. The boy flinched. He would have run if Dale hadn't kept a tight grip on his collar. "He'll spend the rest of his life on Skullbreaker Island."

I stared at the youngster for a long moment. If things had been different, that could have been me. Ancients! I'd done enough stupid things, when I'd been his age, to know how lucky I'd been. Father would have disowned me on the spot if I'd been stealing things, but…I swallowed, hard. The poor boy deserved a whipping, not a death sentence. I'd heard enough about Skullbreaker Island to know that being exiled there *was* a death sentence.

"We'll take him back to his father," I said, firmly. Would Dale argue? Or demand that I took the boy to Sir Griffons? Or…or what? "I don't think he'll be stealing again."

Dale glared. "On your head be it," he said, as he shoved the boy at me and picked up the handbag. I hoped he'd make sure it went back to its owner. "And if you see him again, you can arrest him yourselves."

He nodded to his men. "We'll see you again tomorrow," he added. "Goodbye."

"Charming," Caroline muttered. "Do they ever solve any crimes?"

"They can normally be relied upon to find a suspect," I said. I wondered, sourly, just how many people who'd been marched to the gallows had *really* deserved it. There were truth spells—I knew how to use them myself—but would the City Guard bother? Or would they simply arrest the usual suspects in lieu of doing any actual detective work? "Let me see..."

I gazed down at the boy. "What's your name?"

He had to think about it, I noticed. "Kevin."

"Really?" I didn't believe it. People didn't normally need to think about their own names—or the truth, whatever it was. A delay almost certainly meant a lie. "What would you say if I cast a truth spell?"

"Brian," the boy said, sullenly. I had the feeling that was a little more truthful. "It was a dare."

"Was it?" I met his eyes, evenly. "It wasn't very clever, was it?"

I sighed, inwardly, as I drew his address from him and marched him down the road. Caroline followed, ready to catch him if he tried to run. Brian didn't live anywhere near Water Shallot, but in one of the tenement blocks on the far side of South Shallot. I had the feeling his father was probably a manservant, judging by the way Brian held himself. He wasn't going to be pleased, not when he found out the truth. A criminally inclined son wouldn't make him look very good.

"I didn't mean to do it," Brian moaned. "It was Joe's idea and..."

"Let me guess," I snarled. "You wanted some excitement in your life. You decided it would be funny to steal from someone who seemed to have plenty of money. And then..."

I shook him, none too gently. I knew what my father would have said, if he'd caught me stealing from *anyone*. The thrill would be replaced, sooner rather than later, with the fear of being caught. It would hang over his head until he either became a hardened criminal or confessed...probably to a world that didn't care. Or sent him to Skullbreaker Island. I imagined Brian being shipped there and shuddered. He was too young. It would be a fate worse than death.

We marched him up the stairs and rapped on the door. There was a pause, just long enough for Brian to start shuffling nervously before the door slammed open to reveal a formidable-looking woman. I showed her my ring, explained what had happened and shoved Brian at her. The look on her face suggested he wasn't going to be sitting comfortably for a few days. Better that, I told myself firmly, than Skullbreaker Island. I ignored the shouting as we made our way back down the stairs. Brian's mother wasn't keeping anything back.

"Well," Caroline said, as we stepped back onto the streets. "Did we do the right thing?"

"He was just a silly idiot," I grunted. What were we supposed to be doing now? Go back to Sir Griffons or continue exploring the city? "If he went to jail, it would be the end."

"I suppose." Caroline frowned. "Did the old woman get her handbag back?"

I frowned. I hadn't *seen* Dale give it back to her. And that meant...I sighed, promising myself that I'd check. The old lady didn't deserve to lose her handbag either.

"I'll check," I said. "And now..."

I looked around as we started walking back towards the bridge to North Shallot. The streets felt tense, but not *that* tense. I could see children running and skipping during recess, trying to get as much fun in as possible before they were called back to class. A grim-faced man wearing a mortar board sat by the schoolhouse, smoking something that released an unpleasant-looking green smoke. I felt a flicker of pity. I'd probably driven *my* tutors mad, when I'd been a little boy. But then, I'd hated school with the passion of a million white-hot burning suns. I hadn't started to *enjoy* learning until I'd gone to Jude's.

A broadsheet seller walked past us, offering copies of the latest newspapers. I bought a couple and skimmed through the pages, looking for anything on the Working Men or Prince Jacob. There was nothing on the Working Men—there wasn't even the usual advert for the clubs—but there was quite a lot on Prince Jacob. The foreign prince was apparently a very well-dressed man, who'd fitted perfectly into High Society. The story was so sweet that I felt my teeth starting to ache as I read my way through it, but…it lacked a certain substance. All the people who would normally have provided statements that set the course for the Great Houses and Magus Court were missing. It read as if no one really knew *what* to do with Prince Jacob.

Caroline finished her paper. "Is there ever anything of importance here?"

"Sometimes." I shrugged. "The newspapers are owned by the Great Houses, mostly. They only print what their masters want them to print. There's a handful of printing houses that are more independent, but they don't tend to last very long. Father wanted to open a newspaper, once upon a time, yet…I think the costs were too high. He certainly didn't get past the planning stage."

My ring grew warm. I touched it, lightly. "Adam."

"Adam." Sir Griffon's voice seemed to appear in my head without going through my ears. "I've heard an…interesting report from Captain Dale."

"Yes, sir," I said, carefully. What had Dale *told* him? The truth? Or…or what? "Do you want us to come back now?"

"I think that would be a good idea," Sir Griffons said. "Be back here in twenty minutes."

"I'll back you up," Caroline said, as the ring cooled. "We can both get in trouble."

"Don't," I said. "Better I get in trouble alone."

I sighed as I folded the papers under my arm and started to walk. I'd done the right thing, morally…but legally? Dale had had a point. We'd caught Brian in the act. He deserved punishment. And yet…he didn't deserve to lose everything. A good butt-kicking had been more than enough, I thought. Who knew? Maybe he'd turn his life around and join the Kingsmen. Stranger things had happened.

Caroline snorted. "This isn't the time to be a hero," she said. "Besides, I thought we were supposed to be in this together. Let me share the blame."

She grinned, humourlessly. "Besides, there's probably more than enough blame for both of us," she added. I had a nasty feeling she was right. "We'll both get in deep shit."

I shook my head. "It was my call," I reminded her. "I didn't ask you. I should have, but I didn't. Let *me* take the blame."

"Honestly." Caroline shook her head. "That hero complex will be the death of you."

"And you," I said. "Why did you join if you *didn't* have a hero complex?"

"I wanted a new challenge," Caroline said. "Just like you. Right?"

I nodded, but said nothing.

CHAPTER FOURTEEN

I'd expected Sir Griffons to be furious, despite my explanation. I'd expected everything from press-ups to being stripped of my rank and sent back to the gutter. But instead, Sir Griffons merely listened and then sentenced me to cook dinner for the three of us. I wasn't sure who was *really* being punished—I was an indifferent cook at best, despite high marks in potions—but I wasn't fool enough to argue. I cooked a very basic stew and served it with bread and tea. They ate without complaint.

"Go get some sleep," Sir Griffons ordered, when we'd washed and dried the dishes. "I'll see you both in the morning."

I nodded and hurried upstairs to wash and change into my sleepwear. It was astonishing how the habit of washing quickly had become ingrained, after what felt like *years* of training. I honestly couldn't believe it was only three months. I slipped into bed, trying to ignore a vague sense of unease as I mulled over the events of the day. I had the strangest sensation I wasn't going to hear the end of the whole affair.

The Guard Commander probably bitched to Sir Griffons, I thought, as I drifted off to sleep. *They won't be pleased about me overriding them in public.*

Sir Griffons woke us, what felt like bare seconds later. "Wash and dress, then get downstairs," he ordered. "We have a situation."

I sat up, blinking the sleep from my eyes. The clock insisted it was five in the morning. I was sure it was lying. I hadn't slept at all...had I? Caroline sat up, her hair spilling over her shirt as she stumbled to her feet and hurried into the washroom. I forced myself to stand, ignoring the aches and pains. The hours I'd spent on that wretched horse were starting to catch up with me. I needed a long soak in the bath. I was fairly sure I wasn't going to get one.

"There's been an incident at House Califon," Sir Griffons said, as he thrust mugs of black coffee at us. It tasted vile, but shocked us awake. "Lord Redford has been murdered."

I blinked. I'd heard the name before, but I couldn't remember where. I'd never been inclined to waste my time memorising who was related to whom. It wasn't as if it was going to be important to *me*. I snorted, inwardly. I might have made the wrong call. Lord Redford might be related to someone I knew.

Caroline had a more practical question. "He was murdered in a Great House?"

"Quite." Sir Griffons nodded as he pulled his cloak over his tunic. "Not the easiest place to carry out a murder, I'm sure you'll agree."

We followed him into the courtyard. A carriage was already waiting for us in the gloom, an armsman sitting at the front. He wore a uniform that made him look like a bumblebee. I concealed my amusement with an effort. The Great Houses trained their armsmen very well. They tended to be far more effective than the City Guard, even if they looked absurd in their house colours. I scrambled into the carriage and forced myself to relax, despite a thrill of excitement running through me. This was it! I was going to investigate my first murder! I couldn't wait.

Caroline leaned forward. "What else do we know?"

"Very little," Sir Griffons said. He seemed completely at ease as the carriage rattled into life. "And that's quite interesting, don't you think?"

I frowned. The Great Houses were supposed to be practically invulnerable. Sneaking through their endless layers of wards was almost impossible. A murderer would do better to wait until the victim was outside the wards, at least if they wanted to get away afterwards. I felt my heart sink as I realised the case was going to be political. The murderer might not have gotten away. And that meant...what? A vendetta? Another House War? Or...or what?

The carriage rattled to a halt. Sir Griffons didn't wait for the armsman to open the door. He unlatched it himself and jumped down to the ground. We followed, looking around with interest. I'd known the Great Houses were huge, but the building in front of us made Haddon Hall look tiny. The armsman had parked by the servants' entrance, by the side of the building. I had the feeling that was an unsubtle insult. Sir Griffons ignored it as two tired-looking men materialised by the door. One of them was dressed in a butler's uniform. The other wore a bland suit that bothered me. I wasn't sure why.

"Sir," the butler said. "His lordship will see you now."

"I'll see the crime scene first," Sir Griffons said, curtly. "Take us there at once."

The butler looked as if he wanted to argue, but his companion merely nodded. I wondered just what the relationship between the two men actually was as the butler turned and led us into the hall. I could feel layer upon layer of wards probing at us, scanning our bodies so intimately that it was hard to believe we could smuggle anything into the hall without permission. Beside me, Caroline smiled faintly. I knew what she was thinking. The wards hadn't been enough to save Lord Redford.

It was the first time I'd been inside a Great House and, despite myself, I was curious. The walls were lined with portraits of the great and the good, people I guessed had been important once upon a time but now largely forgotten outside their families. Statues stood everywhere, some so realistic that I wondered if they were family enemies who'd been permanently turned to stone. A handful of servants in drab uniforms gave us a wide berth as we moved down the corridor, up the stairs and through a maze of rooms. The butler seemed to have no trouble navigating his kingdom. I felt lost, as if the wards were interfering with my sense of direction. They probably were. The Great Houses had secrets they didn't want us to see.

The butler opened a door, revealing a large suite. A middle-aged man sat in a comfortable chair, a knife protruding out of his chest. I didn't have to check his pulse or cast any spells to know he was dead. The runes carved into the hilt composed a thoroughly lethal curse. The poor bastard probably hadn't had a chance to cast a counterspell before the curse got him. I frowned as I inched closer, studying the blade. It was tainted by dark magic. I honestly couldn't understand how someone had managed to get it through the wards.

Caroline's thoughts were moving in the same direction. "This was an inside job."

Sir Griffons looked at the butler. "Do you know who did it?"

The butler shifted, uncomfortably. "That's a family matter…"

"Then you'd better take it to the Patriarch," Sir Griffons said. "I want him down here, right now."

He turned back to the body as the butler spluttered in outrage. "Adam, what do you make of it?"

I leaned closer, careful not to touch the corpse. "Cause of death, a cursed blade," I said, slowly. "No other wounds, as far as I can tell. Do I have permission to use forensic spells?"

"Not yet." Sir Griffons looked oddly irked. "Caroline? Do you have anything to add?"

"He was taken by surprise," Caroline said. "There's no sign of a struggle. There's no hint he had any reason to expect attack. He didn't even sense the blade before it was plunged into his chest."

I nodded. The curse was so strong it should have been easy to sense. Lord Redford should have known it was there, even if he didn't know the blade's owner intended to stick it in him. A lack of imagination? Or arrogance? People didn't craft cursed blades for fun. Whoever had carved the runes into the metal had done it inside the house, risking detection if the master of the hall decided to carry out a security scan. I didn't think anyone would take it *lightly* if they detected the blade. It was a weapon with only one purpose. Whoever was cut with it was going to die.

The door opened. I felt a surge of magic as I looked up. A tall man stepped into the room, wearing long dark robes and a grim expression. He looked oddly familiar, but…I couldn't place him. He had a natural air of authority that suggested he couldn't be pushed around, not even by us. I straightened, bracing myself. I'd heard horror stories of what happened to people who found themselves no longer welcome in a Great House. If this was an inside job, the master of the hall might want to cover it up...

"Sir Griffons," the Patriarch said.

"Lord Califon." Sir Griffons nodded, curtly. "I assume you're not going to waste my time?"

"No," Lord Califon said. "We need an independent inquiry into the murder. And the murderer."

"So you know who did it," Caroline said.

Sir Griffons shot her a quelling look, then returned his attention to Lord Califon. "Who did it?"

"Saline," Lord Califon said. "She stabbed her uncle with a cursed blade."

I reeled. *Saline?* I knew her...in hindsight, I should have realised we were going to Saline's house. And she'd murdered her uncle? I couldn't believe it. She'd been an odd duck, but she'd never struck me as a murderer. But... if she'd lived in the house, she wouldn't have any trouble carving the blade and taking it to Lord Redford's room without being detected. I swallowed, hard. Saline might not have *planned* to make her escape, afterwards. I had the feeling I'd been right, when I'd been woken from a sound sleep. This case was *political*.

"Why?" Sir Griffons cocked his head. "Did she say anything to you?"

"She's waiting in a side room," Lord Califon said, without answering the question. "Get your answers from her, before the family council meets. We need to know *why* before we proceed to judgement."

He nodded to the butler. "Escort the Kingsmen to Saline's room and wait outside," he ordered. "And then have Lord Redford's body transferred to the family crypt."

Sir Griffons held up a hand, casting a series of forensic spells. I watched, impressed. There was no magical signature on the blade, as far as I could see, but there *were* fingerprints. Sir Griffons carefully copied them, placing the record on a piece of charmed parchment. They weren't proof of anything—we'd been taught that fingerprints could be faked or simply scrubbed through magic—but they were indicative. If nothing else, they might suggest what the murderer wanted us to think.

"This way, sir," the butler said. "She's waiting for you."

"I'm sure she is," Sir Griffons said.

My thoughts churned as we followed the butler down a long corridor and stopped outside a locked and warded chamber. I couldn't believe that *Saline* had murdered her uncle, certainly not in a manner that made it impossible to hide her guilt. Were we being conned? Or had she been under a compulsion charm? The wards should have spotted that, but I knew through bitter experience that they had their limits. The butler pressed his hand against the doorknob, undoing the locking spells. I felt a gust of warm air flowing around us as he opened the door. The chamber didn't look like a prison cell. It looked rather more like a small bedroom, bigger than mine back home. I felt an odd flush of envy, mingled with concern. A child who grew up in such luxury could be deeply warped by the time she hit adulthood.

Saline herself sat on the bed, staring down at nothingness. Her long brown hair spilled over her nightgown, hands were clasped in her lap...I could sense faint flickers of magic surrounding her, as if she was trying to defend herself against constant pressure. The house wards were probably locking her down, I guessed. Her father—or uncle; I wasn't sure if Lord Califon was her father—had isolated her from the wards. The building no longer welcomed her. I had the odd feeling she probably found it unpleasant.

She looked up at us, her eyes lingering on me. "Adam?"

I winced, inwardly. She sounded years younger, as if she was a little girl again. Her face was blank, yet...there was a looming horror in her eyes. I wondered, despite myself, if someone *had* managed to get a compulsion charm through her defences. It might explain the horror. If someone had used her as a weapon...no one would ever trust her again, not completely. It wasn't fair, but it was true.

"Yes," I said, as gently as I could. "I haven't changed that much, have I?"

"We need to know what happened," Sir Griffons said, calmly. His voice was very professional. "And we need to use a truth spell."

"I understand." Saline looked down. Her voice, when she spoke again, was very low. "I killed him."

Sir Griffons cast the truth spell. "Tell us what happened," he said. "Start at the beginning."

Saline made a sound that was somewhere between a giggle and a sob. "Uncle Redford put a spell on me," she said. The truth spell didn't twitch. She was telling the truth. "He turned me dumb! I couldn't *think*. I just... lost everything. He did it to me."

"I see," Sir Griffon said. He sounded understanding. Very understanding. "And how did you break the spell?"

"Akin broke it." Saline looked up, an odd expression covering her face. It looked like hero-worship. "He got a spellbreaker from somewhere and used it on me. The spell snapped"—she laughed, harshly—"and I was smart again. I promised myself that I'd kill my uncle for his crimes and I did. He put that spell on me!"

Sir Griffons nodded, slowly. "And how did you get the knife into the hall?"

"I made it myself," Saline said. "I did all the pieces separately, then put them together and forged the spellform this morning. I knew where all the blind spots were. I put the knife in a box, carried it up to Uncle Redford's bedroom and stabbed him. He died instantly."

"And you didn't think to report him?" Sir Griffons leaned forward. "Your family wouldn't let him get away with it."

"I didn't have any proof," Saline said. "The spell was completely shattered. I couldn't *prove* what had happened to me. And he was so important that he might have gotten away with it. He had so many friends and supporters and clients and..."

I shuddered. I couldn't think of any *good* motive for casting such a spell on anyone. And yet, it seemed pointless. Saline was hardly going to inherit... I resolved to try to dig into the family affairs, to work out who benefited if Saline grew too dumb to brush her teeth without help. There were hundreds of horror stories about madmen and women in the attics. I couldn't help wondering how many magic-less Zeros had been banished, instead of being put to work. *That* would be ironic. The Great Houses had literally thrown away their one chance to establish themselves as unchallengeable rulers.

Sir Griffons asked hundreds of questions, forcing Saline to go over the affair time and time again. I felt pity for her, pity and sympathy and…I wondered, sourly, what her family would *do*. They wouldn't want to keep a murderer on the books, but they wouldn't want the remainder of the city learning what Lord Redford had done. My imagination provided too many possible motives, each one more horrifying than the last. I'd thought I knew how dark the world could be, growing up in Water Shallot. But I'd been wrong. There were people out there who did the most *horrific* things.

"Remain here," Sir Griffons ordered, when he was finished. "Do either of you"—he looked at us—"have any further questions?"

I tried to think of one, but nothing came to mind. Sir Griffons had covered the entire case quite comprehensively. We knew she'd done it, we knew *why* she'd done it…we found it hard to condemn her. Hell, she'd probably done her family a favour. It would have been a major scandal if Lord Redford had been arrested for his crimes, one even the Great Houses would have found impossible to cover up. I had the feeling House Califon was merely waiting for us to go before they drew a veil over the whole affair.

Sir Griffons led us outside. The butler was still waiting, patiently. I wondered if he'd been spying on the conversation. There was little true privacy in a Great House, if rumours were to be believed. The privacy wards might not stand up to the household charms. I rather suspected Lord Califon would have been listening to us. He had to know what had happened before his family council met. He might find himself stampeded into doing something stupid if he didn't come up with a plan of his own.

"We'll be in touch," Sir Griffons said. His voice was very calm, but I thought I detected an undertone of anger. I wasn't sure why he was so annoyed. "But I think it's a fairly open and shut case."

The butler bowed. "My master will be glad to hear it," he said. *He* sounded pleased. I wondered, sourly, just how close he identified with his masters. "Do you require transport back home?"

"I think we'll walk," Sir Griffons said. "You may escort us to the door."

"Yes, sir," the butler said. He turned away, heading down the corridor. "If you'll come with me…"

CHAPTER
FIFTEEN

"So," Sir Griffons said, once we were through the gates and walking away from House Califon. "What do you make of the whole affair?"

"That poor girl," Caroline said. "He could have done *anything* to her."

"Quite." Sir Griffons nodded. "Once a spell like that got bedded in, he'd have no trouble taking advantage of it."

I stared at my feet. "I don't believe it," I said. "How could he hope to escape detection?"

"The spell would have blurred itself into Saline's natural magic," Sir Griffons said. "In a sense, she would be cursing herself. I'm quite impressed young Akin spotted the curse and did something about it. I wonder…"

He frowned. "He must have obtained an Object of Power from his family," he mused. "A Device of Power might not be strong enough to root out and destroy the curse."

Caroline poked me. "You knew her, didn't you?"

"Yeah." I sighed. I didn't want to think about Jude's, not now. "She was an aristo, back when we were lowerclassmen. I thought…she wasn't a bad person, but she wasn't a very good person either. And then she started to decline. I didn't pay much attention to it."

"Perhaps you should have," Sir Griffons said.

"Perhaps." I didn't want to think about that either. If I'd stumbled across the truth, a year ago, it was a given that no one would have believed me. Lord

Redford would have charged me with slander and crushed me like a bug. It spoke well of Akin, I supposed, that he'd done *something*. I wondered if he'd known Saline intended to kill her uncle. He might be in some trouble if he'd known and said nothing. "There was no reason to think it was anything more than her reaching her peak."

"Perhaps," Sir Griffon echoed. "But you never know what lurks behind the fine walls and finer words of *Polite* Society."

He waved a hand at a mansion. "Behind those walls, all kinds of crimes are committed," he added. "And most of them will never see justice."

I nodded. "Aristos!"

"They're not all bad," Caroline said, sharply. "Saline would still be dumb if one of her friends hadn't helped her."

I said nothing. I knew she was right, but...she wouldn't have *been* dumb—either—if her uncle hadn't cursed her. I promised myself, silently, that I'd give my father a big hug when I saw him again. I'd complained about him time and time again, when I'd been a little boy, but he'd never cursed me. He'd never even forced me to work in his shop! Compared to Saline's parents, whoever they were, he was practically perfect.

"Quite," Sir Griffons said.

I frowned. "So...what's going to happen to her?"

"Our investigation, such as it was, will provide some degree of political cover for Lord Califon," Sir Griffons said. "Our *independent* confirmation that Lord Redford cast illicit spells on Saline will serve as proof he deserved to die. Given that he's no longer around to cause trouble, or rally his supporters to his cause, the family can breathe a sigh of relief and condemn him without having to worry about his response. Saline...will probably get a smack on the behind and then let go."

"Good," I said, savagely. I'd never *liked* Saline—she was an aristo—but she didn't deserve to have her mind twisted and warped by her uncle. "How many people will know the truth?"

"I suspect the full truth will be covered up, before too long," Sir Griffons said. "If some of it leaks out"—he smiled, thinly—"Saline may find herself unwelcome. The family may cut a deal with her so she stays out of the public eye."

"That's not fair," I protested. "She was *cursed*."

"And they can't tell the world she was cursed without admitting what sort of serpent they were clutching to their bosom," Sir Griffons pointed out. "They don't want the rest of the Great Houses turning on them, not now. Things are fragile enough as it is without poisonous suggestions slipping into the open. The city came alarmingly close to another House War last year."

I scowled. "And so there's no closure?"

Sir Griffons smiled. "Lord Redford is dead. His death was thoroughly deserved. Saline will probably get away with it. People will be giving her suspicious looks, depending on how much of the story actually gets out, but she won't face any formal punishment. I dare say there'll be enough closure for everyone involved."

"Yes, sir," I said, sullenly.

I resisted the urge to kick a stone into the gutter as we kept walking. It didn't feel like enough. I wanted the truth to be shouted right across the city. Let *everyone* know what sort of monster had infected House Califon. But Sir Griffons would never let me tell the world. The case was closed—it had barely even been open—but it left a sour taste in my mouth. I remembered what I'd been told, when I'd been recruited, and shuddered. Some cases were never truly closed. And sometimes the truth was buried under a mountain of bullshit.

The streets started to fill with people as we turned the corner and walked past a row of expensive shops. I spotted hundreds of aristocratic women, some wearing the latest fashion in fancy hats. They'd woven their hair into their hats, crafting them in a style that resembled giant clipper ships. I thought they were absurd. Their bodyguards gave us sharp looks—I guessed they recognised potential threats when they saw them—and steered their charges away from us. I tried not to snort in disbelief at just how much their mistresses were buying. The shops were so expensive that price tags were nowhere in evidence. If you had to ask the price, you couldn't afford it.

"Notice the women over there," Sir Griffons said, nodding towards a trio of middle-aged ladies striding down the road as if they owned it. "See the clothes they're wearing?"

I shrugged. The ladies were wearing robes, but...they weren't *real* robes. They looked more like towels wrapped around their bodies than anything else. They were close enough to trousers that I was *sure* the older women would be looking down their long noses at them. I snorted at the thought. It was fine to show most of their breasts, but to show the shape of their legs was a *faux pas* beyond hope of redemption. It wasn't as if they were showing off their *bare* legs. But then, I'd never understood fashion.

Caroline had a more intelligent thought. "They're wearing North Cairnbulg fashions, aren't they?"

"Yes." Sir Griffons didn't sound pleased. "They're showcasing their support for Prince Jacob and his cause."

I leaned forward as the three women vanished into the distance. "Sir... is it *legal* for Prince Jacob to be here?"

Sir Griffons looked pained. "As I understand it, he didn't bother to ask permission. He just moved into the city."

"So he's an unwelcome guest?" I stroked my chin. "Why don't they just throw him out?"

"Politics." Sir Griffons let out a long breath. "It's something you cannot afford to forget in this job."

He led us past Magus Court and stopped outside our building. I watched as he parted the wards, allowing us entry. A single scroll was resting in the letterbox, waiting for us. Sir Griffons picked it up, broke the seal and scanned it quickly. I shared a glance with Caroline. I was morbidly sure that, whatever was in the letter, it was bad news.

"We have been invited to a party in honour of Prince Jacob." Sir Griffons snorted, rudely. "I trust you two know how to behave yourselves?"

"Yes, sir," I said. Sir Muldoon had drilled us in the basics. "I...should we be going? It might embarrass the king."

"It might," Sir Griffons said. "But merely attending a party doesn't imply support for the bastard."

"And no one cares about our opinions anyway," Caroline put in. "We're just…squires."

"And you can be disowned at any time," Sir Griffons cautioned. He passed me the scroll. "If nothing else, it will be a good chance to take the city's pulse. There's more wheeling and dealing at such parties than there is in Magus Court or the stock exchange. We might find out who's in, who's out and who's planning what for the end of the summer."

Caroline frowned. "The end of the summer, sir?"

"That's when young Akin Rubén and Caitlyn Aguirre either have to announce their engagement or end their betrothal," Sir Griffons said. "Whatever happens, things will change."

I nodded, slowly. Even *I* knew the alliance between House Rubén and House Aguirre depended on Akin and Caitlyn turning their betrothal into a real marriage. I wondered, grimly, what they thought about it, now their time was almost up. They couldn't delay much longer. Caitlyn's family couldn't deny her claim to adulthood unless they wanted to claim she was mentally unsound, unable or unwilling to live as an adult. I doubted they'd get very far if they tried. Caitlyn might not have magic, but she was hardly a *cripple*. She'd have no shortage of supporters if she wanted to flee her family and find safety elsewhere.

"But that isn't our concern for the moment," Sir Griffons said. "You two can grab some breakfast, then spend the day exploring the city. We'll go to House Lamplighter this evening."

Caroline took the scroll and read it. "What do we wear?"

"Your formal uniform," Sir Griffon said, curtly. "You don't need to dress up fancy to attend a party."

"Yes, sir," I said. I'd always hated dressing up for formal balls, if only because I hadn't had the money to do it properly. The aristos had always known I'd borrowed my suits and ties. It was worse for the girls. They were mocked if they wore the same dress twice in a row. "Do we have to write a report about Saline?"

"No." Sir Griffon smiled. "That's my responsibility. You can do it yourself when you're knighted."

I headed into the kitchen and put the kettle on. Caroline walked past me and dug into the food preserver, producing bacon, eggs, onions and a hunk of strong-smelling cheese. Sir Griffons watched, expressionlessly, as she cooked omelettes and handed them 'round. I took mine and quickly ate it, enjoying the combination of tastes. Caroline was a much better cook than me. I wasn't too surprised. It was uncommon for boys to be taught how to cook. I'd gotten in trouble, once, for implying that potions brewing was *very* like cooking.

"Have fun," Sir Griffon said, when we'd finished eating. "I'll call you if I need you."

The streets were crammed with people as we walked down the road and crossed the bridge into South Shallot. This time, without the guardsmen surrounding us, people didn't pay any attention to us. I stopped by a stall and bought a pair of sausages in buns, passing one of them to Caroline as we kept walking. The meat tasted very suspicious, the flavour hidden behind mustard and tomato ketchup. I smiled, remembering eating street food when I'd been very young and the family short of cash. The food was cheap, but not always healthy. The buyer ate at his own risk.

"I've never liked big cities," Caroline confessed, as we made our way over the bridge to Water Shallot. "They're too unfriendly."

I frowned. "I've never lived anywhere else," I said, softly. The streets were quieter now. The men were at their jobs, if they were employed; the women were cleaning their houses while their children were at school. The women who lived on the edge of the gentrified region were poor, but proud. They were all too aware of the gap between themselves and the even *poorer* families further south. They'd be terrified if their children brought home suitors from the docks. "The cities have their advantages and disadvantages."

The streets grew darker as we made our way further south. A handful of prostitutes sat on the street corners, whistling at anyone who showed even the *slightest* hint of interest. There was no sign of their pimps, but I knew they were probably watching from a distance. I rather suspected they were wasting their time. The women on the streets were reaching the end of their careers, their short lives coming to a harrowing end. I shuddered as one of them waved at me, her toothless mouth forming something that *might* have been intended as a smile. Her john had probably knocked her teeth out for answering back or *something*. I felt a stab of pity, mingled with horror. If I'd grown up in such an environment, who knew what *I* would have become?

I was tempted to take Caroline to the shop and introduce her to my father and sisters, but I knew better. Instead, we headed towards the docks. The stench of rotting fish grew stronger as we walked, seeping into our clothes and brushing against our bare skin. I saw a dozen posters nailed to the wall, each one inviting us to the Working Men's Clubs. The guardsmen hadn't tried to take them down. I guessed they didn't even know the posters were there. I wasn't even sure the intended audience could read them. Here, schooling was regarded as a waste of time.

We walked across a canal, watching a heavy barge steadily navigating its way down towards the sea. A handful of children worked on the deck, performing tasks I couldn't even begin to comprehend. The barges were almost all family-owned businesses, the children going to work almost as soon as they could walk. I'd heard that the bargemen *hated* the schools, insisting that it was a cunning plan to keep them poor by forcing them to hire outsiders to work their barges. They might have been right, although I knew schooling was important. A man who couldn't read a contract couldn't tell if he was being lied to.

I scowled as we headed through a darkened alleyway. A handful of older men were lying in the shadows, trying to snatch some sleep in the quiet of the day. They were homeless, probably kicked out by families that could no longer support them. Or…or something worse. I remembered some of the horror stories I'd heard and shuddered. Some people thoroughly deserved to be kicked out of house and home. Lord Redford, for one. Saline shouldn't have *needed* to kill him.

Caroline nudged me. "I don't want to worry you," she breathed, so quietly I could barely hear her, "but we have company."

I reached out with my senses, swearing under my breath. There were four men in front of us, three more behind. We'd been boxed in...I glanced at the crumbling iron fire escape, wondering if we could get up to the rooftop, but that would just be trading one trap for another. Either they'd chase us over the rooftops or shadow us on the ground, waiting for us to come down. I felt the magic flowing through me, blurring with Caroline's. Neither of us *wanted* to run away. Instead, we picked up speed. I sensed their surprise as we hurried towards them. They didn't seem to realise we knew they were there.

The four men came into view, three carrying knives. The fourth carried a rusty spellcaster, so degraded that I honestly didn't expect it to be in working condition. I reminded myself, sharply, not to take that for granted. The spellcaster might still be dangerous. I shuddered, inwardly, as the four men leered at us. They intended to rape and kill us both.

"There's a toll you have to pay, if you want to get past," the leader said. He was practically undressing Caroline with his eyes. "And you..."

I lunged forward, striking him in the throat. He emitted a gurgling sound and tumbled to the ground, coughing and choking. The spellcaster hit the ground beside him and exploded in a shower of sparks. The other three started forward, too late. Caroline and I could have stopped them in their tracks with magic. Instead, we tore them to pieces. I laughed, despite myself, as I took the knife off one of them, snapped it in two and flattened him with a single punch. I'd measured myself against Sir Muldoon and the other instructors. I hadn't quite realised just how much of an edge I had against everyone else.

There was a clattering sound behind me. I turned, just in time to see the two behind us turning and running for their lives. They were so scared they'd dropped their knives. They'd never live *that* down, not in the docks. No one would be afraid of them. I snickered as I destroyed the remaining knives, resisting the urge to put my foot on their throats and push down as hard as I could. I'd met too many thugs like them. They were just human vermin, keeping the streets unsafe for locals. I'd be doing everyone a favour if I'd killed them out of hand.

"We'll take them back home," Caroline said, casting a capture spell. "And they can be shipped to Skullbreaker Island."

"Yeah," I agreed. One of the thugs moaned. I kicked him in the chest. "They won't be tormenting anyone *here* any longer."

Caroline checked her watch. "And we'd better hurry," she added. "We have to look our best for tonight."

I groaned. "I hate parties."

"Think of it as a chance to find out what's *really* going on," Caroline said. She winked at me. "And, if nothing else, a chance to eat some really good food."

"And it was supposed to be my turn to cook tonight," I said. "Point taken."

CHAPTER SIXTEEN

I felt ludicrously out of place as I clambered out of the carriage and walked towards House Lamplighter. My formal dress uniform was as uncomfortable as hell, as if it had been designed by a sadist, and I could *feel* aristos looking at me and sneering as they realised I was a commonborn Kingsman. Caroline fell into place beside me, offering me her arm. Sir Griffons had told us to go ahead, promising he'd be there within the hour. I had a sneaking feeling he *meant* he wasn't going to be coming at all.

House Lamplighter glowed in the darkness, every window lit up with an eerie magical radiance. The main doors were thrown wide open, allowing the throng of aristos to move in and out of the mansion as they pleased. I looked around, trying not to sneer at the limitless wealth on display. The dresses the girls wore cost more than my family could hope to earn in a year. And they all looked unique. I shook my head in disbelief as we presented ourselves to the butler, who looked so stiff I half-expected him to have a rod stuck up his butt. He eyed us sardonically, then motioned for us to enter. Caroline managed a polite curtsey. I would sooner have died.

The sound of dance music drew louder as we walked down the steps and into the main hall. Couples were milling about, moving through the steps or haunting the buffet. I looked around for Lady Lamplighter herself—the reports had stated the Great House had a new Matriarch—but there was no sign of her. I felt my heart twist as I spotted a couple of girls I knew vaguely from school, chattering loudly about nothing with their friends. They didn't seem to notice me. I wasn't sure if I should wave or not. Here...they'd probably prefer to pretend they didn't know me. I couldn't blame them. Their parents would ask pointed questions about what they might have been doing.

A passing servant offered me a glass of wine. I took it, muttering a spell to remove the alcohol before I started drinking. Sir Griffons would kill me—probably literally—if I got drunk and made an ass of myself in front of the Great Houses. Caroline caught my hand and turned me around, pointing towards the inner stair. A young man in tribal robes stood at the top, staring down at us.

The herald cleared his throat loudly. "Ladies and Gentlemen, Prince Jacob of North Cairnbulg."

I studied the prince for a long moment, thoughtfully. He was a dark-skinned youth, only a shade or two lighter than myself. His clothes were carefully designed to show off his muscles and make a display of wealth, even though—reading between the lines—I had the feeling he wasn't anything like as wealthy as he claimed. He didn't have his kingdom, not yet. His eyes were alight with intelligence as he strode down the steps, accepting the applause of the junior aristos as his due. The older aristos didn't seem so entranced. I saw a handful turn away, cutting the prince dead in the midst of the crowd. It didn't seem to bother him.

Saline stepped up and asked the prince to dance. I blinked in surprise... that *was* Saline. She looked different now, wearing a long blue dress that set off her brown hair nicely. Clearly, she'd already been forgiven. I guessed that they wanted to thank her for sparing them the embarrassment of a trial. The prince took her hand and led her onto the dance floor. He seemed to be a good dancer. He certainly didn't seem to be treading on her toes.

"Politics," Caroline muttered.

A smarmy-faced aristo—I wanted to hit him on principle—came up to Caroline and asked her for a dance. Caroline accepted and allowed him to take her hand. I felt a surge of jealously, even though I didn't want to dance. I'd had lessons, but I knew I wasn't good enough to go on the dance floor without embarrassing myself. Instead, I turned and walked up the stairs to the balcony. It was as good a vantage point as any. Saline seemed to be having a great time. Caroline...not so much.

She can take care of herself, I reminded myself. *Really. She can.*

I directed my gaze over the dance floor, trying to pick out the alliances amongst the noblemen. There was a surprising lack of *senior* aristos, save for Lady Lamplighter herself. She wasn't much older than *me*, I noted. It was never easy to tell with the aristos, but I'd be surprised if she was over twenty. I wondered if she'd done the right thing by agreeing to host the prince. The older aristos were going out of their way to shun him.

"Adam?"

I turned. Akin stood beside me, wearing a suit and tie. I was surprised he hadn't made more of an effort, although he *was* House Rubén's Heir Primus. He set fashion, whether he wanted to or not. He didn't follow it. I was surprised he'd sought me out. Or perhaps I shouldn't be surprised. We hadn't been invited to the ball because the aristos wanted to see us. We'd probably been invited so they could take our measure before we were knighted.

"Akin," I said. I reminded myself, sharply, that Akin was the best of the aristocratic bunch. It wasn't *his* fault his psychotic cousin had stabbed me in the back before taking a jump off the castle and plummeting to his death. "How are you?"

"Bored out of my mind," Akin said. He held a glass in his hand, but it looked as if he hadn't so much as taken a sip. "This ball is a waste of time."

"Far be it from me to disagree," I said. I turned my attention back to the dance floor. Prince Jacob had moved on to another dance partner and was whirling her though a complex series of steps I could barely follow. Caroline had moved to another partner too. "Why are you here?"

"Someone has to put in an appearance." Akin sounded as if he didn't believe it. "And to make it clear we're interested, without being *too* interested."

I glanced at him. "In the prince?"

"Yeah." Akin let out a sigh. "If he'd asked permission to move here, we would have said no."

"I imagine it isn't doing wonders for your relationship with North Cairnbulg," I agreed.

"No." Akin sighed, again. "He's caught us in a trap."

He said nothing for a long moment. I waited, trying to offer a sympathetic ear. I had the feeling Akin wanted to talk, although I had no idea if he'd been *ordered* to talk. Sir Griffons had told us that parties were often places for passing underhand messages, ones that would be officially denied if anyone heard of it. Akin had never been the kind of person to enjoy playing cloak and dagger games. If someone had told him to pass us a message…the list of suspects was very short. His father was about the only *real* suspect.

"We don't want him here," Akin said, quietly. "But we cannot be seen to giving into pressure—from the capital as well as North Cairnbulg—to expel him either. As long as he doesn't break the law here, we have no formal grounds for kicking him out. And the more we're pressured into expelling him anyway, the more we have to push back."

I sighed, inwardly. The Great Houses deserved to squirm, but not when there was something genuinely *important* at stake. Prince Jacob had tangled them in a political web that couldn't be broken without causing all sorts of problems. The Great Houses wanted—needed—to maintain their independence. They couldn't be seen to be surrendering to the king's pressure without compromising it.

Which means that both the Great Houses and the king want the same thing, I thought, as I considered the implications. *But they're actually blocking each other from obtaining it.*

I looked down at the dance floor. The prince was moving onto a third partner, a young woman in a dress so tight I thought it was going to split open at any moment. Saline was following him, keeping surprisingly close to the prince. I wondered if she knew she was defying the will of her community, or if she was simply establishing her independence. It could be anything. With aristos, who could tell?

"The prince seems to be enjoying himself," I commented, dryly. "What are you going to *do* with him?"

"The decision has been taken to refuse him the support—money and material—he wants," Akin said. "There's nothing to be gained by supporting him, not when it would mean picking a fight with North Cairnbulg. If he wins—if he takes the throne—we don't think he'll be willing to throw out all the trade treaties. His people would rise up against him."

"And you don't think he has a hope," I added. "Right?"

Akin shrugged. "He has a handful of hardcore supporters, who will do just about anything for him, and a slightly larger band of fair-weather friends who will claim they supported him completely if he actually wins the throne. Beyond that…he has no army, no navy beyond a pair of minor warships, no sorcerers…his only real hope is sparking off a rebellion in the hinterlands or bringing in help from outside. Neither one is likely to happen."

"I take your point," I said. Sir Griffons had briefed me, carefully. "The king wasn't pleased when he showed up here."

"No." Akin winced. "The king's grandson is still on track to hold both crowns. He won't want to do anything to disrupt *that*."

"No," I agreed. "I wonder what the prince makes of it?"

"I imagine it doesn't matter," Akin said. We stared down at the dancers for a long moment, our thoughts elsewhere. "I have to go mingle."

"You make it sound like an invitation to your funeral," I said, dryly. I understood the sentiment. "Is Caitlyn coming?"

"No." Akin shook her head. "Politics. She cannot afford to have the prince request help in front of everyone."

I felt a twinge of sympathy. I could understand the prince's position. But…there was no excuse for using politeness as a weapon to manipulate your way into getting what you wanted. I supposed he had to be desperate. Time wasn't on his side. The king's grandson—the heir to both crowns—would be an adult before too long. When that happened, I doubted anyone would give two rusty coppers for Prince Jacob. He'd be well-advised to sell his ships and retire somewhere on the other side of Maxima. His enemies wouldn't care about him if they thought he'd given up his claim to the throne.

"He probably would," I said. "You can sneak out and see her later."

"Not here," Akin said. "Too many eyes would notice."

He nodded to me, then turned and strode away. I watched him go, wondering just how much of what he'd told me had been at someone else's command. Akin was more...likable than the other aristos, but he was still an aristo. I turned back to the dance floor, looking for Caroline. There was no sign of her. I shivered, glancing from face to face. Was she alright? Or...I hadn't liked the boy who'd first taken her onto the dance floor. He could be doing anything with her!

She can take care of herself, I told myself, again.

I walked back downstairs, took another glass of wine and forced myself to mingle. No one seemed to want to talk to me, but it didn't matter. I'd had plenty of experience at listening to people unobtrusively. The aristos talked about everything from trade deals to magical experiments, from who was marrying who to who's marriage was in serious trouble. I heard a couple of older ladies gossiping over the late Lord Lamplighter, a man who'd been under the impression—the very *mistaken* impression—that he had a head for business. It was hard to believe, but—the more I looked around the hall—the more I thought the family didn't have the money to maintain the mansion. The servants didn't look like old retainers. The butler was the only one who looked to have been in the house for years.

Quite a bit of conversation focused on the prince, although most of it seemed to be about how handsome he was rather than the justice of his cause. I had the feeling the prince probably found it a little frustrating. I smirked, then looked up and blinked in surprise as I met Alana's eyes. She stared at me, as if she'd never expected to see *me* here. I supposed she had a point. I'd never expected to visit House Lamplighter either.

I held out my hand before I could think better of it. "Would you care for the pleasure of this dance, my lady?"

Alana gave me a sharp look, then shrugged and took my hand. I blinked, surprised. The girl I'd known at school wouldn't have willingly taken my hand, unless one of us wore gloves. I put the thought aside as I led her onto the dance floor, falling in step with the other dancers. Prince Jacob whirled past us, a girl on each arm. Alana's face twisted with distaste.

"So you're a Kingsman now," Alana said, as we moved in tune with the music. "What are you doing here?"

"I was invited," I said.

"Lucy must have been short on numbers," Alana said. She nodded to the crowd. "It's quite a small gathering."

I looked up. There were at least two hundred people within the hall and more outside, dancing on the lawns or exploring the grotto on the far side of the mansion. It didn't strike me as a small gathering. There was barely standing room only. But Alana's mansion was probably bigger. I had no doubt of it.

"I'll take your word for it," I said. I noticed her hair was still in braids. "When are you going to start your season?"

"My parents will decide," Alana said. Her voice was flat, but I caught an edge of anger in her words. "They haven't made up their minds."

Because they want to arrange partners for you and Bella before you reach adulthood and start having your own ideas, I wondered, *or because they want to delay your other sister's marriage as long as possible?*

I felt a twinge of sympathy. Alana had finished her schooling. It was rare beyond words for a child *not* to be raised to adulthood after they'd passed their exams, unless there was something *seriously* wrong with her. Alana had to feel the shame of still being treated as a child keenly, particularly as her friends started to make the jump into adulthood. I almost felt sorry for her.

Saline appeared behind Alana. "Mind if I cut in?"

Alana let go of my hands and hurried away before I could say anything. Saline grabbed hold and whirled me around the dance floor, grinning from ear to ear. I wondered if the prince had lost his attraction. He was still dancing, a glass of wine in one hand. I did my best to ignore him as Saline held me close. I was suddenly very short of breath. She was so close I could feel her breasts brush against my chest.

"I have to thank you," Saline said. Her lips brushed against my ears. "If you hadn't come when you were called…"

"All part of the job," I said. It wasn't as if I'd done much of anything. Sir Griffons had done all the heavy lifting. "What are you going to do with yourself now?"

"No idea." Saline's grin grew wider. "I might follow the prince to North Cairnbulg. Or I might go on holiday and never come back. Or I might join Louise and go into politics."

I blinked. "Louise has gone into politics?"

"Yeah." Saline looked pensive, just for a moment. "I thought she was going to invite you."

"…She didn't." I recalled her asking me out, back before I'd travelled north to Haddon Hall. Had she something in mind? "What's she doing?"

"I'll ask her to drop you a note," Saline said. "I'm sure she'll be pleased to hear from you."

I wasn't so sure. I was a Kingsman…a squire, to be sure, but I still had duty and obligation. And…I wondered, suddenly, what sort of politics Louise was doing. She didn't have a powerful family, to push her into politics at the very highest level. Her parents were merchants. What was she doing?

"We'll see," I said, doubtfully.

Caroline appeared, looking angry. "Care for a dance?"

Saline grinned. "Me or him?"

"Him," Caroline said.

Saline curtseyed and let go of me. Caroline's expression didn't lighten as she took my hands and led me down the hall. I frowned, wondering what was bothering her. She didn't look remotely happy.

"A couple of young men had wandering hands," she said. "I probably shouldn't have hexed them."

"I don't think anyone will care," I told her. "You probably taught them a much-needed lesson."

"Yeah." Caroline shrugged. "Did you learn anything interesting?"

I frowned. "I don't know," I admitted. It looked as though the party was finally coming to an end. Sir Griffons, standing by the door, caught our eyes and nodded. "I might have."

CHAPTER
SEVENTEEN

"An interesting development," Sir Griffons said, the following morning. "Do you think Lord Carioca Rubén ordered his son to talk to you?"

I hesitated, unsure of myself. "I think so," I said, finally. "But I don't know."

"No one ever does," Sir Griffons said. He'd forced me to go through everything Akin had said with a fine-toothed comb. "At that level, it's hard to tell who's responsible for what. The real movers and shakers never show their hand so easily."

Caroline had a different question. "Adam, do you *trust* Akin?"

I hesitated. "I don't know," I admitted. "Of all the aristos, Akin was—is—the most approachable. I think he was probably the most *decent*. He *was* the one who helped Saline, after all, when no one else could be bothered to do it. But I don't know if *any* aristo can be trusted."

"You can trust them to put their interests first," Sir Griffons said.

"But they're acting *against* their interests," Caroline said. "Prince Jacob being here isn't good for the Great Houses."

"True," Sir Griffons agreed. "But kicking him out isn't going to be good for them either. If Akin's telling the truth, the Great Houses have decided to grit their collective teeth and wait the prince out. Sooner or later, he'll run out of money and move on."

"Unless someone picks up his bills," I pointed out. "He seemed to have quite a few supporters on the dance floor."

"I imagine anyone who does will feel the wrath of their peers." Sir Griffons shrugged. "We'll keep an eye on the situation, naturally, and inform our superiors of our conclusions."

Caroline frowned. "What will they do?"

"That's above your pay grade," Sir Griffons said. "The two of you can do some sparring. I want to…"

The wards chimed. "Stay here," Sir Griffons ordered. "No one would come here unless they needed us."

I glanced at Caroline as Sir Griffons headed to the door. "Maybe they want us to help evict the prince."

"Maybe," Caroline said. "But they couldn't turn a blind eye to us grabbing the bastard off the streets and plonking him on a boat back home."

I nodded, curtly. Prince Jacob was a nuisance. I could understand why the Great Houses wanted to be rid of him. Just by staying in the city, he was a diplomatic nightmare waiting to happen. But, at the same time, I could see why they couldn't simply kick him out. They couldn't afford to look weak. Akin had been right. Prince Jacob had placed the Great Houses in an impossible position.

Sir Griffons returned, looking grim. "Grab your cloaks," he ordered. "We have a case."

He snatched his cloak from the walls, donned it and hurried back to the door. We followed him, as quickly as we could. A carriage was already waiting, the driver looking impatient as we scrambled inside. He barely waited for us to close the door before he cracked the whip and the carriage rattled into life, heading out of the courtyard and down the street. It was midmorning and the streets were already lined with people, but they scattered for the carriage. I didn't blame them. I knew drivers had few qualms about lashing out with their whips if the crowd got in their way. And the bastards tended to be protected from most hexes. I'd found that out the hard way.

"A child has been kidnapped," Sir Griffons said, as we rattled down the road. "It may be political."

Caroline narrowed her eyes. "How do you know, sir?"

"They called us in," Sir Griffons said, easily. "There's almost certainly more to the story than I was told."

I kept my thoughts to myself as we crossed the bridge into South Shallot and drove down a road towards the riverside. The buildings here were poorer, but still expensive compared to Water Shallot. The inhabitants looked as if they were desperately trying to keep up appearances, as if they were trying to make it clear they belonged. I felt a pang of sympathy as I saw a middle-aged woman sweeping the flagstones clear of dirt. The locals lived lives of silent desperation. If they lost their jobs, they would fall all the way back into poverty. It was practically a given that they didn't own their homes.

The carriage rattled into a courtyard and came to a halt. Sir Griffons opened the door, allowing us to jump down to the cobblestones. The building looked like one of the old post stations, where the mail would be delivered and sorted before being passed on to its final destination. Now...I frowned as I read the sign on the door. WORD OF SHALLOT. I'd read the newspaper, back when I was in school. It had been too aristo for my tastes, even though the editor was solidly middle-class. I was pretty sure he was either someone's client or trying to establish himself as a power-broker. But that didn't matter now.

"This way," Sir Griffons said. The door opened as we approached. He held up his ring. "You summoned me?"

"The editor summoned you," the doorman said. "If you'll come with me..."

I looked around with interest as we made our way up a long flight of stairs. The building was larger than I'd realised and *very* oddly designed. I had the feeling they'd worked two or three buildings into one, something that was technically against the law unless someone either got special permission or splashed out one hell of a lot of money in bribes. The upper floors were crammed with printing presses, some powered by magic, some by hand. I frowned as we headed through a warded door. The editor and his family lived on top of their workshop, just like my family. It made me feel a little warmer towards them.

"Your Grace." The editor was a tired-looking man, his face pale with worry. He was so scared that he messed up the title. "Thank you for coming."

"You're quite welcome," Sir Griffons said. If he cared about being addressed by a superior title, he didn't show it. "What happened?"

A sob echoed down the hallway. The editor winced.

"My wife," he said. "She's not in a good state. The healers prescribed potion, but she refuses to take it and…"

"I understand," Sir Griffons said. "But I need to know what happened."

The editor turned and led us down the corridor. "Last night, we put Cathy to bed as normal, before we went to bed ourselves," he said, as he opened a door. "This morning, we discovered she was missing. The wards were cracked open from the outside. Someone spirited her out of the window and…and they took her. They took her!"

I peered into the bedroom. It was larger than my bedroom, but not by much. A single bed, a wooden chest of drawers, a mirror…it looked odd, as if Cathy was small for her age. Or maybe she was already on the verge of outgrowing her room. Nora had needed a new bed five years ago, I recalled. The bed wouldn't be hard to expand. A skilled carpenter would have no trouble. Or maybe they'd just swap it for another one. The locals shared what little they had. It was the only way to survive.

"She did that painting herself," the editor said, pointing to a simple picture of a house surrounded by trees. "It was where she wanted to live, when she grew older."

"You're talking about her as if she's already dead," Caroline commented. "Don't you think she's still alive?"

"There's been no ransom demand," the editor said. "And I have enemies who won't hesitate to kill my child…"

"Maybe," Sir Griffons said. "Adam, what do you make of the hole in the wards?"

I stepped forward, reaching out with my senses and feeling out the damage. The editor was right. The wards *had* been cracked from the outside, cracked so professionally that the alarms hadn't sounded even when Cathy had been removed from the house. They'd practically cut her room out of the building, as if it was no longer protected by the ward network. I felt a flicker of sour admiration. The wardcracker was a professional. I couldn't have done such a neat job myself.

"Professional." I peered outside. The window looked down on a dark alleyway. "I guess the kidnapper levitated himself up, cracked the wards and then yanked Cathy through the window. Probably transfigured her too, just to make sure she couldn't scream. Dropped down to the ground and ran, leaving the wards in a mess. By now, he could be anywhere."

Sir Griffons nodded. "When do you think it took place?"

I shook my head. There was no way to tell. Or was there? "Early morning," I hazarded. If I knew something about such communities, it was that there were eyes and ears everywhere. "Everyone would be asleep. Even the vagabonds in the alleys would be asleep. There'd be no risk of being seen."

"There are no beggars here," the editor said. "We don't let them sleep here."

"Oh," I said. I glanced at Sir Griffons. "What now?"

Sir Griffons looked at the editor. "You're absolutely positive there's been no ransom demand? No demand for *anything*?"

"No, My Lord," the editor said. He sounded as if he was on the brink of despair. "If they wanted something, they'd have told me…wouldn't they?"

"It's only been a few hours," Caroline said. "They might want to let you sweat first."

"Perhaps," Sir Griffons said. "Is Cathy your only child?"

"Yes, My Lord."

"Caroline, go visit the mother and collect a sample of her blood." Sir Griffons produced a bleeder knife from his belt. "I'll take a sample from her father. If she's their only child, there shouldn't be any false positives to confuse the search."

I blinked. "Sir...wouldn't they have hidden her behind solid wards?"

"They might," Sir Griffons agreed, curtly. "But we have to try."

The editor made no objection as Sir Griffons gently cut his skin, allowing a trickle of blood to drip onto a sheet of cloth. Caroline didn't seem to be having such an easy time, judging by the screaming echoing down the corridor. Cathy's mother seemed to believe Caroline was planning to murder her. The editor twitched, as if he wanted to run to his wife. Sir Griffons put out a hand to stop him.

"Check the room," Sir Griffons ordered. "See if we missed anything."

I nodded and started to search the room from top to bottom. It looked and felt very much like my sister's room, when they'd both been younger. The clothes were clearly second or third-hand, save for a simple summer dress that Cathy probably wore to formal occasions. *She* couldn't afford a new dress every day. There were a handful of notebooks, covered with childish scribbles. I was amused to see that she had a habit of writing notes about her schoolmates. She'd be in hot water if they ever found out. I guessed she intended to follow her father into the family trade.

Cathy returned, blood on her knife. "I had to put her in a trance," she said. "Sorry."

"No matter," Sir Griffons said. He took the knife and mingled the two sets of blood together, then smeared them on a cloth. "Cathy should be the only one who shares blood from both her mother and father."

I frowned, feeling unsure of myself as Sir Griffons chanted a spell. I'd been warned that anything involving blood—and human waste—was borderline dark. Only a handful of blood-based spells and potions were legal and almost all of them came with severe restrictions on their use. Sir Griffons had authorisation to use whatever spells he thought necessary, I thought, but...I put the thought aside. I wasn't sure if I should call him on it or not. I didn't know how he'd react.

The cloth twisted, then shaped itself into an arrow pointing to the window. "Interesting," Sir Griffons said. "There was no resistance at all."

"That's a good thing, right?" Caroline peered through the window. "They're not trying to hide her."

Sir Griffons didn't look pleased. "Anyone who could break through the wards here without setting off a dozen alarms would know to hide her behind more wards of her own," he said, coldly. "Either the kidnapper handed her over to an idiot or he's trying to spoof us."

I followed the pointing arrow. It led to Water Shallot. Somehow, I wasn't surprised. There were so many places where everyone minded their own business that no one would give a damn if someone carried a kicking and screaming preteen into one of the crumbling buildings. I peered into the distance, trying to guess where Cathy might be hidden. It didn't seem possible. It could be anywhere along a line that headed down to the docks and out to sea.

There was a rattling sound downstairs. I heard grim-sounding men barking orders, followed by heavy footsteps. Sir Griffons let out an annoyed sound. I winced, even though it wasn't directed at me. Whoever had arrived wasn't someone Sir Griffons wanted to meet. I exchanged glances with Caroline as Sir Griffons plucked the arrow out of the air and passed it to me. I had the distinct feeling he didn't want to show it to the newcomer.

"Take a bearing, when you're outside," Sir Griffons instructed. "Then go somewhere else and take another bearing, so you can triangulate her exact location. And then"—his eyes rested on us for a long moment—"go take a look. No heroics, unless there's no other choice. Remember, we want her back alive."

I felt the arrow quivering in my hand as we were shown to the rear staircase and urged down onto the streets. A handful of black carriages waited outside, their drivers eying us suspiciously as we hurried down the streets. They didn't look like City Guardsmen. There were no insignias on their sleeves, suggesting…what? Armsmen would wear their master's colours. There were no coats of arms on the carriages either. I put the thought out of my head as we crossed the bridge and headed into Water Shallot. The mysterious armsmen were Sir Griffons' problem. *We* had a missing girl to find.

Caroline nudged me as we strode past the Hiring Hall. "If you were hiding a kidnapped girl," she said, "where would you go?"

I considered it, then shrugged. There were just too many possibilities. And, for that matter, too many ways of hiding her. The kidnapper could have transfigured her into a shoe—or something equally innocuous—and left her lying around, secure in the knowledge no one would pay any attention to her. It would require a *very* careful search to find her. The spells wouldn't last forever, unless he used a spellbinder, but it probably wouldn't matter. They'd be making a ransom demand before too long. The arrow quivered in my hand as we slipped into an ally and recast the spell. Cathy looked to be hidden somewhere near the docks.

"That way," I said. I wished Sir Griffons was with us, even though he might have attracted more attention than I would have liked. "Try to pretend to be a local."

Caroline cast an illusion spell around herself. "How do I look?"

"Very poor," I said, approvingly. I cast a similar spell on myself. "Just remember, you're poor but proud."

I kept one hand on the arrow as we headed down towards the docks. The streets grew quieter, save for women washing their clothes and a handful of little kids running around screaming. Their older siblings would be at school, their fathers probably on the boats or working on the docks. I spotted a handful of teenage girls, watched closely by their mothers or aunts. They'd have little freedom, at least until they got married. I felt a stab of sympathy for the poor girls. If my mother had lived, or if my father had been more of a traditionalist, my sisters might have been kept under such tight supervision too.

The arrow quivered again as we reached an abandoned shipping office, attached to a giant warehouse. It looked deserted, but I could feel a quivering ward melded into the brick wall. I was impressed, despite myself. The ward was almost impossible to detect. I would have missed it completely if Sir Muldoon hadn't forced me to push my senses to the limit. And yet, it wasn't good enough to hide Cathy.

I held the arrow as we circled the building, doing our level best to pretend to be lovers searching for a place to make out. The arrow rotated in my hand, insisting that Cathy was inside the office block. It definitely looked deserted, yet...I told myself I couldn't rely on anything. The warehouse was *huge*. There could be a small army quartered inside. I lifted my gaze, allowing the arrow to steer me. Cathy appeared to be on the second floor. I had no idea if she really *was*.

Caroline caught my eye as I eyed the drainpipes. "You want to get inside?"

"Yeah." The doors would be locked and protected, of course, but the upper floor windows might be a different story. Or...would they? Cathy had been taken *out* of an upper floor window, after all. And whoever had done *that* was no slouch. "Contact Sir Griffons. Tell him where we are and what we're doing."

I knew I should wait for orders, or for help, but I couldn't. I couldn't stand the thought of an innocent young girl being held captive. I'd heard enough horror stories, first in Water Shallot and then from my instructors, to know she could be going though utter hell. Her kidnappers might not even care to leave her alive, after they'd got whatever they wanted. Her memories might lead to a short and unpleasant meeting with the city's hangman.

"Follow me," I ordered. "I have a plan."

CHAPTER EIGHTEEN

I put my doubts out of my mind as I walked up to the wall, inspecting the drainpipe carefully. It looked strong enough to take my weight, although I had my doubts. There might be any number of wards designed to toss unwanted climbers back to the ground, perhaps deliberately crafted to inflict serious injury—or death—when the climber crashed to the stone below. No one would care, not in Water Shallot. If you climbed someone's drainpipe, or broke into their house, you took your life in your hands. I'd known enough kids who'd been injured to be wary of the drainpipe. But it didn't matter.

I braced myself, then cast a levitation spell. I drifted upwards, using as little power as possible. There didn't *seem* to be any searching wards, not outside the building, but I knew better than to take that for granted. Someone might cast a cancellation spell at any moment, in hopes of sending me plunging to my death. It might work, too. Levitation wasn't easy, not when you were trying to levitate *yourself*. I kept calm as I reached the window and peered inside. There was nothing moving, as far as I could tell. The glass was covered in muck, rather than a ward. I wondered if that was deliberate. I drew a multitool from my belt and went to work on the window, carefully opening it from the outside. The entire frame came free, pieces of mouldy wood and dust drifting around me as I peered inside. There was a shape on the bed. I glanced down, giving Caroline a pair of hand signals, then threw myself into the room. I expected to be greeted by an angry ward, or a sorcerer, but there was nothing. The room was as dark and silent as the grave.

A chill ran down my spine as I turned to the bed. A young girl—Cathy, I assumed—lay on the mattress, utterly unmoving. I felt a surge of pure anger as I realised they'd frozen her solid. She couldn't even move her eyes. I cast the counterspell as quickly as I could, realising my mistake a second too late. Cathy screamed as her muscles spasmed in agony. The bastards hadn't frozen her so much as locked her muscles solid. The cramps would be unbearably painful. I hastily slapped a silencing spell into space as Caroline came through the window, spellcaster in hand. She had to have assumed the worst. I motioned for her to take Cathy—the young girl would probably find another woman less threatening, right now—and inched towards the door. I'd expected the screaming to bring the kidnapper and his goons running up the stairs, but there was nothing. The entire building was quiet. I reached out with my senses, noting that there were only three wards within detection range. *None* of them felt particularly dangerous. I frowned in bemusement. Surely, they had to have left *someone* in charge of their victim. Cathy wouldn't have been left to starve.

And she would have starved, if they didn't come back and remove the spell, I thought. They could have used a spell that ensured she didn't need to eat, but they hadn't. It was cruel, sadistic and pointless. *Did they decide to run the moment they heard her scream?*

I glanced back at Caroline, then slipped down the corridor. The office block appeared to have been deserted for years. It was nothing like my father's office. There were a handful of broadsheets on the table, all five years out of date. They were chatting about Caitlyn Aguirre as if they'd only just found out about her. I frowned as I found the top of the stairs and inched downwards. It was growing increasingly difficult to believe there was anyone in the building. I was starting to think we'd gotten incredibly lucky.

The warehouse was immense, but empty. The floor was covered in a thick layer of dust. It looked as if no one had visited for years. I couldn't even see any footprints in the dust. I turned and slipped into the next room, spotting a handful of pieces of paperwork on the ancient wooden desk. They looked to be political pamphlets, but I didn't have time to look at them. The entire office building appeared to be empty. I frowned as I hurried back up the stairs, no longer trying to be sneaky. We really *did* appear to have gotten very lucky.

"I've used a pair of painkilling spells," Caroline said, as I returned to Cathy's room. The girl lay on the bed, twitching in an uncomfortable sleep. "But she really needs more help than I can provide."

I heard a rattling sound downstairs and peered out the window. The black carriages were outside, a stream of black-clad men—and Sir Griffons—making their way towards the door. The wards howled in alarm as they snapped, men crashing into the building as if they expected armed resistance. I keyed my ring, muttering a hasty update. Sir Griffons said nothing, but the crashing from downstairs came to an end. I let out a breath as I heard a handful of people making their way upstairs. Sir Griffons stepped into the room, his face utterly unreadable. It dawned on me that we might have made a mistake. He'd warned us against heroics...

But we saved her life, I thought. *Didn't we?*

"Report," Sir Griffons ordered, as another man followed him into the room. "What happened?"

"I saw a chance to sneak into the building and took it," I said, carefully. "And it paid off."

"So I see," Sir Griffons said. He sounded as if he wanted to say something more, but not in front of the stranger. "Well done."

I beamed. "Thank you, sir."

The stranger took a step forward, his eyes lingering on Cathy. He was a tall man, with short white hair and a lined face that suggested he was easily as old as my father. I was *sure* he was an aristo. He wore a simple black outfit, but he wore it with a grace and style that practically *screamed* of an aristocratic upbringing. And he looked at me as if I was something unpleasant he'd scraped off his shoe. There was no greater proof of aristocracy than *that*.

"My people will search the office," he said. "And return Cathy to her parents."

"Of course, Lord Dirac," Sir Griffons said. "You will keep us informed."

Lord Dirac nodded, curtly. "And we will also require statements from yourself and your apprentices," he said. "My staff will take them before you go."

I kept my thoughts to myself as Sir Griffons handed Cathy over to a pair of healers—they seemed to have accompanied Lord Dirac—and took us downstairs. The office was teeming with black-clad armsmen, chatting to each other in low voices as they searched the entire building from top to bottom. They seemed to be doing a professional job of it, although it didn't look as if they were worried about putting the building back together afterwards. I would have been more concerned about that if the building hadn't been deserted before the kidnappers moved in. I wondered, grimly, if we'd made a mistake. If we'd kept an eye on the building, instead of crashing through the window, we might have caught the kidnappers in the act. Instead... they'd hear the building had been raided and retreat back into the shadows.

Cathy might have gotten a look at the bastards, I thought. She was a child, but who knew? Children could have pretty good memories. *She might be able to tell us enough to track the kidnappers down.*

"Tell them everything," Sir Griffons said, as a stenographer appeared to take our statements. "We'll discuss the issue later."

I frowned. "Sir? Who *is* Lord Dirac?"

"Magus Court's enforcer," Sir Griffons said. "One of them, at least. This case clearly has political implications."

I mulled the issue over and over in my mind as I gave the stenographer a brief statement. He didn't seem inclined to ask questions, unlike my instructors when they'd drilled me in making clear, concise and—above all—informative statements. I wasn't sure that was a good thing. Witness statements could be unreliable, even if the witnesses thought they were telling the truth. It took a careful interrogation—sometimes—to sort the wheat from the chaff.

Lord Dirac appeared as soon as we were finished. "We found a boatload of socialist literature," he said, thrusting some of the pamphlets at Sir Griffons. "They might well have been behind the kidnapping."

"Maybe," Sir Griffons said. "Or maybe someone is trying to frame them."

"Maybe," Lord Dirac echoed. "But the *Word of Shallot* has taken a strong stance against the socialists. Cathy could have been kidnapped in a bid to convince the editor to change his tune."

"But they didn't send any demands," I said. "You'd think they'd insist the editor didn't call for help, at the very least."

Lord Dirac gave me a sharp look. "Socialists are not very clever," he said, curtly. "They don't trust the City Guard. They probably assumed the *Word of Shallot* didn't trust the City Guard either."

I kept my thoughts to myself. If there was *anyone* in Shallot who trusted the City Guard…I'd never met him. I didn't even believe he existed. The editor had been lucky or smart enough to get us, instead of the guardsmen. I wondered if he'd been the one who sent the message. The City Guardsmen had never struck me as being smart enough to admit they needed help.

"Keep us informed," Sir Griffons said. "Adam, Caroline…with me."

I took one last look around the abandoned building, then turned and followed Sir Griffons up the streets towards South Shallot. He said nothing as we walked, leaving us to stew in our own thoughts. We'd saved Cathy… hadn't we? But we'd ignored his order to avoid heroics. And yet…I shook my head. The thought of leaving her alone and suffering was unbearable. I had no time for newspaper editors—they filled their papers with lies—but Cathy didn't deserve to be kidnapped and tortured. I hoped Lord Dirac's people would get her safely home. Her parents missed her.

And if Sir Griffons wants to chew me out for saving her life, I thought coldly, *I can take it.*

Sir Griffons said nothing until we were back home. "Make some coffee," he ordered, as he snapped the wards into place. "I'll be back in a moment."

He hurried upstairs, leaving us alone. I shrugged and put the kettle on, then made a big pot of coffee. Caroline poured milk into three mugs, then handed out a tray of biscuits. Sir Griffons returned, looking grim. I felt my heart skip a beat as he took his coffee and swallowed half of it in a single gulp. He didn't look remotely pleased.

"You took a horrible risk," he said, putting the mug on the table. "Are you aware of it?"

I swallowed. "Yes, sir."

"You could have gotten her killed," Sir Griffons added. "You could have gotten *yourself* killed. And that would have been disastrous."

"Yes, sir," I said.

Sir Griffons stared at me. "Is there a *reason* I shouldn't give you both punishment duties?"

I gritted my teeth as his eyes bored into mine. "Permission to speak freely, sir?"

"Granted."

"First, it was my idea." I forced myself to hold his eyes, somehow. "You shouldn't be punishing Caroline for going along with it."

"I can punish her for not talking you *out* of it," Sir Griffons said, coldly.

"Second, it worked." I tried not to look away. "We rescued the victim. We found their base, which is being searched for clues. We may have laid the groundwork for tracking them down…"

"You may." Sir Griffons conceded the point with a nod. "You might also have given them a chance to go further underground. They presumably already know their plan's gone spectacularly wrong."

His eyes held mine for a long second, then switched to Caroline. "You'll find that success brings you great rewards," he said. "But if you fail, you'll find that *everyone* will blame you. You could have gotten both her and yourselves killed. Do you understand me?"

"Yes, sir."

"Good." Sir Griffons leaned back in his chair. "What do you make of the whole affair?"

"It was too easy," I said. "We shouldn't have found her that easily."

Sir Griffons cocked his head. "Explain."

I took a moment to put my argument together. "The enemy was competent enough to take her out of her bedroom, without setting off any alarms. At the same time, they didn't bother to hide her behind heavy wards. It should have been impossible to use a blood-spell to track her down. They could have made us work much harder to find her, if we found her at all. It makes no sense."

"The average criminal is no mastermind," Sir Griffons pointed out.

"Anyone who could steal her from her own bedroom *should* be good enough to hide her, afterwards," I countered. "The kidnapper was clearly an experienced wardcrafter."

"Unless the kidnappers hired a wardcrafter to do the kidnapping and then paid him off," Sir Griffons said. "They might not have realised we'd do a blood-spell."

"They should have considered the possibility," I insisted. "It makes no sense."

"No," Caroline agreed. "Sir...was it a test?"

Sir Griffons looked irked. "We are not in the habit of kidnapping little girls to test our squires," he said. "This was no test."

I winced at his tone. "So...it just makes no sense. If they were idiots, they couldn't have carried out the kidnapping in the first place. But if they're not idiots, they shouldn't have been caught so easily."

"They weren't caught," Sir Griffons reminded us. "The kidnappers themselves remain unknown."

I made a face. "Perhaps they were trying to distract us—or Lord Dirac. What happened while we were busy looking for a kidnapped girl?"

"Nothing, as far as I know," Sir Griffons said. "There's been no report of anything that might require attention from us or Lord Dirac. There's no suggestion that *anything* happened—and if it did, we'd have heard of it."

"Unless they managed to cover it up," Caroline suggested.

"It makes no sense," Sir Griffons said.

"Or perhaps it's a frame-up," I said. "Perhaps the *real* motive was to point the finger at the socialists."

"That's a possibility," Sir Griffons agreed. He unfurled one of the pamphlets from his pocket and spread it out on the table. "But it's not proof of anything."

He studied the paper for a long moment. "Lord Dirac has taken responsibility for hunting down the kidnappers," he mused. "Officially, we're off the case. The *Word of Shallot* must have more clout than we'd thought."

"Or whoever funds it has clout," I said. "Sir...who *is* Lord Dirac?"

"I told you," Sir Griffons said. "He's Magus Court's enforcer. He's responsible for upholding the laws, such as they are. Politically...his job is to give Magus Court some extra teeth. If it actually works..."

Caroline frowned. "Because of the alliance between Aguirre and Rubén?"

"Yes." Sir Griffons looked down at his scarred hands. "Right now, Aguirre and Rubén have the clout to run things to suit themselves. The remainder of the Great Houses aren't going to tolerate that any longer than strictly necessary. I imagine they intend to use Lord Dirac and his men as a wedge to limit the power of the individual Great Houses. It'll weaken them all, in a sense, but Aguirre and Rubén will get the worst of it. After all...if you're at the top, the only way you can go is down."

"I see, I think," I said. It sounded like the aristos were knifing each other in the back. I wondered, absently, if Aguirre and Rubén understood the danger. "How do they intend to get around Caitlyn Aguirre? She's unique."

"For the moment," Sir Griffons said. "Statistically speaking, she cannot be unique."

"You think," Caroline said. "So far, there's been no other Zeros."

"No." Sir Griffons shrugged. "Right now, that isn't our problem. We're going to approach the whole investigation from a different angle."

He held up the paper. "There's going to be a socialist rally at one of the working men's clubs, down in Water Shallot," he said. "You two are going to attend."

I frowned. I wasn't sure I liked the idea of spying on the working men. "Yes, sir."

"I've got to report to my superiors," Sir Griffons said. "You two can write your own reports too. Hopefully, by then, we'll have a copy of Cathy's statement. We might learn something useful from it."

I wasn't so sure. The kidnappers had been *really* odd. Maybe it was just me, but…they'd been a strange mixture of terrifyingly competent and unbelievable *incompetent*. It just didn't make sense. Perhaps someone *was* trying to frame the socialists. I couldn't see any real long-term interest in threatening Cathy's father. The population would be outraged, when the truth came out. I knew people in Water Shallot who'd have no qualms about drowning a kidnapper in the canals and leaving the body to drift out to sea.

"We'll see," Caroline said. "I thought I wouldn't be writing any more reports after I left school."

Sir Griffons laughed, humourlessly. "Paperwork is the bane of our lives," he said. "But your reports will be studied long after you're gone."

"Sure," Caroline muttered. "And people will be writing reports on our reports, under the title of *how not to do it*."

"You can get away with anything, if you win," Sir Griffons said. "Victory has a thousand fathers. Defeat…is all in your hands."

CHAPTER NINETEEN

My father had made it clear, when I was a child, that I was *not* to go out after dark, not in Water Shallot. The streets were decidedly unsafe for a young boy, even one who'd been born and raised in Water Shallot. I'd resented it at the time, but—as I'd grown older—I'd come to understand that the old man had been right. The bars were crammed with dockyard workers and fishermen drinking their sorrows away, the streets were infested with drunkards looking for fights and whores looking for clients…it was no place for a child. Even now, I felt oddly unsure of myself as I led Caroline down the dark street. The street corners were lined with toughs, their weapons clearly visible. A challenge to a fight could come at any moment.

I walked past a pair of stalls selling suspicious-looking sausages, my stomach churning as I breathed in the aroma of fat and rotten meat. The sausages were incredibly spicy, at least partly to blot out the taste of foul meat. They were being sold at cut-rate prices, but hardly anyone seemed interested in buying. I didn't blame the locals. No one could afford to get sick in Water Shallot. Their masters would simply fire them and hire someone else. There was never any shortage of unskilled labour. My father had certainly had no trouble hiring people to work for him when he'd expanded his store.

Caroline took my hand as we turned the corner, passing a line of prostitutes. The women hooted and waved, baring their breasts or sticking out their legs as we passed. I saw a pair of sailors bartering with a girl, haggling over her price. I doubted she'd be very expensive. The high-class brothels were on the other side of town. The other prostitutes cheered as the woman led her customers into a dark alley. I felt sick, wondering if they'd wind up being mugged…or infected with something unpleasant. Father had been so sharp on the subject of seedy whores that I'd wondered if he'd had a bad experience with them, once upon a time. It wasn't something I wanted to think about.

The Working Men's Club was a converted warehouse, midway between the bridges and the docks. It was surprisingly well-lit, magic lanterns drifting in the air as if it was owned and operated by an aristo. Music echoed through the air as we approached, a drinking song properly brought up youngsters weren't supposed to know. I had to smile. There were five official verses and countless unofficial versions, ranging from one about the evils of drink to a celebration of the virtues of drunkenness. I knew more of the verses than I cared to admit, certainly not to my father. He'd have thrown a fit.

There were no guards on the doors, I noted, as we passed through a simple privacy ward and stepped inside. The clubbers didn't seem to care that we'd entered their territory. I looked around with interest, noting that the gaming tables and sporting facilities had been removed for the night. Instead, the crowd was drinking beer and eying the podium. The singer was still belting out the verses, including several I didn't know. I frowned as we pushed towards the bar. The clubbers weren't normally ones for concerts. They preferred to spend their time drinking, gambling and playing games.

My lips quirked. The clubs were intended to keep grown men—and a handful of women, the ones who'd earned their places amongst the men—off the streets. I wondered just how well they succeeded. The older men had wives and families, the younger men wanted a wilder life featuring boozing, prostitutes and potions that were technically illegal. I was mildly surprised the clubs were as popular as they were. Perhaps the older ones wanted time away from the wife and kids. My father might have been the same, if he hadn't lost my mother in childbirth. I'd heard enough older men grumbling about the ball and chain to know some of them lacked perspective.

The bartender gave us both a sour look. "What'll it be?"

"Two beers," I said. Ordering anything else—here—would arouse suspicion. I shuddered to think of what would happen to someone who ordered wine or water. He'd either be the bravest man in Shallot or the stupidest. I supposed it would depend on how well he could handle himself in a fight. "And some peanuts, if you please."

The bartender poured the beers, then shoved a small bowl of peanuts at us. I paid—the booze was cheap, probably to ensure the working men stayed safely drunk—and led the way to the corner. The crowd was growing larger, men—and a handful of women—chatting to each other as they waited. It was standing room only. I muttered a spell to remove the alcohol, then took a sip of the beer. It really should have been poured back in the horse. I couldn't believe there'd been a time when I'd drank beer like water. I'd been young and foolish and trying to impress my peers. Father had put a stop to *that* when he'd caught me. I supposed I should be grateful.

It felt like hours before the singer finally stopped murdering a ballad and stepped off the stage. The musicians took a bow—the audience showed its appreciation by pelting them with peanuts—then hurried into the next room. I felt a twinge of sympathy, mingled with the grim awareness that the working men were tough nuts to crack. They knew what they liked and woe betide someone who tried to give them something—anything—else. Caroline shifted next to me as the crowd pressed against us. There were just too many warm bodies in the room. I'd thought I was used to crowds, but now I was tempted to turn and try to force my way out of the hall.

"And now," a voice boomed, "the moment you've all been waiting for."

I frowned as music started, seeming to come from everywhere and nowhere. The crowd started to sing, practically in unison. I pretended to sing, moving my lips soundlessly as I listened to the lyrics. Whoever had written the song—and the music—had done a brilliant job. He'd reminded us of the hard life of a commoner, while holding out hope that things would change when the working men found their power. It came back, time and time again, to the simple theme. The working men would find their power... and everything would change.

Caroline shifted against me, uncomfortably. I kept pretending to sing, silently grateful there were so many people in the hall that no one would notice I wasn't actually making noise. I was a commoner and yet...the song called to me and repelled me in equal measure. I wasn't sure why. Perhaps it was the simple fact that the singers were steadily losing their individuality, subsuming themselves in a greater whole. I'd read a *lot* about mob psychology, back at Haddon Hall. A *person* might be smart enough to avoid doing something disastrous; a mob might be too consumed in its cause to care what it was doing. And afterwards...the people involved might not understand what they'd done.

The singing went on and on. I'd had no idea there were so many socialist songs. We sang about brave men and women who worked together to build farms and factories, we sang about robber barons getting their just desserts from their former victims, we sang about the importance of unity and the curses we'd pile on anyone who dared betray us...I shuddered as the song grew unpleasantly vindictive, knowing we'd be in deep shit if we were caught. We'd have to fight our way out...

I breathed a sigh of relief as the singing finally came to an end. The crowd was shouting and cheering, all fired up for whatever was going to come next. I looked around, unsure what to expect. A rally, the papers had said. What did it *mean*? I had no idea. Caroline looked as ignorant as I felt. I saw her exchanging glances with an older woman pressed up against her. The woman seemed to be trying to say something, but the noise was so loud I couldn't pick out a single word. I couldn't even read her lips.

A hooded figure stepped onto the stage. My eyes narrowed. The hood and cloak were completely shapeless, but somehow I was convinced the hooded figure was *female*. I couldn't put my finger on it. Perhaps it was the simple fact that she was acting as though she had something to hide. A faint obscurification charm covered her face, casting a veil of shadow over her features. I leaned forward, trying to peer through it. I had the strangest feeling I *should* be able to see her face. I just wasn't sure why.

She reached for her hood and pulled it back in one smooth motion, revealing a very familiar face. I stared in complete and total disbelief as blonde hair spilled down—and around—a severe face. *Louise!* It couldn't be Louise. But it was. Her mouth was set in a grim expression as the crowd cheered. She seemed to be above it all, yet...I shook my head, unable to wrap my head around it. Louise wasn't a socialist, was she? She wasn't a politician...

Saline said Louise had gone into politics, I reminded myself. *She didn't say what kind of politics.*

I shook my head. It was incredible. Louise was a merchant's daughter. She'd been to Jude's...by now, she'd probably *graduated* from Jude's. The ceremony would have been a few weeks ago. She had less in common with the working men than *I* did. And yet, they were cheering her to the skies. I couldn't understand it. There were men in the room who'd sooner paint their faces and wear dresses than take orders from a girl young enough to be their daughter. And yet...

"The system is rigged," Louise said. I was sure she was using a charm to amplify her voice, but I couldn't sense anything. "We know this to be true. The system is rigged against us."

I listened, feeling a twinge of awe, as Louise explained the truth. I'd known the system was rigged—Father had made that clear—but Louise told us how and *why* the system was rigged. The aristos had created a system that put all the power firmly in their hands, keeping everyone else under control even though the city was—in theory—democratic. The crowd muttered angrily as Louise continued, reminding them they were the victims of the aristos. Their lives were *controlled* by the aristos. There was no point in trying to fight.

"They seek to keep us divided," Louise said. "They want us to remain unaware of our power. They want us to remain ignorant, so we don't challenge them. They want...but we can fight back! Through knowledge, through understanding, through patience and force and unity! We can reclaim our birthright! We can reclaim the freedoms they stole from us!"

I stared, unsure how to feel. Her words called to me. I *wanted* a world where I didn't have to bend the knee to the aristos, a world where merit triumphed over breeding. And yet, I knew enough—from my instructors—to fear the consequences of mob rule. The rebels would defeat their enemies and then turn on themselves. Louise might go mad with power—or she might lose control. I wasn't sure which one would be more dangerous.

My eyes lingered on her as she continued her speech. Louise would never be classically beautiful, but...I thought she'd never looked more striking. There was something about her that called to me, something that insisted she was someone to take seriously. I wasn't sure what to make of it. She was just...

Caroline put her mouth next to my ears. "You're staring."

I felt myself blush. "I..."

A low tremor ran through the room. I felt my ears pop, an instant before the bottles behind the bar shattered with a deafening retort. Magic—hostile magic—spilled through the air, brushing through the crowd and sending dozens to the ground. I blocked the itching hex as it passed over me, looking around for whoever had cast the spell. The floating lanterns glowed brightly for a second, then winked out. Darkness fell, like a hammer blow. I heard the door blow in, debris flying in all directions. People screamed as shadowy figures hurled spells into the room.

I started for the stage as the crowd roared like a wounded animal, then hurled itself on the attackers. Magic flared, powerful spells lashing out at the socialists. The screaming grew louder—I sensed one of the magicians die, probably trampled to death—as things grew worse. An attacker stepped up in front of Caroline, half-hidden in the gloom. She cancelled his protective wards, then kicked him in the groin. He was out of it before he hit the ground. I couldn't help feeling it was probably a relief.

"Get out of here!" I shouted at Caroline. "Move!"

I kept moving. The stage was right in front of me. Light flared, revealing two attackers racing towards Louise. She was casting spells of her own, but they seemed completely ineffective. The attackers, whoever they were, knew what they were doing. I summoned a chair from the side of the stage and brought it down on the nearest attacker's head. He crumbled like paper, his comrade turning towards me with murder in his eyes. I blasted his wards with a hex Sir Muldoon had shown me, then followed up with a haymaker that would have stunned an elephant. He went flying. I glanced back, but the darkness was descending once again. There was no sign of Caroline. I hoped she'd had the sense to get out while she could. A whole bunch of people were about to get hurt.

"This way!" I caught Louise's hand and half-dragged her towards the rear entrance. The warehouse wasn't that complex, thankfully. I'd seen enough to guess where the exits actually were. "Hurry!"

Louise let out a yelp as we sprinted down the corridor and onto the darkened streets. A riot had sprung up, seemingly from nowhere. I swallowed hard, unsure what to do. If I'd been on my own, I could have watched for Caroline or sneaked into the shadows and headed back home. But I had Louise with me. Caroline could get out on her own, but Louise? I briefly considered taking her back home, yet...I shook my head. Sir Griffons wouldn't be pleased to see her. And besides, I had no idea who'd attacked the rally. Aristos? I could easily imagine Francis leading a gang of young bucks to attack the socialists. Francis was dead, but there was no shortage of idiots in the aristocracy. I wondered if I'd bashed a chair over his brother's head. Did Francis *have* a brother?

The riot grew louder. "This way," I said, hoping to the ancients I was right. "We have to hole up somewhere."

Louise seemed to be in shock. She didn't try to fight as I pulled her down the street, past two blocks of tenement housing before reaching a cheap and nasty inn. I knew the rules of the place as well as I knew my name, although I'd never been inside. The innkeeper wouldn't ask questions, as long as you crossed his palm with silver. I plucked a pair of coins out of my pouch, paid the woman at the desk and helped Louise up the stairs to our room. We'd be safe in the inn, I hoped. It was unlikely the rioters would burn it down. Hopefully, the riot would break up before the City Guard arrived.

"They...they attacked us!" Louise sounded stunned as she sat on the bed, even though she *knew* aristos could be treacherous. Francis had nearly killed her, too. "They could have killed everyone."

"I don't know," I said. In truth, I had no idea how many people had been injured or killed. There was no easy way to tell, short of going back to the hall and counting the bodies. "It might not be as many as you suppose."

Louise looked up at me, her eyes clearing. "Adam?"

"Yeah." I wondered what I should tell her, if anything. What would she say if she knew I was a Kingsman? "I thought it would be interesting to attend your rally."

"They wouldn't be trying to kill us if they didn't think we were a threat," Louise said. She sounded oddly happy, even though there could be hundreds of people wounded or killed back in the club. "You probably saved my life."

I grinned, pleased. Louise didn't deserve to die. She certainly didn't deserve to die at the hands of a pack of cowards too fearful to show their faces.

"Yeah." I smiled. I'd saved her life. "I guess I did."

Louise stood. "You saved my life and..."

She leaned forward and pressed her lips against mine. I felt my body move, my hands slipping down her back. Her breasts pressed against my chest. I wanted her, with an intensity that surprised me. We'd just escaped certain death. I knew I should be calling Caroline, or Sir Griffons, but...it was suddenly very hard to focus. We were trapped, at least for the moment. And she was so very beautiful. It was suddenly very hard to undress without tearing something.

It wasn't my first time. But it was definitely my best.

CHAPTER TWENTY

When I awoke, I wasn't sure where I was.

I sat up, looking around the room. It was bright outside, the sunlight streaming through a window and mockingly reminding me I'd overslept. The bedroom...wasn't *my* bedroom, not the one I shared with Caroline. Someone shifted next to me and I jumped, half-convinced I'd wound up in bed with Caroline before I recognised Louise. She was naked, her pale skin covered in sweat and red marks. The memories came flooding back as she opened her eyes. We'd been in a riot, we'd escaped, we'd found a place to hide and...

And we slept together. I felt a surge of sudden warmth towards her, mingled with an awareness that I might *really* have fucked up. And not in a good way. *Sir Griffons is not going to be pleased.*

"Adam?" Louise smiled at me, dreamily. "What time is it?"

I reached for my pocket watch and glanced at it. "Eight o'clock, more or less," I said. "I..."

Louise looked down at herself, her cheeks reddening. I watched with a strange fascination as her blush ran down until it reached the top of her breasts. She really was beautiful. I wanted to stare all day, even though I knew I was in deep shit. Sir Griffons was *really* not going to be pleased. *Caroline* was going to be even *less* pleased. I swung my legs over the side of the bed and stood, pacing to the window and peering through the curtains.

The streets below were quiet, too quiet. I didn't like the look of it. They should have been packed with workers heading to the docks and schoolchildren trudging unwillingly to school.

My ring was cool against my bare skin. I wondered what *that* meant. Caroline hadn't tried to call me...I hoped she was alive. She wouldn't have had any trouble breaking contact and getting back to the bridges, would she? Caroline was a powerful and skilled sorceress. She could easily have concealed herself if she couldn't get out of the riot before she was torn apart.

"Fuck," Louise said. I couldn't recall her swearing before, not at Jude's. I supposed that was understandable. The upperclassmen knew spells to wash our mouths out with soap, if we swore too often. I rather suspected Louise had picked up bad habits from the longshoremen. They wouldn't have responded well to a middle-class girl acting like an upper-class toff. "I...fuck."

I had to smile, despite my own concern. If we were caught together...I knew what my father would say. I knew what *her* parents would say. They'd expect us to get married immediately, just in case our little tryst had resulted in a pregnancy. There was no one so strict about unmarried sex as people who lived just north of the docks, where unmarried mothers and fatherless children were common. Her parents would kill me if they thought I'd knocked up their daughter and ran away.

Louise gave me a sharp look. "You're lucky it's the right time of the month."

"Thanks." I tried not to look too relieved. There were potions I could have taken, if I'd thought about it. "I won't tell anyone if you don't."

"Hah." Louise stood, without trying to hide herself. "I guess I should thank you."

I tried not to stare as she walked into the tiny washroom and closed the door. My ring pulsed against my skin, once. I pressed my fingers against the metal, tapping out a handful of codes. I was alive and well, but unable to talk. I hoped Sir Griffons would understand. It would be awkward if he wanted to talk in person. I had no idea how Louise would react if I told her why I'd attended the rally. Or, for that matter, who I worked for. She might take it in her stride or she might hit the roof. I sighed, inwardly. I really did seem to have a talent for messing things up.

It felt like hours before Louise stepped back into the bedroom. I headed into the washroom, granting her what privacy I could as I splashed water on my face and hands. There was no shower, just a basin and cold tap water. My skin crawled unpleasantly, even as I muttered a spell to warm the water. There were people living in the district who didn't have hot and cold running water, let alone showers. They couldn't even use the public baths! I scowled, realising just how used I'd grown to luxury. The days when I'd had to wash in a giant metal tub had been a long time ago.

I walked into the bedroom, half-expecting to discover that she'd left without saying goodbye. Instead, she was seated by the window, staring out onto the streets. I dressed rapidly, muttering a spell to remove a bloodstain from my shirt. It wasn't *my* blood. I was tempted to keep a sample, in hopes of finding whoever had bled on me, but there was no way to know if it was one of the attackers. It might have been one of their victims. I shuddered as I finished dressing, utterly unsure of myself. Violence was far from unknown on the streets of Water Shallot—there were bar fights almost every night—but political violence was rare. I couldn't help thinking it boded ill for the future.

Louise barely moved, her face pale and drawn. I felt a rush of protectiveness that surprised me, even though I *knew* I should be reporting back to my master or interrogating her. Louise might know who'd attacked her, who'd injured and killed dozens—perhaps hundreds—of her supporters. And...I found it hard to believe, despite everything, that *Louise* was the leader of the socialists. She was too young—and female. She was hardly the type of person the working men would take seriously. The women they respected were the ones who worked alongside the men, sharing their burdens and never showing a hint of weakness. Caroline would have done a wonderful job of earning their respect.

"The streets are quiet," Louise said. "It's as if last night didn't happen."

"Yeah." I'd already noticed that for myself. I perched on a wobbly wooden chair, trying to make myself look as harmless as possible. "Louise, what are you doing?"

She glanced at me, sharply, then looked away. "Fighting for justice," she said, quietly. "And struggling to bring down the rigged system."

I winced. There was a wealth of pain in her voice. I understood, better than I cared to admit. Louise and I were very alike. Our families had pulled themselves out of the gutter by their own efforts. We didn't want to pledge ourselves to the aristos, but if we didn't…there were limits to how high we could rise. Louise had the same problem as me, yet…no one had offered to induct *her* into the Kingsmen. She couldn't hope for much if she went back to her father's store. Her education would be wasted.

"It was all Francis's fault," Louise murmured. "He…"

She ran her hand through her blonde hair. "You remember the Challenge?"

"Of course." I gritted my teeth. "I was there."

"Francis betrayed us all," Louise said. She laughed, harshly. "Even his own cousin. Poor Akin was completely blindsided. Stupid aristo. I knew Francis was no good right from the start! There he was, being a complete and utter fool and Akin *trusted* him. I should have told Akin to kick Francis or me off the team. I really wouldn't have minded if he'd booted *me* out."

She laughed, again. "You know Francis was making out with Lindsey?"

I blinked. Lindsey wasn't an uncommon name amongst the aristocracy, but I only knew one Lindsey in my year. "The one who was betrothed to Lord Swinging Dick?"

"The very same." Louise grinned, but I saw tears in her eyes. "The finest blade His Majesty commands. Fought a hundred duels and never even *looked* like losing. Francis could have gotten himself killed…for what? A few moments of pleasure?"

"A shame he didn't," I said, a little more harshly than I'd meant. "What happened?"

Louise looked away. "Francis enspelled me," she said. "He slapped me with a compulsion spell…a *powerful* compulsion spell. He made me help him and I did, screaming on the inside all the time. And afterwards...no one seemed to care. Francis was dead and everyone was trying their hardest to cover up the whole affair. There was no justice."

"Francis is dead," I said, carefully. "The Ancients will handle him."

"If you believe in them," Louise said. She shook her head. "The system is rigged. You know it as well as I do. The whole patron-client system is designed to harvest the very best of the commoners, tying them to the aristocracy while leaving the rest in the dirt. Rose—you remember Rose—will not be using her talents to benefit herself. She'll be using them for her aristo masters. And you know what's worst of all?"

I had no answer. If Francis had used a compulsion spell on Louise that she couldn't shake off...I remembered my training and shuddered. It would have to have been powerful, very powerful. My imagination suggested all sorts of things he could have done, none of which would be remotely out of character. If Francis had been stupid enough to risk picking a fight with Lord Richard, who knew what *else* he'd do? Ancients! Francis's family would have had to pay through the nose to keep Lord Richard from challenging and killing the little bastard. Or maybe they would just have stepped back and let him die. I'd have been sorely tempted to do just that if *I'd* been running the family.

"We don't even know it," Louise said. "Every longshoreman gets a vote, right? They go to the tribal halls every six months to cast a vote, right? But all those votes are diluted. Every longshoreman in the city could vote for something and it would barely even register! And, in the meantime, the Great Houses control the vast majority of *effective* votes. They've tricked us into believing our votes matter, when in truth our votes are effectively meaningless. *That's* the worst of it! We're trapped in a dictatorial system, and we don't even *know* it."

"But people can join other tribes," I said, carefully. "A longshoreman could become a forger..."

Louise snorted. "Without becoming a client?"

She let out a funny little laugh. "You remember Allianz?"

"Vaguely." I remembered an ugly little aristo brat, a year above us. "What about him?"

"He asked me to marry him," Louise said. "He told me it would make me *important*. And yes, I'd have had a vote in the family council. But it would be just *one* vote. The really powerful family members would have *hundreds*."

I tried not to laugh. Allianz had tried to ask *Louise* to marry him? He must have been desperate. I felt a twinge of guilt as I remembered the stories, the whispered suggestions that Allianz was a toad who'd been turned into a man or the victim of a botched transfiguration that—somehow—had never been fixed. He'd been a puny little boy with poor hygiene and worse marks...I would have felt worse, if I hadn't known he'd taken his anger out on the poor lowerclassmen as soon as he gained the power to punish them. And he'd asked Louise to marry him? I didn't see *that* ending well. They'd both dodged a curse there.

"The system is corrupt and broken," Louise said. "And that's why I want to tear it down and rebuild it."

"And you can't do that by working within the system," I mused. I had no idea what I should do. Political organising was hardly a crime. And yet...if she tore the system down, whatever replaced it might be worse. "Who do you think attacked you?"

"The aristos." Louise's eyes shone. "They must see us as a threat. They'd never have bothered to attack us otherwise."

I had the nasty feeling she was right. The aristos—Alana, in particular—prided themselves on ignoring people they considered worthless. They would hardly send out attack squads if they didn't see any real threat. I considered it thoughtfully, unsure—again—what to do. The attackers were committing crimes, but without proof there was no way they could be brought to justice. And Louise was right. The system was rigged. I doubted the bastards would see the inside of a jail cell, let alone Skullbreaker Island. Their parents would call in a lot of favours and they'd be released on a technicality.

"I'm glad you came," Louise said. She stood, brushing down her dress. "Why *did* you come?"

"I was curious," I said. I didn't want to tell her the truth. Not yet, perhaps not ever. "Louise, I..."

"Don't take it too seriously," Louise said. She paced over to me. "I just wanted to feel *alive*."

She brushed her lips against mine, then turned. "I have to get back home," she said. "And so do you."

"Wait," I said. I donned my cloak, checking my spellcaster and other tools were still in place. "Do you want me to walk you home?"

Louise hesitated. I was pretty sure I knew what she was thinking. She was a grown woman. Tongues would start to wag if their owners saw her walking with a young man, particularly one they knew. The rumourmongers would have us married off by the end of the day...I snorted. There were some people I would happily hit with blinding curses—or worse—just for spreading nonsense and making people's lives worse. But, at the same time, the streets were far from safe. Ancients alone knew who might be on the prowl.

"I suppose," she said, finally. "But keep your hands to yourself."

I bit down the urge to remind her that *she'd* started it as we walked down the stairs. The receptionist shot us a knowing look as we reached the bottom, making it clear she knew what we'd been doing. I told myself, firmly, that cursing her would end badly, even if she deserved it. She wouldn't talk. The inn's customers would evaporate like snow in the desert if they thought she'd talk. I tossed her a coin to make sure of it, then led Louise outside. The streets were deathly quiet.

A shiver ran down my spine as we made our way towards the Working Men's hall. It was mid-morning, when everyone should be at work or at school, but the streets still felt unnaturally still. The children who should have been playing in the gutter were nowhere in evidence. We turned the corner and stopped, dead, as we saw what remained of the club. The warehouse looked on the verge of crumpling into rubble. A small army of City Guardsmen were standing on guard, backed up by black-clad armsmen from Magus Court. They didn't look friendly.

Louise caught my arm as we hastily altered course. "What happened to the bodies?"

I shrugged. I had no idea. Normally, no one gave a damn about bodies in Water Shallot. They'd be sold to the medical students for dissection, if they weren't harvested for the illicit potions trade or simply dumped into the canals. Relatives might claim a body, but what could they do with it afterwards? Now...I scowled as it dawned on me the City Guard might be searching for bodies, with the intention of covering up the dead. If a number of attackers had been killed, their bodies might be identified. And who knew what would happen then?

"I think it doesn't matter right now," I said. I wondered, suddenly, if I should take Louise to Sir Griffon. If she'd been identified, she was probably on a wanted list. I tried to tell myself that no one would believe *Louise* was the socialist leader, but that was probably wishful thinking. A number of important aristos were no older than either of us. They'd probably assume the socialists were no different. "We have to stay out of their sight."

I cast a careful charm around us as we headed up towards the shops. The streets gradually filled with people, although I could feel an uneasy tension in the air. The gentrified parts of Water Shallot had good reason to fear their neighbours, who resented being driven out by the newcomers. I wondered, suddenly, what my father thought of the riot. I was tempted to go find him, to learn the word on the streets...I shook my head. Sir Griffons had forbidden it. I was probably in quite enough trouble already.

"I'll go alone from here," Louise said. She squeezed my hand. "If you want to find me again, come visit the shop."

"I will," I promised, although I wasn't sure if I could *keep* that promise. If Louise had told me what she was doing, before I'd joined the Kingsmen, I would have joined her without hesitation. Now...I wasn't so sure. Was I a sell-out? Or was I mature enough to realise that violent uprisings and rebellions tended to lead to more violence? "Good luck."

Louise nodded, then hurried down the street. I watched her go, telling myself she'd be fine. Probably. If her enemies didn't know who she was...

I turned and walked towards the bridges, keeping my eyes open for a cab. I had to get back home and…and what? What was I going to tell Sir Griffons? Or Caroline? I honestly didn't know…

…But if I didn't come up with something quick, I was going to be in *real* trouble.

CHAPTER
TWENTY-ONE

"I suggest you start from the beginning," Sir Griffons said, once I'd returned home and had a proper shower. "And continue until you reach the end."

"Yes, sir," I said. Sir Griffons didn't sound angry, but that was meaningless. "We attended the rally and…"

I described everything that had happened in as much detail as possible, at least until I reached the moment I yanked Louise out of the club. "I thought it would be better to hole up somewhere, at least until I knew what was going on," I said. "And that was what I did."

Sir Griffons cocked his eyebrows. I hadn't lied to him, but I'd left a chunk of the story out. I knew a lie of omission wasn't *that* much better than a real lie. Behind him, Caroline shot me a sharp look. She *knew* there was something I wasn't saying. I braced myself, wondering if she'd ask me in front of our master or confront me privately. She wasn't the sort of person to leave a mystery alone. I would have been surprised if she hadn't already guessed part of the truth.

"I see." Sir Griffons stroked his chin. "How well do you know this…*Louise*?"

I hesitated. "I knew her at school, sir."

Caroline let out a snicker, which she hastily converted to a cough when Sir Griffons *looked* at her. "You seem to know a *lot* of people."

"That's not too surprising," Sir Griffons said. "Everyone who is anyone, in Shallot, goes to Jude's."

I blinked. I'd had the impression Sir Griffons wasn't from Shallot himself, but...I could easily have been wrong. Princelings and squires weren't allowed to read personnel files. Sir Griffins might have grown up in Shallot, then spent most of his career elsewhere. I had no idea. But...he seemed to understand. There was nothing *suspicious* in me knowing many of the city's movers and shakers. I'd been brought up to know the names and faces of the most important people in town.

"She was not an easy person to like," I admitted. "She never had many friends. She nagged, she questioned...I think she got hexed a lot, back in her first year. She was clever, but lacked social skills. Whenever she thought she was right, she was right...all evidence to the contrary aside. She used to slow classes by demanding explanations and then complaining when the explanations didn't suit her. On the other hand..."

I remembered what Louise had told me about Francis and shivered. "She was often picked on by the aristos," I said, carefully. I didn't want to tell them the full story if it could be avoided. "They made fun of her. They...treated her like crap. I think Akin and Saline were the only ones who were nice to her and Akin let her down, somehow. I don't think they were friends after the Challenge was over. Louise was technically on the winning team"—I resisted the urge to grind my teeth in bitter recollection—"but I don't think she got to make use of it. And now she's leading the socialists."

"She *says* she's leading the socialists," Caroline said. "Is she telling the truth?"

"I never thought she was a liar," I said, crossly. "If she says she's in charge, she's in charge."

"Or thinks she is," Sir Griffons said. He was studying me, thoughtfully. "The socialists were never seen as a serious threat. They didn't seem to have appeal, beyond the very lowest levels of society. The people a little higher up didn't seem to want their solutions. Do you think that's changed?"

I frowned. "I don't know, sir," I said. "But whoever attacked the rally clearly thought they needed to be slapped down."

"Yeah." Caroline let out a breath. "I shadowed one of the attackers as he headed home, but the bastard lost me shortly after crossing the bridge into North Shallot. He was no amateur, whoever he was. I'm not sure how he managed to get away from me."

I frowned. Caroline was *good* at tracking people. She'd once followed me all around the estate, despite my best efforts. If someone had evaded her... there were hundreds of concealment and invisibility spells they could have used, but they tended to leave traces Caroline could have followed. Hell, how had her target known she was even *there*? Caroline was so stealthy I hadn't been sure she was behind me and I'd *known* she was supposed to be shadowing me. The attacker, whoever he was, had been good.

"North Shallot," I mused. "An aristo?"

"It proves nothing," Caroline said. There was an oddly sharp note to her voice. "The bastard could have hidden in North Shallot, then slipped back into South or Water Shallot the following morning."

I wasn't so sure. North Shallot was heavily policed by armsmen. Someone who had no business there would be moved along pretty damn quick, if they weren't turned into toads or fish and tossed into the nearest canal. The armsmen had few qualms about doing whatever it took to get rid of unwanted intruders. If the attacker *wasn't* from North Shallot, he either had friends amongst the locals or a striking faith in his ability to avoid the armsmen. I supposed he might be entirely justified. He'd certainly managed to evade *Caroline*.

"No," Sir Griffons agreed. "And Lord Dirac has already claimed jurisdiction. We do not have grounds to continue the investigation."

"Sir," I said. "With all due respect, can we trust them to handle the investigation?"

"Probably not," Sir Griffons said. "But the blunt truth is that we have very limited authority within the city. We have no grounds to interfere unless we're asked"—he held up a hand before I could muster a response—"and the request would have to come from legitimate authority. Magus Court has its man on the case. Lord Dirac will handle the affair."

I frowned. Lord Dirac hadn't struck me as being interested in *justice*. I rather suspected he'd be more interested in covering up the dead, particularly the ones with important names, than bringing them to book. And if he caught Louise…I shuddered. Being a socialist wasn't illegal, but I was sure that wouldn't stop him. Magus Court had a whole string of poorly-written laws that were designed to provide a veneer of legality for just about anything. Lord Dirac could arrest Louise under the Security of the City Act, convict her of something sufficiently vague and ship her off to Skullbreaker Island before anyone could muster a defence. And even if she was rescued from the island, she'd never be the same again. People who were sent to the prison were sent to die.

"So." Caroline sounded a little too bright. "What do we do?"

"Right now, nothing." Sir Griffins reached for his cloak. "I have an appointment at House Samarra. You two can practice your spells until I get back. If a messenger arrives, call me at once."

"Yes, sir," I said. It was hard to hide my relief. I'd expected more questioning. "Can we keep an eye on things?"

"Yes." Sir Griffons held my eyes for a long moment. "And Adam…?"

"Yes, sir?"

"Be careful."

I watched him go, wondering what he meant. How much did he know? How much had he guessed? He'd given me—us—some freedom, but he was ultimately responsible for knighting us. Or washing us out, if we failed. It would reflect badly on him, if we did. I was pretty sure he knew more than he'd admitted. He'd been a Kingsman longer than either of us had been alive. He had to suspect there was something I hadn't told him.

"Well," Caroline said, as she poured herself another mug of coffee. "What *really* happened back there?"

I raised my eyebrows. "What do you mean?"

Caroline snorted. "You slept with her, didn't you?"

"I…"

"Don't bother to deny it." Caroline sat down, facing me. "It's written all over your face."

"Get me a mirror," I said. As jokes went, it was pathetic. "Caroline…"

Caroline let out a breath. "I'm not angry," she said. She *sounded* angry. "I know you have every right to start a relationship with someone outside the order, just as *I* do. But you should have told Sir Griffons you're no longer…unbiased."

"I am unbiased," I protested, a little too quickly. "Caroline…"

"You slept with her," Caroline said. "Didn't you?"

I cringed. It was the most embarrassing conversation I'd ever had, up to and including my father's explanation of the facts of life. I'd wanted to crawl into a hole and die when *that* conversation had finally come to an end, too late to spare me from hours of embarrassment and mind-numbing horror. But this was worse. I felt…I felt as if I'd betrayed her, even though I hadn't. Caroline and I hadn't been together. We weren't *allowed* to be together. It just wasn't fair.

"Yeah," I admitted. "And I talked to her afterwards."

"I'm sure your pillow talk was most interesting," Caroline sneered. "Did you tell her more than she told you?"

"I let her do most of the talking." I ignored Caroline's snort. "She has good reason to hate the aristos."

"Hatred *blinds*," Caroline observed. "And just because she slept with you doesn't mean she's in the *right*."

"I know that." I stood, brushing down my trousers. "I…we…wanted to celebrate being alive! Is that so wrong?"

"No," Caroline said. "But you should bear in mind that she might have been trying to manipulate you."

I shook my head. Louise was almost painfully blunt. She'd never learnt how to cosy up to her social betters and manipulate them, trading favours for patronage. She'd reacted very badly when someone suggested she should do his homework for later favours. I found it hard to believe that Louise had seduced me for later manipulation. For one thing, she would have had to know I was worth manipulating.

I did save her life, I reminded myself. I felt like a heel for even *thinking* it. *And she probably needs a better bodyguard.*

"I don't think so," I said. "I know her."

"And that's exactly why your emotions cannot be trusted," Caroline said. "She takes off her clothes in front of you and suddenly you cannot think straight."

I glared. "And girls are any better?"

Caroline scowled. "We tend to be vulnerable to people who pretend to listen to us," she said, sourly. There was a hint of pain in her voice. "And yes, that can bite us too."

I picked up my mug and carried it into the kitchen. "I think we need to focus on what's actually going on," I said. "Did the aristos attack the socialists because they blamed the socialists for Cathy's kidnapping?"

"The morning papers certainly say as much." Caroline followed me into the kitchen and watched as I washed my mug. "Only a couple of papers even *mention* the riot in Water Shallot. The remainder are screaming about how horrible the socialists are, kidnapping and abusing a little girl. They're practically glossing over her safe return to her family."

I looked up, sharply. "Was she hurt? I mean…apart from the muscle cramps?"

"The healer's report says *no*," Caroline said. "The whole kidnapping doesn't make sense. Why bother kidnapping someone without trying to *keep* them? All they did was take her to the warehouse, lock her muscles and just leave her there. They didn't even *try* to hide her."

"I said as much," I said, a little tartly. "Do you think I was right, now?"

"I never said you were *wrong*," Caroline said, evenly. "But it makes no sense."

I frowned. Maybe it *did* make a certain kind of sense. Kidnap Cathy, then leave her in a building crammed with socialist literature. Blame the socialists for kidnapping her, before using the kidnapping as an excuse to clamp down on the socialists. Or...there hadn't been any *legal* attempt to clamp down, had there? Perhaps the kidnapping was to provide an excuse for attacking the socialists, then clamping down in the wake of a riot and a few deaths. I still didn't know how many people had been killed or wounded. I wondered if *Louise* knew.

"They might have been trying to frame the socialists," I said, outlining my theory. "And then they'd have all the excuse they needed to clamp down."

"That's way too thin," Caroline objected. "The mere presence of socialist claptrap doesn't prove anything."

"It does if people *want* it to prove something," I countered. "There are people out there"—I waved a hand southwards—"who'll assume that a man and a woman walking hand in hand, or even side by side, are in a relationship. The rumours will have them married with children by the time they reach their parents. And they won't stop because they'll want the rumours to be true."

"And Lord Dirac might want to believe the socialists are behind the kidnapping," Caroline said. "I take your point."

"Yes." I turned and opened the stasis cabinet. We'd have to buy more food. We were down to cheese and bread for lunch, unless I wanted to go to the trouble of cooking a piece of meat and preserving it. "One *could* argue that possession of a copy of *Voice of Shallot* means I own the newspaper, but it would be a pretty stupid argument."

"But it would imply an interest in reading the news," Caroline mused. "If I wasn't interested in potions, I wouldn't be reading *Potions Monthly*. A person who wasn't interested in socialism wouldn't be reading socialist journals."

"But that wouldn't make him a socialist," I said. "And even if he considered himself a socialist, he might not be a formal member."

I frowned. The socialists might not *have* a formal membership structure. Hell, it would be a dangerously unwise thing to *have*. Each subsection might be centred on a different club—there were at least thirty Working Men's Clubs in Shallot—and operate largely independently. And then...I wondered just how much power Louise had amassed in a few short months. Had she convinced everyone to go along with her? Or...I remembered just how painstakingly *through* Louise had been, at school. She might have taken over the paperwork and used it to leverage herself into a position of power.

But there'd be limits to how far she could go, I reminded myself. *A secretary commands no real respect.*

"It doesn't prove anything," I added. "But Lord Dirac *wants* it to prove something."

I sighed as we headed up to the duelling chamber. It was quite easy to be branded something that was manifestly absurd and yet maddeningly difficult to refute. The rumourmongers loved to create slanders that were too weak to demand legal action—or a challenge to a duel—but strong enough to weaken someone's future prospects. I'd seen it happen, back at school. A lie could gain strength and credence, the more people who repeated it. And no matter how many corrections the victim tried to put out, he could never rid himself of the lie. Louise and her comrades might have real problems, if they were branded child-snatchers. Even the hardened folk of Water Shallot would turn on them.

If they believed whatever they read in the papers, I thought. The writers were either aristos or commoners sucking up to the aristos. They had little sympathy with the working men and it showed. *The newspapers might kill the story by promoting it.*

I put the thought aside as we practiced our spells. Caroline was clearly in a bad mood and took it out on me, snapping off spell after spell as she chased me around the chamber. I ducked and dodged, firing back spells of my own. Caroline was good. I wondered if someone had been drilling her while I wasn't looking. She'd certainly have kicked my ass if I'd met her six months ago.

"Hold still," she growled, as she slammed a spell at me. I jumped aside, too late. The spell crashed into my shield and threw me to the ground. She darted forward, magic crackling around her fingertips. My weakened shield shattered. She landed on top of me, blue light sparkling as she pressed down on my chest. "Surrender?"

I glared, trying to think of a way out. But there was nothing. She'd sense me mustering a spell and stun me before I could cast it. She had me, bang to rights...

"Yeah." I leaned back, trying to relax. "You got me."

"Hah." Caroline pressed down on me for a second, then rolled off me and stood, brushing down her tunic. I wondered, suddenly, if someone had given her a hard time for wearing trousers. It wasn't as if she could pass for a boy. "Good bout."

I heard Sir Griffons coming up the stairs and hastily stumbled to my feet. "Good afternoon, sir."

Sir Griffons entered the room, his expression unreadable. "Am I to deduce that you spent the last hour beating each other up, instead of practicing your spells?"

"We were doing both, sir," Caroline said. She sounded like my sister, when she was trying to get out of trouble. It worked more often than it should. "We learnt a great deal while trying to beat each other up."

"You are *expected* to work as a team," Sir Griffons said. "*Particularly* when you're tested against other teams. Which will happen, believe me."

I exchanged glances with Caroline. "Yes, sir. Sorry, sir."

"Good." Sir Griffons turned, his lip curling in disgust. I had the feeling it wasn't aimed at us. "We're going to spend the afternoon pressing the flesh. I expect you both to be ready to..."

He broke off. A second later, the wards vibrated an alarm.

CHAPTER TWENTY-TWO

"What the…"

I broke off as the wards vibrated again. A disconcerting sensation swept over me, my head spinning as if I'd been deep underwater and suddenly surfaced at terrifying speed. My ears hurt, then popped so painfully I almost cried out. Caroline rubbed her ears, her face stricken. I had the horrible thought, just for a second, I'd been deafened. It was hard to hear anything. It wasn't until Sir Griffons turned and ran for the door that I realised I *hadn't* been deafened. My ears just felt weird.

We followed Sir Griffons into the morning room. The windows had been covered with wooden slats when we'd arrived and we'd never bothered to take them down. Now, Sir Griffons tore at them until the windows were exposed, peering over the city. A nasty haze hung over the city, flickering with dark magic. Smoke was billowing up from the direction of Magus Court…slightly beyond the weirdly-shaped building, if I was any judge. I glanced at Caroline, her face slack with horror. What the hell had happened?

"Grab your protective cloaks," Sir Griffons snapped. Our master ran down the stairs, moving like a teenager. "Hurry!"

I followed him, snatched my cloak from the hooks and ran outside. Dark magic hung in the air. It was dissipating, but not quickly enough. Dogs howled as we hurried through the gatehouse and up the road towards

Magus Court. I could taste the scent of human agony in the haze. Whatever had happened, it had been bad.

My heart raced as the scene of the disaster came into view. A large building had been badly damaged, its white walls blackened and scarred by dark magic. There had been a gatehouse once, I recalled; the gatehouse was now nothing more than a smouldering crater fuming with dark magic. I shuddered in horror as I remembered what the building *was*. It was a dorm for scholarship students, brought in from the countryside and made to wait until the new term began. I hoped it hadn't been full of new students. The people close to the blast might be lucky if they were *merely* killed.

Sir Griffons raised his voice as a handful of armsmen came into view. "Seal off both ends of the street," he snapped. They were so stunned they followed orders without question. "Don't let anyone in or out until we can get a decontamination team up here."

I peered into the crater and felt my gorge rise. There were a couple of bodies, warped and twisted into a teeming mass of flesh. They were still, yet...somehow, I *knew* they were still alive. The stench was appalling, horrific beyond words. I couldn't help myself. I turned to one side and threw up, emptying my stomach of everything I'd eaten. Beside me, Caroline looked as if she wanted to be sick too. Sir Griffons glanced at us, but said nothing. He seemed to take the horrifying scene in stride.

A senior armsman arrived with a small army of assistants. Sir Griffons directed him to finish sealing off the street, then call for help. I watched, unsure of what I should be doing. My stomach hurt, aching as if I'd been hit repeatedly. I couldn't help looking at the blackened building, at the confused webs of tangled magic that were all that were left of the wards. The disaster, whatever it was, could have killed dozens—if not hundreds—of people. I couldn't imagine what had happened.

"This way," Sir Griffons growled. "Try not to step in anything."

The dormitory courtyard had been surprisingly elegant, once upon a time. Now, it was a tattered mess. The cobblestones looked as if they'd been picked up one by one and then dumped in random locations. The bushes planted near the walls were now warped and twisted messes, as if they'd been blasted with waves of raw magic. It dawned on me, slowly, that that was precisely what had happened. I hoped none of the students had been caught in the blast. Their families would never know what had happened.

That could have been me, if things had been a little different, I thought. I *knew* students from the countryside, boys and girls with enough raw magic to earn scholarships. They were innocents, in every sense of the word. *What the hell happened here?*

Sir Griffons pressed his gloved hand against the door. It shattered at his touch, pieces crashing to the ground. I tasted decay in the air and looked up, warily. The brick looked as if it was starting to crumble, something I would have thought was impossible. I glanced at Caroline as Sir Griffons led the way, picking his steps with extreme care. The floor creaked uneasily, as if it was on the verge of collapsing under our feet and sending us plummeting. Water dripped down from the ceiling, pooling on the floor. The pipes above us had to have broken. I tensed as my foot slipped, the floor nearly giving way. Sir Griffons kept moving, practically hopping as he reached the bottom of the stairs and peered up. A terrified face looked back.

"I'm here to help," he called. "Can you come down?"

The girl eyed him fearfully. She looked unharmed, as far as I could tell, but she wasn't speaking. The stairs themselves looked flimsy, no better than the floor we'd just crossed. Sir Griffons made an impatient gesture and the girl was yanked forward, her tattered dress billowing as she flew through the air and landed in front of us. She was young, probably on the verge of her first year. The terror in her eyes as she clutched at Sir Griffons suggested she wasn't used to magic.

"It's going to be fine," Sir Griffons said. "How many others are upstairs?"

She hesitated, then held up seven fingers. Sir Griffons passed the girl to Caroline, then carefully levitated up the stairs. I followed, trying to ignore the stench of growing decay. The stairwell seemed to be crumbling in real time. I heard a crash in the distance and shuddered. The entire *building* seemed to be on the verge of collapse. It was all we could do to locate the other seven students and levitate them out the window into the backyard. We couldn't take them through the courtyard. The students had almost no protection.

I caught my master's eye as we started to inspect the staff bedrooms. "Where's the staff?"

"They might have been downstairs, caught in the blast." Sir Griffons sounded distracted, as if he had something else on his mind. "Or they might have been escorting others around the city."

I opened my mouth to say something, but closed it sharply as I felt a shudder running through the building. The windows shattered, one by one. I jumped back as the floorboards started to break, a wave of destruction tearing the building apart. Sir Griffins turned and ran, barking orders for me to follow him as the ceiling started to cave in. The outer wall crumbled. I wrapped a combination of levitation and shielding spells around me, and jumped into the open air as the remainder of the building collapsed into rubble. The ground came up and hit me, harder than I'd expected. The raw magic was wearing away at my protections. I grunted as Sir Griffons landed next to me. There was no sign of Caroline.

Panic seized me as I peered into the dust. She'd been ordered into the backyard, hadn't she? But...what if she'd gone back inside? She should have been able to protect herself, yet...an entire building might have landed on her head. I forced myself to remain calm as I peered into the dust, watching it settle. I didn't dare use magic to push it aside. I'd be blowing contaminated dust in all directions.

My heart whooped for joy as I saw Caroline on the other side of the pile of rubble. She was helping the armsmen with the children, trying to get them to wait until the healers could check them. Sir Griffons nodded curtly, then turned and walked back around the crater. A small army of healers, armsmen and sorcerers had arrived, wearing livery from all over the city. It looked as if they'd started to bicker over who was in charge. I looked around for someone the remainder of the aristos would defer to, but saw no one. The *really* important aristos were probably in their mansions, being held prisoner by their armsmen. Their protective teams wouldn't want their principals exposed to raw magic.

"The blast appears to have been largely contained by the wards," Sir Griffons said. He spoke with a natural authority that practically *dared* listeners to disagree. "Only one building was seriously affected. However, I want buildings on all sides evacuated and checked *thoroughly* before their inhabitants are allowed to return."

He spoke on, taking authority with effortless ease. I watched, reminding myself that my father had been right. The aristo is either at your throat, if he feels himself the superior party, or on his knees, if he feels himself to be inferior. Sir Griffons didn't seem to have any doubt his orders would be obeyed. It was a kind of magic, I thought, as he divided up the manpower and sent the healers to inspect the children. The armsmen obeyed without question.

I caught his eye after he'd finished ordering containment wards for the courtyard. "Sir...what happened?"

"This wasn't an accident," Sir Griffons growled. "This was a terrorist attack."

I glanced at him. "Sir?"

"Someone rigged a Device of Power to emit a burst of raw magic—tainted magic," Sir Griffons said. "The infernal device might have been triggered when it was taken through the gatehouse. The wards wouldn't have allowed it any closer to the dorms. If the carrier knew what he was carrying..."

I felt a sinking sensation. If someone hadn't known what they were carrying, they wouldn't have known they were in danger until contact with the wards triggered the device. They would simply have been the first to die. But if they had known...I felt sick. They'd carried out a suicide attack, sacrificing their life to kill dozens of innocents. I tried not to think about the bodies in the crater. They'd never be positively identified. The bodies would probably be dumped in a toxic spell dump and buried under tonnes of limestone to make sure they stayed dead.

The awful day wore on. Caroline and I helped get the children checked, then frog-marched through a decontamination procedure before they were shipped off to Jude's. I hoped they'd be alright. It was hard to be sure. They hadn't taken the brunt of the attack—that would have killed them, if it hadn't turned them into monsters—but they seemed stunned into silence. The bodies themselves were piled into a cart and driven off...I said a silent prayer to their ancestors, knowing their families might never have closure. And we spent hours picking up pieces of the contaminated building and dumping it in iron bins. Sir Griffons worked as hard as the rest of us. By the time night fell, I was so tired I could barely walk.

"They could have killed everyone in the dorms." Caroline sounded stunned. "What were they doing?"

"We have never plumbed the depths of man's inhumanity to man," Sir Griffons said. "Go back home. When you get there, enter through the rear door and dump *all* your clothes in the bin for disposal. Put everything else in a containment chamber—and I mean *everything*—and then go have a shower. We'll worry about disposal later."

My body ached like hell as we limped down the road. The streets were quiet. Magus Court itself had been shut down, the aristos and their cronies having been evacuated long ago. A handful of carts rocketed past, bringing City Guardsmen to help clean up the mess. I was mildly surprised the guardsmen hadn't called out sick. But then, if they'd been slow in responding to a crisis so close to Magus Court, they would probably have been for the high jump. Literally.

The horses neighed in complaint as we stumbled into the courtyard and staggered to the rear entrance. Sir Griffons had explained it was for decontamination, but I don't think he'd expected to have to actually *use* it. The interior room was lined with a thin layer of dust. I reminded myself to clean it, when I had a moment, as I lit the lantern and closed the door behind us. Caroline leaned against the wall, breathing heavily. I had the feeling she felt worse than me. She'd probably had less sleep the previous night.

"Those poor kids," Caroline said. She started to tug on her cloak, but her fingers refused to work properly. "They could have been killed."

I nodded as I undid my cloak. Dust billowed, before sinking to the floor. I shuddered, wondering how much of the dust was contaminated. I'd heard enough horror stories to know the dangers of breathing it in, no matter what sort of protections we used. Normally, a house that was scheduled for demolition would have to be thoroughly demagicked first. And *that* was just common or garden-variety magic.

My fingers twitched uncomfortably as I undressed. It was growing harder to focus, although I knew I had no choice. We *had* to shower before we slept, or we might wind up breathing in more poison. I opened the bin and held it open, allowing Caroline to drop her clothes into the void. I tried not to notice her nakedness. I was in quite enough trouble without it.

"Put everything else in the box," Caroline reminded me. She dropped her ring in the box, followed by a necklace she'd worn since we'd left Haddon Hall. "Sir Griffons will have to clear it."

"He won't be able to call us," I said, as I dropped my own ring in the box. My spellcaster and wallet followed, the latter crammed with money. I wondered if I could get recompensed for the money if Sir Griffons sent it to the toxic spell dump too. "What do you think he's doing?"

"Probably trying to figure out who to blame," Caroline said. She turned and opened the door to the washroom. "And then hoping we get a shot at them too."

I felt my stomach twist as I followed her into the dusty washroom. It was bare and barren, no better than the chamber we'd used at Haddon Hall. I turned on the water, cursing as dusty liquid splashed down before reluctantly running clear. We really *should* have cleaned the chamber before we had to use it. Caroline didn't bother to wait for the water to get warm. She simply stepped into the stream and washed thoroughly. I turned away, trying not to touch her as I let the water wash the contaminated dust away. I still felt filthy, even after letting the water flow through my hair. It was hard to escape the feeling that, in some way, I was still there. My hands felt dusty, as if I'd aged years overnight. I knew I was being silly, but...

My heart skipped a beat. *Was* it silly? Really? I'd been in a contaminated zone. I could have been tainted or...I swallowed, hard, as I glanced at myself in the mirror. My skin felt uncomfortably dry, but otherwise...I didn't look to have aged. I glanced back at Caroline and nodded. She didn't look to have aged either. I breathed a sigh of relief, then turned off the water and muttered a spell to dry myself. There should have been robes on the far side of the door, but they were missing. I made a mental note to replace them too as I hurried upstairs to grab our pyjamas. Who knew if we'd need the chamber again?

And whoever carried out the first attack might carry out another, I thought. Sir Griffons had been right. There were no limits to man's inhumanity to man. People would storm cities, plunder homes, kill men, rape women and children...crimes so awful I couldn't believe they existed, except they did. I'd grown up in Water Shallot. I knew how grim things could be. *What do they want?*

Caroline took her clothes with a nod and donned them, hurriedly. "What now?"

I hung a robe on a hook for Sir Griffons, then shrugged. "I think we should get some sleep," I said. It was dark outside, suggesting it was well past ten. I looked at my bare wrist in bemusement, then mentally kicked myself. The watch was in the box, waiting to be scrapped or decontaminated. I really was too tired. "There's nothing else we can do right now."

"Quite." Caroline headed for the stairs, then stopped and look back. "Who do you think did it?"

"Right now, there's no evidence," I said. If there was anything left of the Device of Power, it had been bathed in raw magic. I doubted there would be any point in studying the remnants in hopes of finding a clue. "And speculation without evidence is pointless."

"They'll blame it on the socialists," Caroline said. There was a hard edge to her voice that made me flinch. "They'll blame it on your *friend*. Don't you think?"

I scowled. I had the nasty feeling she was right.

CHAPTER TWENTY-THREE

I didn't sleep well, even though I'd been utterly exhausted by the time my head hit the pillow. I had nightmares about the bodies caught in the blast, about the men and women who'd been erased from existence... or worse, turned into monsters that couldn't hope to survive long enough to be healed. But...I couldn't believe Louise would do such a thing. I wasn't even sure she knew *how*. Forging Devices of Mass Destruction hadn't been covered in school.

Which is probably for the best, I thought, as I sat up. I *still* felt filthy. *How many of us would have tried to make them?*

The clock insisted it was seven o'clock. I was morbidly sure it was lying. Caroline snored in her bed. I forced myself to stagger to the shower, unwilling to risk going back to sleep. The water cascaded down my body, but I still felt unclean. I had the feeling I'd never feel clean again. My hands trembled as I dried myself—I didn't dare risk a spell, not feeling like this—and donned my tunic before heading downstairs. I could get a mug of coffee before Sir Griffons and Caroline woke. They'd probably be delighted if I put a pot of coffee on for them...

I stopped, dead, as I peered into the living room. I'd assumed Sir Griffons was asleep—he hadn't roistered us out of bed—but he was sitting on the armchair, smoking a pipe and studying a sheet of parchment. I hesitated, unsure of what to do. Go into the room anyway? Or sneak back upstairs and pretend to be asleep? Sir Griffons looked up, his face unreadable in the half-light. I wasn't sure how he managed to read without a lantern.

"You may as well come on in," Sir Griffons said. "The kettle's just boiled."

"Yes, sir." I stepped into the room, closing the door behind me. Caroline didn't need to wake up, not just yet. "I...ah...did you get any sleep last night?"

Sir Griffons shot me a questioning look. "Is that any of your business?"

I winced at his tone, but pressed on. "I thought apprentices were supposed to look after their masters."

"A common delusion." Sir Griffons tapped out his pipe in the ashtray. "Probably spread by lazy masters who wanted servants, rather than apprentices. You're here to learn and work towards your knighthoods, not to serve me. I could hire servants if I was so inclined."

"Yes, sir," I said. "I just thought..."

Sir Griffons laughed. "I know what you thought," he said. "But I'm not a doddering old man *just* yet."

He let out a sigh as I poured two mugs of coffee. "I didn't sleep very well either," he admitted. "I got the latest update before I came back here."

I wasn't sure I wanted to know, but asked anyway. "How many dead?"

"Seven, we think." Sir Griffons took the mug I gave him with a nod of thanks. "There were four men in the gatehouse when the device triggered. Three more—two tutors and one student—remain unaccounted for. They may have been out on the town and simply haven't reported back, but... after what happened, they bloody well *should* have reported back. And the remainder of the students are currently being decontaminated. I'd be surprised if they want to continue their education after *this*."

I sipped my coffee, keeping my thoughts to myself. Magical education could be incredibly dangerous, even without aristos like Francis and Alana making life miserable for everyone who couldn't defend themselves. I'd seen more potions explosions in my first year of schooling than most people saw in an entire lifetime. There were plenty of ways someone could wind up injured, even killed, in magic school. But this...someone had deliberately set out to kill innocent children in the most horrific manner possible. Whoever had done it was a monster.

A thought struck me and I leaned forward. "Do we have a suspect yet?"

"Not yet," Sir Griffons said. "Lord Dirac was blaming it on the socialists."

Somehow, I wasn't surprised. "Louise wouldn't do something like that!"

Sir Griffons met my eyes. "How well do you know her? Really?"

Intimately, I thought. I kept *that* to myself. It wasn't true. I knew her, but…I didn't know what was going through her head. I'd felt the desperation of someone who wanted to get ahead, yet…couldn't without compromising himself and surrendering to the aristos. I didn't want to think it possible, but I couldn't deny it. Louise might be desperate enough to do something *really* nasty.

"They could have targeted Magus Court itself," I pointed out. "It's just down the road from the dorms."

"Perhaps," Sir Griffons said. "Magus Court is protected. It would be tricky to get such a device through the wards without being detected."

I looked down at my hands. It made no sense. Louise…I scowled. I wasn't sure *what* she was doing. She'd talked about tearing the system down. And yet…I couldn't believe she'd murder kids. She'd make herself public enemy number one. The entire population would be screaming for her to be hunted down and executed as a dangerously-insane terrorist. But I couldn't imagine who *else* would do such a thing.

Sir Griffons returned to his thoughts. I watched him as I drank my coffee, wondering what was going through his head. How much did he know? How much did he guess? How much…I wondered, suddenly, if Caroline had told him. Technically, she had a duty to tell her master anything of importance. She might have told him…I thought about it, then decided it was unlikely. Caroline would compromise herself if she ratted me out, even if—legally speaking—it was the right thing to do. No one would ever trust her again.

I finished my coffee and stood, then paced to the window. A faint haze hung in the air, a grim reminder that tainted magic had been unleashed.

I thought I could hear people chattering, despite the silencing wards. If I knew my city, there were countless spectators on the outside of the protective charms, watching as the remains of the dorms were dismantled, decontaminated and shipped to the limestone pits. The entire building would have to be rebuilt from scratch. I wondered, sourly, if Magus Court would consider it a priority. It wasn't as if Jude's was short of living space. There were people who believed the school would one day swallow up the whole city.

The wards tingled. "We have visitors," Sir Griffons said. "Wait here."

I nodded, wondering if I should call Caroline. It was nearly nine o'clock. She had to be awake now, didn't she? Or was something wrong? She'd breathed in the tainted magic too. Sir Griffons returned, looking grim. I felt my heart skip a beat. Something was *definitely* wrong.

"We've been summoned to Magus Court," Sir Griffons said. "Wake Caroline, then get into your dress robes. I don't want to see a *hair* out of place."

"Yes, sir." I poured a mug of coffee for Caroline and headed for the stairs. "How long do we have?"

"We'll be leaving in thirty minutes," Sir Griffons said. "Hurry."

I nodded and practically ran up the stairs. Caroline was lying on her back, her eyes open and her skin glistening with sweat. I guessed she'd slept as poorly as I had. She sat up, heedless of her nudity, and took the coffee I offered with a grateful nod. I hoped it would wake her up. We didn't have time to eat anything more than a ration bar for breakfast.

"We're expected at Magus Court shortly," I said. "You'd better get showered and dressed."

Caroline finished her coffee, threw her covers to one side, jumped out of bed and ran for the shower. I allowed myself a chuckle, even though she'd make me pay for it later, and searched through the wardrobes for my dress robes. They looked as uncomfortable as ever. I pulled them over my tunic. If things went wrong, I could ditch the robes and fight in my trousers. Whoever had designed the robes clearly hadn't thought the wearer might have to run.

Toni used to say that dresses were designed to restrict women, I recalled. I could see her point. If it was impossible to run in a dress, a woman couldn't escape if a man had bad intentions. *Whoever designed the robes probably had the same idea.*

I checked my appearance in the mirror as Caroline hurried back into the bedroom, water drops flying in all directions. I shoved her robes at her, then went downstairs. Sir Griffons—somehow—had washed, shaved and changed into his dress robes in less than ten minutes. I wondered if we should be practicing that, too. I hadn't bothered to shower or shave, and yet he was ahead of me. It didn't make sense.

There's probably a trick to it, I thought. I could get into my regular clothes in less than a minute, but dress robes? Not a hope in hell. *I'll have to ask him. Later.*

Caroline joined us, somehow managing to make her robes look elegant. I resisted the urge to ask *her* how she did it as Sir Griffons led us onto the streets, locking and warding the door behind us. The streets outside were quieter than I'd expected, but there was a crowd in the distance watching the recovery efforts along with a small stream of aristos driving their carriages to Magus Court. I couldn't help thinking they were being lazy. It wasn't as if their mansions were *that* far from Magus Court. A middle-aged man in reasonably good health could walk from the furthest mansion to Magus Court in less than thirty minutes.

They do it to show off their wealth, I reminded myself, as we walked into Magus Court and through a heavily-warded door. *They want everyone to know they're rich and powerful enough not to have to walk.*

The tension in the air was so thick I could have cut it with a knife. Armsmen were everywhere, making no attempt to hide their spellcasters and enchanted armour. It felt as if the merest cough would be taken as a sign to start something violent. Young aristos swarmed the corridors, making it clear to passing eyes they were important, while their fathers and grandfathers make their steady way to the central chamber itself. I shivered, noting the clients dancing attendance on their patrons. If my father had been a little less ambitious, or a little more ready to compromise himself, I could have been one of them. I spotted Akin, walking next to his father, and felt a stab of sympathy. It was clear he didn't want to be there. Akin had never struck me as someone who enjoyed politics for its own sake.

And his sister betrayed her entire family, I thought. I wasn't clear on the details—people who knew the truth weren't talking—but Isabella *had* been sent into exile. They wouldn't have done *that* for a harmless little prank. *Akin's the only heir his father has left.*

I sucked in my breath as we walked into the central chamber. I'd never visited before, not even when Magister Niven had explained how the system actually *worked*. The only students allowed to visit were the heirs and their clients, the ones who would be politically important in the years and decades to come. I looked around, trying to reconcile what I'd been told with what I saw. There were one hundred chairs in the chamber itself, each representing a single tribe, but—above them—there were rows of seats for spectators. Normally, according to Niven, the spectator seats were largely empty. This time, it was standing room only.

The room filled with astonishing speed. Akin and his father occupied a box on the other side of the room. Beside them, I saw Alana and a dark-skinned man who had to be her father. I scowled as I realised he looked a lot like *my* father. It was easy to see, all of a sudden, just how people could believe I was a natural-born son. But it was silly. It wasn't as if there were only a handful of dark-skinned people in Shallot.

The other students know it gets to me, I thought, as the speaker banged for silence. *I should have just ignored it, instead of starting fights.*

"I call upon Lord Dirac, Defender of the Court," the speaker said. His voice was curiously flat, enough to make me wonder if he was a homunculus. It would be as illegal as hell, but we all knew the normal rules didn't apply to Magus Court. "Let him now be called."

My eyes narrowed as Lord Dirac strode out of the shadows and took his place in the centre. I couldn't help thinking of a man standing at the bottom of a pit, unsure if the watchers were going to help him up or start hurling rotten fruits and vegetables. He appeared to be looking straight at me, turning his back on the senior aristocrats behind him. I puzzled over it for a moment, then realised the chamber was charmed. *Everyone* presumably saw him that way. I wondered why the chamber wasn't better designed, then realised—as I studied the seating—that it was intended to convey the impression that the members were equals. I doubted anyone *really* believed it. In theory, Magus Court could bring the Great Houses to heel like unruly dogs; in practice, Magus Court was kept divided by the aristos through careful patronage and blatant bribery. No one could get them moving in the same direction.

Lord Dirac spoke quietly, but his words echoed through the chamber. "Yesterday, unknown forces unleashed the most cowardly and contemptible attack in the history of Shallot. The attack—a calculated burst of tainted magic, carefully primed to be redirected by emplaced wards—killed at least nine people. One of them was an innocent child."

I felt Sir Griffons tense. Nine people? He'd told me seven. Had they pulled more bodies from the rubble? Or had they run the figures and calculated that two more people should have been caught within the blast, even if nothing remained of their bodies? Or had they simply made the figures up out of whole cloth? My instructors had told me that early reports and estimates were almost always wrong. They often had to be adjusted down as the hysteria gave way to more accurate reporting.

"The attack was carried out by the socialists," Lord Dirac said. "They have a long history of cowardly attacks, of kidnappings and murders and brutal assaults...all of which were carried out with the intention of weakening our resolve! I pledge to you that we will *not* weaken! I ask you to vote for a state of emergency, to grant me the powers to hunt down these vermin and bring them to justice. I ask you to take a stand against terror!"

I shuddered, torn between the sense that strong measures were necessary and the fear that they would be abused. It was easy to demand newer and stronger laws, but equally easy to wind up abusing them. A law intended to hunt down terrorists could easily be turned against free speech, opposition politicians and activists...activists like Louise. But no one was interested in *my* opinion. The debate appeared to have been rigged in advance. After

Lords Aguirre and Rubén spoke in favour of the measure, no one seemed inclined to go on the record as opposing harsher laws. Instead, they fell over themselves in praising them.

"Interesting," Sir Griffons muttered. He used a subtle privacy ward to ensure that no one apart from us could hear him. "They must be worried."

I glanced at him. "Why?"

"Aguirre and Rubén don't normally show their hand so blatantly," Sir Griffons said. "Now…they're running the risk of arousing opposition in the long term."

"Bad news for them, I guess," Caroline said.

I said nothing as the vote was taken. The bill passed, ninety-eight to zero. Only two members abstained. I wondered why they'd bothered. Two abstentions wouldn't make a difference. Sir Griffons touched my shoulder as the members started debating the precise measures to be taken against terrorists. Caroline and I followed him out, down the stairs and back to the entrance. Lord Dirac awaited us.

"Sir Griffons," he said. "In line with the state of emergency, I must ask you to stay out of the way."

I clenched my fists. How *dare* Lord Dirac speak to my master like that?

Sir Griffons didn't show any sign of anger. "Is that the will of Magus Court?"

"Yes," Lord Dirac said. "The Kingsmen are to stay out of the affair. This is *our* problem."

"You couldn't track down a kidnapped girl," I said, before I could stop myself. "Let us help…"

Sir Griffons cut me off with a sharp look. "I apologise for my apprentice's harsh words," he said. "Rest assured, I'll beat him this evening."

Lord Dirac nodded. "The Kingsmen are to stay out of the affair," he repeated. "Do you understand me?"

"Perfectly," Sir Griffons said. "The Kingsmen will do as you wish."

He turned and led us onto the streets. "The Kingsmen will stay out of the affair," he said, as we made our way back home. "But you two aren't Kingsmen. Not yet."

Caroline chuckled. "Will he accept that technicality?"

"Probably not," Sir Griffons said. "I need you to find out who was *really* behind the attack. *Without* getting caught. It could end badly."

"Yes, sir," I said.

"And I'll be beating you at chess later," Sir Griffons added. "We wouldn't want to disappoint the poor man, would we?"

I shrugged. "I could live with it."

CHAPTER TWENTY-FOUR

I felt the tension in the air as Caroline and I crossed the bridge into Water Shallot. The people might not be sure of *precisely* what had happened—the broadsheet screamers were insisting that *millions* of children had been killed yesterday, which was unlikely to convince anyone—but they knew *something* had gone badly. The schools seemed empty, as if half the children had been kept home; the streets seemed suspiciously quiet. There weren't many people in evidence, save for the stallkeepers and newspaper sellers. Even the prostitutes were nowhere to be seen.

It is the middle of the day, I reminded myself. I could *feel* unseen eyes looking at us as we made our way down the street. *Water Shallot doesn't really come alive until nightfall.*

Caroline nudged me. "Do you know where to find your friend?"

"Not directly," I said. There *was* a Working Men's Club on the edge of the gentrified region, but I doubted Louise would be there. They probably wouldn't know where to find her, either...and if they did know, they wouldn't tell us. They didn't *know* us. "But I think I know where to start looking."

I felt a rush of memories as we turned the corner and walked past a handful of stalls. They were selling everything from cheap food to books of magic and Objects of Power. The latter practically *had* to be broken or they'd have been taken to North Shallot and sold there. I cast my eyes over a bench of potions, brewed by an old hag who leered cheerfully and me, and shook my head firmly. I didn't need potions that claimed to boost my potency or lengthen my lifespan. I was sure the potions would do the exact opposite of what they claimed. And yet, I suspected she probably had a lot of customers. There was a sucker born every minute.

It felt...odd to be walking towards Louise's shop. Her father had concentrated on selling food and drink, unlike my father who'd bought everything he could in the hopes of finding something *new*. The shop window displayed meat and fish, wrapped in complex preservation wards. I thought I sensed Louise's hand in the magic. She wasn't as innovative as some of the other students I'd known, but she was very good at taking older spells apart and putting them back together so they'd do whatever she wanted. I felt a twinge of guilt as I pressed open the door. It felt as if I was betraying her. And yet...I gritted my teeth. She hadn't been named, as far as I knew, but it was just a matter of time. Too many people had seen her in the destroyed club for her to remain unidentified.

Although the description might be a little vague, I thought. *Blonde and beautiful. It could almost be a description of Isabella Rubén.*

I put the thought aside as I looked around. Louise's father *had* done well for himself. There were rows upon rows of food, drink and spices, some common and some surprisingly exotic. The prices were lower than I'd expected. I wondered if someone was engaged in something underhanded, then decided it didn't matter. Prices had been falling for years, as more and more ships entered the spice trade. It was about time some of the benefits trickled down to the poor.

The shopgirl, standing behind the counter, waved. I studied her for a long moment. She reminded me of Louise, although her hair was a shade or two darker. Louise's younger sister? It was rare for a shopkeeper to hire someone from outside the family if it could be avoided. Outsiders didn't *like* the thought of working extended hours for a pittance. My father had had the same problem, before Toni had grown old enough to work the counter.

"Hi," I said, finally. "Can I speak to your older sister?"

The girl regarded us both with wide-eyed innocence. "Jeanette?"

"Louise," I said, trying to conceal my irritation. "I'm a friend from school."

"A boyfriend?" The girl smirked, then raised her voice. "Louise! Your boyfriend is here!"

I cringed inwardly, trying to ignore Caroline's snicker. I'd done that to Toni. Once. Her revenge had been epic. Louise wasn't *quite* as violent as my older sister, I thought, but she had more than enough magic to punish *her* sister. I felt a twinge of pity for the younger girl, even though she deserved *some* punishment. Louise wouldn't thank her for starting a whole string of newer and nastier rumours. I schooled my face into immobility as Louise clattered down the stairs. Under the circumstances, rumours were probably the least of her concerns.

"Adam?" Louise sounded surprised. Her gaze flickered from me to Caroline and back. "What are you doing here?"

"We need to talk," I said. "Is there somewhere we can talk alone?"

"Leave the bedroom door open," Louise's sister said. "Or I'll have to rat you out to dad."

"If you do..." Louise lifted her hand in a spellcasting pose, then dropped it again. "Keep your mouth shut and I won't tell him you went walking out with that bloke from across the street."

She turned, motioning for us to follow her up a claustrophobic flight of stairs. I felt uncomfortably trapped before we reached the top. The upper floor reminded me of my father's shop, although it was a little more cramped. I reached out with my senses as Louise led the way into a small bedroom, marvelling at just how clean and tidy it was. Louise was just a *little* obsessive. I felt a twinge of sympathy for her sister. It was clear, from the simple fact there were two beds, that they shared a room.

"Leave the door open, but cast privacy wards," Louise ordered. She sat on the bed, her eyes cold and hard. "Who are you"—she looked at Caroline—"and what are you doing here?"

I hesitated, suddenly unsure what to say. It had seemed like a good idea at the time. I hadn't had any difficulty guessing where she might be, but...

but what was I meant to *say*? Louise had every right to be mad at me, given what we'd shared. And yet...

"There's something I didn't tell you," I said. I'd already considered and dismissed the thought of lying to her. "When I left school, I didn't go to work for my father. I went to join the Kingsmen."

Louise stared at me, then drew back her hand and slapped me. Hard. I tasted blood as I reeled. I'd been punched and kicked before, back during training, but this was worse. She'd woven a hex into her palm. It felt as if she'd hit me with a firecracker charm. I could barely think straight. She drew back her hand to slap me again...

"That will do." Caroline held up her hand, ready to cast a spell of her own. "I know he deserved it, but you can't slap him again."

"Traitor," I muttered. My teeth ached. "What...?"

"You utter..." Louise's mouth worked silently, as if she couldn't come up with anything vile enough to call me. I was a little surprised. She'd grown up in Water Shallot. "You...*traitor*."

I held up my hands, palms outwards. "I never joined your cause."

"And what were you thinking," Louise demanded, "when you took me to bed? Who do you think you are? Sir Gadabout, Knight of the Realm?"

Caroline snickered. Sir Gadabout, Knight of the Realm, was a popular series of novels for teenage boys. He spent most of his stories engaged in implausible fights, casting spells that never worked in real life, sleeping with the latest Gadabout Girl and breaking whatever rules stood between him and his target. I'd loved reading the books as a young man, before it had dawned on me that they tended to share the same basic plot and physically-impossible love scenes. Sir Gadabout *had* to be one hell of a contortionist.

"No." I kept my palms steady. "You kissed me first."

Louise produced a spluttering noise, but Caroline spoke first. "It doesn't matter who kissed whom first," she said. "And—as stupidly as Adam acted—it doesn't matter either. What *does* matter is that you are the prime suspect in a terrorist outrage."

"I didn't do it." Louise glared at Caroline. "What the hell do I have to gain by killing hundreds of people?"

"The *official* death toll is nine," Caroline said. "I dare say that wasn't dramatic enough for the broadsheet editors."

"Probably not," Louise said, sourly. "It wasn't me."

I started to say something, but Caroline spoke over me. "We have to be sure," she said. "I need to cast a truth spell on you."

Louise glared. "I have my rights."

"Actually, you don't." Caroline waved a hand south. "Magus Court has formally declared a state of emergency. All rights have been suspended for the duration of the crisis."

"Those *bastards*," Louise said. Her face twisted in angry. "They can't just..."

"Legally, they can." Caroline looked expressionless. "The vote passed ninety-eight to zero."

"The system is rigged," Louise insisted. I knew Sir Griffons would agree. "It wasn't a fair vote..."

"Right now, that doesn't matter either," Caroline said. "Adam believes you're innocent, but you've got him by the short and curlies. I don't know that you're innocent...nor does our master. You have to prove your innocence now or we have to take you into custody, which might be a great deal safer than falling into Lord Dirac's hands."

Louise said nothing for a long moment. "Cast your spell."

Caroline glanced at me. "Would you cast the spell?"

I blinked, then realised Louise would probably be more comfortable if *I* cast the spell. Or perhaps not. She had every reason to think I'd betrayed her, even though I hadn't. Not really. I'd certainly attended her rally under false pretences. I put the thought out of my head and wove the spell, making sure to do it properly. Caroline was watching. She'd know if I made a mistake. And she certainly *wouldn't* give me the benefit of the doubt.

The spell flared to life. "Tell us something true," I said. "And then a lie."

"My name is Louise," Louise said. "And I'm engaged to Akin Rubén."

The air around her turned red. I nodded. The spell was working. I'd been careful not to cast one that would *encourage* her to talk—whatever Lord Dirac said, I wasn't prepared to put her rights aside so easily—but she wouldn't be able to lie. Not to us. I glanced at the open door, tightening the privacy wards. I didn't want her sister overhearing. It would be difficult to explain.

"Louise," Caroline said. "Did you carry out yesterday's terrorist atrocity?"

"No," Louise said.

Caroline nodded. "Did you order it? Or arrange for it to happen?"

Louise scowled. "No."

I breathed a sigh of relief. I'd been sure she was innocent, but…I could have been wrong. And that would have been disastrous. My career would have gone down the shitter before it had fairly begun.

Caroline looked relieved too. "Do you know who carried it out?"

"No," Louise said.

"Good," I said. "I think we have the proof we need…"

"Wait." Caroline shot me a sharp look, then returned her attention to Louise. "Do you…?"

I listened, impatiently, as Caroline asked question after question, varying the precise wording every time. I knew what she was getting at—Louise could hardly admit to carrying out an atrocity if she didn't think the atrocity actually *was* one—but it was still annoying. I could tell Louise was getting angry, even though she answered each question as quickly as possible. I supposed that was another sign she was telling the truth. It took time to think of a lie, time to work out how to maintain it. But, in the end, Caroline sat back and cancelled the spell with a wave of her hand. Louise let out a sigh of relief. She must have been scared we'd ask her questions she didn't dare answer.

"Happy now?" Louise glared at me. "Are you convinced I didn't do it?"

"Yes." I met her eyes. "And I'm sorry."

"I'm glad to hear it," Louise said, in a tone that suggested she wasn't *remotely* pleased. "You're still a bastard."

"Far be it from me to disagree," Caroline said.

"And where the hell did he find you?" Louise demanded. "Tinian's Finishing School?"

Caroline's eyes opened in mock astonishment. "However did you guess?"

I cleared my throat. "Like I said, I'm sorry. And if things had been different, I…I don't know. But things are what they are and we had to ask those questions."

Louise scowled. "What now?"

"We believe you didn't do it," Caroline said. "Do you know anyone who *would*?"

"I don't think so," Louise said. "The movement cannot achieve its goals through violence."

"But you might have a splinter group that feels you *can* win if you turn violent," Caroline pointed out. "Would that group report to you?"

"No." Louise shook her head. "The movement has always been very loose, very decentralised. The Working Men were *always* intended to serve as a political movement, you see. The founders knew the tribes couldn't be relied upon to secure *anything* for the workers, so they devised the clubs. The clubs themselves are onions. The outer layers are pretty much what they say on the walls. People can go there, have a few drinks, make some friends… the inner layers are more concerned with recruiting political activists. But the system was never designed to accept a single centralised leadership structure…"

Caroline cocked her head. "You're *not* the leader?"

"No," Louise said. "I have influence, and respect, but no formal power."

I blinked. "How did you do it? I mean…"

"Being a little girl?" There was a hint of bitterness in Louise's tone. "It wasn't easy. It took me months to make any real headway. I had to convince them I was a working man—well, working *woman*. Too many of them saw me as a kid, at first. Thankfully"—she snapped her fingers, sparks of magic dancing over her palm—"they understood that a magician is a professional worker. And that I had the drive to succeed."

"Clever," Caroline said. "How do you intend to win?"

Louise met her eyes. "That's a secret," she said. "But suffice it to say my plans don't include violence."

"But someone else might have their own ideas," I said. "If you have a faction that *does* want to commit violence."

"It's not impossible," Louise admitted. It sounded as if admitting it was painful. "There are people who have lost their jobs, their homes, their hopes…because Magus Court did something without thinking of the consequences. Or because it enacted legislation to *clarify* disputes that always went one way. But I've always made it clear that *my* faction will avoid violence."

"So while we've cleared you, we can't clear the rest of your movement," Caroline said.

"Anyone who commits violence is *not* part of my movement," Louise said. Her voice was very firm. "And that's a fact."

"Is it?" Caroline smirked. I elbowed her, none too gently. "Have fun explaining that to Lord Dirac."

I held up a hand. "Louise? Who do you think is behind it?"

"Who benefits?" Louise ran a hand through her hair. "We don't. We look like monsters, terrorists. It does nothing for us, while it does a great deal to *harm* us. But I could easily see the Great Houses or Magus Court carrying out the atrocity themselves. They have secrets, big secrets. And they're prepared to do *anything* to maintain their power."

"You can't start throwing accusations like *that* about," Caroline said.

"Why not?" Louise gave her a savage smile. "You came here making them about *us*."

Her smile grew wider. "Where were *you* during the House War?"

"I wasn't here," Caroline said. "And you know it."

I frowned. I'd been a first-year when the House War—the *last* House War—had turned violent. Hundreds of people had been killed as the Great Houses fought, hundreds of people who'd been in the wrong place at the wrong time. Louise had a point. If the Great Houses were ready to resort to violence against their peers, they probably had even *fewer* qualms about turning on the poor. And Lord Dirac…he'd moved with unseemly haste to get the population's rights placed to one side. Was *he* the mastermind? Or was he merely playing his part in a plot masterminded by someone who remained in the shadows?

Or I might be being paranoid, I thought. *The atrocity might have been carried out by a splinter faction after all.*

Louise stood. "I know someone you two should meet," she said, as she smoothed down her dress. "He knows quite a bit about the Great Houses."

I frowned. "Who?"

"Come with me." Louise grabbed her cloak and pulled it on, then led the way back downstairs. "You'll see."

"Interesting," Caroline muttered, as Louise spoke quickly to her sister. "Someone else you know?"

"I don't know," I muttered back. Someone I should meet? Someone I hadn't *already* met? I couldn't think of any *reasonable* candidates. There weren't many people Louise and I both knew who moved in and out of High Society. Akin was the only person who came to mind and *he* wasn't likely to help the socialists. "I guess we're about to find out."

"Yeah," Caroline agreed. She sounded edgy, as if she felt out of place. "Let's just hope it doesn't bite us on the behind."

CHAPTER TWENTY-FIVE

We hadn't been inside for more than an hour, by my estimate, but the streets felt decidedly less safe as we made our way deeper into Water Shallot. I could see City Guardsmen everywhere, standing in small groups as they guarded street corners or paced backs and forth as if they expected trouble at any moment. The locals didn't look pleased to see them. Atrocity or no, it was only a matter of time before violence broke out. I doubted a lone guardsman would stay alive long enough to reach his peers if he was foolish enough to step away from them.

Louise said nothing as we kept walking, leaving my thoughts a tangled mess. My cheek was still throbbing with pain, despite a couple of painkilling charms. She had every reason to be mad, to think I'd seduced her for evil purposes...I shook my head, knowing it hadn't been that way. I hadn't planned on anything, let alone spending the night in her bed. She knew it, too. But...I was pretty sure she didn't want to believe it. People found it easier, somehow, to believe they'd been tricked or conned than they'd simply been the victim of a random and unfortunate turn of events.

Caroline strode next to me, looking around with interest as we reached a set of dingy-looking houses. They'd probably been expensive, once upon a time, before they'd been sold to predatory landlords who'd subdivided them into tiny apartments and crammed tenants in until they couldn't fit any more. Louise walked down the street until she reached the final house, then pressed her hand against the wooden door. There was a long pause—I sensed a low-power, but very elegant ward buzz around us—before the door clicked open. A pale-faced woman with almond eyes stood just inside, dropping a curtsey as we entered the hall. I was pretty sure she was half-caste, the child of a Hangchowese sailor and a local woman. I felt a twinge of sympathy. Her ancestors were unknown. It limited what she could do with her life.

Even in Water Shallot, people still care about the little things, I thought, as the girl led us upstairs. *It just isn't fair.*

I frowned as I looked around. I'd been wrong. This house *wasn't* subdivided into smaller apartment blocks. Indeed, there was a curious elegance about the old-style building that suggested it had once been more than a little expensive. I found it hard to believe, even as I ran my hands along a piece of detailed woodwork that had been melded into the wall. A painting of a blonde girl—around ten years old, I thought—hung on the upper landing. She looked oddly familiar, but I couldn't place her. I'd never seen her in all my life.

The servant opened an inner door, revealing a cosy sitting room. A man sat at a desk, holding a translucent sphere in one hand. I studied him, thoughtfully. He looked like everyone's favourite uncle, with a balding head, a nice smile and a hint of plumpness under his elegant and outdated suit, but there was something in his beady eyes I didn't like. He put the sphere in a drawer and sat upright, his eyes flickering from face to face. I felt as if I was looking at a snake, a snake that could be kind—or poisonous—depending on its whim.

"Louise, my dear," the man said. He had a *very* aristocratic accent. "It's *so* good to see you again."

He glanced at the servant girl. "Four teas, if you please," he said. "And bring a tray of those biscuits too."

The girl dropped a curtsey, then backed out. I felt my hackles rise. We were in the middle of Water Shallot, but the man was acting like he was an aristocrat...no, he *was* an aristocrat. I couldn't imagine anyone developing such an accent unless they'd spent years amongst the aristocracy. And yet, what was he doing in Water Shallot? Who the hell *was* he?

Louise performed introductions. "Adam, Caroline, this is Malachi Rubén."

I blinked. Malachi Rubén had been kicked out of his family, if rumour was to be believed. Even *I* had heard about that. Malachi Rubén...father of Penny, uncle to Akin and Francis...I frowned, again, as I remembered the girl in the painting. No *wonder* she'd looked familiar. It was Penny. She'd probably sat for the painting a few years before she'd gone to Jude's. The nasty part of my mind wondered how they'd convinced her to sit still for the painter. Had they bribed her? Or had they simply frozen her in place?

"I've heard about you," I said, carefully. I had no idea why Louise trusted him. Maybe she didn't. She probably took everything he said with a grain of salt. "How many of the stories are true?"

Malachi smiled. It didn't touch his eyes. "It won't surprise you to know the Great Houses slander their enemies mercilessly," he said. "You can't trust *anything* they say."

I nodded. "So...what really happened and what are you doing here?"

"Someone had to take the blame, after Francis died," Malachi said. "*Someone* had to take the fall, so Carioca and Davys could emerge blameless and Carioca's brat could be confirmed Heir Primus. And so, they kicked me out of North Shallot. They pay me a stipend to make sure I don't go home."

"I see," I said. I wasn't sure I believed him. The Great Houses could be ruthless at times—there was nothing unbelievable about his story—but it would be hard to drive him out of North Shallot completely. There was no single authority that could tell him to go to hell and make it stick. "And what are you doing here?"

"Writing my memoirs and providing help and advice to some people." Malachi nodded to Louise. "I assume you didn't come strictly for the pleasure of my company?"

The servant girl returned, placing a kettle, a tray of cups and a plate of biscuits on the desk. Malachi dismissed her with a nod, then stood and poured the tea himself. I wasn't sure if he'd been born an aristo or simply married into the aristocracy, but he had the manners down pat. I didn't think Akin or Alana could have done it so well. He practically oozed charm as he passed cups to the girls. I muttered a charm to check my tea was safe to drink. It was.

"Yesterday, there was a terrorist attack near Magus Court," Louise said. She sipped her tea with surprising elegance. "We were wondering if you could shed any light on who might have carried out the attack."

"I see." Malachi exchanged a look with Louise. "Magus Court is the most heavily protected place in the city, outside the Great Houses themselves. It would be difficult to get close to the walls without being detected."

"Unless one had inside help," Louise growled. "Someone seems to be trying to frame us for the attack."

"It's possible." Malachi shrugged. "It's also possible that someone could be trying to set off another House War."

I blinked. "Madness."

"And trying to frame the socialists is *what?*" Malachi smiled. Once again, it didn't touch his eyes. "Politically speaking, anyone who wants to upend the balance of power *has* to act now or risk losing their last chance. There's little hope of keeping House Rubén and House Aguirre from formalising their partnership now."

"Because Caitlyn and Akin are due to get married," I said. "What if they say no?"

"She might." Malachi took a sip of his tea. "The chatterboxes are speculating that the only reason she *hasn't* had her season, not yet, is because she *doesn't* intend to go through with the marriage. If her family knew that, they'd have a strong incentive to keep her a legal child for as long as possible. The marriage couldn't go ahead, but the betrothal couldn't be cancelled either. The legal fiction will remain"—he smiled, coldly—"*fictional*."

"Akin won't be very pleased about that," Louise pointed out.

"Quite." Malachi gave her an approving look. "But—in public, at least—Akin has always been a nice young man. He won't try to pressure her or her family to set the date."

I rubbed my forehead. "So you think someone might have staged the attack as an excuse to seize control."

"It's possible," Malachi commented. "It's also possible that someone else carried out the attack and Magus Court leapt to the wrong conclusion."

He met my eyes. "Magus Court is big, young man. It's more than *just* the hundred members and their cronies. It's quite possible there's a faction within the court that wants to take control itself. They may have set out to provoke a crisis. Or…the Great Houses are perfectly capable of being cunning in their own interests. They might have set out to start the crisis…"

"You don't know," I said, flatly.

"No," Malachi agreed. "But I do know that there are factions—and secret operatives—within the Great Houses. And Magus Court. You know Lord Dirac? How do you think he got the job?"

Caroline cocked her head. I had the feeling she didn't like Malachi any more than I did. "Tell us."

"The Great Houses are moving to constrain the currently dominant houses," Malachi explained. "They don't want to endure permanent submission. Creating a layer of investigators with immense powers, led by Lord Dirac, is their response. They intend to use the investigators to pry control out of their enemy's hands. Really"—he looked pensive for a moment—"I'm surprised they haven't already moved to take control of poor Caitlyn."

I blinked. "Because she's unique?"

"Yes. And whoever controls her has a huge advantage." Malachi stroked his hairless chin. "The king might demand she be handed over to him, when she reaches her majority. And what will *that* do, I wonder?"

I finished my tea. "Maybe we're going about this the wrong way," I said. "Maybe we should be looking into where the device came from."

"Building it wouldn't be hard," Caroline said. "You'd just have to put the pieces together…"

Louise gave her a sharp look. "And where would someone living in Water Shallot get the money to buy the pieces? We're not talking about a handful of coppers here."

That surprised me. I kicked myself, mentally. It really *shouldn't* have. But I'd spent seven years at Jude's and a further three months at Haddon Hall, where expensive potions ingredients and forging tools had been free for the asking. Louise was right. A person born and bred in Water Shallot would have *no* hope of buying whatever they needed to make the device. Whoever had made it practically *had* to come from North or South Shallot.

And some of the items they'd need are on the restricted list, I mused. *Even trying to buy them would be a tip-off.*

"There's somewhere you could start looking, if you have time," Malachi said. "Rebecca Travis."

Louise coughed. "*Her*?"

"She's a Bolingbroke client, with a habit of selling discounted potions to people who live in Water Shallot," Malachi explained. "She has the contacts to get her hands on ingredients that might be restricted, if she wishes to obtain them. And...*something* odd happened in Bolingbroke Hall, shortly after the House War. I heard a rumour that said she was involved."

"She's one of the good guys," Louise said.

"You'd be astonished at just how much you can get away with, if everyone thinks you're one of the good guys," Malachi reminded her. "In any case...I hope you found this meeting useful."

I scowled as we stood and donned our cloaks. The meeting *hadn't* been useful, even if we *had* been given a tip. But...I had no idea if the tip was any use. And the hint of other factions within Magus Court and the Great Houses might be useful, or it might be completely misleading. We didn't have any idea if those factions really existed, if they were really involved...

"You spent years in a Great House," I said, to Malachi. "Is it possible there could be a faction that...that is somehow kept secret from the rest of the family?"

"Yes." Malachi didn't sound remotely unsure. "You have to understand, young man. The Great Houses are huge. House Lamplighter is the only real exception and *that* is because they've been in financial trouble for years. The remainder...even the smaller houses have hundreds of members. It's quite possible for them to have a dozen factions, each one convinced that it's alone."

He rang the bell. His servant appeared within a minute, ready to escort us downstairs. I felt a ward pressing against my defences as we walked, making it harder to sense anything within the house. Malachi didn't seem to be powerful, compared to his relatives, but he was skilled. *Very* skilled. I had the feeling he was more than good enough to tie someone who relied on brute force in knots. I nodded to the serving girl as she opened the door and waited for us to leave. She hadn't spoken a single word. I couldn't help finding it a little creepy.

"I hope that was interesting," Louise said, as we made our way back up the streets. "Did you learn anything useful?"

"Perhaps," Caroline said. Her voice was icy. Her lips were so thin they practically vanished. "Or were you just trying to waste our time?"

Louise made a dismissive gesture. "I thought you needed to hear other voices," she said. I couldn't tell if she was being serious. "And to understand that my people could *not* have carried out the attack."

"So you say," Caroline said.

"I let you cast a truth spell on me," Louise snapped. I hastily cast a privacy ward before we attracted attention. "I put my rights aside to convince you of my innocence. What more do you want me to do?"

She wrapped her cloak around herself before either of us could answer. "Now, I've got work to do. Father expects me to take over the store this evening. Or are you going to try and stop me from going home?"

"You might be safer if you came with us," Caroline warned.

"No." Louise scowled at me. "If you need to meet again, send me a message via my father."

She turned and walked away, her back ramrod straight. It took me a moment to realise she half-expected to be hexed in the back. We could arrest her...technically, we had enough authority to do so even without the state of emergency. Lord Dirac would probably not complain—much—if we brought her in. But we knew she was innocent. We couldn't arrest her, even if it *would* keep her safe.

"Your taste in women is appalling," Caroline muttered, as we started to walk towards the bridges. "Did you lose the ability to think as soon as she took off her clothes?"

I felt myself flush. "She's not a bad person."

"She has a cause," Caroline said. "People with causes tend to be dangerous. And you know it."

I said nothing as we passed a row of guardsmen, looking increasingly nervous as they waited on a street corner. It didn't look as if they were planning a raid or...well, *anything*. It looked more like their superiors had thrown them onto the streets to make a show of strength without any plan. The locals *weren't* going to like it. I felt them watching as we left them behind, doing our best to ignore them.

There was trouble in the air. I could feel it.

"Interesting," Caroline mused, as we reached the bridges. "Are they *allowed* to block passage to North Shallot?"

"I think, right now, they can do whatever they like," I said. The guardsmen inspected our rings, then waved us through. "Bastards."

I scowled as we crossed the bridges. The guardsmen were searching carriages and a number of pedestrians, although I noticed they seemed to spend more time searching the young female pedestrians than the men who might be more dangerous. The lawsuits were going to be a nightmare, once the state of emergency was finally lifted. I wondered if they'd have the wit to formally absolve the guardsmen before the suits could be filed. Lord Dirac might not think of it. *I* certainly wasn't going to tell him.

Sir Griffons met us as we reached home. "What happened?"

"We found her," Caroline said. She explained everything, from our interrogation of Louise to our meeting with Malachi Rubén. "She appears to be innocent."

"But still on the wanted list, once they figure out who she is," Sir Griffons said. He held out an envelope. "You have a letter."

I took the envelope and frowned. It wasn't *just* made of the very finest paper. It was scented with perfume…nothing illicit, as far as I could tell, but more than enough to catch my attention. I turned it over and over in my hand, trying to learn as much as I could before I opened it to check my deductions. The handwriting was very feminine, and quite probably aristocratic, but I didn't recognise it. I had no idea who'd written to me.

Caroline's lips brushed against my ear. "Another girlfriend?"

"Shut up." I ignored her giggle as I opened the envelope. Inside, there was a single sheet of scented paper. "It's an invite to a ball in honour of Prince Jacob."

"Charming," Caroline said. "From whom?"

"Saline," I said, surprised. "Tonight. I…I don't think we should go."

"You should," Sir Griffons said. "You've been invited. You should go."

"Sir?"

"We need to know the mood on the ground," Sir Griffons said. "And Lord Dirac can hardly object if you're invited, can he?"

"Probably," Caroline muttered. "Dress robes again, sir?"

"No," Sir Griffons said. "But make sure you wear something nice."

CHAPTER TWENTY-SIX

"You look cute," Caroline said teasingly, as she descended the stairs. "Quite the little aristocrat."

I glared. I'd had to hire the suit from a local tailor, the sort of thing that turned aristocrats into laughingstocks...not that I cared about *that*, of course. It felt disquietingly like I was going back to school: black jacket, black tie, black trousers, white shirt...Caroline, of course, looked stunning in a long yellow dress that hinted at, rather than revealed, her curves. She'd deliberately picked one that would keep a distance between her and any prospective paramours. I supposed it make a certain kind of sense. Too many aristocrats had wandering hands when confronted with someone young, female and deprived of family connections.

They'd be more careful if they knew how much magic she had, I thought, as I held out my arm. She took it and allowed me to lead her into the courtyard. The carriage was already waiting. *She could give almost any aristo a real lesson in manners.*

The driver cracked the whip as soon as we clambered in, spurring the horses out of the courtyard and down the street. I peered out the window, noting how darkness had spread over the city. North Shallot seemed to glow with pinpricks of light, while Water Shallot was awash in darkness. I wondered why the streets looked so dim. It wasn't as if it was *hard* to cast lighting spells. I'd mastered them well before I'd gone to Jude's. Perhaps they just *wanted* to make the streets safe for footpads or *unsafe* for the guardsmen. I assumed they were still on the streets.

Caroline smiled as we turned a corner. "Remember to check in with as many of your old friends as possible."

I groaned. There weren't *many* of my old classmates I wanted to see. Louise was perhaps the *only* person I wanted to see, and there was no way in hell *she'd* be invited. Saline might have planned the party, but I doubted she had control over the guest list. I was mildly surprised she'd invited *us*. It wasn't as if we were aristos. We certainly couldn't *help* her in any way.

Maybe she's rebelling against her parents, I mused. *Or making it clear to her family that she's not going to toe the line any longer.*

The carriage rattled to a halt. I opened the door and peered out. We'd parked below a small mansion, sitting on a mid-sized hillock. I frowned, remembering what little I'd heard about the Greenbank Mansion. The Greenbank Family had deeded it to a social club, if I recalled correctly. And the social club had turned it into a party house. The building was brightly lit, every last window streaming light onto the grounds. A footman stepped up with a foot rest. I smiled and stepped down, then assisted Caroline to descend. It wasn't easy in her dress, but she managed it. I wondered when she'd found the time to practice.

"Well," Caroline said, after tipping the footman. "Shall we go?"

I took her arm. We walked up the path towards the house, trying to ignore the handful of peacocks and other exotic animals the family had gathered to showcase their wealth. I thought I spotted a unicorn in the ill-lit grove, although I didn't believe it. Unicorns were so rare that it was far more likely someone had cast a glamour on a pony. The family could have paid off their debts and then some if they'd sold a *real* unicorn to the zoo.

The noise of music and dancing grew louder as we approached the French Windows. A pair of aristos stood by the door, smiling at all and sundry. I started as I recognised Saline, wearing a long blue dress that set off her eyes. She wasn't wearing any family livery, as if she'd chosen to put her family name aside for the night. I didn't blame her. It was starting to look as though the party wasn't something of which the older folk would approve, if they were forced to take official notice. I felt a twinge of sympathy for the servants. They'd have to clean up the mess before the owners returned to take stock.

"Adam," Saline said. She leaned forward and planted a kiss on my cheek. "So good to see you again."

I concealed my astonishment with an effort. Saline and I had never been *friends*. I had no idea why she'd invited us, unless she wanted to scandalise her parents. There wouldn't be many commoners amongst the guests. Saline might have invited a few dozen clients—and former students—but the smart ones might have found an excuse to stay away. Here, the aristo brats were letting their hair down—literally—and allowing their inner demons to run free. I didn't feel remotely comfortable.

"My pleasure," I lied.

"Prince Jacob will be making his appearance shortly," Saline said, as she exchanged air kisses with Caroline. "I do trust you'll show your support."

"I'll be happy to show my support," I said. It wasn't entirely untrue. I'd be happy to show my non-existent support. Hell, even if I did support him…so what? No one was going to be swayed by *my* opinion. "Why did you throw a party for him?"

"His cause is just." Saline's eyes shone like a woman in love. "And he's so dreamy."

And supporting him upsets your family, I added, silently. Saline had plenty of reason to make her family uncomfortable. And they'd have problems doing anything about it without making the whole story of just what had happened to her public. *I suppose that's why you invited us too.*

I bowed politely, then stepped inside. The doors opened into a massive hall, teeming with aristocrats and servants. I'd attended some parties at Jude's—the parties the staff weren't supposed to know about had been the best—but this was a whole other world. The elegance of the Lamplighter Ball was nowhere in evidence. Aristos glided around the hall, stuffing their faces like pigs or flirting tastelessly with the servants. The men—they were all young, as far as I could tell—wore suits like mine. The women wore dresses that would get them in *real* trouble if they wore them at a formal ball. Caroline was the most conservative dresser within eyeshot.

A serving girl offered us a drink. I took a glass of wine and muttered a charm to remove the alcohol, unwilling to risk getting tipsy or drunk in the midst of such a hostile crowd. They might be smiling now, but they could turn nasty in a heartbeat. The wine wasn't very good, I decided. Perhaps it was an acquired taste. It wasn't as if *I'd* ever had the money to become a wine aficionado.

Caroline squeezed my hand. "See anyone you recognise?"

I shook my head, slowly. Akin wouldn't attend. He was the Heir Primus. He couldn't attend without giving some legitimacy to Prince Jacob's cause. Francis would probably have *loved* the party, damn him, but…he was dead. The others…I thought I spotted a trio of girls a year older than me…it was hard to be sure. They were trying so hard to look older that I couldn't be certain. Besides, I doubted they'd have time for me. They'd never paid any attention to anyone who didn't have a lineage stretching all the way back to the Thousand-Year Empire.

We slipped onto the dance floor and whirled about, losing ourselves—just for a moment—in the tune. There didn't seem to be anyone calling the dances. The dancers just did whatever steps came naturally, although—somehow—they seemed to avoid stepping on each other's toes. I blinked as a girl whirled by, wearing an outfit that looked as if it was permanently on the verge of falling off and pooling around her feet. I supposed the only thing holding it in place was magic—and the eyes of every young man in the room.

"Eyes front," Caroline teased. "Really."

A young man came up to us as the music changed and asked Caroline to dance. She accepted, nodding to me as she allowed him to lead the way. I frowned, feeling suddenly very alone. I didn't belong in this crowd. I was alone in the midst of strangers…

"Adam." I turned and saw Alana standing behind me. "It is you."

I stared at her. Alana shouldn't have been anywhere *near* the party, but here she was, wearing a low-cut dress that showed off her body to best advantage. Her father was going to kill her when he found out, perhaps literally. If my sister had worn something like that, in a party heaving with tipsy young men, my father would have exploded with rage. Toni wouldn't have been able to sit comfortably for *weeks*. I dreaded to think what my father would do to any young man who looked at her twice.

"I got an invitation," I said. I held out a hand. "Would you like to dance?"

Alana shrugged, then took my hand. "I hear you're a Kingsman now," she said, as we moved around the floor. She was a better dancer than Caroline. "How...nice."

The way she said it, as if it was a joke, made my blood boil. "I'm not a man to be laughed at," I said, trying to keep my irritation under control. "I..."

"I know." Alana smirked. "I've heard you try to crack jokes."

I glared. "What are you doing here? You're the Heir Primus."

"I got bored." Alana winked at me. "And I don't want Dad to think I'll do *everything* he wants."

I frowned, surprised. Alana was probably the haughtiest girl I knew, which put her up against some pretty stiff competition, but she was far from stupid. Her father might have paid her way into becoming Head Girl, but she wouldn't have been given high marks in class unless she'd earned them. She knew—she *had* to know—about the complex vortex of politics surrounding Prince Jacob. *Akin* knew. She certainly shouldn't be anywhere near him.

"Never a good idea," I said. "Your hair is still in braids."

Alana's face twisted. I saw a flash of frustration in her dark eyes. "I'll have my season at the end of the summer."

I tried to conceal my amusement. Alana's friends—or cronies, the nasty part of my mind added—would be having their seasons now, while she... formally, she couldn't enter the marriage market until she had her season later. It had to be *really* irritating to know she was being held back, simply because her sister's betrothal couldn't—yet—be converted to a formal engagement. I wondered just how badly she was being teased, by her social equals. They were probably sniggering. I might have done the same, if I was in their shoes.

"I look forward to it," I said. "I'm sure it'll make all the papers."

"You'll have to read about it in the papers," Alana snarled. It *had* to be wearing on her. "You won't be getting an invitation."

"And thank the Ancients for that," I said, truthfully. I'd never attended *anyone's* season, but I'd heard the stories. If I wanted to spend a few days dancing attendance on a girl who'd been declared queen for a day, I'd have accepted one of the offers of patronage that came my way. "I'm sure the stories will be long on boring details about what you wore and short on anything *interesting*."

Alana scowled, just as Saline rang a bell. "Prince Jacob is approaching," she said, her voice hanging in the air. "Please join me in welcoming him."

"Hah," Alana muttered.

She pulled her hand free, then turned and headed further into the building. I snickered, hastily covering my mouth as a handful of aristos turned and looked. Alana's little rebellion clearly had limits. She wasn't going to join the others in welcoming the prince, not when her father would go mental. Alana had two sisters. Cat was—in one sense—a cripple, but there was nothing wrong with Bella. There was no reason *she* couldn't be declared Heir Primus instead.

I pasted a bland expression on my face as Caroline and I joined the throng heading out of the building. Someone had cast a whole *series* of powerful lightspells, illuminating the lawn with an eerie white radiance. My eyes hurt, forcing me to cover them as a fancy carriage passed through the gate. It was covered in gold, real gold. It was so gaudy that the Great Houses would sneer at the carriage if they saw it. And yet...I frowned, inwardly, as I saw another carriage following the prince. Prince Jacob didn't *have* wealth and power. His only hope of gaining support came from pretending he had a hope in hell of regaining his throne.

Except he never really had it in the first place, I thought. Someone would have loaned him the golden coach. I wondered who. *It was his grandfather who got booted off the throne.*

The lights flickered and failed. I looked up, just as a surge of magic—tainted magic—brushed against my senses. People screamed as an eerie, shimmering light overwhelmed the gatehouse. For an instant, reality itself seemed to hang on a knife-edge. I thought I felt blood trickle from my eyes and down my cheeks. That light was like looking into the gates of hell themselves.

A thunderous roar struck my ears. The gatehouse disintegrated, pieces of debris flying in all directions. Prince Jacob's coach was picked up by the blast and hurled towards us, rolling over and over until it plunged into the pond. Swans fled, hooting and howling, as a sheet of warm air washed over us. I could *taste* the tainted magic. Everyone was in terrible danger.

"Get inside," I shouted. No one heard me, not over the sounds of growing panic. I muttered a spell to boost my voice. "EVERYONE GET INSIDE, NOW!"

I glanced at Caroline, then hurried towards the remnants of the coach. Prince Jacob might still be alive. It crossed my mind, just for a second, that Sir Griffons might be happier if I left the prince to die, but…I couldn't live with myself if I did. I jumped into the water, which churned unpleasantly, and tugged at the door. It came free, allowing Prince Jacob to crawl out. He looked shaken, but otherwise unhurt.

"They tried to kill me," he said, as I pushed him out of the water. "They tried to kill me."

"They tried to kill everyone," I said. The wards had absorbed most of the blast—fortunately, otherwise hundreds of young aristos would have been killed—but the tainted magic was still going to be a problem. Everyone would need to be checked before they were allowed to go home. "Stay close to me."

I hurried back towards the mansion. A pair of senior armsmen were arguing with Caroline. I opened my mouth to say something, but she punched the leader out before I could say a word. The remainder nodded hastily, then hurried to carry out her orders. I had the feeling they'd be making hundreds of complaints before the day was through, but it didn't matter. Right now, we had to decontaminate the scene before more people were exposed. The attack could have killed hundreds of people...

Could have, but didn't. I frowned, feeling something nag at the back of my mind. The attack—both attacks—could have been a great deal nastier. If the attackers had thought to shield their devices...they hadn't even learnt from their first attack. *They could have killed a great deal more people with a little forethought.*

I put the thought out of my mind as I helped organise the relief and recovery efforts. The aristos were too stunned to argue, even when we separated the men from the women, then told them to strip down and wash thoroughly before donning clean clothes. I'd never heard so much complaining in my life, not even after the yearly exams came finally—mercifully—to an end. Sir Griffons arrived with a small army of armsmen and sorcerers, ready to decontaminate the remains of the gatehouse and sift through the rubble for clues. I doubted they'd find anything. The entire complex had been bathed in tainted magic.

"They tried to kill him." Saline was sitting by the door as I headed out, looking stunned. "They tried to kill the prince!"

"Perhaps," I said. I wasn't so sure. There were easier and safer ways to assassinate the prince. Hell, if it had happened in the prince's lodgings, there were people in Magus Court who would probably have breathed a sigh of relief. Whatever they said in public, they'd be glad he was dead. "How many people knew he was coming here?"

"Everyone." Saline gave me a wide-eyed look. "The party was in his honour. It was on the invites and...I invited hundreds of people."

I nodded, then winced as Lord Dirac strode into view. There was no way to tell if Prince Jacob had been the target or not—I was pretty sure he would have been killed if the device had been triggered a little earlier—but it didn't matter. The Great Houses were already jumpy. Now...their children had been attacked. I didn't think there were any aristos amongst the dead, but...they wouldn't care. They'd be looking for a way to hit back.

And Louise is still their target, I thought, as I rejoined Sir Griffons. *This is not going to end well.*

CHAPTER TWENTY-SEVEN

"Lord Dirac wishes to speak with us," Sir Griffons said, the following morning. "Go shower, then change into your tunics. I want you to be alert."

I groaned. It felt as if we'd barely gotten any sleep. I wasn't even sure when we'd gotten home, showered in the decontamination chamber and stumbled into bed without bothering to get dressed. My skin prickled uncomfortably, a grim reminder that I'd been brushed by tainted magic. The healers said there should be no long-term effects, but I wasn't so sure. There were too many horror stories about people who lived near the Desolation for me to be sanguine about anything.

"Yes, sir," Caroline said. I didn't know *how* she managed to sound so alert. "Are we going to see him?"

"He's coming to see us," Sir Griffons said. "That bodes ill, I fear."

I nodded. I'd taken the time to skim through the morning papers while eating breakfast and pouring gallons of coffee down my throat. The broadsheets had been utterly hysterical, claiming that hundreds of people had been killed or seriously injured, while the more sober papers—for once—hadn't poured water on the fire. Their editors seemed united in their demand for Magus Court to do something—anything—about the terrorists. A handful were even brave enough to suggest Magus Court didn't know who was behind the socialist threat.

We stumbled upstairs, undressed and plunged into the shower. Cold water cascaded down, shocking me awake. I washed thoroughly, trying to ignore the patches of greying skin on my chest. The tainted magic had left its mark. I ran cold water over the skin, trying to wash it away. It felt weird, like it was no longer part of me. I glanced at Caroline. Her skin appeared to be clear. I hoped that was a good sign.

"Maybe Prince Jacob was the target," Caroline said, as we dried and dressed. "He's certainly got enemies here."

"Not to hear the broadsheets tell it," I said. The majority of the newspapers had glossed over Prince Jacob's involvement. The prince had been rushed off by the healers and I hadn't seen him since. "Everything is the fault of the socialists."

I scowled as I buckled my belt, then checked my pouch and tools. I *knew* Louise was innocent, but...it was quite possible there was a splinter faction that thought it could get what it wanted through violence. Or a faction from Magus Court. Or one of the Great Houses. Or...could it be Prince Jacob, trying to drum up sympathy for his cause? I rather doubted it. The Great Houses were caught in a trap. They *had* to put up with him. But that would change if he started unleashing tainted magic within the city. They'd throw him out on his ear.

If they didn't kill him out of hand. It sounded insane, although I'd heard worse plans that someone had been stupid enough to try. *He'd be putting his entire cause at risk.*

I heard a carriage outside as we slipped downstairs and into the living room. Sir Griffons looked us up and down, then nodded curtly. "Caroline, show them in," he ordered. "Adam, pour us all tea."

"Yes, sir," I said. I disliked serving guests, even though it was one of the duties of an apprentice, but it would just have to be endured. "The *good* tea?"

"Yes." Sir Griffons smiled. "And the good biscuits too."

I heated the kettle, then poured water into the teapot and carried it and the biscuits back into the living room. Lord Dirac looked as if he hadn't had much sleep either, his pale face lined with tiredness. I guessed Magus

Court must have summoned him in the wee small hours, on the assumption he had nothing better to do than answer their questions. I felt a stab of sympathy, despite everything. Sir Griffons had grumbled enough about superiors who thought that harassing their subordinates was the best way to look like they were doing something…he might be a pain in the neck, but Lord Dirac didn't deserve to be harassed with pointless questions. It would keep him from doing his job.

Lord Dirac nodded, politely, as I poured him and his fellows a cup of tea. One of them looked so much like him that I honestly wondered if they were father and son, although the age gap didn't look to be *that* large. Father had been twenty when he'd had me and there was no way I could pass for *him*, not now. Maybe they were cousins. Or brothers. Nepotism was the way of the world in Magus Court. Lord Dirac would run into *more* trouble if he refused to promote his family above all others. The other man was older, his face nearly completely bland.

"We are displeased by your interference," Lord Dirac said. He sipped his tea in the proper aristocratic manner. "You should not have been at Greenbank Mansion."

Sir Griffons raised his eyebrows. "You would have preferred I left the armsmen to handle the crisis on their own?"

"Your apprentices"—Lord Dirac glanced at Caroline and myself—"certainly should not have been there. The party was a political headache even before the atrocity."

"My apprentices were invited," Sir Griffons said. "Or would you have suggested they refused the invites?"

"Many did," Lord Dirac said. "The *important* people found pressing business elsewhere."

No, they didn't, I thought, remembering Alana. She might have legged it when Prince Jacob had arrived, but she'd been there. Hundreds of people had *seen* her there. *Don't you know she was there?*

I kept that thought to myself as Lord Dirac leaned forward. "There is a state of emergency," he said. "Magus Court will not tolerate interference in its affairs."

"I was unaware that saving lives was illegal," Sir Griffons said, with an affected casualness that was nothing of the sort. I knew him well enough to tell he was annoyed. "And my apprentices *were* invited to the party. It would have been incredibly rude to tell the organisers that they couldn't make it."

Lord Dirac ignored him. "By the terms of the Shallot-Tintagel Treaty," he said, "I must formally request that the Kingsmen withdraw from the city at once."

"I see." Sir Griffons said nothing for a long chilling moment. "And you feel that chasing *us* out of the city will help you find the terrorists?"

"Magus Court believes so," Lord Dirac said. "We intend to protect ourselves."

"I see," Sir Griffons said, again. "Might I remind you that the *last* time we were withdrawn from the city, you wound up with a full-fledged House War?"

"Magus Court has made up its mind." Lord Dirac's face was so expressionless that I couldn't tell if he believed what he was saying. "You Kingsmen have twenty-four hours to leave the city or, in line with the treaty, we will evict you."

"I formally protest," Sir Griffons said.

Lord Dirac stood. "Magus Court has made its decision," he said, as he beckoned for his assistant to follow him. "I trust you will comply."

"If that is your wish." Sir Griffons glanced at Caroline. "Escort them out, if you please."

He leaned back in his chair as Caroline led Lord Dirac and his assistant to the exit. I stared, utterly unsure of what had just happened. Throwing *us* out of the city wouldn't help in the slightest, would it? I couldn't believe it. *We* weren't the ones blowing up the city. Magus Court had to have lost its collective mind. They should be hunting down the terrorists. They should be letting us *help* hunt down the terrorists. They shouldn't be wasting time hurling us out.

"Sir," I said. "Are they...?"

"Wait." Sir Griffons held up a hand. "When Caroline comes back, we'll talk."

I forced myself to calm down and drink my tea as Caroline returned, her face pale. "Sir," she said. "Are they mad?"

"I wanted to ask that," I said. "Are they mad?"

"You tell me." Sir Griffons looked at me, sardonically. "Why might they give us the boot, now?"

I thought about it. Lord Dirac didn't know we'd interrogated Louise. He didn't even know who Louise *was*. I was pretty sure he would have made a terrible fuss if he'd known. And yet...why would they order us to stay out of the investigation, then order us to get out of the city itself. It made no sense. They were hunting dangerous terrorists who'd shown a frightening lack of concern about civilian casualties. This wasn't the time for petty power games. They wanted—they needed—all hands on deck. It didn't matter who caught the bastards as long as *someone* did.

"I don't know," I admitted, finally. "Are they *that* unhappy we attended the party?"

Caroline had another idea. "They're going to do something bad and they don't want outside witnesses."

I blanched. "You mean..."

"They've already declared a state of emergency and suspended everyone's rights," Caroline said. "What's to stop them—now—from searching Water Shallot from top to bottom? From casting truth spells on everyone who falls into their clutches? From using dark magic to track down the terrorists and kill them..."

"And, in the process, shattering the socialist movement beyond repair," I finished. I could see it now. Louise and her comrades would be arrested, interrogated and shipped off to Skullbreaker Island without a trial. They might be innocent, but so what? No one came back from Skullbreaker Island. "They're using the atrocities as an excuse for a purge."

I looked down at my hands. "Sir...we have to stop them."

"We need to uncover who's really responsible for the atrocities," Sir Griffons agreed. "Shallot has always rested on a knife-edge. The various tribes moved in uneasy harmony. If that gets broken, now, the results are unlikely to be pleasant. If we can catch the people responsible, we can convince Magus Court to back down before it provokes a full-blown revolution."

I nodded. For all of its flaws, the system enjoyed the support of the population. They wouldn't react well if they were stripped of their rights, their ancient liberties and—most importantly of all—their voice in the city's affairs. If faith in the system collapsed, there would be blood. I wondered if the Great Houses knew they were playing with fire. They were the most powerful magicians in the world, but they weren't the *only* ones. Louise and I were hardly the only sorcerers to come out of Water Shallot.

"Which means we need to track down the source of the devices," I said. "And quickly."

Caroline had a different question. "How are we meant to do that when we've just been ordered to leave the city?"

Sir Griffons let out a long breath. "I can leave," he said. "I *have* to leave. But you two can stay."

"On a technicality," I said.

"Yes." Sir Griffons met my eyes. "I won't lie to you, either of you. The technicality won't impress Lord Dirac, if you're caught. You might wind up arrested—or worse. If you want to leave the city instead...I'll understand. I won't hold it against you."

I didn't need to think about it. Shallot was *my* city. I wasn't going to leave while a bunch of bloodthirsty monsters tore it apart. There were innocent people at risk, people who might be killed or brutalised as Lord Dirac searched for the socialists. My *family* lived in the city. So did almost everyone I knew. *Someone* had to stay and fight for them. I wasn't going to run.

"I'm staying, sir," I said. "Caroline?"

"I dread to imagine what you'll do if left unsupervised," Caroline said, with a hint of a smile. "I'll stay with you."

"Then you'd better move now," Sir Griffons said. "Lord Dirac will be here in twenty-four hours, just to make sure we've gone. Take some money, take some tools, and stay in touch. I'll try to convince His Majesty to authorise an intervention force. The Great Houses may change their minds if all hell breaks loose."

I swallowed. "Yes, sir."

"Keep your rings," Sir Griffons said. "But make sure you tighten the charms on them. You do *not* want to be caught."

My stomach shifted uneasily as we hurried up the stairs to pack. I'd never considered becoming a fugitive. I'd always been too proud to steal. Father would have probably killed me if I'd considered a life of crime. But now...if we were caught, we would be in trouble. Lord Dirac would be entirely within his rights to keep us prisoner until the state of emergency was lifted—or worse. We could find ourselves on the way to Skullbreaker Island. His Majesty wouldn't make a fuss. Our presence within the city wasn't legal. It would suit everyone—including our superiors—to turn a blind eye.

But it has to be done, I thought, as I changed into a labourer's outfit. Sir Griffon had clothes for every occasion. *No one else is going to do it.*

"Make sure you hide some money about your person," Caroline said. She passed me a pouch, crammed with gold coins. We'd have to get them changed. Golden Crowns were rare in Water Shallot. "And hide your tools in your bag."

"Yes, Mum," I said. "I won't forget."

My stomach twisted again as I dropped the spellcaster, spellbinder, spellbreaker and multitools in the bag. If I was caught with them...the City Guard would assume I was a cat burglar or a safecracker. Perhaps even the wardcrafter who'd kidnapped Cathy...it felt like years ago. I hoped she was recovering—I kicked myself, mentally, for not inquiring—as I pulled my bag over my shoulder and looked at Caroline. She looked like a housewife, complete with a pinafore and her hair worked into an elaborate bun that made it clear she was married. I hoped no one realised she *wasn't*. People could get very unpleasant if they thought they were being given mixed or false messages.

"Cute," I commented. "But your hands are a little too smooth."

Caroline made a face. "And what do you suggest I do about them?"

"Use a glamour," I suggested. A lower-class woman would have spent most of her life cooking and cleaning with her hands. Caroline's hands, on the other hand, didn't suggest any kind of manual labour. "And don't make it obvious."

Sir Griffons was waiting for us downstairs. "Use the rear door and make sure you cast an obscurification spell before you leave," he said. "And wherever you stay, make sure you ward it as thoroughly as possible."

"Yes, sir," I said. "We could always stay with my family."

"If you feel that's wise." Sir Griffons met my eyes. "Don't forget just how much trouble you could bring down on their heads."

"Yes, sir." I lowered my eyes. "I won't forget."

We cast a handful of spells over ourselves, then walked out the back door. There was an edge in the air, fewer people on the streets as we made our way to the bridges. I was uncomfortably aware of eyes following us, men and women thinking we didn't belong anywhere near North Shallot. The obscurification charms were working too well. I twisted them carefully, trying to avoid notice. It didn't work. The stares didn't go away until we crossed the bridge into Water Shallot.

Caroline glanced at me as we walked past the shops. "You think they'll just let us rent a room, no questions asked?"

"Yes." I grinned at her. "We pay. They give us whatever we want."

A line of guardsmen marched past us as we headed further into Water Shallot, holding their weapons at the ready. A couple looked to have been in the wars. I guessed citizens had stood on the roofs and hurled slates at the guardsmen. They glowered at us, but said nothing. They'd probably had enough trouble for the day. I said nothing as we chose a seedy-looking inn and stepped inside. The innkeeper wouldn't ask any questions. It was quite clear he was bending the law, if not breaking it outright. His inn was so cramped that a single fireball would probably turn it into a towering inferno.

I spoke briefly to him, crossed his palm with silver, then accepted the room keys and allowed his serving girl to lead us upstairs. The room was cramped and smelt faintly of illicit potions, but I didn't care. Let him think we were running away from home or having an affair. I didn't care. It would provide cover for our *real* activities.

"That girl isn't old enough to go to school," Caroline observed. "I'd be surprised if she was in her second decade."

"Kids here start working young," I said. I was surprised she didn't know that. My sisters -and I—had been working from the moment we could toddle from place to place. "It's cheaper to put your kids to work than hire someone who might want to be paid a living wage."

Caroline looked discontented, but kept her thoughts to herself. I wondered, not for the first time, where she'd been born and raised. Somewhere outside Shallot, I knew, but where?

I put the question aside as I unpacked my bag. "The devices had to come from somewhere," I said, again. "And we know where to start looking."

"Assuming you trust Malachi Rubén," Caroline said, tartly. "He's a creep. If he told me it was sunny outside, I'd be sure to carry an umbrella."

"It's a good place to start," I said. I finished warding the room, concealing most of our tools under the bed. The innkeeper might try to search our bags…I smiled. He'd be in for a nasty surprise if he did. I just hoped he didn't send his daughter to search instead. "Shall we begin?"

CHAPTER
TWENTY-EIGHT

Someone—Magister Niven, I thought—had once told us that we didn't know what we had until it was gone. I'd never understood that saying until we crossed the bridge into South Shallot. Normally, it was rare for anyone to be searched, let alone arrested, as they moved from Water Shallot to South Shallot. Now...we had to endure the attentions of the guardsmen as they checked everyone who thought they had business in South Shallot. I wanted to kill the bastards as they groped us both, then sent us on our way. They didn't *have* to be so unpleasant.

I was still in a vile mood as we walked past Jude's and headed towards Broadway Avenue, where the magical traders did their business. It had fascinated me as a young boy, starting my first term at Jude's, although I'd rapidly come to realise that the storekeepers were quite happy to cheat students who didn't have the wit to realise they were being overcharged. I scowled as I walked past a bookshop, remembering how the owner had chased me out years ago. It wasn't a lending library, he'd said. But I'd barely been able to afford even the *basic* textbooks for each year. It just wasn't fair.

The street seemed almost deserted, somewhat to my surprise. It was summer, I supposed. I'd only ever visited while Jude's was in session. I stopped outside the apothecary and frowned. The sign above the door—TRAVIS—looked as if it was permanently on the verge of falling down. The window was crammed with small jars, labels advertising everything from herbal teas to basic solidified potions. I'd known students who swore by potions to sharpen their memories before exams. I might have been tempted myself, if I hadn't known the effects rarely lasted long enough to be useful. The invigilators never allowed us to bring learning aids into the room, anyway.

I pushed the door open and stepped inside. Caroline followed. The scent of spices and herbs wafted across my nostrils, making me think—suddenly—of home. I wasn't sure why. Father might *sell* spices, but he rarely used them. It wasn't until Toni had learnt to cook that we'd had anything more adventurous than bland fish and blander chicken.

A small girl stood beside the counter, eyeing me with a perplexed expression that—I was sure—concealed a sharp mind. I thought she was actually some years older than we were, but she was so slight it was hard to be sure. She didn't *look* like a potioneer. I would have bet good money she was actually a shopgirl. Her hair glistened too brightly for it to be natural. Toni had experimented with hair-colouring potions too. They'd never looked natural.

"Good afternoon," she said. Her voice held a surprising hint of North Shallot. "What can I do for you?"

"We'd like to speak to the manager," I said. I pushed as much authority into my voice as I could. "Rebecca Travis?"

"She's in the brewing chamber," the girl said. She started towards a wooden doorway, then stopped herself and turned to face me. "Who should I say is calling?"

"The Kingsmen," I said, holding up my hand so she could see the ring. "We'll see her upstairs, if you don't mind."

The girl twitched, then opened the door and scurried into the next room. I winced, feeling like a bully. The poor girl might have a hint of an aristo accent, but I was pretty sure she didn't have even a *hint* of aristocratic blood. I guessed she'd grown up in one of the Great Houses, probably as a servant's daughter. She might have picked up the accent without ever being told it was unseemly. If she'd been a child, it was unlikely the adults would have tried to beat it out of her.

"If you'll come this way," the girl said. "She'll see you now."

I looked around with interest as she showed us into a well-equipped potions lab. Two walls were covered with shelves, lined with hundreds of jars of potions ingredients. A sink and disposal tube sat in one corner, next to a small collection of cauldrons and measuring jugs; a large door, coated with iron, presumably led down to the ironhold. A single lantern hung high overhead, a candle burning bright within the glass. Rebecca Travis clearly didn't take risks. A magical light might not affect the brewing, but why chance it? There were limits to how many wards she could weave around such a small chamber.

Rebecca Travis herself was striking. She stood behind a table, eyes resting on a bubbling cauldron. She was tall and willowy, her almond eyes, long dark hair and tinted skin marking her as a half-caste. She wore a simple dress that was covered in potion stains, concealing her curves in a manner that reminded me of Louise. She was definitely a few years older than either Caroline or myself, yet she looked timeless. There was something odd about her, although I couldn't put my finger on it. It wasn't her appearance. It was something else.

"Welcome," she said, carefully. She'd been born and raised in Water Shallot. The accent was unmistakable, even if it had been diluted slightly over the years. I felt a rush of fellow-feeling. She might have accepted patronage, but she'd clearly done well for herself. It was no small achievement for an ancestor-less half-caste. "Please give me a moment."

I watched as she poured a pinkish liquid into a large bottle, then sealed the top with a simple charm. It smelt of flowers, suggesting she was brewing perfume. I hoped she wasn't breaking the laws on just how much enchantment one could weave into perfume. It was quite easy to blend a basic love potion into a perfume, then sit back and enjoy the results. It was also thoroughly illegal.

Caroline had the same thought. "I trust that perfume is legal?"

"It's a slightly modified version of Flower in Bloom," Rebecca told us. "It doesn't break any of the laws."

"As long as it isn't mixed with a handful of others," Caroline pointed out. "What *else* are you selling your customer?"

Rebecca's eyes flickered up, then down. "Just Flower in Bloom."

"Good," Caroline said.

I cleared my throat. "We need to ask you some questions," I said. "First, why *have* you been selling discounted potions in Water Shallot?"

Rebecca seemed surprised by the question. "Because the people there need them, but cannot afford them," she said. "I devised a handful of tricks to make mass-production possible. My overhead is covered by sales here."

"For which you charge full price," Caroline said, flatly. "What *sort* of potions do you sell?"

Rebecca studied her for a long moment. "Do you have a warrant?"

Caroline made a show of lifting her eyebrows. "A warrant?"

"A warrant," Rebecca repeated. "A court order authorising you to ask questions and demand answers…"

"There's a state of emergency underway," Caroline said. She was careful not to suggest we were operating alone, technically against orders. "We have authority to ask whatever questions we like."

"Oh." Rebecca's lips thinned, as if she was considering telling us to go to hell anyway. "I sell strengthening potion, contraceptive potion, smoothing paste and…"

"Nothing more interesting?" Caroline cocked her head. "Nothing…*special*."

"No," Rebecca said. "Why?"

"Have you sold *anyone* anything special?" Caroline pressed her advantage. "Anything that might release a surge of magic?"

Rebecca's eyes narrowed. "What are you asking?"

I leaned forward. "You run an apothecary," I said. "Have you been asked to source something—anything—from the restricted list?"

"Of course." Rebecca eyed me, warily. "I get requests for illicit ingredients all the time. And I tell them, when they fail to produce the right paperwork, that I can't sell them what they want. They generally stamp off in a rage."

"I can imagine," I said. "Who and why?"

"Students, mostly," Rebecca said. I had the impression there was something she wasn't telling us. "The aristos generally have their own apothecaries. They don't need me."

"Even your patrons?" Caroline met her eyes, staring her down. "Do they ever ask you for anything?"

"No." Rebecca scowled. "We rarely talk."

I frowned. That couldn't possibly be true. Setting someone up in an apothecary—particularly here, so close to Jude's—was *expensive*. *Very* expensive. House Bolingbroke might be wealthy enough to buy and sell a hundred apothecaries without ever noticing the price, but they wouldn't invest so much money without demanding *something* in return. Rebecca was lying to us. She *had* to be. I felt my previous goodwill drain away. She was trying to lie to us.

"You're lying," I said. My voice sounded ugly, even to myself. "I *know* you're lying."

Rebecca lowered her eyes. "I am not."

I stared around the room. "Tell me something," I said. "If I was to search your ironhold, how many illicit ingredients would I find? Dragon Scales? Basilisk Eyes? Powdered Unicorn Horn? Human *Blood*? Would I find enough to justify throwing you in jail?"

"I have permits for everything in the shop," Rebecca said. Her voice shook. "And blanket permission to work with rare and expensive—even restricted—ingredients."

I kept my face hard, even though I felt like a heel. I was pushing her… was I any different, really, from a guardsman who wanted to take advantage of his uniform? I was trying to find a bunch of terrorists, but…I pushed my doubts to one side. I needed answers. I needed to know what she was lying about. And why.

She couldn't have lied about getting blanket permission, I told myself. *That would be a matter of public record. We'd have no trouble checking.*

"Someone supplied the potions ingredients that were used to unleash a surge of tainted magic," I said. "*Two* surges of tainted magic. Did they come from you?"

Rebecca straightened, meeting my eyes. "I didn't supply anything to anyone without a valid permit."

"Good." I let out a breath. That was true, I thought. I was starting to think we'd been sent on a wild goose chase. Except…she *had* lied to me about something. Or she'd chosen not to mention something. "Do you have a register of customers?"

"Yes." Rebecca turned to the door. "Jill! Bring the red book!"

The shopgirl hurried into the room, carrying a large red tome. Her eyes flickered from me to Rebecca and back again, hardening as she realised I'd upset Rebecca. Jill seemingly had a crush on her boss…I wondered, absently, if Rebecca was aware of it. She hadn't cut her hair short. But then, neither had Jill.

I opened the book and skimmed the last few pages. Rebecca had better handwriting than I did. She'd had to read every permit and sign off on every purchase. My eyes narrowed as I read the list. She'd handled everything necessary to unleash a burst of tainted magic and then some. My eyes slipped to the ironhold door. Had she sold something off the books? Or had she been robbed? She was in South Shallot. There were so many magicians in the district that, in some ways, she was being terrifyingly lax.

"As you can see," Rebecca said, "everything was pre-authorised."

"So it seems," I said. It *was* possible Rebecca had been tricked, that she'd been given a forged permission slip, but that would hardly be her fault. "Have you lost anything? Or had it stolen?"

"People don't steal from this shop," Jill said. I nearly jumped. I'd forgotten she was there. "We have protections."

"We've never lost anything," Rebecca confirmed. "And all our records are in order."

"Quite." Maybe we were wasting our time. "Tell me, do you know someone called Malachi Rubén?"

Rebecca shook her head. "No."

"I met him once, at Bolingbroke Hall," Jill put in. "He wasn't a very nice man. He never got invited back."

I frowned. Malachi Rubén had sent us to Rebecca. Had he been trying to be helpful or…or what? Take revenge on House Bolingbroke? We hadn't found anything that might be embarrassing to the family. If it was a plot, it had clearly misfired. Or…

Caroline made a hand signal. *We're wasting time.*

I studied Rebecca for a long moment. She'd lied to me about something. What?

"If you were looking for something you couldn't get legally, something on the banned or restricted list," I said carefully, "where would you go?"

Rebecca flinched. It was barely perceptible, but it was there. *She* clearly hadn't been raised in a Great House. Whoever had raised her hadn't taught her to conceal her true feelings. And that meant…I'd put my finger on something important. I just needed to tease it out.

"I'm sure I wouldn't know anything about that," Rebecca said, carefully. "I…"

"I think you do," I said. "I think you'd have an idea where to look, even if you never actually did. And I think you could tell *me* where to look."

Rebecca stared at me for a long moment. "And if I refuse to talk?"

"We have the power to force you to talk," Caroline said, coldly. Her voice betrayed no hint of our weakness. "Where would you look for something on the banned list?"

"I wouldn't," Rebecca said. She looked at the ground. "But, speaking *completely* off the record, I might ask Zadornov."

I blinked. I'd heard that name, although only in whispers. He was a big man in Water Shallot, but…I knew very little about him. He was supposed to be behind everything that happened in the district, yet…I'd never even been sure he was *real*. He was a shadow, a cipher...I shivered. It was disturbing, somehow, to know there was some truth behind the rumours.

My eyes narrowed. "And *you* know Zadornov?"

"My old master knew him." Rebecca seemed to have given up all hope of keeping anything from us. "He purchased a handful of restricted ingredients from Zadornov. That was six years ago, more or less. I haven't heard anything from Zadornov since."

I figured she was telling the truth. "How would you contact him now?"

"I don't know." Rebecca met my eyes. "And if he knew I'd talked to you..."

"We won't tell him," I said. "You have our word."

"Hah," Rebecca said. Her eyes went cold. "I...the last I heard, he'd taken over the loan shark con. Completely, I mean. You could probably get a line on him if you shook them up a little, but...you might also get turned into mice and fed to the cats. Zadornov...he was genial, when I met him, but he was a very dangerous man. I can't imagine he's mellowed since then."

I felt a flicker of sympathy. If the rumours and whispers were even remotely accurate, Rebecca would be in real trouble if Zadornov thought she'd betrayed him. He might even have pressed her, once or twice, to do favours for him over the last few years. The Bolingbroke connection might be enough to keep him away... or it might not. The Great Houses might not have touched someone like Zadornov with a ten-foot pole, but they might be quite happy to let Rebecca serve as the middleman. Was *that* why Malachi Rubén had pointed us at Rebecca? Or was I overthinking it?

"Thank you for your time," I said, stepping back from her. "We're sorry to bother you."

Rebecca didn't look pleased. Beside her, Jill shot me a look that should have turned me into a pile of ashes. If she'd been Alana, I would have considered it a very real possibility. I bowed to Rebecca, then led Caroline back through the door and into the shop itself. The collection of ingredients was impressive enough, but the row upon row of prepared potions, salves and medicines were stunning. Rebecca really *had* done well. And we'd come and bullied her. I told myself that we'd had no choice, but I wasn't sure that was true. Malachi Rubén might have sent us up the garden path.

"So," Caroline said, once we were outside. "What now?"

I felt my stomach rumble. "We get something to eat," I said. It was mid-afternoon. I hadn't eaten anything since breakfast. It felt like days had passed since we'd left Sir Griffons. "And then we go looking for a loan shark."

I scowled. Father had warned me that it would be better to become a prostitute than sell myself to a loan shark. He'd actually been a *lot* more graphic, when he'd explained how the scam worked. The interest was so high that the debt literally could *never* be paid off. It was just like becoming an aristo's client, only worse. I wondered, sourly, if Rebecca had run the risk of falling into Zadornov's clutches. Her old master might have sold her for drink.

I should see if I can figure out her story, I thought. I'd never *heard* of Rebecca Travis. If she was good enough to be snapped up by House Bolingbroke, I should have heard of her. *I'm sure there's something missing here.*

"And then...what?" Caroline smiled, coldly. "Do we let him lead us to Zadornov?"

"I was thinking we'd force some answers out of him," I said. I had no qualms about hurting loan sharks. They sent the leg-breakers around if someone missed a single payment. The entire community would cheer if the loan sharks were fed to *real* sharks. "And then let him take us up the chain to Zadornov."

"And then?" Caroline smiled. "Do you think we can get answers out of him?"

I nodded as we entered a small diner. "Yeah," I said. "I'm pretty sure we can."

CHAPTER TWENTY-NINE

It was raining by the time we returned to Water Shallot, great drops of water that splashed our cloaks and threatened to seep into our clothes, no matter what charms we used in a futile attempt to stay dry. The streets emptied, hundreds of people scurrying for what little cover they could find in the shops, clubs and alleyways. The only people left on the streets were the guardsmen, looking increasingly damp despite their caps and waterproof cloaks. I would have felt sorry for them if I hadn't known they were making things worse. I was pretty damn sure the local hard cases were already plotting ways to drive the guardsmen out.

And yet the streets are probably safer than they've been in years, I thought, as we hurried into the lower districts. The stench of rotting fish was almost overwhelming. *I wonder if anyone's grateful for their presence.*

"The loan sharks have an office down here," I said, grimly. "Follow my lead."

Caroline shot me a sharp look, then nodded. Something was bothering her, although I didn't know what. She'd been very quiet over lunch. I wondered if she was having second thoughts about our plan. We were alone, miles from any hope of support. If we ran into something we couldn't handle, we were dead—or worse. A smuggler who'd survived for years in Water Shallot wouldn't have done it by being a nice, reasonable sort of person.

I put the thought to one side as we stepped into a grimy alley and eyed the shop. It was tiny, the building looking vaguely as if it was being squashed between two *larger* buildings. The golden globes in the window—cheap brass, naturally—marked it as a combination of pawnshop and several other trades that preyed on the desperate. I shuddered, remembering the horror stories I'd heard as a kid. The rentmen were genial souls, as long as you paid them. If you didn't—if you couldn't—out came the sticks. There were some men wandering the markets who'd been crippled for non-payment of debts. I hated to think what might have happened to the women.

The door chimed as I pushed it open. Inside, the shop was even *smaller*. There was barely any room for a handful of grown men. The shelves were lined with goods, put in pawn by people desperate to make their rent for the month. I frowned, wondering how much the stuff was worth. It probably wasn't worth very much, even if the pawnbroker was honest. I was pretty sure the man behind the counter had undervalued everything that had crossed his desk.

"Hello?" The loan shark looked like a kindly old grandfather. "Can I help you?"

I met his eyes, daring him to challenge us. "Take me to Zadornov."

He blinked. He made no visible motion, but the wards flickered. Two burly young men appeared, wearing black tunics and caps. The boys, I knew; the leg-breakers. I glanced at Caroline, then hit the first with an overpowered stunning hex. He flew back and crashed against the far wall. The second lifted his hand, too late. Caroline turned him into a stone and kicked him out the door. I wondered, vaguely, where he'd find himself when the spell finally wore off.

The loan shark's jaw dropped. "What...?"

"Take me to Zadornov," I repeated. I felt no guilt at pushing the man around. I had no doubt he made people suffer, just because they couldn't pay their rent. Once you were in their clutches, it was very hard to break free. "Now!"

The man stared at the stunned bodyguard, his eyes flickering between us. I glared at him, willing him to believe that I was ready to do *anything* to force him to comply. And yet...I knew what he was thinking. Zadornov wouldn't be happy if he took us to him. The loan shark would probably bear the brunt of Zadornov's displeasure. I found it hard to care. The man deserved worse than either I or Zadornov could give him.

"Fine." The loan shark grabbed his coat. "If you'll come with me."

"And no funny business," I warned. "It might work out well for you if you take us there without any tricks."

I was pretty sure that wasn't true, but it didn't matter. The loan shark closed the shop, then led us through a twisting maze of streets until we reached the older warehouses by the canals. I was aware of eyes following us, but no one moved to bar our way. I wasn't too surprised. The loan shark was a big man. No one wanted to risk his displeasure, save Zadornov himself. I wondered, idly, if Zadornov had set the man up or if he'd simply taken over once the loan shark was in power. The man had folded rapidly, when we'd confronted him. Most bullies collapsed when faced with someone stronger and more ruthless than themselves.

They're cowards at heart, I reminded myself. *The trick is to hit them hard enough to bring that to the fore.*

The loan shark led us into a warehouse and spoke, briefly, to a man wearing a dockyard worker's outfit. The man eyed us both, then vanished into the backroom. I waited, my heart pounding. The warehouse was surrounded by magical protections, slowly coming to life as they realised they had intruders. I braced myself, ready to fight my way out if there was no other choice. The loan shark could have led us into a trap. Or Zadornov might decide to kill us both...

"This way." The *faux* worker returned and indicated the door. "Come."

We followed him through the door, up a rickety flight of stairs and into a small office. A man stood in front of a desk, studying us with a cool and collected expression. He was slightly shorter than me, muscular with broad shoulders, a pale face with dark hair cut so closely to his scalp that he was almost bald. His clothes marked him as a manual labourer, but they were made of a fine cloth no labourer could have hoped to buy with less than a decade's wages. My eyes narrowed. A nobleman, pretending to slum with commoners? Or someone who wanted people to think he was a nobleman? But only a nobleman could afford such an outfit for day-to-day life.

Or a smuggler, I reminded myself. *He's probably rich enough to fund a Great House.*

"Well," Zadornov—it had to be Zadornov—said. "A pair of Kingsmen, coming to call on *me*."

I frowned, surprised. We hadn't told anyone who we were.

Zadornov smiled. "You're wearing rings," he said. He made a dismissive motion at the loan shark, who was hastily escorted out. "The charms you have on them are good, but…not good enough."

He waved a hand at the sofa. "You went to some trouble to see me," he said. "What do you want?"

I glanced at Caroline, feeling flat-footed. I hadn't expected Zadornov to see through us so quickly. I'd intended to try to probe him gently, to see what he might have to say before I tried to pressure him. This was his territory. We might not get out alive if he decided to have us killed. But there was no point in trying to be subtle. He'd seen through us.

"So far, there have been two terrorist attacks in North Shallot," I said, carefully. "And, in response, Magus Court has declared a state of emergency and put a small army of guardsmen on the streets. They're already searching carriages heading into North Shallot from Water Shallot and they're planning to extend the searches to barges and ships moving up and down the river. I submit to you that their searches won't be good for business."

Zadornov cocked his head. "And you think I need to worry about the City Guard?"

"You might have to worry when they put armsmen on the streets too," I pointed out. "You cannot bribe them all."

"Maybe," Zadornov said. "Are you sure?"

"They're looking for the person who built the terrorist devices," I said, ignoring the question. "And you are one of the people who could supply the components. They'll come for you."

Zadornov's face became expressionless. "Maybe," he repeated. "Are you *sure*?"

"Yes." I met his eyes, even though it felt as if I was locked in a staring contest with a dangerous snake. "Sooner or later, someone will talk. Someone always does."

"Perhaps." Zadornov looked me in the eye. I could sense a hint of magic in his words. "How did *you* know where to find me?"

"You have a file in the office," I said, carefully. I didn't let his spell get a grip on my mind. Besides, it was probably true. We just hadn't been able to *look* at the files since Sir Griffons had been ordered out of the city. "It was quite informative."

"I see." Zadornov's face was so bland that I couldn't tell if he believed me. "But not informative enough to lead you here."

"No," I said.

Zadornov smiled. "What do you want?"

I looked at him. "I want clear answers," I said. "Truthful answers."

"They come at a cost," Zadornov said. I wondered, idly, just how many hundreds of crowns he'd try to charge us. "What do you have to offer me?"

"An end to the affair before Magus Court pulls your operation up by the roots and dumps you on Skullbreaker Island," I said. "If we can catch the people responsible, the state of emergency can come to an end. You'll be safe."

"Provided I keep paying bribes," Zadornov said, amused. "Very well, truthful answers. I didn't supply the materials to make the infernal devices."

I blinked, surprised. "You didn't?"

"No." Zadornov looked at me, evenly. "I concede I have no way to *prove* it to you, but lying is hardly in my best interests. Is it?"

"No." I glanced at Caroline, who frowned. "Do you know who *did*?"

Zadornov looked oddly offended. "If it didn't come from me, then it came through more...legal channels," he said. "I didn't supply it. The other smugglers don't have *my* contacts. I think you have to look elsewhere."

I cursed under my breath. If Zadornov was telling the truth...I turned it over and over in my mind, trying to understand. He had good reason to tell the truth...I thought. Zadornov wouldn't have survived for so long if he hadn't been ruthlessly pragmatic. He wanted the state of emergency lifted before it crushed his business. And yet, if the materials hadn't come from Zadornov, where *had* they come from? The Great Houses? Or...or where?

"So it would seem," Caroline said. She sounded resigned. "Do you know who built and triggered the infernal devices?"

"It was none of *my* people," Zadornov said. "Of course, there are factions within factions and splinter groups within splinter groups. It could be anyone."

He grinned at me. "I hope you found our chat informative."

"It was very useful," I said. It felt as if we'd wasted our time, although... we did know, now, that Zadornov hadn't supplied the raw materials. We'd eliminated one possible suspect. And I found it hard to believe he'd lied. Zadornov stood to lose a great deal if the state of emergency led to mass civil unrest. "Thank you for your time."

"I would be very interested to know what my file had to say about me," Zadornov said. He held out a hand. "Can I trouble you for a copy?"

"No." I couldn't tell if he was serious. Was he pulling our legs? Or trying to see if we could be bribed? He'd *love* to have a pair of Kingsmen on the payroll. "We can't take the files out of the office."

"How terrible." Zadornov stood. It was clearly a dismissal. "Don't bother coming back here. You won't be welcome."

"Understood," I said. The door opened, revealing another man in black. "We'll be seeing you."

The man led us down a different flight of stairs and pointed us at the door. Something ran down my spine as we stepped through the door and into a barren alleyway. My eyes narrowed. There weren't any homeless sleeping in the rough, not here. It wasn't normal. The sense that something was wrong grew stronger as we made our way through the maze of streets. Caroline picked up on it too. I could sense her concern as we turned a corner and ran into a trap.

"Well," a voice said. I recognised the thug Caroline had transfigured, surrounded by a handful of other leg-breakers. I didn't have to look behind me to know there were others standing there. "Look who *we've* found."

I reached out with my senses, carefully. There were at least four behind us, two powerful enough to bleed magic in all directions. They hadn't been formally trained, as far as I could tell, but it didn't matter. Four behind us, five in front...I gritted my teeth. Caroline and I were good, but not *that* good. My head spun, trying to think of possible options. Perhaps if we levitated, we could hop along the roof until we reached more civilised territory...

Caroline cleared her throat, nervously. "What do you want?"

I hid my amusement with an effort. Caroline was *never* nervous. I thought she was overdoing the act. The thugs didn't notice. Their grins grew wider as they stared at Caroline, undressing her with their eyes. I shuddered, inwardly. I didn't know if Zadornov had set us up—there was certainly no way we could prove it—but it was a matter of honour for them now. We'd humiliated the thugs. They wanted revenge.

"I want a little kiss," the thug said, nastily. He licked his lips, his gaze crawling over her breasts. "And then we'll let you go."

Caroline walked forward. I stared, unsure what she had in mind. She didn't intend to *kiss* the thug, did she? The thug leered, wrapping his arms around her as their lips met...and blue-white light flared. He screamed in agony as magic crackled around him, every cell in his body ablaze with pain. I didn't hesitate. I summoned the strongest spell I could and hurled it behind me, slamming all four thugs into the nearest wall. I thought I heard bones break under the force of the impact, but I didn't have time to check. Caroline knocked down two more, forcing the others to scatter. Her would-be rapist hit the ground, groaning in pain. I could practically *smell* burning flesh.

"Run," Caroline said.

A thug loomed in front of me, so big and muscular that I was sure he was mainlining dangerous and illicit potions. I clenched my fist, muttered a spell and then punched him in the jaw. The magic strengthened my blow. I felt his jaw crack as he spun and hit the ground. I hoped Zadornov would pay for reconstructive magic as I jumped over the thug and ran up the alleyway. No one tried to chase us. I grinned at Caroline, forgetting—just for a moment—how close we'd come to disaster. If Zadornov had intended to quietly dispose of us, he'd failed completely. And I wasn't going to forget it either.

No proof, I reminded myself. There would be nothing to tie Zadornov to the thugs. I was sure of it. His narrative would insist the thugs had attacked us without orders, just to get a little revenge. *And we'd have no grounds to interrogate him under truth spells.*

I caught her eye as we slipped out of the dockside and up into the more civilised part of Water Shallot. "What the hell did you do to him?"

"The Alderman Curse." Caroline puckered her lips at me. I couldn't help flinching. "It's a trick I learnt at school. If someone tries to steal a kiss..."

I grimaced. "No one ever told *me* about those spells."

"Probably for the best." Caroline let out a long breath. "The boys who find out about them...well, let's just say they find out the hard way."

"You'll have to teach my sisters," I said. Water Shallot would be a great deal more civilised if *every* woman knew those spells. "They'd be happy to learn."

"You could probably reinvent it for yourself," Caroline said. She winked at me. "It isn't a hard spell to cast. It just requires concentration and focus."

"I see." I considered it for a moment. It wasn't *easy* to remain calm and focused when one was under attack. A woman who was being harassed might not be *able* to cast the spell, even when her virtue was at stake. But the mere *threat* should be enough to convince people not to press. "My sisters could probably master it with ease."

A thought struck me. "Where did you go to school? I never asked."

Caroline opened her mouth, then paused as we heard a sound from up ahead. It sounded like an angry crowd. We turned the corner and peered at Louise's shop. The crowd was mustered at the far end of the road, shouting and screaming as the City Guardsmen—and Lord Dirac's armsmen—searched the shop. Angry men came from all directions, carrying makeshift weapons; women were hurrying away, some dragging preteen children. It felt as if all hell was about to break loose.

"The raids have started," Caroline said. "I guess they know who Louise is now."

I nodded, curtly.

CHAPTER THIRTY

"Stay back," I muttered as the crowd grew larger and angrier. "We don't want to get caught here."

"Teach your grandmother to suck eggs," Caroline muttered back. We inched towards the rear, trying to keep our eyes on the store. "I know what I'm doing."

The crowd's muttering grew louder as a middle-aged man and woman, their hands cuffed behind their backs, were escorted out of the store and shoved into a black carriage. Louise's parents, I guessed. Her sister and a young boy I didn't recognise were dragged out moments later, their hands cuffed too, and shoved into another carriage. I shuddered, feeling sick, as the guardsmen slammed the doors closed. The kids wouldn't know anything about their older sister's politics. They'd be held captive until the state of emergency came to an end, for nothing. Unless…I winced as the guardsmen started to ransack the store. They might be used as leverage to force Louise to surrender herself.

"Shame," someone shouted. A shower of bricks and slates rained down on the guardsmen. "Shame!"

"This way," I snapped. The crowd was surging forward, pushing and shoving as it tried to get to the guardsmen. They'd have cast wards to seal off the store and protect themselves, but I doubted they could shield themselves completely. "Hurry!"

The roar kept growing louder as we broke free and ran down the street. The other shops were slamming closed, iron shutters rattling into place. A handful of magicians were hastily casting spells to protect themselves and their property; others, without proper training in magic, were reliant on cold iron and good intentions. I saw a pair of men holding bludgeons, ready to fight if the mob overwhelmed their outer defences. They had no choice. The City Guard wouldn't come to their rescue at the moment.

"They didn't catch Louise," Caroline said. "Where do you think she is?"

I shrugged. We didn't *know* Louise hadn't been caught. If the raid had snatched her up, she would have been whisked back to North Shallot quicker than...well, anything. And yet, I had the feeling Caroline was right. The guardsmen wouldn't bother to arrest Louise's parents if they had an infinitely more valuable prisoner. Lord Dirac might have other ideas, but even *he* would have trouble compelling the guard to do more than the bare minimum if they'd thought they'd already won.

A man, wearing a long brown cloak, caught my eye. There was nothing suspicious about him, yet...I frowned, my instincts warning that he was somehow important. My eyes lingered, trying to see what had caught my attention. There was something oddly familiar in the way he moved...no, *she* moved. I walked over to her, already knowing who was under the hood. There was no one else it *could* be.

"Louise," I said.

Louise looked up at me, sharply. Her face was slightly blurred behind a charm. It would have fooled me if I hadn't known her. "Did you bring them here?"

"No," I said. "We have to get off the streets."

"This way." Louise headed down the street, without bothering to look back. "Come or not, as you please."

I exchanged glances with Caroline as we followed Louise through a maze of streets until we reached a small, backstreet pub. It looked rough. It was mid-afternoon and the regular drinkers were clearly already drunk. The bartender looked up, spotted Louise and nodded curtly as she led us up a flight of stairs and into a small meeting room. I checked around as she removed her cloak, her blonde hair damp. She looked as if she'd been through hell.

"They raided the club again," she said, as she dried her hair with a charm. "I was lucky to escape. And then..."

She sagged, slightly. "What'll happen to my family?"

Caroline cast a handful of privacy wards. "Do they know what you've been doing?"

"Dad knows...*something*," Louise said. "The others, no."

"I guess they'll be held until the state of emergency is lifted," Caroline said. I had the feeling she was trying to be comforting. Under a state of emergency, suspects could be dispatched to Skullbreaker Island without trial. "Do they know about *this* place?"

Louise shook her head. "No," she said. "Only the most senior amongst us know about here."

I frowned, considering it. The pub was well-hidden, concealed within a maze of alleyways that would make it difficult for the guardsmen to reach the entrance without being spotted and attacked by the locals. By the time they got here, Louise and her associates could be on their way to South Shallot. And yet, I had my suspicions. *Someone* had clearly identified Louise. Someone...I knew it hadn't been me. Or Caroline. Did she have a spy in her movement?

Probably, I thought. The Working Men predated Louise by decades. *Someone* could have been quietly watching the movement for Magus Court. Or someone else, upset by Louise's rise to power, could have ratted her out. It wouldn't be the first time someone turned traitor because they felt they'd been slighted in some way. *And whoever betrayed her might be still on the prowl.*

"We were trying to track down the source of the infernal devices," I said, sourly. "So far, we've drawn a blank."

"I didn't do it," Louise said. "I made some quiet enquires. If someone did...they're keeping very quiet about it."

"As is to be expected," Caroline said, curtly. "What are you going to do now?"

Louise frowned. "The runners should be on their way," she said. "And they'll tell us what's going on."

She stood, produced an odd-looking spellcaster from her tunic and started to cast a series of complex privacy and obscurification charms. I watched with quiet admiration. Louise might lack the brilliance of some of our fellow students—our *former* fellows, I reminded myself—but she was skilful enough to adapt the charms to serve her needs. Anyone who entered without the right counter charms would have problems remembering anything they saw in the chamber, whoever they were. I'd never seen anything like it, not outside a handful of demonstrations at school. Louise had definitely been taking lessons on the side.

I stood by the wall and watched as a handful of runners came in, gave their reports and left. The news wasn't good. A dozen clubs had been raided, the inhabitants either arrested or kicked out; the locals were responding by attacking guardsmen on the streets, driving them away from the guardposts or simply harassing them until they gave up and fled. The guardsmen had also raided over twenty homes and stores, most having no connection whatsoever to the socialists. I saw Louise frown as she put the picture together. It made no sense.

Caroline nudged me. "What do you want to do now?"

I shrugged. I didn't know. We'd drawn a complete blank. I mulled over possibilities, but came up with nothing. If the Great Houses had built the infernal devices...I scowled. It was starting to look as if someone had set out to create an excuse for declaring a state of emergency. If that was the case, they'd succeeded brilliantly. My fingers touched my ring. We should probably report to Sir Griffons, but what could we tell him? The only fact we'd established was that Louise was not responsible for the devices.

"Stay here, for the moment," I said. If someone had betrayed Louise, that person might be on his way already. "We might find a clue."

Caroline didn't seem impressed. "Where *else* might someone find the components to make an infernal device?"

"Jude's, perhaps," I said. The school had always been a little lax with expensive or dangerous potions ingredients. They were so wealthy they could afford to coat the entire school in dragon scales and never notice the cost. "If someone stole from the school…"

My voice trailed off. I doubted it was possible. Not easily, at least. Jude's might be a ramshackle old building, but there *were* hundreds of protections lining the walls. The staff might turn a blind eye to upperclassmen scaling the walls at night, but that would change if they thought the upperclassmen were stealing supplies. I made a mental note to check on it, when we had a moment. There might be a way to get supplies out of the school if they were packed in a warded trunk.

I rubbed my forehead as I watched the socialist leadership gather. They looked old, save for a couple of young men and Louise herself. I felt a twinge of contempt, mingled with pity. They were old enough to be Louise's grandfathers, yet they'd accomplished nothing. She'd done more than they in less than four months. I looked from genial face to genial face, wondering which was the spy. It would probably the one I least suspected. My lips curved into a smile. *That* would be Louise.

The leadership talked, and talked, and talked. Louise and the other youngsters seemed to have problems taking control of the conversation. The older socialists were talking about dogma and ideological issues that meant nothing to me, while Louise and her allies wanted to *do something*. I was starting to think I knew why the socialists had accomplished so little. My eyes moved from face to face, wondering if the oldsters had been bribed to bog the socialists down in ideological talk. If they were scrabbling over details that made no sense to the rest of us, it was no wonder the movement had never really taken off. What did a starving man care about dogma? Louise was practical enough to know better.

And that makes her a target, I mused. *Which one of you bastards is the spy?*

I shook my head, slowly, as the meeting finally came to an end. The *real* meat of the matter—apparently—hadn't taken long at all. I wasn't surprised. It was the idle chitter-chatter that wasted so much time. I wondered if they'd been *trying* to waste time. The people on the streets would turn away from the socialists if they refused to provide proper leadership.

Louise watched them go, then stood and came to me. "We're going to be carrying out a protest march," she said. "We're going to make it clear we won't stand to be pushed around."

I frowned. "A protest march?"

"Yeah." Louise looked at me. "A march through Water Shallot, into South Shallot and then back again."

Caroline stiffened. "Is that wise?"

Louise looked back at her, coldly. "Do you have a better idea?"

She waved a hand at the wall. "We have rights, except those rights have been taken away! We have freedoms, except those freedoms have *also* been taken away. And if we just let it happen, without protest, we'll lose them forever!"

I swallowed. I knew she was right, but...a protest march could easily turn into a bloody disaster. I could see a hundred ways the march could go wrong. And yet, Louise had to do *something*. The population outside was angry. Either that anger had to be steered into something productive or...I shuddered. If the runners were right, guardsmen were already being attacked. The cycle of violence was going to keep on building up and up until something exploded. It might already have reached a savage denouement.

"There's a public ban on protests," Caroline pointed out. "You'll be greeted by force."

"A ban which is illegal, because we have no real representation in Magus Court." The frustration in Louise's voice made me wince. "What else are we supposed to go? Grin and bear it?"

"I don't know," Caroline said. "But you could let us get on with finding the *real* terrorists?"

Louise looked me in the eye. "Do you even know where to begin?"

I shook my head. "No," I said. "We *could* check the rest of your socialists under truth spells..."

"There'd be a riot," Louise said. "Why?"

"One of them is a traitor," I said. "I *really* hope your obscurification charms hold."

Louise looked as if I'd just insulted her ancestors. "Those men kept the fire alive over the last few decades," she said. "They're above suspicion."

I exchanged glances with Caroline. Our instructors had drilled it into us, time and time again, that *no one* was above suspicion. The criminal might be the lowest of the low or...he might be the highest of the high. There were monsters in all walks of life, people who had worked themselves into a position where others protected them or chose to overlook the warning signs because they were from good families or they prayed regularly or something—anything—else that could hide a monster. Louise couldn't be sure her fellow leaders were trustworthy. Some people would sooner see the side lose than watch someone else lead it to victory.

"You can't be sure," I said, bluntly. "How did the guardsmen know about you?"

Louise's lips twisted. "I always assumed the secret would get out, sooner or later, if it wasn't *already* out. I've been making speeches for nearly a year!"

"You started while you were in school?" I remembered, suddenly, just how many times she'd sneaked out after class. "That's...impressive."

"The Challenge convinced me that *something* had to be done," Louise said. "I joined the socialists shortly afterwards."

I made a face. That added a new wrinkle. Magus Court might have known about Louise for months, but done nothing. I could see their point. Louise wasn't the sort of person they would have expected to gain influence in the Working Men's clubs. She was scholarly enough to be distracted, and ultimately neutralised, by ideological debate. And...she hadn't really accomplished anything, not yet. Magus Court might have decided to simply leave her alone until the infernal devices started exploding.

"Interesting," Caroline mused. She sounded impressed. "How do you intend to win?"

"I have a plan," Louise said. "But right now...we have other problems."

"You do," I agreed. "Do you trust your comrades?"

"We're not aristos," Louise said. "We don't backstab each other."

"Aristocrats are not the only people who knife their allies in the back." Caroline sounded irked. "Can you look me in the eye and tell me the people here"—she waved a hand at the wall, indicating Water Shallot—"don't backstab each other?"

"That's different," Louise said, weakly.

Caroline smirked. "No. It's not."

I kept my thoughts to myself. Caroline had a point. Water Shallot would be a much nicer place to live if the strong didn't prey on the weak. And yet, what betrayals there were came from utter desperation. The young betrayed the old, the poor betrayed the even poorer...it wasn't a game. I remembered the aristos gambling for absurdly high stakes or playing games with lives and shuddered. *They* couldn't lose, whatever they did. They wouldn't find themselves homeless, or enslaved, or at the mercy of a merciless creditor. They had no conception what life was like for the poor.

"Wait a couple of days," I said. "It might give us time to track down the terrorists."

Louise's eyes narrowed. "It will take a couple of days to organise the march anyway," she said. "And to get everything ready."

"Good." I met her eyes. "We have to catch the terrorists before all hell breaks loose."

"Adam, all hell has already broken loose," Louise said. She turned and went to the drinks' cabinet. "And we have to do something."

She poured herself a drink. "You want something?"

"No, thank you," I said. We were on duty. "Are you going to stay here?"

"Probably." Louise took a sip of her drink. "You're welcome to stay, you know."

Caroline elbowed me. "We shouldn't be staying here," she said. "Unless you'll let us run checks on your comrades."

I shot her a sharp look, but said nothing. It struck me as the smartest thing to do.

"It'll cause a riot," Louise said. "I *told* you it'll cause a riot."

"And without it, someone will betray you," Caroline said. "Who can you trust?"

Louise shrugged, then led the way through a concealed door and into a small bedroom. I admired the charms hiding the compartment, although the effect was somewhat spoilt by two midsized windows. Anyone who compared the exterior of the building to the interior would know there was a concealed room, unless the charms hid the windows as well as everything else. I suspected it wouldn't work, if someone searched the building from top to bottom. The windows opened onto an alleyway, two floors below. I was oddly reassured to see homeless sleeping below us. They'd have fled if the guardsmen were bearing down on us.

"I've slept in worse places," Louise said. "I had to share a dorm with Ayesha and Zeya McDonald."

"You poor thing." I had to smile. Ayesha and Zeya McDonald had been so snooty that they made Alana look like a commoner. "That must have been terrible."

"I'm sure the comfortable beds made up for it," Caroline said. She looked around, her eyes narrowing. "We'll continue our investigation. You can... start laying your plans."

"Thanks." Louise's voice dripped sarcasm. "I didn't know I needed your permission."

I held up a hand before Caroline could say anything. "We have to catch the terrorists," I said, for what felt like the hundredth time. I couldn't afford to forget that. I couldn't allow myself to become distracted. "And that..."

Something flickered, outside in the gloom. I looked up, an instant before the window shattered...

...And a man in black crashed into the room.

CHAPTER
THIRTY-ONE

I grabbed Louise by the arm and yanked her behind me, propelling her towards the door as the man in black stabbed with a spellcaster. A flash of green light shot past, splashing harmlessly against the wall. I cursed under my breath—an assassination spell, rather than something more destructive—and threw back a spell of my own. The assassin muttered a word I didn't recognise as the spellcaster shattered, then cast another spell. I felt it *dong* against my wards, sending me stumbling back. He was *strong*.

"Get Louise out of here," I shouted to Caroline. "Go home. I'll deal with him."

The assassin threw himself forward, slamming into me. I fell back as our wards collided, our magics grappling on a dozen levels at once. He was trying to *kill* me. I gritted my teeth, then compressed a pressure spell and threw it at him. The force of the impact should have smashed his bones to powder. Instead, he flew back and landed neatly on the far wall. I was reluctantly impressed, even as I hurled another spell that shattered the wall into powder. I didn't think *I* could have pulled that off.

Caroline hurried past, catching hold of Louise and rushing her down the stairs. I hoped she'd have the wit to take Louise to our inn, then put the thought out of my mind as the assassin ran across the ceiling and dropped down on me. I caught his arm and twisted it, trying to hurl him to the floor.

He rolled, dodging a blow that should have smashed him flatter than a pancake. His answering blast missed me by bare millimetres—I felt a wave of heat prickling my skin—and tore through the ceiling. The entire building shook. I heard shattering windows and falling debris in the distance. I hoped—desperately—that Louise and Caroline had made it out.

The assassin growled, his magic curling into a whip and lashing out. I sidestepped it, then jumped forward. Power shimmered around me as I punched him again and again, each blow powerful enough to break bones. He countered with a technique I'd never seen before, the air around him hardening for a few brief seconds…just long enough to block my blows before I killed him. The building shuddered again, the wooden floor starting to give way underneath our feet. I cursed as he slammed a punch into my chest, hurling me back. I heard more falling debris as the assassin stood, magic crackling around his hands. He was going to kill me…

I summoned my own magic and threw myself forward, slamming into him with all the force I could muster. We plunged back, smashing through the remnants of the wall and falling down to the alley below. I thought I saw him grimace as he hastily cast a levitation spell, a fraction of a second too late. The impact knocked the wind out of both of us. I forced myself to stagger to my feet, silently thanking Sir Muldoon for his lessons. He'd made me work to build up my endurance. The assassin seemed to have similar training.

He rolled to his feet, his hands moving in a complex pattern. I sensed the curse building and ducked, casting a levitation spell on everything within reach as a nasty-looking flash of eldritch light shot past. Homeless people ran in all directions as my spell scooped up debris and threw it at him, trying to punch through his wards. He wove a complicated protective spell as I channelled two extra spells of my own, throwing more and more magic into the morass. I gathered myself, then ran forward. His spells snapped and snarled at both of us. I smirked, remembering my instructors. They'd cautioned me—time and time again—about the dangers of accidentally mixing up my targets. The assassin hadn't had time to protect himself from his own spells.

I shoved forward, bringing my magic into close contact with his. His face twisted into a snarl as I pushed harder, trying to rip his spells apart. It was an endurance test now. The loser would be the one who ran out of magic first. I felt my head start to pound as I whaled on him, shaping my magic into a sharp knife to cut through his wards. His hand came up, twisting oddly. I barely had a second to see the tiny spellcaster in his palm before he jabbed it at me. The fireball threw me back along the alley, dumping me in a muddy puddle.

"Bastard," I managed. I should have seen that coming. The assassin, whoever he was, was no slouch. "You…"

The assassin stood and stalked towards me. I tried to stand, but my body was hurting too much. I felt cold, cold and wet as he raised his hand. I could sense a curse crackling around his fingertips. I swallowed, hard. I wasn't going to die, not before I'd earned my spurs. I reached out with my magic, yanking on what remained of the pub's wall. A shower of debris crashed down. He glanced up, deflecting the debris and giving me a chance to pull myself up and throw myself on him. I pulled a cuff out of my belt and shoved it against his chest. His magic sparkled and died. I didn't *need* to wrap it around his wrist…

His eyes hardened, then went blank. His entire body relaxed. I blinked in surprise. A trick of some kind? Or…or what? His eyes were completely blank. He looked like a newborn baby, not a trained assassin. I carefully cuffed him, then searched his outfit. Another tiny spellcaster, no bigger than a small pencil; a spellbreaker…a couple of Devices of Power I didn't recognise…and a small pouch of money. There were no papers, no clue as to his name. I sat back, studying him. His face was completely unknown.

He had some training, I thought. It was a colossal understatement. He'd come within bare seconds of killing me. *An aristo? Or…what?*

"Get up, scum," I ordered, stiffly. "Who are you?"

He said nothing. He made no move. His mouth opened, emitting a trickle of drool. I recoiled in disgust, a chill running down my spine. He could have been faking it, but…I leaned forward, casting a diagnostic spell. There was a hint of magic—a potion—in his mouth. When I took a sample, the magic dimmed. I shuddered as I carefully preserved as much as I could. The potion—whatever it was—was clearly dangerous.

"Fuck," I muttered. "What am I going to do with you?"

I hesitated, then cast a transfiguration spell and turned him into a small statue. It wouldn't last, but I needed to move. The guardsmen might have heard the commotion, wherever they were. The entire pub was on the verge of collapse. I shoved the statue and his gear into my pocket, then turned and ran. I couldn't afford to be caught, not now. The guardsmen would ask questions I couldn't even *begin* to answer.

Louise would have been killed, if we hadn't been with her. My heart twisted at the thought. Louise had good marks in defensive magic, but the assassin had been an order of magnitude more dangerous than anyone we'd duelled in class. *Someone told the bastard where to find her.*

I felt my body start to ache as I made my way through the alleyways, finally emerging a little too close to my father's shop for comfort. The streets were deserted, even though night was falling rapidly. A handful of bodies lay on the corner, battered into bloody pulps and stripped naked. I shuddered as I recognised one of the guardsmen we'd met, back before the first infernal device had detonated. It looked as if they'd been beaten to death by overwhelming force.

"May your ancestors bless you and take you," I said. No one deserved to die at the hands of a mob. "And may you be welcome in their hallowed halls forever."

I wanted to do *something* for the bodies, but there wasn't time. Instead, I forced myself to start moving. The pain was growing stronger, making it harder to concentrate. My side felt as if I'd been repeatedly punched. It was getting harder to breathe. I wondered if I'd been cursed as I reached the inn, stumbling through the door and heading up the stairs. The receptionist said nothing. We were paying through the nose for privacy. My legs threatened to give out as I reached the top of the stairs, parted the wards and crashed into the room.

"Adam!" Caroline caught my arm as I nearly collapsed. "What happened?"

"I got him." I pulled the statue from my pocket and shoved it at her. "He's not quite himself."

Caroline nodded and pressed a bottle of water to my lips. Louise was sitting on the bed, staring at me. I must have looked terrible. My face was black and blue, my cloak was soaked in muddy water...I probably looked unrecognisable. The water tasted so pure I wanted to keep drinking. I nearly snapped at Caroline when she pulled the water away.

"Help me get undressed," I said. My fingers felt numb. "Check me for damage."

Caroline nodded and went to work. "You've got a couple of broken ribs and a whole collection of bruises," she said, as she undressed me carefully. "Give me a moment and I'll heal you up."

Louise stepped over to me. "What happened?"

I focused as Caroline started casting healing spells. "He nearly killed me," I said. The entire fight was a blur. "I got the drop on him. Got the cuff on him. And he just...went blank."

"Blank?" Louise helped hold my arms so Caroline could heal the bruises. "What do you mean, *blank*?"

"He looked and acted like a baby," I said. My body felt better, but the aches and pains were still gnawing at my mind. "I couldn't get anything out of him."

"Have a wash," Caroline said, once she'd finished. "And then we'll look at your prisoner."

Louise let out a gasp as I removed the rest of my clothes and stumbled into the bathroom. I didn't know why she was so surprised. She'd seen me naked before. Perhaps she was just surprised I'd undressed in front of Caroline. The shower was as pathetic as I'd expected—it dribbled so weakly that I would have had a better wash if I'd danced in the rain—but at least the water was warm. I eyed the growing collection of bruises on my skin as I towelled down, feeling a little bit stronger. The assassin had come far too close to ending my career before it was begun.

"Put him in a containment circle," I said. The assassin hadn't tried to free himself from the spell, which was odd. Students learnt such spells very quickly or they spent much of their schooling as frogs or statues or whatever. "And then we can see what we can learn."

Caroline set up the circle, then muttered the counterspell. The statue warped and twisted, then morphed back into the assassin. The man stared at the ceiling, unmoving. I thought for a moment he was dead, before I saw the steady rise and fall of his chest. He was breathing, but not much else. Caroline leaned forward, casting a handful of spells. Her dark eyes narrowed as the results came back. I could tell she didn't like them.

"There's very little brain activity," she said. "I'd say he was in a coma if his eyes weren't open."

Louise leaned forward. "Is he faking it?"

"I don't think so." Caroline sounded doubtful. "It would be like pretending to be dead by committing suicide."

"Ouch," I said. "Who *is* he?"

"I don't know," Louise said. "A Rubén? He's got the blond hair."

"Wrong shade," Caroline said. "House Rubén prides itself on golden hair."

I nodded. Akin—and his disgraced sister—both had golden hair, hair so bright it practically shone under the sunlight. Every Rubén was blond, save for those who'd married into the family. The assassin, however, wasn't *that* blond. His hair was more sandy than golden.

My eyes looked him up and down as Caroline carefully undressed him. His face was bland, utterly forgettable. There was no hint of strong character or crippling weakness, nothing that would make him stick in my mind. His hair was short, probably tinted…his eyes were blue, his nose just a *little* too small. I could have passed him on the street and never taken notice of his presence. I supposed that was what someone would have wanted, in an assassin. A man who could walk into a house and kill without being noticed would be very useful indeed.

Caroline poked him with her magic. "Very healthy, probably a combination of heavy training and exercise mixed with potions. Quite muscular... strong enough to give someone a hard time without magic. No obvious injuries, beyond the beating he took today, save for some traces of internal scarring. I'd say he undertook a training regime like ours."

Louise coughed. "Are you saying he's a Kingsman?"

"No," Caroline said. "I'd say he was trained as a lone operator."

"By whom?" I scowled. There weren't many suspects. "What are we dealing with here?"

I listed the options, one by one. "The Great Houses—or Magus Court—could have trained him," I said. I looked at the assassin's collection of tools and nodded to myself. "The King could have trained him too, I suppose. But there aren't many other possible suspects."

Louise looked up. "Prince Jacob?"

"He wouldn't want to kill *you*," Caroline pointed out. "You're *nothing* to him."

"And if he did have a trained assassin on his payroll, he'd have bigger and better targets," I said, before Louise could snap at Caroline. "He'd be killing people in North Cairnbulg."

"True," Caroline agreed. "Zadornov?"

"What?" Louise stared at her. *She'd* clearly heard of the man. "Zadornov?"

"We had a bit of a run-in with him," I said. I didn't want to tell her everything. "But I can't see him sending a trained assassin to get us."

"He certainly has reason to want us dead," Caroline pointed out. "We're assuming Louise was the target. But it could have been us instead."

"Perhaps," I said. I wasn't so sure. Zadornov would presumably prefer an uneasy stalemate to an all-out war with the Kingsmen. Magus Court wouldn't shield him if King Rufus wanted his head. There were certainly no political considerations that might mandate standing up to the king. "But it would be one hell of a risk."

"True," Caroline said.

She studied the potion in the assassin's mouth. "I've never seen anything like this," she said. "Have you?"

"No." I'd never had the knack for potions. I'd mastered the basics to pass my exams, but I lacked the insight that would have made me a Potions Master. I couldn't even *begin* to analyse the mystery potion. "What do you think it *does*?"

"I don't know," Caroline admitted. She put the sample back in stasis. "We need an expert. A *real* expert."

I frowned. "Rebecca Travis?"

"She's still studying for her mastery," Caroline said. She smiled when I shot her a questioning look. "Didn't you *notice* the paperwork on her desk?"

"No." I shook my head. "And we don't know if we can trust her either."

Louise leaned forward. "What about Magistra Loanda?"

"...Good thought," I said. "Although she *did* give me a few hundred million detentions."

"You exaggerate," Louise said. She laughed, sweetly. "It was only a *hundred* million detentions."

"You're both mad," Caroline said. She rolled her eyes at us. "And besides, do we have any other options?"

I considered it, but drew a blank. There were no other Kingsmen in the city. We might not have *time* to take the sample out of the city. And the vast majority of Potions Masters within Shallot were either aristos or aristo clients. Magistra Loanda was the only one I could think of who didn't have strong ties to the aristocracy. Hell, she had a long-standing rivalry with Lady Sorceress Sofia Aguirre. She might help us, if only to embarrass her rival.

"I'll go tomorrow," I said. It was already dark outside. I doubted it would be safe to try to cross the bridges tonight. Besides, I needed a rest. My body was reminding me just how close I'd come to being killed. "In fact, I'll go alone. Louise needs a bodyguard."

"And I'm elected?" Caroline didn't look pleased. "Why me?"

"Because you'll cause less comment if anyone sees you, I suppose," Louise said. She didn't look pleased either, but at least she wasn't trying to argue. Instead, she pointed to the assassin. "What are we going to do with this fellow?"

"We keep him in stasis," I said. I wasn't sure the assassin could eat or drink anything, in his current state. It was starting to look as if his brain had been wiped clean of *everything*. "And see what Magistra Loanda has to say."

"Good, I suppose," Louise said. She grinned, suddenly. "So tell me... which of us is getting the bed?"

"You two can share," I said. "I'll sleep on the floor."

Louise winked at Caroline. "You've got him well trained."

"Oh, shut up," I said. I cast a spell, putting the assassin in stasis. "We'd better get some sleep. Tomorrow is going to be a whole new day."

"Yeah," Caroline said. "And all hell is going to break loose."

CHAPTER THIRTY-TWO

Caroline was right, I decided as I walked to the bridges. All hell *was* on the verge of breaking loose. The streets were dominated by angry men, while the schools were closed and the vast majority of shops were under heavy guard. I hoped the students I'd tutored were safe, wherever they were. There were no women or children in evidence as I passed through the gentrified section, then crossed the bridges. A small army of guardsmen kept watch on the far side. It looked as if they'd chosen to withdraw from the remainder of Water Shallot.

I passed through the guardpost and hurried down towards the school. I'd skipped graduation—I'd been at Haddon Hall, I thought—and I'd assumed I'd never return, but now...I shook my head, feeling oddly out of place as I approached the gatehouse. Skullion stood there, glowering. For a moment, I thought he'd known I was coming. It took me long seconds to realise he probably gave everyone the same treatment.

"Yes?"

I reminded myself, sharply, that Skullion could no longer intimidate me. "I'm here to see Magistra Loanda."

"Really?" Skullion looked as if he didn't believe it. "A student comes back, unable to live in the outside world?"

"No." I controlled my anger with an effort. "I need to consult with Magistra Loanda."

Skullion pressed his fingers against his amulet. There was a long pause. I waited, knowing he was communing with the wards. I'd always suspected the tutors had ways to communicate they'd never discussed with us. I supposed they had no choice. They weren't meant to supervise our every move, but they had to be ready to step in if someone did something really dangerous. The upperclassmen couldn't be expected to do everything.

"She's in her lab," Skullion said, without any detectable emotion. "She'll be pleased to see you there."

He stepped to one side, allowing me to walk through the gates and up to the school. Jude's looked as ramshackle as ever, a collection of buildings that had steadily merged into one giant mess, but I couldn't help feeling as though I was coming home. I'd practically lived at Jude's for the last seven years. I could have applied to join the tutoring staff, if I'd seen no other options. I'd just felt that would have been a waste of my talents. And I'd hated the thought of trying to teach twenty or so students at once.

The corridors felt eerily empty as I made my way down to the potions' lab. A handful of servants were scrubbing the floors, carefully removing all traces of last year's batch of potions disasters. I felt a stab of pity, mingled with bemusement. I'd washed the floor myself often enough during detention. Perhaps Magistra Loanda thought we students hadn't done a good job. Or, more likely, she thought the floors needed to be properly scrubbed after term finished for the summer. I smiled as I peered into her private lab, seeing her sitting at a heavy wooden table. A cauldron of golden liquid was bubbling in front of her.

"One moment," Magistra Loanda said, without looking up. "I just have to put this on to simmer."

I took a chair and waited. Magistra Loanda looked like a stern old lady—she was easily the oldest tutor in the school—but no one ever took her lightly. We'd never been allowed to forget that it was a great honour to have her tutoring us in potions. There weren't many people who matched her breadth of knowledge, let alone her skill. I was mildly surprised she wasn't selling her talent to the highest bidder. Maybe she'd thought she wanted to be more than an aristo's private brewer. Or...

"Adam." Magistra Loanda fiddled with the cauldron, then stood and paced over to me. "I assume you're not seeking a reference?"

"No," I said. I showed her my ring, then pulled the potions sample out of my pocket. "I was hoping for a consultation."

Magistra Loanda's eyes narrowed. "Can I ask why?"

"I need this potion identified," I said. "And I need a countermeasure."

"I see." Magistra Loanda said nothing for a long moment. I wondered, suddenly, just how much she'd been told. Tutors talked, but did they talk about me? "Let me have a look."

Her face darkened as she sniffed the sample, then drew an alchemical spellcaster from her pocket and cast a handful of spells. I watched, grimly, as she drew out smaller samples and poked at them for a few seconds, then dropped the remainder of the sample in an empty cauldron. I tensed, reminding myself it was all part of the procedure. We hadn't been able to take a proper sample. There was a good chance the sample was contaminated.

Magistra Loanda looked up at me. "Where did you get this?"

"I'm not at liberty to say," I said. "What *is* it?"

"It wipes memories," Magistra Loanda said, stiffly. "*Every* memory. A person who drank the potion would lose *everything*, up to and including the memory of how to live."

"You've seen this before," I said.

"There's a girl in the asylum who's somewhere around thirty years old," Magistra Loanda said. "Mentally, she's six. She took a dose of the potion and it wiped out her entire life. Her handlers have been trying to re-educate her, in the hopes it would bring back the lost memories, but so far they've failed completely. She's a child in an adult's body."

I cursed under my breath. "There's no cure?"

"None that we've been able to find." Magistra Loanda studied the cauldron thoughtfully. "I kept abreast of the affair, after the House War. We never figured out who'd invented the potion. Stregheria Aguirre was not a

Potions Mistress. We were pretty sure it wasn't *her* who came up with the potion, but..."

She frowned, expressively. "I take it someone used the potion?"

"Yes." I told her as much as I dared about the assassin. "We need to find a way to get his memories back."

"I doubt you'll succeed," Magistra Loanda said. "I'll play around with the sample you brought me, if you like, but I don't think I'll get anywhere. We never managed to work out how the potion actually works, let alone how to counter it. House Aguirre threw a lot of money and resources into it and drew a complete blank."

I scowled. "House Aguirre?"

"Stregheria Aguirre certainly commissioned the potion," Magistra Loanda said. "And she betrayed her entire house."

"I see," I said. "And there's *nothing* you can do?"

"No," Magistra Loanda said. "Those memories? There's a very good chance they're gone for good."

I shuddered. There were plenty of memory charms that stole memories, for reasons both good and bad, but almost all of them could be countered. I'd been taught how to look for missing memories during training, although we'd been warned not to try to bring them back without a proper mind healer in attendance. But this...I felt a pang of sympathy for the assassin, even though he'd tried to kill me. His life had been utterly destroyed. I doubted anyone was going to waste time trying to rebuild his mind...and, even if they did, the new personality wouldn't be *him*.

"I'll play around with the sample, if you leave it with me," Magistra Loanda said. "But otherwise..."

"Please," I said. I needed answers, but I doubted I'd get them from her. "And if you could keep the sample to yourself, I'd be very grateful."

Magistra Loanda nodded. "Come back in a week," she said. "But I really can't promise anything."

I nodded, then pulled the tiny spellcaster out of my pocket. "Have you ever seen anything like this before?"

"It's a focusing tool," Magistra Loanda said. She took it, turned it over and over in her hand, then passed it back to me. "They're used in specialised charms work. But this one is surprisingly small."

She shrugged. "It could have come from anywhere."

"Thanks," I said. "I owe you one."

I stood, bowed and made my way back out of the school, memories mocking me. I'd had some good times at Jude's. Skullion nodded curtly to me as I passed the gatehouse and headed down the street, back to Water Shallot. The guardsmen made no attempt to bar my way as I crossed the bridge. Clearly, they were only concerned about people heading *out* of Water Shallot. I made a mental bet with myself that the bridges to North Shallot were sealed completely, then shrugged. Right now, it didn't matter. It might keep things quiet if the guardsmen stayed on the other side of the river.

But they won't stay there for very long, I thought. *Blood has been shed now.*

The streets beyond the bridges were quiet, but I could see men carrying weapons and readying themselves for a fight. The vast majority of stores were closed, despite hungry people banging on their shutters and shouting for the storekeepers to open up. I was tempted to swing by my father's shop and see if it was open, but I didn't have time. Instead, I made my way down to the docks. I might just get some answers from Malachi Rubén. The only question was…could his answers be trusted?

"I need to speak to your master," I said, when Malachi's servant opened the door. "Please."

The girl nodded, then led me up the stairs and into Malachi's chamber. I couldn't help noticing that he'd doubled or tripled the wards protecting his house, as if he expected death and destruction to sweep over Water Shallot within the next few days. He might well be right. I was surprised he was still here. Whatever the terms of his banishment, they presumably didn't include standing still and waiting to be murdered. He could easily have left the city if he wished.

"Young Adam," Malachi said. He sounded as if he'd expected me. I was fairly sure he hadn't. "What can I do for you?"

"Tell me about Stregheria Aguirre," I said. "And what she did."

Malachi's lips drew back in a savage smile. "How long do you have?"

"Long enough," I said. I had to get back to Caroline—we'd planned to meet for lunch—but I didn't have a deadline. "What did she do?"

"Stregheria Aguirre was a horrible woman who thought she should wield power," Malachi said. "House Aguirre didn't agree. She simply couldn't be trusted, they said, to wield power responsibly. Power and authority passed down to Joaquin Aguirre, the High Magus, and Stregheria got sidelined. She didn't like it."

"Charming," I muttered.

"Quite," Malachi agreed. "She started plotting. She made contact with the Crown Prince, who'd also been denied power and authority, and made common cause with him. They were midway through their planning when they discovered Joaquin's daughter had a rare, apparently unique, talent. She could make Objects of Power."

He smiled. "Stregheria had Caitlyn kidnapped, although no one knew it at the time. She badly underestimated the little girl and her friends. Caitlyn managed to escape and get back to the city. Undaunted, Stregheria and the Crown Prince put their plan into operation anyway. They triggered a House War and used it as an excuse to bring the Crown Prince's troops into the city. Their intention was to take control, ship in *more* troops from North Cairnbulg and eventually march on Tintagel itself. King Rufus wouldn't have any time to prepare a defence, particularly against Objects of Power, before his world came crashing down."

He shrugged. "The plan failed," he said. "They didn't manage to take control of Jude's. Caitlyn broke free—again—and led the students to retake the school. You were there, were you not?"

I nodded. "Yeah."

"Caitlyn killed Stregheria, somehow. No two rumours agree on precisely *what* happened under the school. Akin killed the Crown Prince. The coup crumbled and most of the plotters were rounded up. Isabella"—his face twisted—"was sent into exile. And that was that."

I blinked. I'd heard the rumours, but...I'd never really grasped the *full* scale of the plan. It had seemed unbelievable. And yet...

My stomach churned. I knew people who'd been killed in the House War. They hadn't been aristos. They'd been ordinary people, unlucky enough to be in the wrong place at the wrong time when Stregheria made her bid for power. I believed it. Aristos didn't care about commoners who were caught in the middle when they went to war. Stregheria had left hundreds of bodies in her wake. Most had never been formally remembered. Only their families had mourned.

"And then what?" My voice was harsh. "What happened to the rest of the plotters?"

"They were tried, convicted and...punished," Malachi said, evenly. "The aristocrats who'd backed the Crown Prince were either executed or sent into exile. King Rufus blamed the Crown Prince's circle for leading him into treason. The Crown Princess was stripped of the custody of her son and ordered back to North Cairnbulg."

"And here?" I looked down at my hands. "What happened to her supporters?"

"Most of them were executed," Malachi said. "A couple committed suicide. Isabella was about the only one to escape severe consequences and that was only on account of her age. Her father"—his lips twisted—"found it convenient to blame everything on Stregheria. It wasn't as if Stregheria was alive to argue."

"And so she got away with it," I snarled.

"Quite," Malachi agreed.

I met his eyes. "Did any of the plotters survive?"

Malachi laughed, humourlessly. "If they did, they kept it very quiet. The Great Houses were in a murderous mood. Even now...if anyone survived, no one knows it."

"So they could still be out there," I mused. There was no way to be sure, but the memory-wiping potion couldn't be a coincidence. "What are they doing?"

"Probably keeping their heads down, while awaiting their opportunity to cause trouble," Malachi said. "What else would you like to know?"

I barely heard him. The pieces were finally fitting together. It was clear the plotters had the ability to build infernal devices. It was also clear they had a Potions Master or a Master Brewer on their team. And...they had a handful of assassins and thugs under their command. And...I shuddered. It was starting to make a certain kind of sense. Push for a state of emergency, trigger off a riot...and take control in the chaos. If Malachi was right, Stregheria had pulled together an alliance of the discontented. They might have survived her death.

And the memory-wipe potion ensured that anyone who was caught was unable to talk, I thought. There were charms—compulsion charms—that could ensure someone took the potion if there was no way out. If there was no cure...I shivered. The plotters might have a cure. Or they might have lied and told their people that there was a cure...

"I know everything," Malachi said. "What else would you like to know?"

I snorted. "Who's behind the plot?"

"I wish I knew," Malachi said. "I know *practically* everything."

He paused. "But if you want a guess..."

I narrowed my eyes. "Who?"

"People don't risk overturning the gameboard if they're winning," Malachi said. "And they don't risk it—even if they're losing—unless they expect the defeat to be fatal. *That's* when they start trying to rewrite the rules. The people who stand to lose, when the Rubén-Aguirre alliance is formalised, are the people who are most likely to be behind the plot. Who loses out? Answer that question and you'll have your plotters."

"I see," I said. "And who *does* lose out?"

Malachi bared his teeth. "Davys Rubén. Or Petal Rubén. Or...there's probably a bunch of people in House Aguirre who also stand to lose. Wouldn't it be funny if they came up with a joint plan to bring the alliance crashing down before it was too late?"

"You don't know," I said. Malachi had every reason to hate his family. His *former* family. And yet, did that make him *wrong*? I wished, for the first time in my life, that I'd spent more time studying the Great Houses. Knowing who was related to whom might have come in handy. "It could be anyone."

"It will be the losers." Malachi shrugged. "Why rock the boat if you're *winning*?"

I nodded, coldly. It *did* make sense. The aristos wouldn't hesitate to set off a war. They'd be certain of victory. Why *not* set off a war? They wouldn't care about how many people got caught in the gears and mashed to a bloody pulp. They wouldn't care about...I shuddered, remembering Sir Muldoon's horror stories. There was nothing *romantic* about war. I'd seen the last House War. *This* war was going to be worse.

"Thank you for your time," I said. "I'll show myself out."

Malachi rang a bell. "My servant will show you out," he said. "And good luck."

I eyed him, suspiciously. He wouldn't have told me anything that could be easily disproved. I was sure of it. But...it was quite possible to say something completely misleading, without actually lying. Malachi had chosen his words very carefully. It was possible there might be a cell within House Rubén—or House Aguirre—that wanted to trigger a war and destroy the alliance. It was also possible the real plotters came from somewhere else.

The serving girl led me downstairs. I looked around, wondering what was behind the closed doors. It could be anything...Malachi might be living in Water Shallot, but it was clear he wasn't short of funds. House Rubén paid him a stipend to stay away. I wondered what he'd really done, before he'd been kicked out. Perhaps I could ask Akin...

And you'd never be sure if you could trust his answer, I thought, as I stepped onto the streets. The door closed behind me with an audible *thud*, the wards slipping into place a second later. *But that's true of everyone these days, isn't it?*

CHAPTER
THIRTY-THREE

The streets felt even darker as I made my way from the docks, following one of the canals as it headed up to the inner warehouses and the river beyond. There were no barges traversing the murky water, no sailing boats or canoes making their way up and down the canal. It felt wrong, somehow. I shuddered as I realised what it meant for the locals. If the canals were shutting down, if the bargemen and dockyard workers were not being paid, it wouldn't be long before they started to run out of money. Too many people lived on the edge for anyone's peace of mind. They'd be heading to the pawnbrokers and the loan sharks before the week came to an end.

I shivered as a cold wind blew across the canal, icy water splashing against my face. The idea of thousands of people becoming slaves to the loan sharks was bad enough, but it could be worse. A great deal worse. If food started to run out...what then? Water Shallot didn't produce its own food. Even the *fish* stayed away from the polluted waters. If people started to starve...I looked at the grim tenement blocks, wondering how many people were already on the verge of starvation. My family had been well-off, by the standards of Water Shallot, and we'd run short of food once or twice. I shuddered to think how it could be—would be—worse for the poorest amongst us.

The path twisted as I approached a bridge, inviting me to either walk under the road or step up to the road itself. I hesitated, then clambered onto the bridge. My father had often told me never to follow the canals under the bridges and, even now, I feared what I might find. There were supposed to be entire *worlds* down there, under the city. I found it hard to believe that hundreds of people might be living in the sewers, but it was true enough that some people went under the bridge and never came out again. I wouldn't feel safe without a small army at my back.

I sucked in my breath as I kept walking, the cold air gnawing at me. The streets were eerily quiet. I saw a pair of naked bodies lying in an alley, but I didn't dare check for signs of life. Guardsmen, perhaps, or merely homeless who'd come off worse in a fight. Their clothes would have been stolen and sold to the poor and desperate. There was no room for sentimentality in Water Shallot. The aristos might have superstitions about wearing second-hand clothes. The poor couldn't afford to have qualms. I...

"Stop," a voice barked. "Stop!"

A spell slammed into my back. My entire body went limp. I crumpled to the ground. I tried to muster a counterspell, but I'd been caught by surprise and—before I could cast the spell—I found a cuff wrapped around my wrist. My magic shivered, then vanished. A sense of tiredness threatened to overcome me as my hands were bound, then I was rolled over. I found myself staring at one of Lord Dirac's armsmen.

Shit, I thought. I'd been distracted. I'd *practiced* being aware of my surroundings, damn it! If nothing else, Francis had taught me to be wary at all times. *I...*

My body twitched. The spell was wearing off. I still felt oddly tired and heavy, as if I'd been hexed or dosed with a sleeping potion. My captor yanked me to my feet as a black carriage rattled up, then picked me up and shoved me into the compartment. It was larger than I'd realised, clearly designed for transporting prisoners. I moaned as my captor wrapped a chain around my ankle. Escape was clearly going to be tricky.

"Be quiet," he growled. Another black-clad man glared at me. "You're under arrest."

I swallowed, hard. My voice felt thick and ungainly, as if it was no longer mine. "On what charge?"

My captor eyed me, coldly. "On the charge of harassing a city merchant, remaining within the city despite clear orders to leave and whatever other charges develop in the course of our investigation."

He stepped back as I cursed under my breath. Rebecca. I'd pushed her hard and...she'd made an official complaint. Of *course* she had. Her shop was in South Shallot, not *Water* Shallot. The City Guardsmen had taken her seriously. And so had Magus Court's enforcers. Rebecca was a Bolingbroke client. They'd probably lit a fire under Lord Dirac. I guessed they'd told him to drop everything until I was in jail.

My mind raced. Rebecca...or Zadornov? He might have ordered his loan shark to make a complaint, gambling that it would get me removed from the city. He might...I shook my head. There was no way to know. And it didn't matter. I couldn't afford to go to jail, not now. Sir Griffons would not be pleased. The political implications would be disastrous. If nothing else, Magus Court could use my presence to score points on the king.

The door banged shut. I heard the armsmen scrambling into the front seat. The carriage shuddered, then started to move. I wondered, as I twisted as best as I could, just where we were going. It would take at least fifteen minutes to drive to the bridges, even with the streets practically empty. And if people had seen them yank me off the streets...it was quite possible they'd try to free me. I shuddered, despite myself. The armsmen were just doing their jobs. They didn't deserve to be beaten to death by an angry mob.

I stared at the cuffs. The band wrapped around my left wrist was the real problem, but...I forced myself to think. Cutting my hand off wasn't an option, not here. I wasn't carrying a knife. And yet...I twisted and squirmed, trying to get my hands on the spellcaster. I couldn't channel magic through it, but there was still a charge within the wood. It might just be enough to unlock the cuff...I gripped the spellcaster in my fingers, then carefully jabbed it against the cuff. There was a surge of magic, powerful enough to make my fingers *sting*, and the cuff came free. I breathed a sigh of relief, then hastily freed myself. The handcuffs and the manacle were easy to remove with magic.

Move, I thought. The hatch was closed and warded. Unlike most ward designs, it was crafted to make it difficult to remove from the inside. They'd taken precautions in case a prisoner managed to break free. *Don't give them any time to react.*

I gathered myself, then carefully unpicked the wards. Alarms howled as the spells came undone, the carriage coming to a halt before I could cancel them. Whoever had crafted the wards had added a charm to raise the alarm if they were opened, even if whoever opened them was *meant* to be there. I kicked the hatch open and jumped, ducking a spell that flashed above my head. The armsmen reacted quickly, too quickly. I threw back a hex of my own, using the carriage for cover as I scanned the street. We were nearing another bridge...

The carriage lurched, nearly toppling over and crushing me. I cursed—they were using their carriage as a weapon—and cast the brightest light spell I could. They staggered back, rubbing their eyes as they tried to cast cancelation spells. That wasn't going to get them anywhere, not in a hurry. I hadn't hit them with *blinding* spells. I jumped back, then turned and ran towards the bridge. I wasn't going to risk injuring or killing them. They were just doing their jobs.

Another spell crashed out at me. I blocked it as I reached the bridge. The churning water below looked sickly-gray, as if someone was dredging the river somewhere north of Shallot. I took a breath, then cast a breathing spell and jumped into the canal. The cold struck me like a hammer as I forced myself to swim under the bridge, my eyes stinging as I tried to stay underwater. They wouldn't come after me, would they? I didn't believe it.

My lungs started to hurt, spell or no spell, as I reached the surface. It was dark and cold...I saw a pair of children living under the bridge, staring as I treaded water. My heart went out for them as I kept swimming, ducking back under the water as I came out from under the bridge and kept moving. The foul water would make it harder for the guardsmen to catch me, I was sure. They didn't have the numbers to place a guard on *every* possible way out of the water.

I surfaced again, my lungs gasping for clean air. The breathing spell didn't seem to be working. I wondered, as I turned and peered at the water, if there *was* oxygen in the canal. There certainly *should* have been. It looked as if no one was chasing me, but I kept swimming regardless. I had to keep moving until I reached cover. A barge drifted by the side of the canal, a teenage girl sitting in the prow. I waved to her, then pulled myself to the edge and scrambled out of the canal. The girl stared at me, then vanished inside the barge. I didn't blame her. I could be anyone.

And most smart people don't go swimming in the canal, I thought, as I muttered a pair of spells to dry myself. My cloak and tunic were horrifically stained. There was no way I could pass them on to anyone, not now. If I'd ruined my clothes as a kid, my father would have been enraged. We didn't have the money to waste anything. *He'd have thought I'd done it deliberately.*

I looked up as an older man stepped out of the barge. "Who are you?"

"None of your business," I said. "Do you have a set of clothes I could buy?"

"A cloak," a man said. "And you get your ass out of here at once."

I nodded, passed him a silver piece and took the cloak he offered me. It was a tatty thing, but it would do. I wrapped it around myself, cast a pair of illusion spells to conceal my face and started to walk. The air felt colder, somehow. I kept a wary eye open for more guardsmen—the bastards had found me somehow—as I walked. I saw nothing, even when I got a glimpse at the bridge I'd used as a diving board. I hoped the armsmen had headed back to the bridges. I felt a twinge of pity. Lord Dirac was going to blast them both for incompetence.

They should have taken my spellcaster, I thought. *And everything else I was carrying too.*

I stayed in the shadows as I made my slow way back home. The streets were starting to liven up, long lines of shoppers forming outside the shops. A crowd was shouting curses at a storekeeper who'd taken advantage of the chaos to raise his prices, demanding that he put his prices back to normal or else. I hoped he'd have the sense to do as they wanted before it was too late. Desperate people wouldn't hesitate to take what they needed if they thought they were being cheated. I heard the crowd grow louder as I walked away. It sounded as though the storekeeper wasn't smart enough to realise the danger.

Father wouldn't be so stupid, I told myself, as I heard the sound of a beating drum. *What the hell is that?*

I blinked as a line of guardsmen walked up the street, the leader beating the drum. The guardsmen had weapons in their hands, ready to fight... they looked like soldiers, not guardsmen. I frowned, wondering if they *were* soldiers. It was unlikely—Magus Court wouldn't have asked for troops—but still...I put the thought out of my mind as the streets cleared rapidly. Pieces of debris rained down from high overhead. I turned and ran down the streets as more and more rioters appeared from nowhere, ready to give the guardsmen a very hard time. I wondered if my arrest and short detention had made matters worse. Too many people had seen me run from the armsmen and jump into the canal...

The sound grew louder, somehow, as I turned into the alleyway and made my way towards the inn. The innkeeper had slammed the shutters into place, but the receptionist opened them as soon as she recognised me. I hoped she hadn't noticed I was wearing a new cloak. Who knew *what* sort of conclusions she'd draw? I suspected she probably *had* noticed. People who weren't observant tended not to live very long in Water Shallot. If nothing else, she'd need to be able to tell the difference between tough and *dangerous* men.

I breathed a sigh of relief as I made my way up the stairs. Caroline and Louise were safe. The inn would have been smashed to pieces, literally, if the guardsmen or armsmen had come calling. Or another assassin...I shuddered, remembering what Magistra Loanda had told me. The assassin couldn't even *feed* himself, let alone tell us what we wanted to know. He might as well be dead. Suicide was a mortal sin—the Ancients would reject anyone who took their own life—but someone who wiped his own memory?

The thought nagged at my mind as I undid the wards. Would there be two versions of the assassin in the afterlife? Or would they both be rejected?

There's no way to know, I told myself. *And we don't have time to wonder.*

The door opened. Caroline sat on the bed, a spellcaster aimed at me. I raised my hands as she stared at me, her magic probing mine before she relaxed—slightly—and returned the spellcaster to her belt. I breathed a sigh of relief as I closed the door, then looked around for Louise. She stepped out of the washroom, holding another spellcaster. I nodded to her. She gave me a sharp look, then nodded back. I guessed she hadn't forgiven me.

"What's it like out there?" Louise picked up her coat. "I have somewhere to be."

"Tense," I said, carefully. I didn't *want* Louise gadding about on her own. "I got arrested."

"What?" Caroline stood. "What happened?"

"I got snatched off the street," I explained. I ran through a brief explanation. "I think I lost them, but I can't be sure."

"That's not good," Caroline said. "If they're looking for us…"

Louise shrugged. "Right now, I have places to be," she said. "Or are you going to try to keep me here?"

"The streets aren't safe," I said. "The guardsmen have started to march patrols through the streets again. There's a brewing riot…"

"Then I have to take control before matters fall out of my hands," Louise said, briskly. "If I meet you both back here this evening…?"

I hesitated. I had a lot to discuss with Caroline. And I didn't want to have that discussion in front of Louise. But, at the same time, I didn't want Louise to go outside. Lord Dirac's men were looking for her. If they caught her, they'd ship her off to Skullbreaker Island without bothering with a trial. They wouldn't care she was innocent. They'd be far more concerned with depriving the socialists of their most effective leader.

"We'll see you this evening," Caroline said. "Be careful who you trust."

"I will." Louise didn't look pleased. "I still can't believe it. I *know* my comrades."

"Akin thought he knew Francis," I reminded her. "And Francis betrayed his cousin for...what? Laughs?"

"Yeah." Louise grimaced, as if she'd bitten into something nasty. "Point taken."

I scowled, feeling everything start to catch up with me. "Don't tell them where you're staying and *don't* tell them where you'll be," I warned. "They'll tell their masters and then you'll be dead. Or wishing you were."

Louise nodded, cast a glamour on herself and headed out the door. I watched her go, hoping and praying she'd be fine. Part of me wanted to keep her in the room, but she wouldn't stay of her own accord. We'd have to imprison her and...I didn't want to do something that would turn her into an implacable enemy. My feelings were a mess. I didn't know how I felt about her. Or anyone.

"Well," Caroline said. She sat back on the bed. "What happened?"

"It's an aristo plot," I said. I ran through everything, from what I'd learnt from Magistra Loanda to what Malachi Rubén had told me. Stregheria Aguirre was dead, but she still cast a long shadow. "They're planning to cause an uprising, then use it as an excuse to take complete control."

Bitterness welled within me. "I suppose it should have been obvious," I said. I knew aristos. They didn't give a damn about commoners. "The infernal devices were carefully planted. No one got killed...no one *important* got killed. Saline's party? They placed the device to make sure none of their little brats got killed."

I glared at my hands. Why was I not surprised? People who rigged the game in their favour would have no qualms about resorting to mass murder if they thought they were going to lose control. "I should have seen it coming. You just can't trust a fucking aristo."

Caroline stood, slowly. Her eyes met mine. "Adam...I *am* an aristo."

CHAPTER
THIRTY-FOUR

For a moment, I thought I'd misheard.

"What?"

"I am an aristo." Caroline stared at me, evenly. "And *you* are being a prat."

I stared at her, my head spinning. Caroline *couldn't* be an aristo. She'd been recruited for the Kingsmen! She had magic and power and a gritty determination never to give up...I couldn't believe she was an aristo. None of the aristos I'd met came close to her. Alana had been cruel, Francis had been a traitor...even *Akin* lacked Caroline's heart and soul. It couldn't be true.

And yet...I forced myself to think coldly, logically. Caroline knew magics I hadn't known existed. Caroline had been strikingly comfortable in the Great Houses. Caroline had danced with an ease and skill that suggested she'd been dancing almost as soon as she knew how to walk. Caroline had...I swallowed, unable to process what I'd been told. It was true. It couldn't be true. It was true...

"How?" I wanted to say *something*, but my brain refused to work. "How *can* you be an aristocrat?"

Caroline's voice was very even. "Father was a high-born brat, little older than yourself when he sired me. Mother was a serving girl who had dreams of rising above her station. She didn't realise she could get pregnant...they had something of a falling out, after she realised what had happened. Father formally acknowledged me, but Mother...she didn't want me to grow up in a

Great House. Father paid for us to live in Caithness. When I turned twelve, I went to Grayling's and studied there. I've been told it's nothing like Jude's."

"I thought it was a finishing school," I said, numbly. "One of those places that specialise in turning young ladies' brains into mush."

"I studied hard," Caroline said. "Miss Grayling is harsh, unbelievably so. But she's also a good teacher. My marks were as good as yours, perhaps better. The Kingsmen recruited me shortly after I finished my exams."

"But..." I had to think, to find the words. "If you're an aristo, why did they try to recruit you?"

Caroline shrugged. "I gave up my family ties," she said, simply. "It wasn't as if I was going to inherit anything. I'd seen enough of my family to know I didn't *want* to spend my days looking pretty and doing nothing. When the Kingsmen came calling, I said *yes*."

I swallowed, hard. "I don't understand..."

"No, I suppose you don't." Caroline held up a hand, cutting me off before I could say a word. "I get it. I really do. You grew up in a place where the only *real* way to get ahead was to become someone's client. And then you went to Jude's, where every aristocrat you met was as unformed as yourself. You saw them at their worst and never at their best. You said it yourself. The only aristo you met who was remotely decent was *Akin*, who was just as unformed as you. And you never realised you'd met me too."

"I..."

"Let me finish," Caroline said, eyes and voice sharp. "I understand. I don't blame you for hating aristos when you were a child. You had every reason, just like Louise, to resent a rigged system and to hate those who'd rigged it. But you know what? You have to grow up! You have to realise that aristos are just like everyone else. There are good aristos and bad aristos, and you need to learn to tell the difference."

She let out a breath. "You sided with Louise. Not because you slept with her, but because you *agreed* with her. You think, deep inside, that she's right. You let your feelings blind you. You told yourself that you weren't, but you were. You took a serious risk to prove her innocence. You sided with her, without admitting it to yourself, because you thought she was in the right. Didn't you?

I had no time to answer before she went on.

"But you cannot let yourself be blinded by your feelings. You cannot let your sympathy for Louise blind you. You cannot let your hatred of the aristos blind you. You have to step back and look at the world dispassionately. *That's* what we're expected to do. People have to trust that we'll render objective judgement. If they lose that faith, they won't trust us any longer. Why should they?"

I clenched my fists. "Did the people who had their businesses ruined because Magus Court passed legislation to *clarify* the issues deserve it?"

"No," Caroline said. "But just because someone is part of your tribe doesn't mean they're a wonderful person."

She shook her head. "You know it's true. It's easy to side with our own people. It's never easy to believe that someone from our family, from our community, is a monster in human form. Or merely an asshole. But that doesn't make it untrue. You had the same lessons I did. You *know* it to be true."

"Fuck," I said. I didn't know how to feel. "I didn't know."

"I was surprised you didn't notice," Caroline said. "The Alderman Curse is an aristocratic spell."

"Which doesn't get taught to commoners," I snarled.

"You might be surprised," Caroline said. "Really."

I forced myself to take a step back, controlling myself. If Caroline was an aristo…she'd saved my life, time and time again. And I'd saved hers…I'd cut off my wrist to save her life. And…my head spun. If I'd known her as a young girl, would I have liked her? I'd met Alana when we'd both been twelve. Would I have liked Caroline when *she'd* been twelve? I gritted my teeth, unwilling to admit—even to myself—that I'd made a complete fool of myself. Caroline was right. I'd allowed my hatred to blind me.

"I'm an idiot," I muttered.

"Not an idiot," Caroline corrected. "Just unformed. And immature."

I glared. "Didn't you do some idiotic things when you were a child?"

"Yes," Caroline said. "But I'm not a child any longer. And neither are you."
She took a breath. "We need to put this behind us and move on," she said. "Please."

I studied her for a long moment. Who *was* her father? Would I recognise the name? Or was he someone who…I told myself, firmly, that it didn't matter. Caroline had more than proved herself since I'd known her. I wasn't going to ask. She could keep it to herself as long as she wished.

"I'll try," I promised. "And I'm sorry."

"Me too," Caroline said. "We should have had this discussion earlier."

I sat down, tacitly changing the subject. "There's no way we'll get anything out of our prisoner," I told her. "Magistra Loanda insisted there was no cure."

"She might be right," Caroline said. "There are plenty of spells to cure wounds, but they're a little pointless if the victim is already dead. And without a bigger sample of potion, they might not be able to devise a countermeasure."

I nodded. "And so we're sunk," I said. "We can't ransack House Aguirre and House Rubén to catch the plotters."

"If they're *from* House Aguirre and House Rubén," Caroline pointed out. "They could be from any of the Great Houses. There are *hundreds* of aristocrats who have no power and no hope of getting it. Why do you *think* I didn't want to stay?"

"I never thought about it," I said. I'd wanted a challenge. I'd assumed Caroline was just the same. "We *could* take the prisoner to Lord Dirac. If he recognises him…"

"He'll throw us both in jail," Caroline said. "And we couldn't be sure he'd try to identify the assassin."

"Perhaps we should sit down and read the society pages," I said, sourly. "We could see if anyone's dropped out of sight recently."

"Only if we're desperate." Caroline grimaced. "Ninety percent of what you read in the society pages is made up of whole cloth. It's practically all nonsense. What little truth they manage to get right is buried under a mountain of bovine faecal matter. No one cares, either. They just want to pretend they're in the know."

"You make it sound so charming," I said. "People spread rumours in Water Shallot too."

"Quite," Caroline said. She winked. "See? We're just like you."

"Except you have more money," I said. I didn't want to ask, but I saw no choice. "Do you think your *father* could help?"

"I doubt it," Caroline said. I heard a twinge of bitterness in her voice. "He's got too many other problems right now."

I nodded. "Sorry."

Caroline shook her head. "I don't see any other option…"

I stared at the confinement circle for a long moment. "People come up with new potions and counter-potions all the time, right?"

"Yeah." Caroline looked at me. "What do you have in mind?"

"We know someone in Louise's inner circle is a spy," I said. "And it practically *has* to be one of the leaders. They're the only ones who didn't have their brains scrambled by the wards. That person betrayed her. He must have told the assassin where to find her. Right?"

"Yeah," Caroline said, again. "Unless they got very lucky and shadowed us to the inn…"

"I don't think so," I said. "The assassin could have caught us earlier, if he'd known where to look."

I smiled, feeling the plan come together. "Louse tells her inner circle that we managed to counter the potion. Perhaps I threw him into stasis quickly enough to keep him from swallowing a permanent dose. The assassin is a bit confused, but his memories are intact; we're holding him prisoner until we can use him as a bargaining chip. Magus Court wants him, so we can use him."

"I'm sure that'll surprise Magus Court," Caroline said, dryly. "What do you have in mind?"

"The assassin had to know his superiors," I said. "If he's an aristo himself, he probably knows far too much for their peace of mind. They'll want him back, quickly, before he can spill the beans to Magus Court. They'd probably also want to know what happened when he drank only a small dose of potion. Their Potions Master might want to vary the recipe."

"You think they'll come for him," Caroline said. "And then what?"

I took a breath. "I take his place and let them take me," I said. "You follow at a discreet distance."

Caroline met my eyes. "Do you know how many things could go spectacularly wrong?"

"Yeah," I said. "I know."

"Hah." Caroline snorted, rudely. "What's to stop them hurling an infernal device into the room and blowing you into the next world?"

"They'll need to know what we know," I said. I smiled, feeling slightly more confident. "The only way they'll know what we know is by interrogating their assassin. If they blow me up, they won't know what we know."

"Which is nothing," Caroline said, coldly. "They'll lose nothing by killing you."

"They won't know that," I reminded her. "Whatever they're doing... they cannot afford to be noticed. Not now. If Magus Court finds out about them, they're screwed. They need to know what we might have learnt, and what we've done with the knowledge, or they might as well pull up stakes and flee the city. There's no point in sticking around when their plan is heading for disaster."

"I don't like it," Caroline said. "Once they realise they've caught the wrong person, they'll kill you."

"I have faith in you," I said. "And I do have my own small powers."

"You could barely handle a single assassin," Caroline snapped. "What happens if you run into two of them?"

I met her eyes. "Do you have a better idea?"

"...No." Caroline glared. "But this is madness."

"I can't think of anything else," I said. "And we're running out of time."

Caroline crossed her arms under her breasts. "We'll make the preparations," she said. "And if we come up with something else, while we're doing it, we'll do that instead."

I nodded. "Let me get a shower first," I said. I started to undress, then stopped. "What were you and Louise doing while you waited for me?"

"Talking about you." Caroline smirked. I thought she was joking. "You were *such* a little brat when you were at school."

"I was not," I protested. "She didn't know me that well!"

"Well enough." Caroline's smirk grew wider. "She had a *lot* of interesting things to say."

I snorted as I stripped off my stained tunic, turned it into ash and dumped the remnants in the bin. "We're going to need new clothes, sooner rather than later."

"Next time, perhaps you should just run," Caroline said. "Why did they arrest you?"

I sighed. "Either Rebecca or the loan shark must have filed a complaint," I said. "And they put me right at the top of the wanted list."

"You weren't very nice to Rebecca," Caroline said. "Were you?"

"Neither were you," I countered.

"No," Caroline agreed. "But you were worse."

I felt a twinge of guilt as I grabbed my towel and headed for the shower. Rebecca…I kicked myself, mentally. I'd seen her as a sell-out, as someone from Water Shallot who'd taken the offer of patronage instead of working her way to the top. But…she made potions for the poor, people who could never have afforded them if they were sold at regular prices. She was a better person than me. I promised myself, silently, that I'd apologise to her after the terrorists were in prison and the whole affair was over. Caroline was right. I'd been a total prat. Worse, I'd allowed my feelings to blind me.

The water darkened as it washed the muck from my skin. It smelt thoroughly unpleasant. I wondered why neither Caroline nor Louise had mentioned it as I scrubbed vigorously, then towelled down. A new tunic awaited me as I opened the door. I shot Caroline a grateful look as I pulled it on. She hadn't *needed* to fetch it for me.

"I'm still thinking about other plans," Caroline said, as we started to draw blood from our prisoner. "We *could* do a blood test. See who he might be related to."

I grimaced. "How many people do you know who'd let us play with their blood?"

Caroline scowled. "Point taken."

Akin might, I thought. He might listen to me, at least, if I tried to convince him to give us a blood sample. *But no one else would.*

I put the assassin's blood in the base potion, then keyed it to the spellbinder. We couldn't have the effects failing ahead of time. An Object of Power would have made it so much easier, but…I doubted Caitlyn Aguirre would make one for us in a hurry. She was probably working to upgrade her family's defences. I wondered if I should envy or pity her. Her gift made her important, but it brought too many weaknesses for my peace of mind. I wouldn't want to be her.

There was a knock on the door. Caroline opened it. Louise stepped into the room, looking tired. She'd changed clothes, donning a dress and scarf that made her look several years older. She was carrying a cloth bag of food. I felt my mouth begin to water. I hadn't eaten much since breakfast.

"The raids have restarted," she said. "Two of my comrades have been scooped up."

"Crap," I said. "Has there been any word about your family?"

"Nothing." Louise passed Caroline the food, then sagged against the wall. "Their captors haven't tried to use them as leverage, not yet. It doesn't make sense."

"It does," I said. "But that doesn't matter right now. We have a plan."

"A very dangerous plan," Caroline said, curtly. "And it needs your help."

"We have to move fast," Louise said. "The protest march will be starting tomorrow morning."

I cursed. "You can't hold it back?"

"No." Louise shook her head, then recovered the bag and produced a small array of sandwiches. "It was all I could do to keep it from happening *today*. The mood on the streets is *vile*. There were dozens of people screaming and shouting for violence. I'm not sure we can keep the protest march from turning into a nightmare."

"Particularly if someone decides to make matters worse," I said. There were hundreds of violent men in Water Shallot. They wouldn't need much prompting to turn the march into a bloody nightmare. The City Guard would have all the excuse it needed to crush the marchers by force. "We need to move. Fast."

Louise nodded as she passed me a sandwich. "I quite agree," she said. "What do you have in mind?"

Caroline leaned forward. "When's your next meeting with your…comrades?"

"Tonight." Louise smiled. "The location is going to be a secret until the last possible moment. I don't want word getting out too soon."

"Good," Caroline said. "I'm glad to hear you're taking security seriously."

"John and Hammond have been arrested," Louise said. "I don't think either of them were known to the guardsmen until now. Someone not only betrayed them, they revealed their homes and families. They've *all* been arrested."

The anger in her voice didn't surprise me. We'd both been to Jude's. The lowest of the low amongst the students had always been the tattletale. The person who pretended to be a friend, while ratting you out to the upperclassmen or the tutors. To accuse someone of betrayal was to start a fight. No one could let that pass. But here…Louise had good reason to be angry. She didn't even know who to blame!

"I have a plan," I said. "But I need your help."

"Of course," Louise said. She gave me a faint smile. "What do you want?"

I told her.

CHAPTER THIRTY-FIVE

I felt...dull.

My body felt heavy, too tired to move. I knew it was a side-effect of the potion, a side-effect I could push away with a simple charm, but it was surprisingly hard to resist. I lay on the bed, staring up at the ceiling and telling myself the plan was going to work. It had to. The protest march was due to start tomorrow morning and if we didn't catch the terrorists... I shuddered. Anything could happen. Louise had organised stewards for the march, but I doubted they could keep the crowd under control. Water Shallot hadn't been so angry since King Rufus had signed a fishing treaty with North Cairnbulg. The riots had lasted *weeks*.

I kept my mind focused as the seconds ticked away. The socialist safehouse had been largely abandoned, if only because it was known to the entire leadership. I hoped they wouldn't see anything suspicious in Louise using it as a makeshift prison. The spy—whoever he was—had had plenty of time to report to his masters. I went through everything Louise had told me about the leadership, but couldn't pick a possible suspect out of the crowd. It wasn't a surprise. No spy ever born had *spy* on his resume.

The seconds started to feel like hours. I was dimly aware of the darkness outside starting to shade to light. The sun was coming up, peeking over the distant mountains and beaming rays of light into the city. Worry gnawed at my mind. Had our plan misfired? Or had we simply missed our chance?

The mystery terrorists and their backers might have already fled, their work done. Or they might have calculated that the potion would have worked perfectly, even if their assassin was frozen in his tracks. I didn't think they could afford to take the risk, but I could be wrong.

My body felt even heavier as dawn broke over the city. Caroline and I had done everything we could to give me a fighting chance, but it was starting to feel like we'd wasted our time. The terrorists couldn't come looking for me in broad daylight. They were much more likely to hurl an infernal device into the building or simply toss a vapour bottle crammed with poison into the room. It was funny how the plan no longer seemed like a brilliant idea. I'd thought it was wonderful, until I'd found myself trying to carry it out.

A rustle ran through the air. I tensed, wondering if the terrorists were finally here. It was dawn. The guards would be at their lowest ebb. The citizens outside the walls would be trying to get a few more minutes of sleep before they woke and began their day. Sir Muldoon had told me that dawn was often the best time to mount an attack, although he'd added a warning that most armies knew it and prepared accordingly. Louise's people didn't seem to be *quite* so well trained. I wondered, as the sound of faint footsteps grew louder, if they knew what they were doing. It was easy to claim to be great until one was actually put to the test.

They'll be used to violence, if nothing else, I told myself. *They grew up in Water Shallot.*

The door opened, so quietly I *knew* they had to be using silencing charms. I lay there, silently praying to my ancestors that they wouldn't test the glamour surrounding me. They *had* to believe I was their assassin or...I didn't dare brace myself, even as I felt them approach. One man...no, *two*. They might have come to take me home or...they might stick a poisoned blade in me and run. I hoped Caroline was ready to intervene, if they *did* look like they were trying to kill me. I wasn't in any state for a fight.

A figure crossed my line of sight. I stayed as still as I could. He was a tall man, dressed in a black outfit charmed to be hard to see. I'd seen invisibility cloaks, back at Haddon Hall, but this was different. I was impressed. The man could walk through a crowd and no one would notice, as long as he was careful not to attract attention. The spells reminded me of the ones on my ring. People wouldn't notice as long as their attention wasn't drawn to it.

The figure looked down at me for a moment, then cast a simple levitation charm. I floated into the air and hovered an inch or two above the bed. The figure caught me, pulled me over his shoulder and turned to the door. I caught a glimpse of a second figure as I was carried out of the room, down the stairs and through the entrance hall. The guards lay on the floor, unmoving. I felt a pang of guilt. It was hard—impossible—to tell if they were dead, or merely stunned. If they were dead...

I stayed still as I was carried down the street and around a corner. A hansom cab stood at the bottom of the road, waiting for us. My eyes narrowed sharply. Hansoms weren't unknown in Water Shallot, but they were rare. The kidnappers risked attracting attention by driving through the city. And yet, I could see their point. The cab was practically unnoticeable anywhere *outside* Water Shallot.

"Put him in the back," the second figure ordered. "Hurry."

I gritted my teeth as I was unceremoniously dumped in the rear of the cab. The door slammed closed. The driver cracked his whip, loudly. I reached out with my senses—carefully, very carefully—as the cab rattled into life and headed down the street. It was hard to make out anything beyond the presence of three trained magicians. The charms surrounding the cab were subtle—someone on the outside would probably be unable to sense them—but they were strong. I drew in my senses and waited. There was nothing else I could do.

The cab twisted and turned. I tried to guess at the route, but it was impossible. That only worked in stories. There was a brief sense of rising and falling, suggesting we'd crossed a bridge, but...which bridge? I couldn't tell. Were we in North or South Shallot? I made a silent bet with myself that it was South Shallot. The guardsmen hadn't forced us to stop. My lips tried to smile. It would have been ironic as anything if the guardsmen had inadvertently rescued me from my kidnappers.

But I wanted to be kidnapped, I reminded myself, as the carriage lurched again. *They're taking me where I want to go.*

The ring pulsed against my bare skin, a reminder that Caroline was following me. I hoped she wouldn't have any trouble crossing the river and catching up. It was possible the cab had a permit to pass through the guardposts without being stopped, although…they'd have to stop, wouldn't they, to show the permit? I wasn't sure. Very few guardsmen would dare to question an aristo. There were criminals who'd pulled off all kinds of heists because no one had stopped to check their credentials. As long as they looked like aristos, they'd be taken for aristos.

I smirked as the carriage came to a halt. There was a brief snatch of muffled chatter—I couldn't make out the words—before the carriage lurched forward again and stopped. I hastily composed myself as I heard someone rattle at the door, throwing it open with a bang. Whoever had come for me wasn't messing around. He cast a levitation charm and guided me out the carriage and through a wooden door as if I was a sack of potatoes. I studied the wards as he levitated me on. They were strong, alarmingly strong. It felt as if we were in a Great House.

My captor hovered me into a room and lowered me onto a bed. The bedding felt almost sinfully comfortable. I could see a lantern drifting over my head as two more figures studied me. One wore a mask that obscured everything. The other was oddly familiar. I drew in my breath as I placed him. He'd accompanied Lord Dirac when he'd ordered Sir Griffons out of the city!

"Well," the man said. He spoke with a pure aristocratic accent. "You may as well sit up."

I held myself still, despite a flash of panic. It looked as if my glamour—my *blood-based* glamour—had failed. Or…my mind raced, wondering if I'd let myself be carried right into a trap. If the glamour hadn't held up…I cursed, mentally. Caroline was on the way, but would she arrive in time? I had the awful feeling I'd sentenced myself to death.

"The glamour is a good one," the man said. "Your spells were quite effective. But—obviously—you're not one of mine. I know who you are."

I pushed the effects of the spell aside and sat up. I was in a large chamber, sitting on a bed. I looked behind me and confirmed there was a third person standing in the shadows. He wore a mask too. The speaker smiled as I turned my attention back to him. He was as bland as his assassin, his face utterly unremarkable. I reached out gingerly and confirmed that he was protected with powerful wards. I'd be stopped in my tracks—or killed outright—if I tried to attack.

"I'm glad you've decided to be reasonable," the man said, as if he'd been reading my thoughts. "I *so* hate it when people are unreasonable."

I felt a surge of hatred. "Who are you?"

"Anton Bolingbroke, at your service." The man gave a slight bow. "You won't have heard of me."

"No," I said. *That* was odd. Most aristos assumed that everyone knew who they were and got cranky when they discovered it wasn't true. I kicked myself, mentally. *Caroline* hadn't wanted anyone to know who she was either. "What are you doing?"

"I thought we should have a chat," Anton said. "Your trick was quite clever. It *did* fool us, right up until you failed to resonate properly with the wardlines. I take it the *real* Gavin had his memory wiped?"

"Yes." There was no point in denying it. "We couldn't get anything out of him."

Anton nodded to his companions, who turned and left. "I'm being a poor host," he said, once they were gone. "Would you like something to drink? Or eat?"

I stared at him. "And what would you put in it?"

"If I wanted to dose you with something," Anton pointed out, "I wouldn't need to trick you."

I scowled. "What are you doing?"

"I think we have interests in common," Anton said. "We should be working together."

"Really," I said. It was unbelievable. I told myself, sharply, that I needed to keep him talking until Caroline arrived. "And what would those interests be?"

Anton summoned a chair with a wave of his hand and sat down. "You are a Kingsman, sworn to uphold His Majesty," he said. "I am a servant of Magus Court, sworn to protect the Court against its enemies. And we have a common enemy."

"We do?" I thought, fast. "The socialists?"

"Correct." Anton leaned forward. "You have to understand. The socialists represent the most serious challenge to Magus Court—and His Majesty—in centuries. They have to be stopped."

I studied him for a long moment. He seemed to believe what he was saying, although *no one* reached such heights without being able to lie convincingly. And yet, I found it hard to believe. Louise might have galvanised the socialist movement, but it didn't represent a threat to Magus Court, let alone His Majesty. She didn't have the power to turn her movement into a serious threat. There was no way the socialists could take control of the city, could they?

"They're not a threat," I said, carefully. "It wasn't *them* who detonated the infernal devices."

Anton shook his head. "You misunderstand. The system is designed to absorb talented newcomers such as yourself. It works because the people with the ability to damage the system are actually brought *into* it. But the socialists want to overthrow the entire system and replace it with something new. They're a threat to the established order."

"They couldn't challenge the Great Houses," I said. "They're not *that* strong."

"Not yet," Anton said. "But that's already changing. The movement is spreading. There are already socialist cells in cities right across the kingdom. They have to be stopped."

"And so, you framed them," I said. "Why? Who are you?"

"I told you," Anton said. "I'm a servant of Magus Court."

I met his eyes as the pieces fell into place. "It's more than just the socialists, isn't it?"

Anton looked back at me, his face expressionless. "What do you mean?"

"The alliance between the two most powerful Great Houses leaves the rest of you in the cold," I said. Malachi had said as much. "If the alliance is formalised, permanently, you'll have a choice between accepting permanent subordination or fighting a hopeless war. Sir Griffons said"—I smiled—"that Magus Court was trying to find a way to either prevent the alliance or weaken it. You planned the state of emergency to give you an excuse to do just that."

"True enough." Anton's blank expression didn't waver. "And it *is* in His Majesty's interests too."

I grinned. "How so?"

"Right now, there is only *one* source for Objects of Power," Anton said. "Whoever controls Caitlyn Aguirre will have the power to utterly dominate everyone else. Do you think the idea of taking control of the entire kingdom *hasn't* crossed her father's mind? Or her future father-in-law? The king's armies will be powerless against Objects of Power. If we take control of her, we can render her harmless."

By killing her, I thought. I shuddered. I'd only known Caitlyn for a few months, but she'd never struck me as someone who deserved to die. *They're going to kill an eighteen-year-old girl just to secure their power.*

I looked down as a thought stuck me. "You *did* mean to kill Prince Jacob, didn't you?"

"Yes." Anton didn't look remotely sorry. "Coming here, the way he did... it caused all sorts of problems. We wanted him gone, but...we couldn't be seen to bow to the king. If he'd been blown up it would have solved the problem rather nicely."

I kept my voice steady, somehow. "If you didn't mind killing him," I said. "And dealing with the diplomatic consequences..."

"And what would *those* be?" I heard a hint of irritation in Anton's tone. "Prince Jacob is a headache for just about *everyone*. No one will waste their time firing off formal protests, let alone doing something effective, if he dies on our streets."

"You saw it as a chance to kill two birds with one stone," I said. "What does Stregheria Aguirre have to do with all this?"

Anton's eyes narrowed. "Nothing. She's dead. She died six years ago."

"But you use the same potion," I said. "You're what's left of her conspiracy, aren't you?"

"In a manner of speaking," Anton said. "Let us just say that…there are groups within the Great Houses, within Magus Court itself, that work together to tackle problems that affect us all. Like Prince Jacob. Like the socialists. Like an alliance that will permanently shatter the balance of power. Some of us lent our support to Stregheria Aguirre. We backed off, sharply, when it became clear she'd failed."

I shook my head. "Does Lord Dirac know about you?"

"No." Anton smiled, rather thinly. "It was decided that it would be better if he remained in ignorance of our existence."

"And he doesn't know he's hunting you," I said.

"No." Anton stood, brushing down his trousers. "And once the protest march turns into a riot, he'll stamp on the socialists for us."

He met my eyes. "Now, you have a choice," he said. "You can assist us, thus satisfying your duty to His Majesty. Or we'll hold you here until the whole affair is over."

I thought, fast. Anton was no fool. He knew he'd told me too much. He'd have to take precautions to make sure I didn't betray them, if I chose to assist them. An oath, perhaps. Or a modified potion. I wasn't sure how it'd react with the protections I already had. The Kingsmen had trained me well. And yet, if I refused, I suspected he'd kill me on the spot. We weren't meant to be in the city. No one would ask too many questions if they dragged my body out of a canal, if they ever found it. There were plenty of ways to make sure no one ever found a corpse.

"This is madness," I said. "There's no way His Majesty will agree…"

"You might be surprised," Anton said. "The socialists represent a threat to everyone. His Majesty will be pleased if they are broken and discredited."

He turned and walked to the door, then stopped. "You can wait here," he said. "As long as you behave, you'll be treated well. If not...well, we do have ways to keep you under control."

"You're a monster." It was hard to keep my voice from shaking. I'd never met anyone quite so callous. "How many people have you killed?"

"Fewer than *will* die, if the socialists take control," Anton said. The confidence in his voice was striking. "Or if we have another House War. The last one was quite bad enough."

He stepped through the door and closed it, firmly, behind him.

CHAPTER
THIRTY-SIX

The moment he was gone, I sprang off the bed and searched the room. It was strikingly bare for a chamber inside an aristocratic dwelling. The bed itself was secured to the floor. I couldn't pull the legs or slats free to make an improvised weapon. The rest of the room was completely empty. There was no wardrobe, no chest of drawers, no mirror...I wondered, absently, if we were in a safehouse. Anton and his little group—I had no idea if he'd been telling the truth or not—probably wouldn't base themselves in a genuine Great House. They'd want somewhere that couldn't be shut down so easily.

My mind raced as I inspected the door. It was locked and warded shut. If Anton was telling the truth...I could believe it, I decided. My instructors had warned me that secret groups tended to lose contact with reality and start thinking they—and only they—were all that stood between their people and utter destruction. I'd asked what kept the Kingsmen from having the same problem and gotten a lecture on cheek for my trouble. Reading between the lines, I'd had the feeling we *did* have the same problem. The only thing that kept it under control was strict rules on what we could and couldn't do.

I touched my ring, wondering if I dared call Caroline. Where *was* she? The ring was pulsing out a locator signal, but I was behind solid wards. The signal might be blocked. Or she might be trapped in Water Shallot. Or...my imagination provided a dozen possibilities, each worse than the last. I put them out of my mind as I probed the wards, cursing under my breath as I realised how solid they were. They'd be easy to take apart from the outside, naturally, but anyone on the inside was thoroughly trapped.

Or maybe not, I thought. The lock was more complex than I'd expected—the Great Houses preferred magic to physical locks—but it wasn't *that* hard to pick. I poked and prodded at the keyhole until the lock snapped open. The door itself refused to open—the wards were firmly in place—but it was a start. *This is going to be painful if it doesn't work.*

Gritting my teeth, I pulled my pen from my pouch, pressed the tip against my arm and pushed hard enough to break the skin. Blood welled up, threatening to drip to the floor. I muttered a charm, giving the blood a life of its own. The liquid glided forward and pressed itself through the keyhole. My awareness went with it. There was no one on the far side. I wasn't too surprised. The wards were tough, very tough. I hadn't even *known* one could animate blood until I'd gone to Haddon Hall. Anton had good reason to be confident in his prison.

And he probably needs his people elsewhere, I told myself. He'd said the protest march was going to turn into a riot. He probably had ringers in the crowd, ready to start hurling curses and hexes at the guardsmen. *His base might not be too heavily guarded.*

I thrust my awareness through the blood, grimly aware the magic was starting to fade. I wasn't sure what would happen if it collapsed while my awareness was focused on the far end of the blood, but I didn't want to find out the hard way. I might be thrown back into my body or I might be trapped *outside* permanently. I'd seen a couple of ghosts. There was no way I wanted to end up like that. I rotated my awareness and cast a spell, unlocking the wards from the outside. The door crashed open. I breathed a sigh of relief and jumped through, muttering a spell to vaporise the blood. I didn't want to leave *that* lying around.

The wards quivered in alarm. I recoiled, shocked. I'd thought I'd tricked them. I braced myself, ready to fight...but no one came to throw me back into the cell. It dawned on me, as I heard the sound of running footsteps above, that I *hadn't* triggered the alarm. Someone – Caroline?—had attacked the house. The guards were running to defend their walls.

I inched down the corridor, keeping a wary eye out for trouble. It looked as if I'd been concealed in the servant wing. The walls were as bare as the prison cell. They looked vaguely unfinished, as if whoever had designed and built the house couldn't be bothered to install facilities for the servants. I glanced into a sideroom as I passed and saw a row of bunks. They didn't look large enough for grown adults. I'd been too big for them when I'd been twelve.

Flickers of magic echoed through the house as I reached a flight of stairs. A pair of black-clad men lurked at the bottom, readying spells I didn't recognise. I shaped a spell in my mind, then blasted them both in the back. They tumbled like bowling pins. I was tempted to steal their clothes, but I didn't have time. Instead, I took samples of their blood and hurried up the stairs. The wards might not be smart enough to realise that someone was in two places at once. Anton might not have a live-in wardmaster on the payroll.

Someone would have to agree to spend the rest of his life here, I thought, as I reached the top of the stairs. The flickers of magic were growing stronger. *And who'd want to do that?*

I kept moving, reaching out carefully with my magic. *Something* was going on up ahead, something bad. I sensed dark magic—black magic—crackling on the air. The spells were banned, but the Great Houses had always been a law unto themselves. I hoped they'd thought to take precautions. Black magic wasn't *just* dangerous because it was cast with bad intentions. It was dangerous because a warlock could become addicted and lose his sense of right and wrong. The Great Houses should know better. I hoped they'd planned to deal with a newborn warlock before he became dangerously insane.

Magic flickered back at me. I recognised the signature. *Caroline* was there! I hurried forward, throwing caution to the winds as I ran into the entrance hall. Two sorcerers stood there, dark lightning crackling around their hands. I could feel the bad intentions as they hurled the spells towards

Caroline, shielding herself as she pushed into the house. I summoned my magic and yanked their feet out from under them, sending them both sprawling to the floor. The black lightning surged up as they lost control, threatening to consume them. I ran past the sorcerers as they started to scream. There was nothing I could do. The forces they'd unleashed would kill them if they didn't manage to retake control.

"Adam," Caroline called. She looked tired, but happy. Her tunic was in rags. "You're free!"

"I broke out," I said. I sensed, more than heard, more people running towards us. "We have to get out of here!"

Caroline nodded, then unhooked a potions bottle from her belt and hurled it into the hallway. There was a flash of light, followed by a roar of thunder that made my ears ache. I saw the ceiling start to cave in as Caroline grabbed my arm, yanking me back. I cast a glamour over myself as we ran through the hall and out the door. The spell wouldn't keep them from noticing me—nothing could do that, now they knew we were there—but they'd have problems knowing *precisely* where we were. Hopefully, it would make us harder to hit.

My ears rang as we ran through the gate and down the streets. I looked around, frantically trying to work out where we were. We were on the southern side of North Shallot, I thought, only a short distance from the shops, cafes and beaches. Caroline held my hand tightly, casting a series of glamours. Passersby stared at us, their noses twitching in disapproval. We didn't look *remotely* like people who belonged in North Shallot.

"I think we're clear," Caroline said, as we reached the beach. A handful of children were playing in the waves, watched by nannies and governesses. They looked carefree, even though the entire city was on the brink of chaos. "I'm sorry it took so long."

"Don't worry about it," I said. We sat down on a bench and stared out to sea. "Where *were* we?"

"A townhouse, I think," Caroline said. "I didn't have time to look up the records and see who owns it."

I scowled. "Anton Bolingbroke," I said. "He had some very interesting things to tell me."

Caroline nodded as she removed a flask from her belt. "What did he say?"

"There's a group within Magus Court that wants to trigger a riot," I said. I outlined what Anton had told me, piece by piece. "And use that as an excuse to clamp down on their enemies."

"Interesting," Caroline said, when I'd finished. "Do you think he was telling the truth?"

"I don't know." I stared at my hands. "He was quite keen to convince me to join him."

Caroline laughed. "He doesn't know much about you, does he?"

"No." I shook my head. "I didn't get the *impression* he was lying, but…"

"Yeah." Caroline peered out to sea. "He could have been lying. Or he could have been repeating a lie someone else told him. We don't know."

I rubbed my aching sides, feeling unsure of myself. "He said—he was quite insistent—that His Majesty *also* wanted the socialists crushed. He figured they posed a threat to the king as well as Magus Court. And… what if he's right?"

Caroline cocked her head. "What *if* he's right?"

"I…" I swallowed, hard. "I don't know."

My mind was a mess. I didn't know *what* to believe. The Kingsmen were meant to uphold law and order, but…what if King Rufus *wanted* the socialists crushed? What was my duty if my ultimate superior *wanted* Anton's plan to go ahead? And yet…I shook my head firmly. The law couldn't stand if the lawmakers themselves abused it. The socialists had done nothing wrong. They hadn't detonated the infernal devices, they hadn't set out to riot…

"If someone is guilty, they have to go to jail or face the hangman," I said. I'd promised myself I was going to fight for justice. "But if someone isn't guilty…it isn't fair to frame them, or to invent new offences, just to bring them to heel. The system itself will collapse."

I looked at her. "We have to stop them," I said. "Don't we?"

"Yes." Caroline winked. "We've certainly received no orders to let the plot go ahead. Sir Griffons could have taken us out of the city, if he'd wanted the plotters to succeed. He didn't have to leave us here..."

I stood, brushing down my tunic. It was torn and stained. My arm ached, a grim reminder that I'd bled myself only a few short minutes ago. I muttered a healing charm, hoping I had enough magic left for it to work. Caroline watched, her eyes concerned. A spell that involved blood—even the caster's blood—was always borderline dark. I might wind up paying a price for what I'd done.

"We have to tell Lord Dirac," I said. "And then..."

I froze. We had no proof. There was nothing we could take to him, nothing that would prove our story. Anton Bolingbroke would laugh in our faces. We could use truth spells and swear oaths on our ancestors and... and it wouldn't be enough. We'd be arrested the moment we contacted Lord Dirac. And then the protest march would become a riot and the crackdown would go ahead.

And they wouldn't stop, I thought. Anton had hinted the king would be happy, but I doubted it. Once the plotters had taken control, they'd need to *keep* control. They might not kill Caitlyn after all. They might try to use her to threaten the entire kingdom. *They'll unleash a civil war, rather than give up their power.*

"We can't prove anything," I said. "We *can't*."

"There *is* the damage to the townhouse," Caroline pointed out. She sounded as unsure as I felt. "And we do have the assassin..."

I shook my head. By now, Anton would have put together a cover story. It didn't matter what it was, as long as it was convincing. Lord Dirac would have no reason to pry any further. He'd just arrest us and...no, that wouldn't do. We couldn't rely on anyone. I didn't think we even had time to call our superiors. What could *they* do about the riot?

"We have to get there," I said. "Quickly."

Caroline caught my arm. "It might be too late," she said. "There were already people on the streets when I left Water Shallot."

"We have to hurry," I said. I wasn't about to give up. Not yet. If we could stop the riot, we could keep the plotters from taking control. There'd be time to gather irrefutable proof. Or contact our superiors and ask for help. Sir Griffons would listen, at least. He might have some good ideas. "Come on!"

Caroline touched her ring. "We need to report first," she said. I saw her gather herself, composing her thoughts. "Give me a moment."

She pressed her finger against the ring, then started to outline everything that had happened since we'd been left in the city. I felt cold as we started to walk, wondering what Sir Griffons would say when everything came to an end. We'd done as we'd seen fit, but it was clear we'd made a whole string of mistakes. We'd probably also pushed our authority to the breaking point—and then crossed the line. He'd have done a much better job, I was sure. It was hard to believe, despite everything, that he'd be fine with everything we'd done. He might dismiss both of us without a second thought.

I picked up speed as we hurried through North Shallot. The people on the streets were either aristos, wealthy commoners or their servants. They looked…content, browsing the shops as if they didn't have a care in the world. They didn't *know* there wouldn't be a third infernal device…I wondered, sourly, if Anton had quietly reassured his superiors. It was so much easier to predict when and where a device would explode if *you* were the one setting them. I felt a flash of hatred. The bastard had killed children—*children*—for his petty power games.

A middle-aged woman in fine clothes walked past us, followed by a pair of servants who were utterly loaded down with expensive bags. I felt a stab of pity as the mistress berated her servants for being lazy and slow. The servants would probably join the socialists, if they thought they could get away with it. I couldn't blame them if they did. It was suddenly clear, more than I cared to admit, that Anton had a point. The socialists crossed class and tribal lines, drawing in supporters from both the lower and middle classes. They could turn society on its head if they wished.

And Anton prefers to resort to force than tackle the problems leading to socialism, I thought, as we reached the bridges. They were closed and barricaded, a small army of guardsmen and sorcerers ready to repel attack. I couldn't hear *anything* on the far side of the barricade. The march was intended to go through South Shallot, not North Shallot. *They're panicking over nothing.*

A guardsman blocked our way as we started to cross the bridge. "The bridge is closed. Go home."

I hesitated, trying to decide what to do. If I showed him my ring, we'd probably be arrested on the spot. There were enough guardsmen and sorcerers within eyesight to make resistance completely impossible. I glanced at the churning waters, wondering if we should jump in and swim again. But...we'd be hauled out within seconds. There were just too many people who could intervene.

I drew myself up to my full height. "Do you know who I am?"

The guard looked doubtful. He didn't know me, but that proved nothing. "No...?"

I felt a flicker of guilt. "I'm the special representative of Lord Joaquin Aguirre," I said, in the most imperious manner I could muster. Francis would have been proud. "I have orders to enter Water Shallot and collect items for His Lordship. Unless you want to stand in my way...?"

"It isn't safe," the guard said, carefully. I'd put him in an awful position. He might think I was lying, but what if he was wrong? Lord Joaquin Aguirre would demand the guard's dismissal for standing between his agents and their mission. No guardsman in his right mind wanted such a powerful enemy. Even checking my credentials would be risky. "My Lord..."

"I have my orders." I lowered my voice, slightly. "I'll be back before you know it."

The guard opened a door within the barricade. "Good luck, My Lord."

I felt another pang of guilt as we passed through the door and crossed the bridge. I'd lied to someone who was only doing his job. But I didn't have a choice.

Caroline nudged me as we entered Water Shallot. "You'd make a good aristo," she said, snidely. "You've really mastered the entitled bastard act."

"And I deserve a kick up the backside," I said, as we started to run. Time was not on our side. "Come on, hurry!"

CHAPTER THIRTY-SEVEN

My sides started to hurt, again, as I raced through empty streets towards the gentrified district and the bridges beyond. No one was in sight, not even the guardsmen or the prostitutes, but I heard a rumbling sound of anger from the bridges. The sound grew louder as we ran faster, fearing the worst. It struck me, as I ran, that it might be impossible to keep the protest from turning into a riot. There were too many people who saw violence as the only answer in Water Shallot. They'd already started killing guardsmen. They wouldn't hesitate to lash out if they came under attack.

My breathing slowed as we ran to the waterside, passing dozens of shuttered and warded shops. I saw faces in the window, staring at us and the gathering marchers. I sucked in my breath as I saw them, realising—for the first time—that they were more than just socialists. Men, women and children, dressed in their finest clothes. They looked as if they were going to pay their respects to their ancestors, not taking part in a political demonstration. I felt a lump in my throat as we slowed, passing a pair of stewards who held out signs. I'd spent most of my life complaining about Water Shallot, but not *everyone* who lived there was a criminal, a loan shark or a monster in human form. The vast majority of the inhabitants were decent people.

I frowned as we headed towards the bridges. The stewards—men and women in red cloaks—seemed to have things under control, although I suspected their control wouldn't last if all hell broke loose. They were telling everyone not to carry weapons, but that wasn't going to happen. Men concealed weapons under their cloaks, women carried daggers on their belts...I saw an able-bodied man carrying a walking stick that was almost certainly a disguised rapier. Or possibly even a spellcaster. If the protest was attacked, the protesters were prepared to fight back.

Caroline nudged me as we hurried on. "How many people are here?"

I shrugged. It was hard to tell. The crowd was shifting too rapidly—people coming, people going—for me to be sure. I shuddered as I saw a handful of small boys running through the crowd, either caught up in the excitement or taking advantage of the chaos to pick a few pockets before they were caught. I hoped it was the former. I didn't want to have to intervene as the crowd beat a tiny pickpocket to death.

"Thousands, perhaps," I said. It felt as if the entire district had turned out for the march. I knew it was unlikely, but still..."I don't know."

We kept moving as someone—a middle-aged man—started to speak, his voice booming. He reminded the crowd of their rights as citizens and castigated Magus Court for even *thinking* they could take them away. Louise was a better speaker, but I had to admit he had power. The crowd murmured its anger as the speech went on and on. It looked as if they were on the verge of pushing forward and marching across the bridges without waiting for the order.

Louise herself was at the front, surrounded by a small army of toughs and runners. I thought I recognised some of the toughs, boys I'd known on the streets before going to Jude's. I was mildly surprised they listened to Louise, even though she *was* a sorceress. Perhaps she'd made it clear the cause came first, always. Or maybe she'd had to use magic to assert herself.

"Adam," Louise said. She drew us forward, motioning her cronies to stay back. "What happened?"

"You have to stop the march," I said. "You're going to be attacked!"

Louise paled. "Are you sure?"

"Yes." I didn't have time to tell her everything. "You can't give them the chance to make an example of you. I..."

The crowd roared as the speaker finally came to an end. Lines of people surged back and forth, threatening to overwhelm the stewards and head for the bridges. The waves of emotion were so strong that I knew, deep inside, that *no one* would be able to stop the crowd when it ran out of patience. Louise might understand what I was telling her, but…she couldn't stop the crowd. And if she walked away, she'd destroy herself. No one would ever take her seriously again.

"We have to do it," Louise said. "If we back down now, they'll know they can keep us under control."

"Listen to me," I said. "They're going to crush you."

Louise met my eyes. "Either we make a stand for our rights, here and now, or we lose them," she said. "What would you choose?"

I bit my lip as Louise turned away, heading for the box. I understood, all too well. I'd learnt the hard way that you had to stand up to bullies. If you gave them what they wanted, they just demanded more and more until they found something you simply *couldn't* give. But here…I swallowed, hard. Louise was going to lead her people into a trap. They were going to be hurt or killed or…I didn't know what to do. There was no way I could stop her. The crowd would tear us apart.

Caroline caught my hand as the crowd roared again. "We have to protect them."

I nodded, stiffly. Louise spoke now, her calm voice echoing over the crowd. She told them things could be different, if they reached out and took what was theirs. I felt another lump in my throat. If I hadn't joined the Kingsmen…my eyes scanned the crowd, picking out a handful of familiar faces. I'd have been one of them, if I hadn't gone elsewhere. I was tempted to wonder if I'd made a mistake. And yet…I shook my head. If I hadn't joined the Kingsmen, I wouldn't have tracked down the plotters. Sir Griffons knew who they were. He'd find a way to expose them even if Caroline and I died today.

Louise jumped off the box and started to march towards the bridges, her long hair blowing in the breeze. The crowd surged forward, the stewards desperately trying to keep the people under control. I glanced at Caroline, then walked on the edge of the crowd as Louse led them up the road. A chant started to echo, the beat thrumming through the air. I understood—I sympathised—and yet I found it terrifying. The crowd wanted what it wanted, and wouldn't hesitate to turn on anyone who denied it. The people on the far side of the river had to be quaking in their shoes, hastily locking their doors and firming their wards. They wouldn't be *pleased* about the marchers coming into their territory. I just hoped they'd have the sense to keep their heads down.

The wind grew colder as the crowd marched across the bridge. The handful of guardsmen on duty seemed to have decided to stand aside, instead of trying to block the crowd. I breathed a sigh of relief, even though I didn't think it was a good thing. The guardsmen could have barricaded the bridges to South Shallot as thoroughly as the bridges to North Shallot. Instead, they seemed to be allowing the crowd to march towards Jude's. I didn't like the look of it. They could have prepared a killing ground somewhere ahead of us.

"The plan is to march around South Shallot and then return to the bridges," Caroline said, as a pair of stewards hurried past us. I concealed a smile as I saw they were dropping leaflets in mailboxes. I didn't think anyone would bother to read them, but it was worth a try. "Louise said she wanted to make a point, without being too provocative."

"I hope it works," I said. Clearly, Caroline and Louise had talked about a lot of things. "The march itself is provocative. The locals will hate the marchers coming up here."

I frowned as I studied the crowd. They might have been wearing their finest clothes, but...I felt their anger. It was more than just their lost rights now. It was everything, from poor housing to corrupt guardsmen preying on the people they were supposed to serve. I suspected it was just a matter of time before the socialists started patrolling the streets, even if it ran the risk of bringing them into conflict with people like Zadornov. The loan sharks might find themselves forced to run for their lives if *everyone* turned on them. I was surprised the idea hadn't occurred to Louise. There wasn't *anyone* in Water Shallot who *liked* the loan sharks. Even hardened criminals saw them as utter bastards.

"I don't know," I said. The crowd was marching past Jude's and heading down towards the shops. They didn't seem concerned that the streets were completely empty. The shops were all tightly buttoned up. Rebecca's shop was as dark and cold as the rest. I hoped she was safe. I still owed her an apology. "The crowd might turn nasty."

I felt my heart start to pound as we reached the far side of South Shallot. A low murmur ran through the crowd as they saw North Shallot, the Great Houses glowing in the bright sunlight. It looked like the promised land, a land forever denied them. The armsmen would confront anyone who looked as if they didn't belong, arresting them or marching them out if they didn't have a good explanation for their presence. I heard the mutterings get darker, the stewards starting to lose control. The crowd surged towards the next set of bridges, even though Louise was marching up the road. I hoped she'd have the sense to run if the stewards lost control. They had the authority, but not the power.

"What?" Caroline looked up, sharply. "Something's happening…"

I sensed it too, a moment later. A surge of magic…for a moment of pure horror, I thought it was another infernal device. The entire crowd would be slaughtered in a heartbeat if someone detonated something like that in the midst of the march. Instead…I looked up as a hail of spells crashed down on the marchers, spells of nasty compulsions along with childish pranks. Dark-clad figures appeared out of nowhere, flaming whips in their hands. The crowd howled, coming apart into an angry mob. I swore as middle-aged men charged the newcomers, screaming their defiance. They were going to be killed effortlessly…

Louise turned, casting a protective spell as two attackers closed on her. They slammed her to the ground, their magic holding her down. I ran forward, readying a spell of my own. The attackers turned, too late. I threw one of them into the river with a modified levitation spell, then punched the other in the head. His charmed mask provided some protection, but not enough. Louise stood, her eyes flashing murder. She hurled a nasty-looking spell past me. I turned, just in time to see it strike another dark-clad man. He staggered, then collected himself. Caroline blasted him before he could do more than glare at the three of us.

"Get out of here," I shouted at Louise. The mob was surging like a cornered animal. I saw people smash their way into a shop, either looking for somewhere to hide or simply maddened by the spells. Magic crashed from person to person, pushing them to the breaking point. Raw emotion lingered on the air. A person who didn't realise he was under attack wouldn't be able to protect himself. He wouldn't know his emotions weren't real. "Hurry!"

A small girl fell to the ground. I cast a summoning spell, yanking her to me an instant before she could be trampled. She was crying as I caught her, then passed her to Louise. Two more attackers ran towards us, hurling dark magic into the crowd. I glanced at Caroline and stepped forward as more attackers appeared. Our magics blurred together as the attackers lashed into us. We fought by instinct alone, fighting as one. They outnumbered us, but they couldn't match us. I smacked one down, muttering a charm that should have shattered his teeth. He staggered, face blank as he hit the ground. I'd smashed the potions capsule in his teeth. The others recoiled, giving us a chance to take the fight to them. I knocked the leader down with a charged punch, then threw another one into the river. I didn't know if he could swim, but it didn't matter. He was out of the fight, at least until he managed to get out.

I caught my breath, looking around as more spells pelted down from overhead. There were people on the roofs, casting spells with dark intentions. I reached out with my magic, brushing against their wards. They were protected against my spells, but...I summoned a gust of wind, blowing them to the ground. One of them didn't react in time to save himself and hit the ground with a sickening thud. The others managed to land, too close to the maddened crowd. They were battered to death before they could defend themselves.

Glass smashed, shattered windows hitting the ground. I cast a protective charm as I stared around, hoping the mob could be steered away from the bridges and back to Water Shallot. It looked impossible. Dark spells were still flickering through the crowd, driving them mad. I thought I saw smoke on the far side...maybe a building had caught fire. Magic crackled behind me as more attackers appeared, holding spellcasters. They raised and fired as one. Fireballs slammed into the mob, driving it back into South Shallot. I cursed as I mustered my magic and lashed out at them, my head starting to pound as I pushed my power to the limit. The riot was going to leave South Shallot utterly devastated. Anton and his fellows would have all the excuse they needed to crack down on the socialists.

The attackers turned and directed their fire at me. Blood trickled down my nose as I held my wards, somehow deflecting the fireballs or exploding them before they could touch me. Fireballs weren't difficult to handle, if you knew what you were doing. But they knew...I felt their spells change, digging into my wards and tearing them open. I felt pain stab into my head, an instant before Louise's allies blasted them. They'd come within seconds of killing me.

Caroline caught my arm as I stumbled, nearly hitting the ground. "The guardsmen are coming!"

I glanced up, forcing myself to ignore the worsening headache. A small army of guardsmen, wearing armour that would not have been out of place on a battlefield, was advancing across the nearest bridge. They were banging their staffs against their breastplates, the sound sending chills down my spine. The saner marchers, those not affected by the spells, were already backing off. I saw Louise urging women and children to run as the men prepared to fight the newcomers. A dark-clad figure pointed a spellcaster towards the guardsmen and let rip. I swore as the fireballs evaporated against their armour. They wouldn't show mercy now. They thought they'd been attacked by the mob.

"Fuck," I swore.

I sagged against the wall, exhausted. There were more guardsmen approaching now, ready to beat the mob into submission. The mob was girding itself to fight. I saw men picking up discarded weapons and readying themselves to use them. There were bodies everywhere, people injured or killed in the fighting. Men, women and children...I stared numbly at a black-clad body, battered into a bloody pulp. Anton had sent him to die. I wondered, morbidly, who he'd been. A natural-born son? Someone who wanted to be important? Or merely someone too stupid to wonder about what he was doing. I was sure I'd never know.

Caroline leaned next to me, casting a weak shield as the roar grew louder. I could hear people smashing through shop windows and terrorising the locals. Anton had succeeded, better—perhaps—than he'd intended. No *wonder* he hadn't bothered to chase us when he'd escaped his custody. He'd already won. No one would listen to us, not after the riot. I turned, just in time to see a bunch of stewards run for their lives. I supposed they were the smart ones. There was no order now, no hope of anything but a bloody slaughter. I knew we should be running too. I just didn't want to turn and run for my life. It would feel like I'd turned my back on everyone.

Reality seemed to shiver. I looked up, sharply. A letterbox was glowing...no, not *glowing*, it was...I wasn't sure what it *was* doing. It seemed more real than everything else, like a light in an endless darkness. I heard Caroline suck in her breath, ice washing down my spine as I realised it was an infernal device. Anton had pulled out all the stops. The rush of tainted magic would finish the riot, killing us as well as hundreds of rioters and guardsmen. Anton's crimes would be buried forever. I could *feel* the magic coil through the air, readying itself to strike. And there was no time to run...

Without thinking, I threw myself forward and jumped onto the device.

CHAPTER THIRTY-EIGHT

Magic—tainted magic—crackled around me.

I could *feel* it burning at my wards, its mere *touch* threatening to corrupt every last one of my protections. It buzzed around me, alluring and repulsive in equal measure. I knew, even as I struggled to reshape my wards, that I might have made a terrible mistake. We'd been taught how to channel magic at Haddon Hall, but *this* was an order of magnitude more powerful—and dangerous—than the spells we'd shaped and cast back there. And it threatened to overwhelm me. I felt as if I'd jumped into the middle of a ward network, without bothering to shield myself. My hair stood on end as the magic surged.

No, I thought. The tainted magic was almost a living thing. I had a weird impression of a snake drawing back to strike. Magic itself seemed to be recoiling…I felt as if I was on the edge of a great discovery, if I had time to look. *That's not going to happen.*

I reshaped my wards, tearing the device's protective charms apart before they could shatter on their own. The magic surged forward, a terrifying blast of random magic—of tainted magic—that threatened to crush me. I'd heard horror stories of people caught up in magic storms. They emerged *changed*, if they emerged at all. The tribes that lived on the edge of the Desolation were people who could never go home again, or so I'd been told. The tainted magic had turned them into monsters.

The magic boiled against my protections, then surged up as it found the easy way out. I breathed a sigh of relief, despite the burning sensation in my skin, as the device detonated. A pillar of tainted magic lanced into the sky. I thought I saw a bird fly into the magic and fall like a stone, but...I couldn't be sure. I might have been hallucinating. All that mattered was that the magic wouldn't hurt anyone on the ground. There was no one in the sky who could be hurt.

I sagged as the device spent itself. My skin itched terribly. I wanted to scratch. My legs gave out and I fell back, landing on the hard cobblestones. It was hard to see—my eyes hurt—but it sounded as if the riot had come to an end. The tainted magic would have sent everyone, rioters and guardsmen alike, running for their lives. I hoped I'd managed to save them. There would be no stopping the chaos if the awful magic had killed hundreds of guardsmen.

A gentle hand touched my back. "Adam," Caroline said. "Are you alright?"

"No," I managed. My voice broke. It was like being an adolescent again. "I feel ghastly."

I leaned into her touch as I fought to centre myself. My head was spinning so madly that I felt as if I was going to collapse to the ground, even though I was *already* on the ground. The ground itself was shaking, tiny earthquakes running through the cobblestones. I couldn't tell if they were real or if I was just imagining them. The city wasn't built on an earthquake zone. The buildings would be falling like dominos if there was a real earthquake. Or so I thought.

Another blurry figure came into view. "Adam? What happened?"

I started. "Sir Griffons?"

My head span. Sir Griffons had been ordered out of the city. He couldn't be here. But the voice was unmistakable. A trick? A trap? Or...I felt my ring grow warm as Sir Griffons pressed his fingers to my forehead, muttering a charm. My vision started to clear. I looked up, half-afraid of what I might see. Sir Griffons knelt next to me, eyes grim. I smiled, despite everything. He was *real*.

"You're out of uniform," he said. It took me a moment to realise he was teasing me. "Don't try to move until you feel ready for it."

I looked down at myself. My tunic was in rags. The cloth itself seemed to have shifted and changed. My skin itched as I realised how close I'd come to death. Or mutation. I wondered, suddenly, what my father would have thought if he'd had a monster for a son. What would he do? Keep me? Or send me to the Desolation? It might be the kindest thing he could do. People weren't kind to the different. And *someone* would certainly try to chop me up for potions ingredients.

My mind was wandering. I centred myself. Again.

"You came," Caroline said. "What happened?"

"We called Magus Court," Sir Griffons said. "Called in a few favours. Convinced them to let us return, with reinforcements. We should have been here sooner, but…someone over there"—he nodded towards North Shallot—"was stalling. I think they'll be in deep shit when Magus Court puts the pieces together."

I wasn't so sure. We still didn't have any real proof, did we? Anton Bolingbroke would dismiss our accusations and then…I shuddered. He'd slip back into the shadows and bide his time, waiting for the next chance to take power. Magus Court wouldn't believe the charges without some very solid proof. Even if they did…my blood ran cold. How many of them would secretly *approve*?

"We don't have any proof," I muttered. "All we did was buy time."

I stumbled to my feet, leaning on Caroline as I looked around. A handful of Kingsmen had arrived and were directing operations, pointing the rioters back towards Water Shallot while keeping the guardsmen on the bridges. A small army of armsmen had arrived and were checking the nearby buildings for contamination, while carrying away the bodies and stacking them by the riverside. I tried to estimate how many people had been killed and drew a blank. Louise had led thousands of people across the river. I had no idea how many of them had stayed with her when the riot began. There was certainly no sign of Louise herself.

She was escorting children back to the bridges, I thought, bitterly. *She should have gotten out of range before it was too late.*

"It'll just make things worse," I said. "Who's going to trust *anyone* after today?"

"We'll see," Sir Griffons said. He smiled, as if he knew something I didn't. "Don't try to do anything. Just wait."

I looked down at myself. My chest was exposed. My skin was covered with an ashy webbing...I shuddered, realising it was dead skin. It itched, terribly. I wanted a shower and a nice long sleep, but...I stumbled forward, heedless of my orders. I wanted to help. I *needed* to help. I owed it to the dead I'd failed to save.

Bitterness ran through me as I saw a handful of small and broken bodies. No one was going to trust again, not after this. Water Shallot would be restive for decades. Louise—or her successor—would have all the cause they needed to raise the mob. And South Shallot wouldn't be much better. I saw a broken building being evacuated and scowled. The locals wouldn't be happy. The entire city felt as if it was on the verge of a breakdown. I didn't want to *think* about what might happen when shock and horror was replaced by anger.

I glanced at Sir Griffons as he spoke briefly to another Kingsman. He was going to fail me. He was going to kick me out. And why should he not? I'd failed. I'd pushed the limits as far as they'd go—and a little further—for nothing. I'd failed to stop the riot; I'd failed to gather the proof we needed to arrest Anton and...I'd failed. Hundreds—perhaps thousands—of people were dead, because of me. I hoped Caroline wouldn't pay the price for my failings. I promised myself, silently, that I'd fall on my sword for her. She deserved someone better than me.

A pair of healers checked me over, gave me a potion to drink and hurried away again. I watched them go, numb. They shouldn't be wasting their time on me. Didn't they know how badly I'd failed? I sipped the potion, grimacing at the taste. It would keep me alive, long enough for me to be dismissed.

And then...I looked down at the bloodstained cobblestones. What was I going to do with my life?

"Look sharp," Caroline said. "We have company."

I looked up. Lord Dirac was approaching, escorted by two men. An armsman...and Anton Bolingbroke. I felt a surge of pure anger. My magic was low, but I could cast a killing spell at point-blank range. There were spells that would punch right through his wards and take him out. They'd cost me my life—they were rare, because they killed both the target *and* the caster—but I didn't care. It wasn't as if I had anything to live for. I'd failed. The best I could hope for was being dishonourably discharged.

Caroline put her hand in mine. I glanced at her, then tried to concentrate. If I could cast the spell...

"The socialists tried to blow themselves up," Anton said. I wondered, suddenly, if he recognised me. My face itched. If it was as ashy as my chest... he might not recognise me. "Thankfully, your man managed to save us all."

"Indeed," Sir Griffons said, coldly.

"We will, of course, push for the arrest of the remaining socialists," Anton continued. "The guardsmen are already readying themselves for their mission. They will put Water Shallot into lockdown, then go house-to-house until the socialists have been rounded up..."

"Your authority has already been terminated," Sir Griffons said. "Magus Court has rescinded your operational charter."

Anton blinked. Beside him, Lord Dirac was completely expressionless. It looked as if he wasn't surprised. I wondered, suddenly, just what Sir Griffons had said to Magus Court. He trusted us—I thought—but our word wasn't enough to convict anyone. Anton was a *Bolingbroke*. Magus Court would close ranks around him, the moment they realised he was under threat. They wouldn't let outsiders dictate to them.

I felt a hot flash of anger. "You did it," I snarled. "You planned it all."

Anton's eyes narrowed. He knew me now. "We do not have time for nonsense."

"You built the infernal devices," I charged. Sir Griffons made no move to stop me. "You killed *children*. You tried to kill Prince Jacob. And here, you started a riot. Your people attacked the crowd and..."

"Bored and foolish young men." Anton made a show of inspecting his fingertips, before turning his attention to Lord Dirac. "A tissue of lies, designed to cover their incompetence."

"Perhaps," Lord Dirac said. His eyes bored into me. "Do you have any proof?"

I swallowed, hard. "There are truth spells. And drugs..."

"The lad is a fool," Anton said. "There isn't a truth spell that cannot be circumvented by a powerful sorcerer."

Sir Griffons shot me a smile. "Adam. Are you still wearing your ring?"

I held up my hand. "Yes, sir," I said. "Why...?"

"The rings have quite a few functions that are not common knowledge," Sir Griffons said, coolly. "For one thing, they record and transmit everything that happens to them—and their wearer. Lord Anton's little rant was recorded. Magus Court was *quite* interested to hear we *did* have proof."

Anton paled. "Lies," he said. "I..."

"Your people will verify it for themselves," Sir Griffons said. "And then you will face..."

He cast a spell, slashing through Anton's wards and freezing him. I blinked in surprise, my dulled mind barely following as Sir Griffons yanked open Anton's mouth and removed a fake tooth. Caroline let out a sigh of relief as Sir Griffons pocketed the tooth, then checked the rest of Anton's teeth. He'd tried to wipe his own memory, to preserve his secrets and give the rest of his team a chance to hide. But he'd failed. The Kingsmen—and Magus Court—would get his secrets out of him. I wondered, sourly, how many of them would ever be revealed to the general public.

"I didn't want to believe it," Lord Dirac said, as Sir Griffons cast a complex web of spells on Anton. "I thought he was my ally."

"He had an agenda of his own, clearly," Sir Griffons said. "Be very careful when you put him in a cell. He'll have contacts who'll want to kill him before he can talk."

"Of course," Lord Dirac said. "I never thought..."

"No," Sir Griffons said. "It's never easy to think the worst of your friends."

I looked from one to the other, wondering why they were talking like... *friends*. They were rivals, weren't they? Magus Court and the Kingsmen were permanently at odds. But they had interests in common too. They had to work together. I supposed they lost nothing by being civil. And...I glanced at Caroline. Not *all* aristos were bad. Lord Dirac...I promised myself I'd give him a chance. I wouldn't assume he was a bad guy simply because he was an aristo.

Lord Dirac summoned a carriage. "I'll be taking him back to Magus Court," he said. "Do you want to accompany me?"

"I might have to," Sir Griffons said. "You never know who can be trusted, these days."

I caught Lord Dirac's eye. "Are you going to send the guardsmen into Water Shallot?"

"No." Lord Dirac studied me for a long moment. "They've been ordered to stay on the bridges. Hopefully, things will quiet down in a few days."

Sir Griffons nodded, curtly. "Adam, Caroline, go back home," he said. "Get a shower, change your clothes and have a rest. Or start writing your reports. I'll expect to see detailed reports from the pair of you by tomorrow evening."

I studied my ring. None of my tutors had so much as *hinted* that the rings recorded everything we said and did. I wasn't sure what to make of it. The ring on my finger had recorded Anton's confession, but it had also recorded my tryst with Louise and everything else I'd done since I'd put it on. I shuddered, realising how easy it would be to abuse such spells. The potential for mischief—or tyranny—was terrifying.

"You saw everything I saw," I said. "Didn't you?"

"But we need to know what you were thinking," Sir Griffons said. "The rings can't read your minds. We know what you did, but we don't know why."

He nodded to us, then scrambled into the carriage. I let out a breath as they rattled away, then turned to look at the bodies. There were hundreds, including a number in black. Anton had sent them to die…I wondered, wryly, if he'd become the most hated man in Shallot when *that* little fact leaked out. His agents had been aristos. Their families wouldn't be amused when they realised he'd intended to kill them. Bored and foolish young men they might have been, but they were still aristos.

A thought struck me. "Malachi knew something," I muttered, as we started to walk over the nearest bridge. The guardsmen, wisely, didn't get in our way. "That's why he sent us to Rebecca."

Caroline gave me a sharp look. "That *could* be just a coincidence."

"Rebecca's a Bolingbroke client," I reminded her. "And Anton *is* a Bolingbroke. If it's a coincidence…what are the odds?"

"We'll figure it out, if we're still on the case," Caroline said. She shrugged, dismissively. "Right now, we have other problems."

I nodded as we passed Magus Court. The buildings, from the towering office blocks to the giant mansions, were surrounded by heavy wards. North Shallot was eerily quiet, as if the locals expected to be attacked at any moment. Only a handful of shops were open, with nary a customer in sight. I told myself it would do the locals good. They needed to feel the fear that had gripped the rest of the city. It might give them some empathy for their fellow man.

The wards around our building parted as we stepped through the gatehouse and walked around to the back. My skin started to itch, again, as we stepped into the decontamination chamber and stripped down. I was covered with dust and ash. Skin cells flaked off as I stepped into the shower, allowing the water to wash me clean. I still looked odd, I decided. My face was a mess. No wonder Anton hadn't recognised me at first. I wondered if my skin would ever return to normal. It didn't seem likely.

"Let the healers take a look at you," Caroline advised, when I said that out loud. She looked me up and down, then shrugged. "There's nothing visibly wrong with you. You haven't grown an extra leg or turned into a woman or dropped dead on the spot. You *should* be fine."

"Hah," I grumbled. I towelled down, grateful my skin had stopped itching. "I'll be marched to the Desolation before you know it."

"You weren't transfigured into a monster," Caroline pointed out. She slapped me on the back. "You'll be fine."

I shook my head. Sir Griffons would be back, soon enough. And when he did...I felt my stomach churn. If he'd seen everything, he knew how I'd failed. He wasn't going to be pleased. I was sure of it.

At least I saved thousands of lives, I thought, as I headed up the stairs to bed. Our bedroom looked unchanged. *That has to count for something, doesn't it?*

But, in truth, I wasn't sure.

CHAPTER THIRTY-NINE

"This is a preliminary inquest," Sir Griffons said, the following morning. "We need to go through a few details."

I stood in front of the table, my hands clasped behind my back to keep them from shaking. I'd expected Sir Griffons, but not Lord Dirac, Carioca Rubén and Joaquin Aguirre. The three aristos studied me, expressions totally unreadable. I supposed I did look a *little* like Joaquin Aguirre. It must have come from my father. My mother looked completely different.

And he looks a little like Caroline, I thought. It was hard to be sure, but there *was* a hint of Caroline in his face. *Is he her father? Does Alana know she has a half-sister?*

I put the thought aside. I wasn't going to ask, not now. If Caroline wanted me to know, she'd tell me. If not...it was none of my business. And besides, I might be wrong.

"You correctly identified Anton Bolingbroke," Sir Griffons said. "How did you do it?"

I took a breath, then outlined the full story. The assassin, who'd wiped his memory; the spy, who'd ratted Louise out to her enemies; my plan, to convince them that the spy *hadn't* wiped his memory and force them to attempt to recover him. I wondered, suddenly, what had happened to the poor bastard. I guessed he was still in the socialist safehouse. No one had tried to transport him to prison.

They listened carefully, asking me a handful of questions. I had the feeling that Carioca Rubén and Joaquin Aguirre *respected* each other, but didn't *like* each other. That boded ill for Akin and Caitlyn, I supposed. It was never fun when the in-laws didn't get along. I told myself, firmly, it wasn't my problem as I outlined how we'd escaped Anton Bolingbroke and fled to try to stop the riot. We'd failed…but at least we'd saved thousands of lives. I'd read the report. The device would have killed everyone within a mile if it had detonated as planned.

"Anton attempted to convince you to stand aside," Lord Dirac said. "Why didn't you?"

I swallowed. "His plan was utter madness," I said. "And it was wrong."

"It came very close to succeeding," Joaquin Aguirre commented. "His supporters—not all of whom *knew* what they were supporting—were poised to take control of Magus Court."

His expression darkened. I felt a stab of sympathy, despite everything. His daughter would have been kidnapped or simply murdered, if Anton had taken control. Everything he'd worked for would have collapsed. And then…I wondered if Anton would have stepped into the light, or if he'd continued to run things from the shadows. It would be difficult for people to revolt if they didn't know who they had to revolt *against*.

There were a handful of other questions, then the senior lords stood. "We'll be in touch," Joaquin Aguirre said. "But thank you for your service."

I nodded, feeling unaccountably vulnerable. Caroline was…somewhere else. Sir Griffons had called her down first, then sent her away. I hoped that wasn't a bad sign. Maybe he was just trying to make sure we told him the same story, when he asked us. But…the rings would have told him everything we'd done, if he checked. I had the feeling he had other reasons for talking to us separately. I just wished I knew what they were.

"Stand at ease," Sir Griffons said. "You may pour yourself a drink, if you like."

I didn't relax. Much. "Thank you, sir."

Sir Griffons studied me for a long moment. "You were on your own for three days," he said. "You were operating without supervision. How do you think you did?"

"Poorly." I didn't think there was any point in lying. "I made a whole string of mistakes."

"Indeed?" Sir Griffons cocked his head. "Explain."

"I let my feelings blind me," I said. I assumed he'd watched everything. "I let myself get too close to the socialists."

Sir Griffons chuckled. "I suppose that's *one* way of putting it."

I silently thanked my ancestors that my reddening cheeks weren't visible. "I let my feelings get in the way, again, when we visited Rebecca Travis. I...I treated her poorly. And then I risked my life—and Caroline's life—in confronting Zadornov. I could have gotten us both killed. And then I risked everything—again—to let them kidnap me. If they'd been a little smarter, or a little more secure in their potion, the scheme would have failed. I could have been killed, or worse."

"You seem to have a good grip on your mistakes," Sir Griffons said, tonelessly. "What do you think I should do to you?"

"They were *my* mistakes," I said. "Caroline...went along for the ride."

"I think you do her an injustice," Sir Griffons said. "But that's not the first time you did her an injustice, is it?"

"No, sir." I hung my head in shame. "I was a little prat."

"You were...unfinished," Sir Griffons said. "That's not uncommon amongst people your age. Very few of them know what they want to be... and even if they do, they rarely *are*."

He smiled, his eyes never leaving mine. "But you never answered my question. What do you think I should do to you?"

I swallowed, hard. "I think you should dismiss me."

"Indeed?" Sir Griffons didn't look away. "Do you feel you failed so badly?"

"Yes, sir," I said.

Sir Griffons said nothing for a long moment. "First, berating you is *my* job, not yours," he said. "It is *customary* to wait a few years before you start scheming to take your superior's position."

I blinked. "Sir?"

"Second, you made mistakes. *Everyone* makes mistakes. You *also* managed to recover from them. You executed a plan to reveal the conspirators and carried it out. Yes, you failed to stop the riot. But that wasn't through lack of effort on your part. You did everything you could."

He paused. "You did push the limits of what we're allowed to do, when it comes to demanding information from people. Trusting anything from suspects like Zadornov or Malachi Rubén was dangerous. Bullying Rebecca Travis was a more serious mistake, even if you thought you had good reason. I trust you've learnt something useful from that little...wrong turn?"

"Yes, sir." I frowned. "But she *is* a Bolingbroke client, sir, and Anton is a Bolingbroke himself."

"Magus Court will determine if there's a link between them," Sir Griffons said. "We've had our eye on Malachi Rubén for the past few months. There are rumours"—he shrugged—"suffice it to say that anything he says should be taken with extreme care. We may never know what happened between him and the rest of his family, but it had to be serious. They exiled him to Water Shallot."

"Yes, sir," I said. "Do you think he was just trying to cause trouble?"

"I'd say he succeeded," Sir Griffons said, dryly. "And your...*friend*... Louise should be careful what she takes from him."

"I'm sure she understands, sir," I said. "What's going to happen to *her*?"

"Nothing." Sir Griffons studied his hands for a long moment. "We know she didn't build the infernal devices. We know she didn't *intend* the march to turn into a riot. The state of emergency has been lifted, her family has been released, compensation will be paid...officially, she's in the clear. I dare say she'll either continue her career or step back into the shadows. It isn't our concern."

He cleared his throat. "You made mistakes. So did Caroline. However...I feel—and my superiors agree—that you do not deserve to be discharged. You admitted your mistakes and did your level best to recover from them. You're not ready to be knighted, yet, but you're on the way."

I breathed a sigh of relief. "Thank you, sir."

Sir Griffons shrugged. "We're going to be heading to Caithness in a few days, once we've filed our reports. There are...issues up north that require investigation. I suggest you spend the next two days with your family. There's no way to know when you'll see them again."

Or at all, I thought, grimly.

"You did well, given the limitations you faced," Sir Griffons added. "Not perfectly, but well enough."

"Thank you, sir," I said. "I...what's going to happen to Anton Bolingbroke?"

"Good question," Sir Griffons said. "They're interrogating him now, steadily peeling back his defences until they get the truth. They'll uncover the remainder of his supporters and deal with them. I dare say they'll be quietly disowned, at the very least. A handful will probably be transported to Skullbreaker Island. No one will try to defend them."

"Good," I said. "And will the public ever know the truth?"

Sir Griffons gave me a sharp look. "Maybe. Maybe not. We'll have to wait and see."

I shook my head. "It feels so...so *inconclusive*."

"Our cases often are," Sir Griffons said. "We find out who's guilty and then...our superiors tackle the matter quietly, rather than enforcing public punishment. People are disowned and sent into exile, while the system lives on. It's never easy punishing people for *political* cases. Push too hard and the entire edifice might crumble."

I couldn't keep the bitterness out of my voice. "Is that a bad thing?"

"How many people work, directly or indirectly, for House Bolingbroke?" Sir Griffons didn't wait for me to answer. "How many clients do they have? How many people depend upon them? And what would *happen* to them if

House Bolingbroke collapsed? Thousands—tens of thousands—of people would be thrown out of work. The economic shockwaves would threaten the remainder of the Great Houses. They might not be *able* to pick up the slack, let alone hire the newly-unemployed. They might remain unemployed for years..."

His voice hardened. "What would you prefer? Quiet punishment for the guilty? Or a public punishment that shatters House Bolingbroke and puts tens of thousands of people out of work?"

"Quiet punishment," I said. "But it doesn't seem fair."

"The world isn't fair." Sir Griffons shrugged. "The guilty will be identified. Hopefully, they'll be a rogue cross-house faction. The Bolingbroke—and all the others—will profess surprise that it happened and purge the faction from their house. And the employed will remain employed."

"I hope you're right, sir," I said.

"It isn't wrong to be idealistic," Sir Griffons said. "But you should be aware of the practicalities too. Idealism without practicality always ends in tears."

He stood and poured himself a cup of tea. "I've already spoken to Caroline," he said. "She'll be accompanying us to Caithness. I hope that'll please you."

"Yes, sir," I said. "We work well together."

"Dismissed," Sir Griffons said. "Make sure you're back here by Thursday evening. We'll be leaving on Friday."

I saluted. "Yes, sir."

It was hard not to run as I turned and left, heading upstairs. My thoughts were confused. I wasn't sure what would be better. Public or private punishment? But the latter...I scowled as I stumbled into the living room. If punishment wasn't public, outsiders would think the guilty man had gotten away with it. But if punishment *was* public...I didn't know. Sir Griffons and his superiors had made the call. I just hoped Shallot would be able to live with it.

Caroline looked up as I entered. "How was it?"

"It could have been worse," I said. I wondered what Sir Griffons had said to *her*. "Did you finish your report?"

"Yeah." Caroline held out a sheaf of papers. "And we just got the preliminary report on the riot. It's not pleasant reading."

"No." I took the papers and started to skim through them. "It wouldn't be."

My stomach churned as I read. It was very precise in places and strikingly vague in others. There was no mention of Anton Bolingbroke or his cronies. There was only a faint reference to the infernal device. The entire riot was blamed on agitators who'd slipped into the crowd and wreaked havoc. I wondered, bitterly, just who the writer thought he was fooling. Too many people had seen Anton's cronies at work for them to be casually erased from history.

"One hundred and seventy people dead, officially." I suspected that was an understatement. "And over four hundred people injured."

"As well as thousands of crowns worth of damaged or destroyed property," Caroline said, softly. "It would have been a lot worse if you hadn't stopped the infernal device."

I nodded, my scalp itching. "Do they really expect people to believe this?"

"They're trying to establish a narrative, while they purge Magus Court," Caroline said. "I dare say Carioca Rubén and Joaquin Aguirre will bring the wedding forward as quickly as possible."

"Yeah." I shook my head. "They won't be inviting us, will they?"

"They'll have to give the Aguirre girls a season first," Caroline said. "You never know. We might get invited to that."

"Alana wouldn't want *me*," I said. "She spent seven years looking down on me."

Caroline snorted. "Being an aristo means you don't get to control your guest list," she said, darkly. "They'll be inviting people they really can't stand because of politics. The people who *don't* get invited will be terribly insulted. And then they'll make it known."

"You'll make me feel sorry for them," I said, as I poured myself a drink. "Stop it."

Caroline shrugged. "The rich and powerful cannot understand the poor. They cannot understand why poverty leads people to make terrible decisions. It makes them see the poor as stupid, because—from their point of view—stupid decisions are stupid decisions. But the poor cannot understand the rich either. They don't see the social obligations, or how failure can lead to utter disaster…"

"But at least they have money," I said.

"Don't count on it," Caroline told me. "House Lamplighter is so short of ready cash that it's anyone's guess when it's going to fall to pieces. They're bleeding family members and don't have any clients worthy of the name. They certainly don't have any prospect of *getting* more, either. The smart money says their heiress will either marry for money or loot the estate and vanish. Either way, she'll be in a lot of trouble."

"I'll take your word for it," I said. I sipped my drink. It was odd to think that a Great House might be terminally short of money, but…I shrugged. It wasn't my problem. "I have to see a couple of people. After that…do you want to meet my family?"

"If you like." Caroline grinned at me. "Should I be concerned about your siblings?"

"Just tell them we got married twenty years ago," I said. I winked at her. "They'll spend at least an hour spluttering before they realise it's impossible."

Caroline laughed. "Siblings," she said. "Yours are probably better than mine."

"They're hard workers," I said. I wondered, suddenly, if I was right. If Alana, Bella and Caitlyn were Caroline's siblings…I felt a stab of pity. That wouldn't be pleasant for anyone. "What about yours?"

"They can be hard workers too," Caroline said. She took back the report. "I've got a few things to do before we go. I'll meet you in Water Shallot at six?"

"Sounds like a plan." I glanced at the window. "Call me if you're going to be late. The streets might be jammed."

"We'll see," Caroline said. She frowned, suddenly. "The guardsmen won't stop you now, will they?"

I laughed. "They probably still want to arrest me," I said. I had no idea if the arrest warrant was still valid. Lord Dirac *should* have cancelled it, but he had other problems right now. I was probably at the bottom of his list. "I'd better get dressed for another swim."

"Try not to drown," Caroline said. She met my eyes, suddenly. "And when you're talking to Louise, be honest."

I made a rude gesture, then turned and headed into the bedroom. The knapsack I'd packed a week ago—it felt like years ago—was still in Water Shallot, but I'd had to leave behind a couple of outfits. I donned a simple tunic and trousers, then checked myself in the mirror. My face still looked odd, as if I'd covered myself in chalk dust. The healers had promised it would return to normal, but it was hard to believe. It just wasn't normal. I cast a glamour to hide it, then turned away. My family would probably notice—they knew me well enough to see through the illusion—but hopefully everyone else would turn a blind eye. They'd probably think I was just using the spell to make myself look better. It took years for teenage boys to realise it simply didn't work.

"See you," I called, as I headed downstairs. Caroline didn't look up as I passed. "Have fun."

Sir Griffons was sitting in his office, writing a report. I felt a pang of guilt for leaving him, even though I'd already done mine. I hoped it was as clear and comprehensive as his superiors wanted. I'd done my best to list the reasoning behind my decisions, but it was painfully clear—sometimes—that there hadn't *been* any real reasoning. It was one of my mistakes. And now...

You'll learn from your mistakes, I told myself. I'd forced myself to go through them all, first on my own and then with Caroline. *And one day you will be knighted.*

Shaking my head, I stepped out the door and walked onto the streets.

CHAPTER
FORTY

South Shallot felt oddly quiet, I decided, as I walked across the bridge and past the scene of the crime. The vast majority of the damage had already been cleared up, I noted; the only lingering traces of the riot were a handful of scorched buildings and a pile of rubble where one particularly rickety building had been. A handful of guardsmen stood on duty, looking over piles of flowers people had distributed along the riverbed. My heart twisted as I turned and walked towards the shops. My beloved city had changed, perhaps beyond repair. There was a new tension in the air. Anton Bolingbroke might have the last laugh after all.

I put the thought aside as I reached the shops. They were open, but largely empty. I hesitated, feeling unsure of myself, then walked up to the apothecary and pushed open the door. Rebecca was standing behind the counter, carefully weighing out small cloth bags of beetle legs. She looked up, almond eyes going wide when she saw me. I felt a pang of guilt. She had to think I'd come to make her life miserable again.

"Can we talk?" I spoke as gently as possible. "Please."

Rebecca looked at me for a long moment, then nodded curtly. She didn't seem inclined to take me into the back room. There was no sign of her shopgirl. I held myself still, trying to communicate that I was no threat. But I was sure she didn't believe me.

"I owe you an apology," I said. "I treated you poorly and...I have no excuse."

"No," Rebecca said. Her voice was very quiet. "You don't."

It crossed my mind, suddenly, that she might not accept my apology. And why should she? I'd thrown my weight around with no thought to the possible consequences. I'd been desperate, but...I knew better. Now. I'd been blinded by my feelings. Caroline had been right. I'd acted poorly and now I had to deal with the consequences.

"I'm sorry," I said. "Someone gave me your name and I ran with it."

Rebecca's lips twitched. "You weren't the only one."

I nodded. I guessed she'd already been visited by Lord Dirac. "Do you *know* Anton Bolingbroke?"

"No." Rebecca ran a hand through her long black hair. "I might have met him, back when I was working in Bolingbroke Hall, but...I don't remember him."

"I see," I said. "Is that a good thing?"

Rebecca smiled. It was strikingly endearing. "Yes. The ones I remember...most of them were thoroughly unpleasant."

"I can believe it," I said. "Forgive me, but I need to ask...did you invent or brew a memory-wipe potion?"

"No." Rebecca bit her lip. "Master Travis did."

I blinked. "Master Travis?"

Rebecca looked down at the counter. "He was my master, before...before he was killed. He did commissions for clients, *special* clients. One of them was a memory-wipe potion. I found the notes in his vault after his death. I don't know who commissioned it."

"I think I do," I said. I'd thought Travis was Rebecca's father. It had never occurred to me that he might have been her master. "Did Lord Dirac ask the same question?"

"Yes." Rebecca looked up at me. "He took the notes."

"Ouch," I said.

"I never did anything with them," Rebecca said. "There was no cure, as far as I could tell. The potion didn't seem to have any valid use."

"Beyond ensuring someone couldn't talk," I said. I had to smile. No wonder Magus Court had never traced the brewer. He'd lived and worked in Water Shallot before he was killed. They probably hadn't thought to look there. "Did you ever consider trying to brew a cure?"

"I never had time." Rebecca gave me a shy smile. "I'm still working towards my mastery."

I nodded. "Good luck," I said. "Can I ask one final question?"

Rebecca frowned, then nodded. "Go ahead."

"You're a Bolingbroke client," I said. "Why don't you work for them directly?"

"I was given the shop and patronage as a reward." Rebecca visibly hesitated. "I can't tell you much more, but…suffice it to say I have no real obligations to them."

"They were paying back a debt," I said. What *had* Rebecca done for them? It could have been anything, anything at all. "I…thank you."

I bowed. "I'm sorry," I said, again. "And if there's anything I can do for you, don't hesitate to ask."

The wards crackled around me as I pushed open the door, stepped back onto the streets and headed down to the bridges. I felt oddly better, as if I'd been absolved. Rebecca had no reason to like me—and it was quite possible we'd never see each other again—but at least she'd heard my apology. I mulled over what she'd told me as I crossed the bridges, passing a barricade someone had thrown up a day too late. If Master Travis had provided the memory-wipe potion to Stregheria Aguirre…

Clever, I thought. *No one would have looked for a Potions Master in Water Shallot. They certainly wouldn't have considered him capable of inventing a new potion, let alone putting it into production.*

It made sense, I told myself. Master Travis could have been killed to bury Stregheria Aguirre's tracks, once he'd outlived his usefulness. I suspected further investigation was pointless, but I made a mental note to suggest it anyway. It might be interesting to see what *else* Master Travis had brewed over the years. If he'd been that good, he could have done almost anything.

The streets were grim, I noted, as I walked towards Louise's shop. The people were fuming. They'd been shocked, but…it wouldn't be long before they became angry. There were already posters everywhere, calling the people to stand up and fight for their rights. I had a feeling Louse's plan had already fallen by the wayside. The people wanted revenge, not a nonviolent struggle for freedom.

I smiled as I noticed the shop was being repaired. Workmen were swarming around the building, patching up the damage. The stocks had already been replenished. Sir Griffons had probably had a few words with someone about it. I nodded to myself as I pushed open the door and stepped inside. It might go some way towards mending fences.

Louise's sister winked at me. "Hello, Louise's boyfriend!"

I resisted the urge to hex her. "Is she upstairs?"

"Yeah." The girl winked at me. "Are you her boyfriend? Really?"

"Just a friend," I said, firmly. "Can I go up?"

"Sure." Louise's sister smirked. "Try and surprise her."

I made sure to make as much noise as I could as I walked up the stairs and peered into her bedroom. Surprising a sorceress was a good way to be turned into a frog—or worse. Louise was sitting on a wooden stool, writing in a notebook. It looked as if she was writing a speech.

"Hi," I said. "How are you?"

Louise looked up at me, her expression vague. I couldn't tell if she was pleased to see me. We'd shared so much, yet…she had good reason to be angry at me. And everyone else. Her cause had been damaged. It might even have been broken beyond repair.

"Tired," she said. "I heard you saved thousands of lives."

"At a cost," I said. Her eyes narrowed. She knew me well enough to see through the glamour. "But it was worth it."

"Good." Louise sounded tired. Tired and depressed. "I'm glad. I really am."

I wanted to hug her. But I didn't dare.

"We caught the person behind the infernal devices," I said. I was fairly sure she knew it already. "Everyone knows you were framed."

"Everyone?" Louise shook her head. "Nothing is ever going to be the same, is it?"

She waved a hand at the tiny window. "Sure, everything *looks* normal out there. Nothing has changed. But you know what? *Everything* has changed. We can't go back to pretending that peaceful protest is enough. If they were prepared to kill their own people to get at us, what *else* are they prepared to do?"

"The only aristocrat they meant to kill was Prince Jacob," I said. "I heard he'll be leaving the city."

Louise managed a humourless laugh. "Do you blame him?"

I shook my head. Prince Jacob probably knew—or suspected—he'd been targeted. And besides, he'd gotten nothing beyond a few vague words of sympathy from the Great Houses. They certainly hadn't promised him material or monetary support. He'd be wise to leave the city as quickly as possible, before he was ordered to leave. The Great Houses didn't have time for him.

"Things are going to change again," Louise said. "I haven't given up."

"I didn't think you would," I said. "And I..."

She cut me off. "You...weren't entirely honest with me that night, were you? You didn't tell me the truth until much later."

I rubbed my cheek. "You slapped me. Hard."

"You deserved it," Louise said. She stood, brushing down her skirt. "Whose side are you on?"

"I swore an oath to uphold the law," I said. "And..."

"And what do you do," Louise demanded, "if the law itself can be rewritten? Or if your superiors order you to *break* the law?"

I said nothing. We'd been warned there were illegal orders—and we'd be in deep trouble if we obeyed them—but it was clear that refusing to obey wouldn't be easy. Our superiors could make our lives very difficult if we didn't follow orders. What would I have done, I asked myself, if I'd been ordered to assist Anton Bolingbroke? I liked to think I would have said *no*. But...I didn't know.

"Stay with me," Louise said. "Join me. Join us. Fight for our rights. Or go. Leave now and don't come back."

My heart twisted. I wasn't in love with her. I was sure of it. But I *did* like her. She was...brave and determined, as well as beautiful. I knew she rubbed people the wrong way—she'd been more isolated than me at school—but she meant well. There was a bit of me that wanted to take off the ring and join her, walking away from the Kingsmen. But...I knew it would mean breaking my oaths. I wasn't ready to become foresworn.

"I can make things better, from the inside," I said. "And..."

"You're not the first person to say that," Louise said. She reached for her cloak and pulled it on. "Goodbye, Adam. Don't come visiting again."

I stared at her, feeling...I wasn't sure how I felt. I understood her point. She couldn't afford to trust someone with divided loyalties. And yet, I felt angry at being dismissed so casually, at being ordered out of her life. How *could* she? I'd put my career on the line for her. I wanted...I wasn't sure what I wanted, either. It wasn't as if either of us were going to have a normal life. She was going to lead the socialists and I...

...I was going to Caithness.

"I'm sorry," I said.

Louise's gaze was very hard. "Goodbye."

I bowed, then retreated back down the stairs. Louise's sister waved cheerfully as I walked past and headed for the door. I had a feeling she was going to be teasing her older sister...*that* wasn't going to work out well. I heard footsteps coming downstairs as I left the shop. Louise...needed to rebuild her cause. I hoped she managed to catch the spy before he did any more damage.

"Goodbye," I said, quietly.

I started to walk, heedless of where I was going. There were more posters covering the walls, promising everything from more protest marches to more direct action. A pair of prostitutes waved cheerfully, their smiles turning unpleasant as they realised I wasn't interested. I tasted fish in the air as I crossed a canal, wondering if I'd gain anything from confronting Zadornov or Malachi Rubén. I had so many questions. But Sir Griffons had hinted the latter was under investigation. I might get in trouble if I got involved.

My thoughts raced as I turned away, striding up the canal walkway. Too much had happened, too quickly. I felt as if I'd been a fool, even though Caroline and Sir Griffons had assured me I'd learnt from my mistakes. I'd done all right, in the end. And yet…oddly, I couldn't wait for Friday. I'd never been to Caithness. It would be somewhere new, somewhere I had no family ties. Who knew what I'd find there?

I turned and started to stride back towards the bridges. It was nearly six. Caroline would be waiting. I wondered what my family would make of her. Bringing a girl home had only one meaning, unless the girl had been a friend since childhood. My father would understand, I thought. My sisters would pretend otherwise.

"Hey," Caroline said. She was standing by the bridge, her dark eyes wary. "How did it go?"

I looked around. "I don't feel like I belong here any longer," I said. "I can't wait for Friday."

"I'm not surprised," Caroline said. "Sooner or later, we all have to grow up."

"Hah." I gave her a sharp look as we started to walk. "What did Sir Griffons say to you?"

"That we both still had a lot to learn," Caroline said. "And that we made a good team. *And* that we won."

"Barely," I said.

"Anton Bolingbroke is in jail," Caroline said. "The crisis is over. Thousands of lives have been saved. The guilty will be punished. Even if they somehow escape, or get away with it, Magus Court knows what they tried to do. You know what? I'd count that as a win."

She squeezed my hand. "And if it wasn't for you, it would never have happened," she said. "How many people owe you their lives? We won."

"Yeah," I said. "I suppose I'd count it as a win too."

I stopped outside the shop. Thankfully, it hadn't been damaged. "Are you ready to meet my family?"

"Yes," Caroline said. "I'm ready."

"Then let's go." I pushed the door open. "I'm sure they'll love you."

THE END

THE ZERO ENIGMA WILL CONTINUE IN:
The Lady Heiress

AFTERWORD
ONE

I have a bit of a confession to make. I wrote an afterword on Class Privilege before I actually started writing *The King's Man*. It drew some interesting comments from my readers, not all of whom agreed with it (of course) and not all thought it fitted with the book. It *is* a little more adult (and controversial) than the story itself. And so I went backwards and forwards on including it before finally deciding to put it after *this* afterword (as well as hosting it on my site, where I could include the links).

It's hard to exaggerate how much a role class plays, both in a fictional city like Shallot and the real world. Adam and Louise have good reasons to resent the system, which forces them to either submit themselves to the aristocracy (by accepting their patronage) or work twice as hard to achieve half as much. Their shared prejudice against the Great Houses is rooted in their early lives—and the simple fact that the system really *is* rigged. And if you cannot win, why *not* flip the table? Why *not* try to tear the system down?

Your mileage may vary, of course.

And now you've read the book, I have a favour to ask.

It's getting harder to earn a living through indie writing these days, for a number of reasons (my health is one of them, unfortunately). If you liked this book, please post a review wherever you bought it; the more reviews a book gets, the more promotion.

CGN.

AFTERWORD
TWO

I'm going to start with a question many people will find, for all sorts of reasons, highly controversial. Bear with me a little.

Does 'white privilege' even exist?

It seems to, based on the sheer number of think pieces published in a vast number of reputable (and not so reputable) journals and suchlike arguing that it does. There is no shortage of people telling other people that they have privilege, then offering to run courses training them to acknowledge they have privilege and then...and then *what*? There is no clear answer to that question, largely because the people who run such courses don't want to put themselves out of business.

First, let me try to answer my original question. Does 'white privilege' even exist?

My answer is rather nuanced. I have indeed experienced a degree of 'white privilege.' But I had that experience in Malaysia, which is *not*—by any reasonable measure—a white-majority country. Whites make up a very small percentage of the overall population, smaller still outside the bigger cities. (When I lived in Kota Kinabalu, I was the only white person in the apartment block.) This 'white privilege' came with a price, literally. When I shopped alone, in places where there were no price tags, the price was generally higher than when my (Malay) wife and I shopped together. Whites are generally assumed to be wealthy in Malaysia, which is one of the reasons the whole 'beg-packing' phenomenon is regarded with a mixture of bemusement and annoyance. It's also true that I got more respect from the local police than other immigrants, who seemed to believe it was unlikely that any white person in Malaysia would be anything other than a perfectly legal immigrant. I was allowed to walk through a checkpoint for illegal immigrants even though I do not look *remotely* Malaysian.

In Britain and America, however, the question of 'white privilege' is a great deal more thorny. By definition, a racial (or sexual or religious or whatever) privilege must apply to the vast majority of people who fit the bill. White privilege can only exist if the vast majority of white people have it (in the same sense, perhaps, as men can be said to have 'penis privilege' and women can be said to have 'vagina privilege'). And it is by no means apparent that the vast majority of white people possess privilege. It certainly doesn't seem to provide them with any real advantages. Indeed, in some ways, it provides quite the opposite.

The 'privilege-checkers' are fond of citing Peggy McIntosh's famous 1989 essay, '*White Privilege: Unpacking the Invisible Knapsack.*' McIntosh lists 26 of what *she* calls the daily effects of white privilege in her life, putting race ahead of any other factor. However, the list is deeply flawed. Not, perhaps, because it is inaccurate in *her* case, but because it is inaccurate for so many others. We might break down her 26 effects as follows:

True (of the vast majority of white people): 6, 9, 17, 20

False (based on non-racial factors): 1, 2, 3, 4, 8, 11, 13, 15, 21, 23, 25

Dubious: 5, 7, 12, 14, 18, 22, 26

Flatly Untrue: 10, 16, 19, 24

Many of her effects—the false or dubious effects—are oddly slanted, drawn from her personal experience rather than more generalist experiences. #8—"*if I want to, I can be pretty sure of finding a publisher for this piece on white privilege*" is laughable from almost *any* other point of view. Finding a publisher is *not* easy and only someone who'd spent most of her life in academia would argue otherwise. #19—"*if a traffic cop pulls me over or if the IRS audits my tax return, I can be sure I haven't been singled out because of my race"*—is odd because it is quite difficult to see who is driving a car or written the tax return until the drunkenly-driving car is pulled over or the auditor checks to see if the person claiming a million-dollar income is *really* drawing in so much money. In both cases, there can be ample grounds for suspicion long before the person's race is clearly recognised.

Others are flatly untrue, depending on personal conditions. There is no way #1 fits me unless I cut my wife, my mixed-race children and all my in-laws out of my life. The only way someone could fit #2 is through having vast amounts of money and a certain amount of social clout. And really, one doesn't *need* to be a different race to have neighbours who are not friendly or even neutral (#3).

It is fairly easy to believe, therefore, that McIntosh was simply wrong.

John Scalzi, the well-known science-fiction author, had a different way of looking at it. He put forward an essay entitled '*Straight White Male: The Lowest Difficulty Setting There Is,*' in which he compared growing up a 'straight white male' to playing a computer game on a very easy setting. This is a more solid argument than the invisible knapsack, as it is less tightly bound to specific advantages, but it suffers from a number of flaws. Most notably, the obvious response is something that boils down to "I'm a straight white male and my life has been anything but easy and therefore Scalzi is wrong." This isn't really helped by the simple fact that most 'easy' settings are *really* easy. I tend to agree with this: my life wasn't easy, even though—yes—I am a straight white male.

It might be better to say that the advantages of being a straight white male are negated by being a friendless nerd with poor social skills, no gift of the gab and a shortage of money. Indeed, one can even argue that 'friendless nerd' is right at the bottom of the social hierarchy. Scalzi's argument is better, as he's talking in general terms, rather than specifics, but it still has problems. People don't think in generalities when they're suffering and react badly to people who say they *should*.

In a sense, both McIntosh and Scalzi are talking from a position of privilege. They recognise their own privilege, their own advantages, but they don't realise that other white people—straight or not—don't share their advantages. (Scalzi did address this point in his 'Double Bubble Trouble' essay.) This lack of empathy leads to problems when they both fail to realise that other white people face other problems and don't, in any real sense, have privilege. It's quite easy to reap the benefits of certain issues—immigration, globalisation, etc—without realising that others, the people you don't see, are suffering the disadvantages. It is easy, for example, to push eco-friendly power plants if you're rich enough to pay the increased bills. If you're poor, if you're already spending money you don't have just to stay alive, why would you support anything that raised your costs?

And, when activists ask white people why they deny their privilege, could it be that they don't *have* any privilege?

It is true enough that most power and wealth in the Western World rests in the hands of white men. They make up the majority of political leaders, corporate directors, etc. However, it is *also* true that the political-financial elite is a very tiny fraction of the whole. The wealth and power they hold is not shared amongst the remainder of the straight white male population, let alone the *entire* population. One may argue that wealth and power can be averaged out and so there *is* an even distribution of such things, but this doesn't work in practice. It is true, to use a simple analogy, that some writers make fortunes (JK Rowling, George Martin), and this suggests that *all* writers make fortunes, yet this isn't actually correct. The vast majority of writers *cannot* sustain themselves by their writing alone.

From the outside, looking in, this may not be obvious. But from the inside, it is so painfully obvious that any practically any writer who heard a suggestion he's one of the super-rich would laugh hysterically...and then dismiss the speaker, on the grounds the speaker is too ignorant to be taken seriously. And he'd be right.

It is this lack of perspective that gives rise to identity politics and the problems they bring in their wake. A broke white guy, suffering the sort of poverty and deprivation that is commonly associated with the Third World, is not going to accept the suggestion he's privileged. And why should he, when he *isn't*? A writer struggling to enter the field and make a career for himself is not going to like suggestions that writers should be published on any other basis than writing skill. Why should he, when it works against him (even if he appears to be given an unfair advantage)? Indeed, one of the most ignorant statements I had to deal with was a suggestion that I was privileged for attending boarding school. The school in question was deeply deprived, lacked the facilities to offer more than very basic classes (to the point that certain career options were foreclosed before I knew I wanted them), and was infested with bullies. If being beaten up and/or insulted just about every day is privilege...I can't take anyone who makes that argument seriously. And why should I?

This leads to bitter resentment. People who don't have any privilege, in any real sense, resent it when they're told they *do*. People struggling to survive and build a career for themselves hate it when they're told they have to work harder than others, as compensation for crimes they didn't commit (and weren't, in many cases, committed by their ancestors). The idea that victimhood justifies further rounds of victimisation is bad enough, but when it's aimed at people who didn't commit the original victimisation it is considerably worse. Why *shouldn't* it be resented?

Perversely—but unsurprisingly—the growing awareness of 'identity' and 'diversity' fuels racism. The more people are aware of different groups within society, the more they draw lines between themselves and other groups. The more people see other groups as having an unfair advantage, one that comes at their expense, the more they hate and resent it. And the more inclined they are to believe that other groups bring their misfortunes on themselves, rather than being the victims of forces outside their control. People who feel they're being nagged and pressured into making endless concessions resent it. Of course they do. And when they feel they're being treated unfairly, they want to push back.

And they do, by arguing that other groups have privilege too. Male privilege is countered by female privilege. White privilege is countered by black privilege. Christian privilege is countered by Muslim privilege. Etc,

etc...it's all a terrible mess that promotes tribalism and encourages a cold war between groups that ensures old wounds will never close, with an endless series of 'atrocities' to keep the cycle going.

Or, as someone more cynical than myself put it, divide and conquer.

...

But there is, it should be noted, a very real form of privilege. *Class* privilege.

Indeed, pretty much all of the time, the person discussing 'white privilege' is actually talking about 'class privilege.' A person born into a higher class has more privilege than a person born into a lower class, regardless of the colour of their skin. Obama's daughters will have more privilege, for the rest of their lives, than a random white guy born in flyover country. If you look back at the *Invisible Knapsack* essay, you'll note that most of the effects credited to 'white privilege' are actually due to 'class privilege.' They would actually be true for someone born to wealth and power, who would be—in the West—almost entirely white.

A person with 'class privilege' has more than just money. He has *connections*. He grew up knowing the movers and shakers—and the next generation, who would become movers and shakers in their own right. He probably met hundreds of celebrities, media personalities and many more, people who are either important or *think* they're important. The upper classes are a *de facto* aristocracy. They marry amongst themselves; they rarely interact with people who are lower than themselves. People like George W. Bush would probably not have risen so high if they hadn't been able to draw on their family's connections. They can also count on the unspoken support of their fellows, even those who are technically on the other side, as long as they're not too poisonous. Class protects itself.

One of the few things I will agree with the privilege-checkers on is this: the person at the top, however defined, often doesn't realise what it's like for the people at the bottom. It is easier, from one's lofty vantage, to divide people into subsets (race, gender, etc) than recognise that each and every person is an individual in his or her own right. However, this also has the massive downside that the people at the top are often unaware of their own ignorance (like the person who insisted that going to boarding school was a sign of privilege) or how their well-intentioned words and deeds come across to others.

The point is that, if you're on the top, it is easy to do a great deal of damage to the people at the bottom even if you have the best of intentions. If you are well aware of your own 'white privilege'—which is actually 'class privilege'—and not a particularly deep thinker, you might assume that everyone who happens to share your skin colour *also* shares your privilege. A moment's rational thought would be enough to put the lie to this, but such people are rarely deep thinkers. They grow up in an environment that does not encourage it.

Imagine, for the sake of argument, that a wealthy—and liberal-ruled—suburb wants to embrace renewable energy. The environment will be protected, but the costs of electric power will go up. This is not a issue for the wealthy, who don't mind paying an extra £100 per month, but a serious problem for the poor. They don't *have* the money to pay for power, leaving them powerless…collateral damage of a well-meaning, yet seriously misguided attempt to help. If you lack the experience to realise that other people are different from you—and not just poorer than you—you will wind up accidentally hurting them.

Percy: Oh, come now, Baldrick. A piffling thousand? Pay the fellow, Edmund, and damn his impudence.

Edmund: I haven't got a thousand, dung-head! I've got 85 quid in the whole world!

If you live in a bubble, and most people with 'class privilege' do tend to live in a bubble, it's easy to fall into the trap of seeing people by their group, rather than as individuals. It requires close contact to separate the members of a different 'tribe,' for what of a better term, into separate people. If you don't have that contact, it's easy to start thinking that 'all X are Z' and other fallacies that are strikingly hard to lose. It's also easy to start hurting the people who lack your 'class privilege'—and to feel, when they object, that they're in the wrong.

The average senior politician, for example, has a great deal of 'class privilege.' He or she also has a great deal of *protection*. So do the very wealthy. People like Bill Gates can afford to live in giant gated communities, places where they never have to come into contact with the great unwashed. They enjoy a degree of *safety* that someone living in a poor and deprived community does not share. A member of the protected class, as Peggy Noonan put it, is protected from the reality of the world he/she helped create. They can argue that a serial killer shouldn't be executed, on the grounds that the death penalty is immoral, but they're not the ones at risk. The ones who *are* at risk—the unprotected; the poor, the people who cannot afford private security—feel otherwise. And then they're insulted by the protected, who cannot understand their point of view.

This tends to lead to amusing moments of naked hypocrisy. The wealthy are all in favour of immigration, diversity and suchlike as long as they don't have to endure the downsides. If they do—if there's even a *chance* they might have to endure the downsides—they change their minds very quickly and shout "NIMBY!" This hypocrisy rapidly becomes sickening, which is at least part of the reason Americans voted for Donald Trump in 2016. The three main candidates for the Democratic nomination for 2020—Bernie Sanders, Elizabeth Warren and Joe Biden—all live in areas that cannot, by any reasonable sense of the word, be termed 'diverse.' Indeed, they're pretty much majority-white…and expensive enough to preclude the average Trump voter from moving there.

Unfortunately, merely exposing the hypocrisy is rarely enough to stop it.

In theory, we live in a meritocracy, in which a person with sufficient merit can rise to the top. In practice, we live in a world where people lucky enough to have the right parents have a genuine edge over the rest…an edge so pronounced that they are rarely aware of what life is like for people at the bottom. This breeds contempt for the lower classes, a contempt that is being increasingly returned. This is not a good thing.

Throughout history, there is a pattern that tends to repeat itself. A very competent man, someone who climbs to the top, will be followed by a son or grandson who is foolish enough to fritter away everything his ancestor built. In Britain, for example, there was a long string of very competent monarchs being succeeded by fools or weaklings. Why would this happen? Put bluntly, the competent monarchs had to struggle to earn their power and, by the time they were secure, they understood the *limits* of their power. Their successors, born to power and privilege, lacked that awareness. They pushed the limits too far and often got their fingers burnt. But very few of them truly suffered for their crimes. They had 'class privilege.'

...

This is the crux of many of our modern-day problems. On one hand, our political-financial-media-etc elites have become disconnected from the *real* world and consumed with a distrust, even a hatred, for those who do not share their views and the wealth that insulates them from the consequences of their own actions. On the other, society has become infected with the virus of 'identity politics,' which makes it impossible to put the past in the past and, perhaps more importantly, focus on what's important. On one hand, we have a steady move towards a *de facto* aristocracy that cares as little for the 'commoners' as any of their more formal processors; on the other, we have a rise in nationalism and radicalism that could easily lead to disaster.

Why? Well, I'd like to put forward a quote that—I think—explains the growing problem.

"And when Johnny doesn't get the job and gets frustrated and complains about it he's told that he shouldn't be bitter because he has all the advantages and privileges of being a white male. So here he is at age 22 or 23 wondering exactly which advantages he's had all along here because for every major event he's had in the last 5 years, he's been shot down because of his race and/or sex.

"If he'd been passed over at one stage by 1 point, people like Johnny would probably shrug it off. But after a while when you see people stepping in line ahead of you at every line you go to, at some point Johnny has to start wondering when he gets to compete on even terms. But the answer to that from affirmative action advocates is "never".

"You saw it happen once and you kind of shrugged it off which, I think is pretty normal. Would you have the same response be if that was the 30th time you'd seen it? And what would be your response if each time you saw it happen was a building block towards another future event? Isn't that what we refer to as "systemic"?"

There are people who will say that the above quote is nonsense, that it isn't true. But that doesn't matter. What matters is that people believe it.

If you were born in some really high-class area and you happen to be white, there's a good chance that you have a lot of privilege. But if you happen to be born white in *Hillbilly Elegy* country, you might reasonably ask why *you* don't have white privilege? And then you might ask why people who have never worked a day in their lives insist that you *do* have white privilege? And *then* you start thinking that these people are, at best, as ignorant and stupid as the person I mentioned above…and, at worst, that they are racist class warriors out to destroy you.

Is it any surprise that people like that voted for Donald Trump?

The point most privilege-checkers forget, I think, is that most people are self-interested. They may not be *selfish*, not in the sense they will gleefully steal candy from children, but they will put their self-interests first. Why would anyone vote for policies that will make their lives harder? It's not easy to get a job at the best of times. Why would anyone want to make it harder?

But it gets worse. The curse of identity politics is that it encourages people to think in terms of their identity—and 'white male' is an identity. Instead of coming together as a united human race, we are being divided into tribes and *judged* by our tribes. What may seem, to the people at the top, a scheme to redress historical disadvantages scans very differently to the people at the bottom. *They* see it as nothing more than racism. Not *reverse* racism, *racism*.

If you stack the deck against one group, for whatever reason, you are engaged in racism. Whatever excuses you use, whatever historical justifications you invent, you are engaged in racism. Instead of dampening racial tensions, you are inflaming them. You are harming the people least able to cope with it, pillorying them when they dare to protest...and then acting all surprised when they vote against you. *Drowning men will clutch at any straws!*

Look, I am a student of history. I know that injustices have been perpetrated throughout history. I know that people have often gotten the short end of the stick because of things—skin colour, gender—beyond their control. But one does not redress such injustices by perpetrating them on someone else. *That* merely makes them worse.

As a writer, I am not scared of even competition. If a writer outsells me...well, good for him. But if that writer has an unfair advantage that isn't connected to writing—being black or female or whatever—it bothers me, because I can't compete.

I've been told that, throughout history, writers were largely WASPs. That might be true. But it isn't my fault, nor is it the fault of everyone else like me, and there is no reason that we should be made to pay a price for someone else's misdeeds. And, for that matter, it is not fair on non-WASP writers to have to face the suspicion that the *only* reason they were published was to fill a quota. Why should *they* have to pay a price because someone with more power than sense thinks that quotas are a good way to rectify historical injustice?

As a historian, I am well aware that women generally got the short end of the stick throughout history. But, as the father of two boys, I don't want programs that profess to rectify this injustice by piling injustice on *my* sons. Why on Earth would I want them to be at a disadvantage? And, if I have a daughter at some later date, I don't want *her* to suffer a disadvantage either. And everything I know about history—and human nature—tells me that she will.

Coming to think of it, my kids are mixed-race. Do I want them to go through their lives unsure where they really belong? Or if they don't have a tribe of their own? Or to have to waste their time calculating precisely where they stand on the indemnity politics roster?

A few years ago, I saw a marriage come to an end. And the reason it came to an end, from what I saw, was that both the husband and wife were fond of dragging up the past, from minor to major offences, and neither one could move past it and travel into the future. All relationships go through bumpy patches, but it is immensely frustrating to have the past dragged up and thrown in your face time and time again. At some point, people just stop caring. They get sick of being told that they cannot put it behind them and move on. And so they get bitter and they end up curdled.

And they start saying *"why should I care about the injustice done to them when no one cares about the injustice done to me?"*

We need to put quotas—and suchlike—behind us, once and for all. The past must remain in the past. We need to ensure a level playing field, with everyone having an equal shot at everything from education to jobs; we need to ensure that the laws apply to everyone; we need to prove, as best as we can, that the best person for the job *got* the job. I don't say it will be easy, because it *won't* be easy. But it has to be done.

I'll let Dale Cozort have the last word:

"If you look around the world you'll notice something. The real dead-end basket case countries and regions are usually the ones where old injustices or perceived injustices are most remembered and most important to people. [SNIP] None of this is to say that ignoring history is good, or even that ignoring old injustices is good. The reality though is that both the villains and the victims of history are for the most part dead, or have one foot on the banana peel... [SNIP]...The other reality is that dwelling on those old injustices tends to lead to situations where the guys who would normally be holding up convenience stores end up running around with AK-47s and RPGs in the service of one side or the other in the dispute.

"When that starts happening on a major scale, anyone with brains and/or money heads for the nearest exit. You end up with a downward spiral as jobs evaporate and people fight ever more bitterly over the remaining scraps of value. And of course a whole new generation of injustices are created, which will undoubtedly be used to justify the next round of victimizations. 'Get over it' isn't the perfect answer. It does have some downsides, but it does work."

Christopher G. Nuttall
Edinburgh, 2020

Printed in Great Britain
by Amazon